... Award for *Pillow Talk* and was shortlisted for the RNA Contemporary Romantic Novel Award 2012 for *Chances*.

At school, Freya was constantly reprimanded for day-dreaming – so she still can't quite believe that essentially, this is what she is now paid to do. She was born in London but lives in rural Hertfordshire with her family and other animals, where she writes from a stable in her back garden.

To connect with Freya and hear about events, unique competitions and sneak previews of what she's writing, join her at *www.facebook.com/freya.north* or log onto *www.freyanorth.com* and find out more.

FREYA NORTH

Pip

HARPER

Harper
An imprint of HarperCollins*Publishers*
77–85 Fulham Palace Road,
Hammersmith, London W6 8JB

www.harpercollins.co.uk

This paperback edition 2012
1

First published in Great Britain by
William Heinemann 2003

A catalogue record for this book is
available from the British Library

ISBN: 978-0-00-746225-4

Printed and bound in Great Britain by
Clays Ltd, St Ives plc

MIX
Paper from
responsible sources

FSC
www.fsc.org

FSC™ C007454

For Mum and Dad

We never know the love of our parents for us till we have become parents.

Now I know! Thank you.

ONE

'*T*here's really not that much difference between lap dancing and doing what I do,' Pip McCabe proclaimed in a very matter-of-fact way over a robust but imaginative dinner that her uncle Django had spent the afternoon preparing in celebration of his three nieces' weekend visit home to Derbyshire. Django spooned a large portion of something alarmingly beige on to his plate and appeared to contemplate it at length. In fact, he was considering his eldest niece's words, wondering if he'd misheard, wondering if Pip had changed jobs; wondering, basically, what on earth he was going to do with her. Pip's two younger sisters, Fen and Cat, sniggered into their semolina. Django had proudly called it 'polenta'. But that was imaginative both with the truth and with the ingredients of the dish itself.

The three sisters tactfully referred to it as 'polenta' because they, too, were being imaginative with the truth as well as heedful of the chef's sensitivities. Having been brought up single-handedly by their uncle Django, the McCabe girls were well accustomed to his eccentricities and loved him all the more because of them. He devoted the same imaginative attention to idiosyncratic detail in his dress sense as to his cooking. The sisters saw nothing untoward about pea soup with tuna and stilton, or rhubarb crumble with Jelly Babies instead of rhubarb. They had never gone hungry and their taste buds had developed a commendable and valuable robustness. Nor did they think it odd that a man in his late sixties should dress in the souvenirs of his colourful past. Today, as Django dolloped polenta on to his plate and enlivened it with a hearty slosh of Henderson's Relish, he tucked his paisley cravat (he'd partied with the Kinks in the 1960s) into his cambric shirt, and loosened the enormous buckled belt he'd acquired at some free festival or other, currently holding together a pair of jeans Clint Eastwood would have coveted for a Spaghetti Western.

'Philippa,' he said, chewing thoughtfully, 'I *implore* you to elaborate.'

'Not much difference at all, really, between lap dancing and my line of work,' Pip mused whilst masticating. 'Same attention to make-up, same use and abuse of one's body. Strutting one's stuff for money. Having often ghastly punters to deal with. Always being gawped at. I'm pretty much a painted lady, too – quite literally.'

Her family regarded her. Everyone chewed. They all thought to themselves that they were sure polenta was meant to melt in the mouth, not glue the hinges of the jaw together. If Jamie Oliver was to be believed. It tasted good, though, and surely that was the point.

'It's a new take on polenta,' Django reasoned out loud. 'A polenta for the Millennium.' Privately they each wondered how long he could credit (or blame) his experiments in the kitchen on the Millennium. As his jaw worked energetically, his mind turned to the vagaries of his niece's career.

'The main difference between my work and lap dancing,' said Pip, holding her fork aloft for good measure, 'is the working hours. Because, of course, I tend to work days and not nights.'

The McCabes observed with awe how the polenta on Pip's fork defied both gravity and her expressive hand movements to adhere with such determination.

2

'Surely the main difference,' Django said, sipping sherry from a teacup because he had used the sherry glasses earlier to measure olive oil and Tabasco, 'is that you wear substantially more clothes when you perform.'

Django, Fen and Cat were momentarily unnerved by the fact that Pip's confirmation was not immediate.

'Yes,' she responded at length, 'and no.'

'No?' Fen asked.

'No?' Cat echoed but with a raised tone.

'No!' Django boomed as an order, not a question.

'I've modified my motley,' Pip shrugged. 'Somewhat skimpier – it's spring, after all.'

*   *   *

'God, I wonder whether to move back,' Cat said, with an audible lump in her throat, as the sisters journeyed by train away from rural Derbyshire and Django, back down to their lives in London.

'Listen, it's still very early days for you,' said Fen, thinking that actually Cat's split with her odious boyfriend hadn't come a moment too soon. 'Why don't you see how you feel after the summer? After all, it's been a long-held ambition for you to follow the Tour de France as a journalist – give it your all.'

'God,' Cat sighed. Her dream-come-true was now more like a nightmare-in-waiting, such was the low ebb of her self-esteem.

Pip regarded her youngest sister and decided in an instant that humour was essential. 'Think of all those bronzed thighs, all that testosterone, the lashings of Lycra!' Cat couldn't help but giggle. Pip felt she could now introduce a little common sense. 'You've wanted to get up close and personal for years. Here's your chance. It'll be an excellent opportunity for someone in your position – further your career as a sports journalist plus get over Bastardwanker. And, of course, you never know whom you might meet.'

'I'm off to Paris soon myself,' Fen announced, 'also to be surrounded by mouth-watering male physiques. Not in Lycra on bicycles, though,' she all but apologized to Cat.

'You're a weirdo,' Pip teased. 'The men you salivate over are all marble and bronze sculptures.' Fen, an art historian, found nothing remotely weird in her penchant for the work of Rodin and his followers and she screwed up her face and poked her tongue out at Pip in protest.

'Well, I have no plans for Paris or pedallers,' Pip said in such a tone as to suggest that she wouldn't want to cross the Channel anyway, 'but I, *too,* am due to be surrounded by men.' She opened a packet of salt-and-vinegar crisps and offered them to her sisters. 'Holloway, actually,' she said, with such gravitas that she might well have said Hollywood. 'I'm doing a show for a young man called Billy. And all his mates.'

TWO

'*B*illy Billy Billy,' Pip chants under her breath whilst putting on a hair band and laying her make-up out in front of her, 'Billy's the birthday boy. He's the blond one in the Gap sweatshirt.' She stares at her reflection in the mirror she always takes with her. She's learned from experience not to trust other people's mirrors – distortion, however subtle or slight, could have utterly drastic consequences. So, wherever she performs, regardless of the size of her audience, the length of her performance, the shortcomings of the venue or the fee she charges, Pip always demands of her client a changing-room with good natural light and a suitable surface other than her knees on which to prop her mirror. Today, she is in Holloway. The gentrified side; where fashionable young folk with large sums of money have been buying up the gorgeous terraces from elderly owners who paid 'two bob' for their homes decades ago.

'Billy's the birthday boy,' Pip murmurs, applying her slap, 'blond hair, Gap sweatshirt.' She stares at her face.

I remember, when I was fourteen and had bought my first eye-shadow – admittedly bright green – Django saying, 'Philippa, you're pretty enough without make-up!'

Now look at me!

'Positively garish,' she mutters, wielding a bright red lipstick with gay abandon and adding a final flourish of powder to set the lot. She scoops her hair into two schoolgirl bunches, tying large polka-dot ribbons on each. She puckers up her lips and blows her reflection a pantomime kiss. 'Well, this is for Billy,' she says, standing and springing up and down as a warm-up. 'He'd expect nothing less from me. He's the birthday boy.' She hops lightly from toe to toe, jiggling her arms and fingers. 'Gap sweatshirt. Blond hair.' Pip clears her throat and hums 'Happy Birthday' very fast. She's ready.

'She's great,' Zac Holmes, who's been watching quietly from the back of the room, murmurs to the man standing next to him. 'I must get her number. So many of her ilk can be such a let-down – and pricey, too. You sometimes don't get what you pay for.'

They watch as Pip does the splits. Billy and his mates gasp with delight. The man next to Zac gives her a round of applause and chuckles, 'Do you reckon she has business cards to give out?'

Zac feels tired. He rubs his eyes, wondering why he's wearing contact lenses and not his glasses. His eyes feel dry and uncomfortable. It's suddenly all a bit too noisy and frantic for him. He'd rather not be in Holloway; he'd rather be diving into a gorgeous cool swimming-pool in the Caribbean, soothing his eyes, refreshing his limbs. But chance would be a fine thing. He hasn't taken a holiday for over a year. He stifles a yawn. He really ought to go home. He has work to do, despite it being the weekend; regardless that it's the first weekend he's officially had off in weeks. Billy's birthday was fun for a couple of hours but Zac has had enough now. He doesn't much like Holloway. He's never really cared for birthdays. He let his own thirtieth come and go without so much as a quick drink with colleagues after work, let alone a celebration with friends or family. And that was almost five years ago. Birthdays. Bollocks. Yes, he's going to go.

The show now over, Billy and the gang are guzzling down the drinks and tucking into the grub. Zac is hungry but doesn't really fancy anything on offer. He'll grab something on his way home to Hampstead. Someone knocks a drink over and it soaks Zac's right trouser leg. No one seems to notice, let alone apologize. It really is time to go.

'Happy birthday, Billy old man,' Zac says, turning on the charm and ruffling Billy's hair boisterously. 'I have to go. I'd love to stay but I can't. I have to work.'

Someone else is vying for Billy's attention and another drink is sent flying.

'Have a great party,' Zac continues. 'Happy birthday.'

'Where's Tom?' Billy asks, not seeming too bothered if Zac stays or goes.

'He was hoping to come,' Zac says, 'really wanted to. But he hasn't been feeling too well.'

'Say "hi" from me.'

'Happy birthday, Billy,' Zac repeats.

Alone, out in the hallway, Zac rummages around for his jacket. He has a headache lurking and is muttering 'Nurofen' under his breath. He's suffered with his headaches a lot recently. He searches his pockets but finds only Marlboro Lights. Why does he always carry cigarettes when he rarely smokes more than two a day and doesn't know why he even smokes those two anyway?

'Stupid fucking idiot,' he hisses at himself.

'Language!' chastises a female voice.

Zac turns around. Who? Oh. Her. Without the make-up, eyes still quite a startling blue-green. Dressed down in jeans. Upright, not doing the splits. Hair in a plain pony-tail. She's smaller now, close to and not in costume.

'I didn't recognize you with your clothes off,' says Zac and then cringes. 'I mean, with your clothes on. I mean, in jeans.'

She laughs. 'Did you enjoy the show?'

'Great,' Zac answers economically. He really doesn't feel much like chatting. He's hungry and headachy in Holloway when he'd so much rather be home alone in Hampstead.

'Thanks,' the girl says, with grace.

'Have you a card?' Zac asks, remembering he wanted one though now wondering why.

'Sure,' she says, and one seems to materialize, as if by magic, from what appeared to be the swiftest snap of her fingers.

'Ta,' says Zac, not looking at her, pocketing her card without even glancing at it. He's at his car. He gets in and drives off. Doesn't give her a backward glance nor even so much as a 'goodbye'. His headache is threatening to consume him.

Pip McCabe thinks he's rude, though. She stands on the kerb side, watching him drive away – too fast.

THREE

You can tell a lot about a person by the friends they keep. You would think you could tell a lot about a person by the clothes they wear and the place they live. However, you'd be hard-pressed to guess what Zac does for a living by analysing his dwelling, his dress or his disposition. Each is at odds with the other and none are remotely representative of the stereotypes traditionally associated with Zac's particular vocation.

Take a look around his flat. To say it sings with colour is an understatement. It's not so much a symphony of colours as a full-blown rock opera. To forgo the approved, if ubiquitous, muted heritage hues predominantly deployed by fellow Hampsteadites was no act of rebellion, no salute to the Shock of the New on his part. Zac simply opted for oranges and turquoises and citrus greens and parma violets because they are his favourite colours. Leyland Paints groan when he comes into the store. He spends a fortune there because he is so exacting. 'No. I said ultramarine and I mean *ultra*,' he'd complain and they'd have to spend a morning adding a dribble of this and a drip of that until Zac nodded and grinned and proclaimed something along the lines of 'Turquoise-tastic! Fan-bloody-brilliant! Ultimate ultramarine. Ta.'

Zac's inspiration comes not from the *Sunday Times* 'Style' section, certainly not from *Changing Rooms*, not from hip clubs, but really just from his own predilections. Zac is in no pretentious pursuit of retro-psychedelia; nor is his home an arty-farty appraisal of the merits of kitsch. Objectively, elements of his colour schemes are indeed psychedelic and some of his furniture and objects are quintessentially kitsch. But he only chooses what he loves. He doesn't refer to style magazines. In fact, when he flicked through a copy of *Wallpaper* at a friend's house, he thought it so brilliant that he started chuckling because he genuinely assumed that the magazine was a parody on other style magazines. He was quite horrified to learn it was serious. 'But it's so far up its own arse,' he'd reasoned, 'they might as well call it *Toiletpaper*.'

Zac doesn't read about art but he does love to look at it. He didn't consider trend when he was choosing colour for his walls and furniture for his rooms but he did pay homage to Matisse. Zac simply loves colour for its own sake. He loves the greenness of green, the blueness of blue, and he finds great expanses of solid colour incredibly satisfying. He cannot comprehend how colours can be in and out of fashion. He loves it that he cannot fathom how colour can convey movement, rhythm and mood. It's a mystery he is content to be awestruck by.

My job's stressful. The building is grey. I want to come home to energy and a place that – I don't know – grins. Turquoise and orange have always made me feel positive. Green makes me feel refreshed. What's all this crap about blue being a 'cool' colour – cool in what respect? Cold? Or hip? Pardon? I just find blue relaxing. Swimming-pools and cloudless skies.

Zac goes for things he really likes the look of. He loves things that amuse him. His acid yellow PVC banana beanbag chair is just as comfortable as his black leather Eames lounger. He knew the Eames was almost vulgar in cost but what price ultimate comfort for reading papers or snoozing or chilling out with a beer? The Eames serves much the same purpose as the banana chair but the banana chair was forty pounds. Zac didn't think it a 'bargain', he simply thought 'funky chair, great colour, really comfortable', bought it on the spot and took it home on the bus. He doesn't own a coffee-table so it's just as well that he doesn't buy sumptuous coffee-table tomes. Though he loves the feel of his Folio editions of fables and myths, he also devours commercial paperbacks. His book shelves are crammed with them. 'What's wrong with Grisham or Herbert?' he might say. 'They're bloody good reads.' He sometimes rereads Wilbur Smith and he really quite liked *Bridget Jones's Diary*. He read it on the tube going to and from work. He was aware that people stared at him. He didn't care.

It's always open house at Zac's. His flat just has a subliminal effect of putting people in a good mood. He doesn't officially entertain but he has the sort of personality and the type of place that encourage people to pop in. Male friends stop by for a beer or two if they've had a crap day at work or a row with a wife or girlfriend. And those very same wives and girlfriends pop in if they've walked their feet off perusing Hampstead's shops. Zac tells them to 'take a load off'; while he fixes them a juice, they revolve a while in the Eames, or snuggle gratefully into the bizarre banana chair. If their kids have thrown tantrums at the Finchley Road Sainsbury's, they're dragged in to let off steam at Uncle Zac's; scampering around his flat, throwing themselves on to his large low bed, rolling off on to the tufty orange rug by the side, coming back into the living-room to snuggle on Mummy's lap and gaze at the lava lamp or quietly snigger at the massive painting that's allegedly of mountains but really looks like a large pair of blue bosoms.

Ah, but have a look inside Zac's wardrobe. It's like an archive for Gap. Beige, navy or black. No deviation. Trousers, shirts or pullovers. He owns one suit. It's currently at the dry-cleaner. It's navy. He never wears it by choice;

only if he must – a meeting with specific clients, a wedding, a funeral. His underwear is unremittingly black and blue.

His kitchen reveals his obsession with gadgets which he affectionately calls 'toys'. A top-of-the-range fully automatic espresso machine, a sixties-inspired juicer, an impressive if intimidating array of Global kitchen knives, all manner of high-shine stainless-steel utensils hanging from hooks above the granite worktop. His fridge-freezer is, of course, one of those cavernous walk-in American machines that do ice and cold water and can take a whole sucking pig plus the apple. There is no pig inside, just a staggering array of ready-meals. Does this man work for M&S? No? He must have a discount card, then, surely? No? Does he have substantial shares in the company, then? Or is this simply what you'd call brand loyalty? Or is it just plain laziness? No wonder that all his utensils and gadgets look so pristine – they've never been used. He has no need of any of them. You do not need a mandolin from Divertimenti to prepare an M&S ready-meal. The only things requiring any chopping are the tomatoes (aesthetically still on the vine) and, of course, the oranges for the juicer (despite the fact that there are cartons of fresh juice, every conceivable variety, in the fridge). His friends' offspring like the cupboard over there best; it contains the most astonishing variety of biscuits, chocolates and crisps. Have a peek in his kitchen bin – nothing but chocolate wrappers and cartons from his shove-it-in-the-oven-at-190-degrees meals. Zac Holmes hides nothing. He is totally at ease with his likes and dislikes and the choices he's made.

'I like figures,' he said ingenuously on a recent date with a Canadian girl who's the cousin of one of his friends. 'I really love getting my teeth into them.' The Canadian girl was so charmed by his open personality, so taken with his slate-grey eyes, handsome face and naturally athletic physique, that she told him her figure was honed to perfection because she worked out five times a week and could they please get the bill right now, though their main courses had not yet arrived, so he could take her back to her hotel and get his teeth into *her* figure. Zac obliged. He doesn't like to disappoint people. And he does love figures. He didn't let her down back at her hotel. He didn't get his teeth into her but he certainly employed a fabulous technique of nibbling and sucking.

Zac likes sex very much. He has quite a lot of it. To him, it's a colourful, fun, recreational activity and he's rather good at it. He doesn't mind at all that over the last three years or so sex has not led to deep and meaningful relationships. He's had two of those during his life. One from his late teens to his early twenties, the other in his late twenties. He's not now shying away from commitment. And, nearing thirty-five, though he does, of course, have a past, it is one with which he is at peace. If there is any baggage, he certainly doesn't look on it as a burdensome weight on his shoulders. He hasn't been in love these past five years. But his life hasn't lacked for it. He's loved his last five years, loved the sex he's had – the quick flings, the threesome, the three-month dalliance, the couple of six-month demi-relationships. He hasn't met the right girl because he really isn't looking. Sex wouldn't be the better for it. Nor does his life want for lack of it. So, being single is neither a problem nor a conscious decision. However, because he's not on the lookout, he might well not recognize Her.

In all probability he certainly wouldn't recognize Her if she came dressed as a clown: all stripy tights, mismatched lace-up shoes, a short frilly ra-ra skirt, pigtails sticking out starchily at odd angles. And a face powdered white, eyes delineated with black diamonds and star shapes; a comedy smile; a nose with a very red tip.

But there again, why would an artist like Pip fall for a chartered accountant?

In fact, how would their paths cross anyway?

They crossed the once, at Billy's party. But by next year, Billy probably won't want a clown. He'll want to take a posse to the cinema. Or McDonald's. Or both.

And so, when Zac came across Pip's card a few days later, it had been through a hot wash, fast spin and tumble-dry. It was frayed and faded when he found it, half stuck to the back pocket of his jeans. He could just make out 'Clown and Children's Entertainer'. After some scrutiny, he reckoned the name was Merry Martha. The phone number remained legible. But he didn't make a note of it and he put the card in his kitchen bin without another thought.

FOUR

*P*ip McCabe's flat, like Zac's, gives away little about the career of its owner. There's nothing remotely zany or even vaguely theatrical about the interior. It's neither colourful nor quirky. Though the basement flat is a small space, it doesn't seem cramped on account of Pip's aversion to clutter. No ornaments. The pictures on the walls are non-representational, frameless and subdued in colour. Photos held in stylish thick glass sandwiches are of her family, though Pip herself features in few. Pip's home is an essay on calm; gradations of neutral hues for walls, floors and soft furnishings. The stripes and spots and frills and flounces and plastic and kitsch of her clowning – her clothes, her props, her funky chunky shoes – are immediately and neatly stored as soon as she returns from work. There's never any leftover washing-up to be done. There's never a damp towel left scrunched on the bathroom floor. The bed is made as soon as she's left it. Not that it even looks that crumpled when she rises each morning.

Pip's favourite drink is red wine. She doesn't care for white, for champagne or for spirits. She likes a good Rioja best of all. And she has the utter confidence to happily drink it – and sometimes quite a lot of it – in her spic-and-spandom, with not one spillage to date. Maybe her training as an acrobat has something to do with it. At work, she flops and flaps and fools around but such japery is attributable to consummate physical control; at the centre of her slapstick and tumbling are balletic grace, athletic stability and acrobatic control.

When Pip McCabe is out and about, at work or at play, she is the life and soul, she's the girl who gets things going, she tells the first joke, she's the last to leave. When Pip McCabe is at home, however, she wafts around quietly with music playing softly. She's happy with the solitude, confident with quiet, content in her own company. Alone in her flat, she provides the best audience in front of which she can truly be herself. She's entertaining; she's a children's entertainer. But she'd really rather not entertain at home. Which was why Mike, her last steady boyfriend, left her. She never let him in. The door to her flat and entry to her heart remained closed.

She's a great illusionist, is Pip McCabe. Her home isn't Conran, none of her stuff is from stockists recommended by *Elle Decoration*. Rather, she has a cunning way with calico bought cheaply from Berwick Street and furniture bid for at Tring Auction Rooms. If she wasn't a clown by trade, Pip could well earn her living as an invisible mender. However, that's not to say there aren't a couple of flaws, a little fraying, in her own fabric. But she'd rather keep them invisible and try to fix them in her own way and in her own time.

There are two nights a week when Pip would rather not be at home, absolutely never alone if she is. Tuesdays and Thursdays are exhausting for her though she works a maximum of four hours in the afternoons on these days and never as Merry Martha. Pip won't ask for support, for help, for company, but she tries to ensure that her evenings on these days are occupied. Pizzas are good, movies are better, a fair few drinks in a raucous bar is the ultimate, watching *Friends* at a friend's home will do and she has even been known on one or two occasions to have people round to hers, Rioja at the ready and comfort food aplenty. This Thursday she quite fancied seeing her sisters but Cat is in bed with flu and doesn't want a visit, much less to provide company, and Fen is suddenly up in Derbyshire again, assessing sculpture in a private collection. Pip turned to her honorary sister instead.

'Megan?' she phoned.

'Philippa McCabe,' Megan responded, thinking to herself *But of course, it's Thursday*. 'I was going to call you. Do you want to do something?'

'Sure,' Pip said casually, as if she had only been phoning for a chat but Megan's suggestion of meeting up was most appealing and how convenient that she herself happened to be free. 'What do you fancy?'

'To be honest,' Megan said in a lascivious whisper, 'I fancy a bit of Dominic. He's the brother of Polly's boyf, Max – you've met them. But I don't think he's on the menu tonight – so I'll settle for pizza.'

'Sounds good to me,' Pip laughed.

'Or alcohol,' Megan interjected excitedly, as if she'd overlooked its existence.

'Either,' said Pip.

'Both!' Megan declared and they arranged to meet at Smorfia in West Hampstead.

Pip settled down to a bath, dipping her body deep into the water, right up to her lower lip.

Wash the day away. Soothe. Cleanse. Breathe.

She closed her eyes on the day just been and what she had seen. She opened her eyes and stared at the taps. She could be in West Hampstead in less than half an hour.

The waiters flirted extravagantly with the two women. Megan was a regular and Pip had been often. The restaurant was small – friendly, noisy and smelt heavenly. Megan and Pip filched food from each other's plates and chatted nineteen to the dozen, though on occasion this meant talking with their mouths full.

'Was it tough today?' Megan asked, tearing a much larger slice of Pip's pizza than she'd intended.

'It was,' Pip confirmed, helping herself to Megan's *pappardelle*, 'particularly.' Megan didn't ask more and Pip didn't elaborate. Pip enquired about this Dominic chap and Megan swooned off on elaborate tangents, describing potential wedding cake design and fantasy honeymoon destinations.

'Has he asked you?' Pip enquired.

'Asked me what?' Megan responded.

Pip thought about it. 'Anything? Your favourite colour? If you snore? If you'll marry him?'

Megan laughed heartily. 'He hasn't even asked me out yet,' she admitted, raising her eyebrows at herself, 'let alone kissed me, never mind asking me to marry him. But hey, I'll live in hope. Or in day-dreamland at the very least.'

'Well,' said Pip, slightly histrionically due to a fast-flowing Chianti and a lot of garlic in the food, 'if you ask me, day-dreams endanger reality.'

'You're too bloody cynical for your own good,' Megan pouted, 'and for mine.'

'No, I'm not,' Pip protested, 'I'm just sensibly circumspect.'

'Bollocks!' Megan retorted, because Pip was her best friend so she was allowed to. 'Your mum ran off with a cowboy when you were a kid and bang! you don't believe in true love!'

Pip chewed thoughtfully. 'I'm fine about love. I just don't trust men with a penchant for rhinestones and rodeos!'

They chinked glasses and laughed.

Megan picked a large glistening black olive from her friend's pizza, scrutinizing it admiringly before popping it into her mouth. Pip mopped at Megan's sauce with some leftover *bruschetta*. 'The thing about love,' she said with her mouth full, 'is that it requires one to get naked.'

Megan looked a little blank. 'Well, if you leave your clothes on, you tend to get a little messy.'

'But that's my point,' said Pip. 'Once you've laid yourself

bare, it often becomes messier.'

Megan looked baffled.

'Reveal?' Pip said first, tipping her head one way. 'Or conceal?' she continued, tipping her head the other way. 'I guess I'd rather keep covered up than expose myself.'

'But you have a great physique,' Megan protested artlessly.

'I'm talking metaphorically,' Pip laughed. 'God, I forget you work in numbers not words.'

'Being a maths teacher doesn't make me an emotional moron,' Megan sulked – but not seriously.

'Of course not,' Pip said, 'but you *do* fall in love too easily and you get hurt.' Over the years, Pip had witnessed Megan in pieces several times. Privately, Pip felt Megan's experience in terms of quantity and variety thus counted for little; certainly it hadn't paved the way to happy-ever-after. Pip found it difficult to fathom how someone who had been badly burnt by love's flame could continue to thrust herself into the fire.

Megan pouted through Pip's silence but was quietly relieved that Pip was keeping her misgivings to herself. Megan topped up their wineglasses and winked lasciviously. 'Well, I bet you I've had more fun and frolics than you with your "I don't need a man" bollocks.'

'But I don't!' Pip attempted to proclaim though it was met with another energetic 'Bollocks!' from Megan. '*Seriously*,' Pip remonstrated.

'Well,' Megan said, 'just as well, then, isn't it? Because working as a clown called Merry Martha doesn't really make you millions and dressing like a clown called Merry Martha really isn't going to have the men flocking. At least, no male over the age of eight.'

'Ouch!' Pip winced theatrically because she didn't want Megan to know that her words had actually confronted her more than anticipated. Megan had meant no malice. Like many around Pip, Megan had become used to her friend shunning romance, wealth and the panoply of either. And, like those closest to Pip, Megan knew Pip would actually benefit from a little of each.

'Share a pudding?' Pip suggested, changing the subject.

'How about share each other's – order one each? Asking me to choose between *pannacotta* and *tiramisu* would be the same as asking me to choose between George Clooney and Brad Pitt.'

'Hmm,' Pip mused, 'I was going to choose fruit salad.'

'You're just trying to be wholesome!' Megan said astutely. 'Live a little!' Soon enough, she was swooning over desserts and Dominic in equal measures.

'I hope it happens for you,' Pip said sincerely whilst wielding her spoon with gay abandon between the two bowls. 'He sounds lovely. And suitable.' Megan raised her glass and her eyebrow. 'Thing is,' Pip said, because the wine was enabling her to do so, 'I say I don't need money because, in truth, I've never wanted – let alone needed – anything I can't afford.' She sipped contemplatively. 'I like bargain hunting. I rather like doing upholstery. I get a kick out of people asking "Heals?" and me saying "Hell no, house clearance".' Megan spooned the last of the *pannacotta* into Pip's mouth. 'And I say I don't need a man,' Pip continued, 'because I've never felt for someone enough to really feel that life wouldn't make sense without them.' She ran her finger around the *tiramisu* bowl though their spoons had already scraped at practically every vestige of the dessert. 'I guess,' she said thoughtfully, 'I've managed to reach the grand old age of thirty without ever being in love.'

Megan contemplated this. She chinked glasses with Pip. 'You know what, McCabe,' she said, 'to be honest, that's no bad thing.' Megan sighed. 'Sometimes being in love is more hassle than it's worth. Way too costly.'

Deep down, that's what Pip had long had a hunch about. 'You see, for me,' she said, pouring the last of the second bottle of wine into their glasses, 'there are nice blokes like good old Mike for every now and then. And in between times,' she whispered, eyes wide for dramatic effect, 'there are vibrators.'

Megan shrieked with laughter. The other diners turned and stared.

Pip snorted into her wine. Paulo, the young waiter, had eavesdropped the conversation. He decided it prudent and hopefully profitable to present the girls with complimentary Sambucas.

'*You get what you settle for*,' Pip murmured softly. It was the early hours of Friday morning when Pip finally decided to go to bed. She'd been sitting up with a bottle of Evian, waiting for her living-room to stop revolving at such an alarming rate. 'If I settle for anything less, I'll be the one who pays.' The revolutions of the room had slowed to approximately three per minute. 'Anyway, you don't enter your thirties without a fair weight of baggage from your twenties. And I'm not having someone else's dumped on me. I'm absolutely not unpacking it for them. I don't *do* baggage and that's that, really. Simple.' The room was settling nicely into one revolution per minute. 'Vibrators it is, then.'

The room is stationary. And silent. The Evian is finished and Pip feels hydrated enough to see what lying down feels like. 'Friday Friday,' she says to herself, trying to recall her timetable as she walks through to her bedroom.

Face painting at Golders Hill Park, lunch-time. Party in Chalk Farm at tea-time.

You could have a lie-in, Pip.

Me? God, no. If I have spare time, why on earth fill it with doing nothing? I have loads to do. I can find loads to do.

Can you face being horizontal?

Let me see. Not too bad.

Are you all right in the dark?

Yes. I'm not afraid of the dark.

Pip is in bed. Lying still in the dark. She loves her bedroom. No clutter. Walls the colour of oyster mushrooms. Thick curtains the colour of *crème caramel* and behind them, cream roller blinds at the window the colour of cappuccino froth. She bought the blinds in the Habitat sale; the curtains were a freebie from a set-designer friend of hers. They had been on a BBC costume drama and had required a fair bit of deft needlework from Pip. The blisters and pricked finger-tips had been a small price to pay for such hallowed curtains. She laid the carpet herself. It doesn't quite fit but her strategically placed furniture hides this from view. It looks like sisal but is much kinder to bare feet. The massive rusty stain that enabled Pip to purchase it for less than a quarter of the price is conveniently straddled by her bed. Her bed has a birch, Shaker-style headboard, very simply panelled and beautifully made. She picked that up for next to nothing as it had a split right through it. But she worked with wood filler and sandpaper and stain; it took her a month, but now you can't see the join.

However, what she loves most of all about her bedroom is something she had to pay full price for – indeed, over the odds – and that is the remarkable quiet considering her flat's proximity to Kentish Town Road. This had cost her the asking price for the flat two years ago. Though most of her pennies go straight towards the mortgage and Camden Council's absurdly high council tax, she doesn't begrudge a penny. It might be a small space subdivided by stud walls, but it is her own place, her haven, and she loves it.

Pip submits herself to the stillness and silence and stares upwards to where the ceiling ought to be though she can't determine its surface in the darkness. She tells herself it is now Friday, that Thursday was indeed yesterday. But in effect, it still feels very much Thursday that she is closing her eyes and going to sleep from. Right now, her evening with Megan doesn't seem as current as the afternoon preceding it. Sure, Megan and she talked about life, love and the universe. And vibrators. But none have the resonance of her afternoon.

'Night-night, little ones,' she says out loud, 'see you next week.'

FIVE

i

George Saunders is nine years old. He is into his sixth month on Reynolds, the renal ward at St Beatrix's, the children's hospital in the City affectionately known at St Bea's. He's uncomfortable and fed up. And now he's agreed to having his eyes tested because they're about the only part of him that haven't been tested. He thinks they're fine. But he wouldn't be surprised if they're poorly. Everything else seems to be.

'Well, here we go, then,' the doctor says. 'Cover your left eye – that's right – what? Yes, I know it's your left one – I said that's right, right? Good, use that hand, right? Or that one, left – we're not testing your hands, are we? Right. Left! Whatever. Ho-hum. Just shut that eye and tell me what's written on this card.'

George stares at the card held in front of him.

'i,' says George.

The doctor is making those stern contemplative muttering sounds that they are famous for. 'Right. Now please cover your right eye with the other hand. Lovely. Can you tell me what's written on this card?' Another card is held in front of George. He looks at it, then looks at the doctor. He really doesn't want to smile but invisible magnets haul the corners of his mouth up towards the mobiles dangling from the ward's ceiling. He reads the card again.

I

'Um, i,' he says, stifling a giggle.

The doctor looks at him sternly. Regards his mother, too. And nods sagely at the ward sister who is hovering. 'I declare that there is absolutely nothing whatsoever wrong with this young man's "i"s,' the doctor says. And then the doctor takes out a hammer and starts bashing George's arms. George giggles as the hammer makes funny beeps and dongs on impact. After all, the tool is made of red and yellow plastic and is light as a feather. 'Now look what you've gone and done!' the doctor chastises. 'Nurse! Nurse! Quick, call the doctor! My nose! My nose!'

The nurse laughs. 'Incurable!' she declares and walks away.

George is smiling widely. The doctor's nose, bright red at the best of times, is flashing. 'Quick!' George is told. 'Give me your bed and your tubes and those things that do all that bleeping – I need them more than you!'

'Are you coming back next week?' he asks, very interested in the stickers the doctor has just given him, having magicked them from behind George's ear.

The doctor regards the young patient. 'Yes. I reckon so. Perhaps. If I can switch my nose off.'

'Brill,' says George. 'See you then, Dr Pippity. Bye!'

'Good aftermorning,' says Dr Pippity, clicking her heels together and saluting so clumsily that she clonks herself in the eye. Her nose continues to glow on and off. She points at her gift of stickers: 'Don't eat them all at once!' she declares. She turns from George and walks away, jauntily, with a peculiar skip every step or so. 'Pippitypippity,' she mutters as she goes. 'Pip. Pip. Good aftermorning!' She settles herself quietly into a chair by the bedside of a small girl who feels too poorly to move, let alone speak. But, in a glance, Dr Pippity clocks a glimmer of welcome in the girl's eyes. So we'll leave her sitting there awhile, performing simple and silly tricks. She's carefully placed a magic wand in the little girl's hand. It's one of those trick sticks that segments and collapses. Dr Pippity is feigning frustration with her bed-ridden assistant. Who, in turn, now has eyes that hint at a sparkle.

The shift is over. Dr Pippity is exhausted but as she makes her way to the small room she uses to change in, she skips and 'pip pip's everyone she passes; the sounds of squeaks and bells emanating at random from any of her many pockets; her nose lighting up every now and then, apparently much to her consternation.

Her changing-room is basically a glorified cupboard along a corridor on the ground floor. Dr Pippity doesn't mind. There's a sink. A small table to prop her mirror on. A stool. She removes her nose. She takes off her slap and in doing so, emotionally wipes away the tougher parts of her day. She hums softly as she unbraids her hair from the taut pigtails. Her scalp feels both sore and relieved. She runs her fingers through her hair, amused, as always, by the kinks and curls that will take a few hours, if not a wash and blow-dry, to calm down. It proves to her that her naturally straight hair suits her best. It still amuses her to remember how she longed for a perm in her teenage years and how she cursed Django who forbade it. The hippy in him, however, was happy for her to experiment with henna ('If it's herbal it's harmless! If it's organic don't panic!' being one of his favourite maxims). Unfortunately, henna turned her mid-mousy brown to garish barmaid orange in the space of half an hour. It took half a year to dull down and fade. Pip has decided to be at peace with her natural colour ever since. She keeps her cut softly layered and shoulder length. It may be mousy and straight, but it's glossy and frames her face becomingly, crowning her features well.

From her doctor's coat pockets she lays out the tools of her trade and wipes everything with antiseptic cloths. A comedy stethoscope. Five different types of magic wand. Small red foam balls that, with a little surreptitious rubbing between the palms, or a heartfelt 'abracadabra' from a child, metamorphose into a selection of miniature animals. A huge pair of plastic scissors. Handfuls of stickers. The squeaking plastic hammer. She takes off her doctor's coat. It's a real doctor's coat, in thick white cotton, but embellished with colourful patterns on the pockets and with her name, 'Dr Pippity', emblazoned on the back like some kind of patchwork tattoo. An intricate circuit and a couple of AAA batteries enable her to make the squeaks and dongs. She takes off her luridly striped pinafore, with the flowers on springs attached to the kangaroo-style pouch, the badges dotted here and there with 'I am 8' and 'smile' and various cartoon characters. She peels off her tights – she customized this pair so that one leg has multicoloured dots and the other has wriggling lines. She showed them off that afternoon, very forlornly, to a girl with no hair up on Gainsborough, the cancer ward.

'I've not got no hair no more,' the child had told her. Dr Pippity had sat beside her and stretched her legs out. 'This leg here,' she showed the girl, 'has the multicoloured measles.' The girl gingerly placed a finger over the spots to check. 'And this leg *here*,' Dr Pippity declared, 'has *worms*!' She'd been able to muster a giggle from the girl. The girl hadn't giggled for days. It felt good. For Dr Pippity. For the nurses. For the children in the beds to either side. But especially for the little girl with cancer and no hair. And she was the point.

'And that's the point,' Dr Pippity says as she takes off her tights and puts on a pair of navy socks instead. 'That's my job.'

The clothes and the bits and pieces that accessorize Dr Pippity are placed carefully into a really rather dull beige holdall. Pip checks her reflection and wipes away a smudge of slap that she'd missed. She pops her mirror into her bag, tucks her white shirt into her jeans and leaves the room, closing the door quietly. Not that there's anyone to disturb. The wards are all upstairs. She walks through the main entrance, not now recognized by anyone, though many of them would know her at forty paces in her slap and motley.

Zac did a swift double take when Pip passed him, but he didn't linger or even look back. Over the years, he has known so many people at the hospital – as faces, or as names, too, or even well enough for a quick conversation – that he doesn't think to try and place Pip. He's got things on his mind, anyway. So has she, she didn't notice him at all.

'Fen? It's me.'

'Hiya, Pip.' The sisters chatted on their mobile phones as they left work; Fen walking away from Tate Britain, her older sister hovering near the ambulance bay.

'Fancy a film?' Pip asked, pronouncing it 'fill-erm' as is a McCabe tradition. But Fen explained she had 'a bit of a date' and would Pip mind awfully therefore if she didn't. 'A bit of a date?' Pip teased. 'Which bit – just the arms and torso of some poor sod? Oh, for God's sake, tell me it's a real hunk, not just a hunk of sculpture you've fallen for.'

'Shut up!' Fen protested lightly. 'It's only that Matt bloke, the editor of the Trust's magazine, *Art Matters*,' she justified. 'I'm still just the new girl at work, remember. Nothing to read into – it's just a quick drink.' However, Pip was sure that there was a veritable novel to read into. Fen could sense her older sister's smirk. And Pip knew her younger sister was blushing slightly.

'Be good!' she warned her. 'And if you can't be good—'

'—be careful,' groaned Fen, finishing off another McCabe-ism.

'Have you spoken to Cat today?' Pip asked. 'Is she OK?' Fen hadn't. 'I'll give her a call,' Pip said, 'cook her something hearty and wholesome.' Deep down, Pip would have preferred someone to do the looking-after her. It was a Tuesday, after all. But she'd never ask. Certainly not her younger sisters. As eldest sister, she had duties to them, responsibilities – in lieu of their mother who had left them to cavort in Colorado.

'Are you off, Pip? Off duty? Off home? Off somewhere else?' Pip turns. It's Caleb Simmons, all chocolate eyes and husky voice and olive skin smoothed over exceptional cheekbones.

'Just wondered if you wanted to go for a quick drink? I'm through for the day,' says the brilliant young paediatrician, ruffling his immaculately tousled hairstyle. Handsome enough for a role on *ER*. Compassionate to the children, patient with the parents, charming and courteous to the nurses, to the hospital staff, to the clown doctors and to the janitors alike. He'd asked her the same question a couple of weeks ago. Today, she gives him the same answer she'd given him then.

'Sorry,' says Pip, with an apologetic shrug, 'I already have plans.'

No, you don't.
I do. I just haven't quite made them yet.

'Another time, then,' Caleb suggests with equanimity and a dashing smile. With hands in his pockets, his white coat flowing out behind, he turns back to the hospital, sharing banter with the porters and patients he passes.

Pip went to see her youngest sister, Cat. And had a draining evening. Cat was heartbroken, now at the stage of denial and daft hope. She begged to be allowed to phone him. Pleaded with Pip to promise that this was a bad dream and she'd awake soon. Prayed that they'd get back together. Yet if Pip could grant wishes, she wouldn't allow a single one of Cat's to come true.

'He was horrid to you,' Pip tried to reason without lecturing, 'he was a nasty piece of work. You are going to be fine. I know it doesn't feel that way right now, but I promise you that there will be a time when you breathe a sigh of relief that your life has no place or space for him.'

Cat looked absolutely flabbergasted. 'I don't believe you,' she sobbed. She didn't believe a word Pip tried to say, didn't want to believe her, didn't eat a mouthful Pip had prepared. In protest, Pip wanted to shake sense into her sister, to yell home truths at her. But she didn't. She was trying hard to be sensitive and diplomatic, although, after the day she'd had, she really didn't feel like counselling Cat. But she did. It was her duty.

You should have said 'yes' to that lovely Caleb Simmons.
Then what would Cat have done without me?
Exactly as she did with you there.
Caleb's not the answer.
But he might be a nice little diversion. A handsome distraction.
I haven't the time. Or the inclination, to be honest.
Honestly? Really.

SIX

*S*o that's who it is. I remember. She was the clown at Billy's party. She did that extraordinary juggling thing whilst doing the splits. She told terrible jokes which the kids loved. Didn't I take her card?

Zac was over at the drinks machine when two clown doctors bustled into Out-patients, creating merry havoc in their wake. From his quiet vantage point outside the fray, he recognized Dr Pippity as being the clown from his nephew's party – albeit with toned down make-up, wearing a doctor's coat and performing at a very different venue today. He sipped his coffee by the machine, watching the clowns at work, enjoying the children's reaction to them. Though the clowns brought colour and a certain cacophony with them, there was a moving gentleness to their gestures and jokes.

'Hey ho and what's your name? Is it Mildred? Or perhaps Millicent?' Dr Pippity asked, shaking the hand of a small boy in Out-patients who she'd seen before up on the wards. Eczema. His skin looked so sore but she gauged in an instant that a level of physical contact would be right. So she shook and shook his hand, operating a hidden squeak in her pocket. 'Dear, oh dear, would you listen to that! I'd say your elbow needs some grease!'

'My name's *Tom*,' the child protested, having a giggle at his squeaky elbow, 'not Mildew or Militant.'

'Of course it is!' Dr Pippity exclaimed, clasping her hand to her head and setting her nose alight in the process. She almost fell over, whilst rolling her eyes. 'And Tom is a very fine name. My brain has run out of battery. Can you help start it again?' She handed the boy her toy hammer and pointed to two positions on her forehead, much to his delight. 'How old are you?' she asked. 'One hundred and thirty-two?'

'No, I'm almost six years old,' he said, as if to a simpleton. 'I live in Swiss Cottage.'

'In a *swish* cottage, hey!' Dr Pippity gasped. 'Is there room for me?' The boy said he didn't think so and the clown doctor pretended to cry, blowing her nose into an enormous polka-dot handkerchief.

'Sorry,' Tom shrugged.

'Do you like Kylie Minogue?' asked Dr Pippity, merry once more. Tom shrugged. 'Britney Spears?' The child dipped his head in a fairly noncommittal way.

'I like Hermione,' Tom offered, 'from Harry Potter.'

Dr Pippity scratched her head, looking perplexed.

'Her-my-oh-knee,' Tom elucidated.

'Your knee? Her knee? What knee? Oh! Hermione! Well,' said Dr Pippity, 'I have a present for you, a lovely picture of Hermione on Harry's Potty. For you to colour in.'

Tom looked happy and expectant. Dr Pippity presented him with the picture. Tom stared at it and tried very hard not to look disappointed, and then not to smile. A grin triumphed over a pout. 'It's *you*!'

Dr Pippity looked horrified. She looked from the picture to herself. 'Good golly — you're right!'

'Thanks,' said Tom, looking at the picture; he was secretly starting to like Dr Pippity just as much as Hermione. And certainly more than Kylie or Britney.

'Ta-ta, ta-ra, toot-toot!' sang Dr Pippity. 'I must be on my way.' And with a hop, skip and a jump, she left Out-patients for her ward rounds.

'Look!' Tom showed off the picture to his father who had returned to his son's side with a cup of water from the vending machine. 'You missed her – she's funny! Last time, she made me a tortoise from a balloon. Is she a real doctor, Daddy?'

'A real clown doctor,' Zac replied, taking a nearby leaflet publicizing the Renee Foundation by whom Dr Pippity was trained and funded. 'Have you seen her before, then?'

Tom nodded. 'A couple of times on the ward. And when Mummy brought me last time, that clown lady was here.'

Zac nodded and kissed the top of Tom's head. 'Laughter is brilliant medicine.' Out-patients now seemed dull and down without the clown.

'Yes,' said Tom, 'that's what the nurses say, too. And it doesn't sting like creams.'

'If it stings today,' Zac said, 'you squeeze my hand and say any swear-word you like. Though you're so brave I doubt whether you'll need to.' He could see Dr Pippity down the corridor by the main entrance, standing on one leg. Really quite a nice leg, actually. Despite the lurid tights and clumpy, bright orange DMs.

'Can you buy me some new crayons,' Tom asked, 'after they've done me?'

'Magic word?' Zac prompted.

'Please-please-please-thank-you.'

'Have you heard of these hospital clowns?' Zac is in Marylebone, eating Lebanese with friends. 'I took Tom for his appointment today and there were a couple working. They're amazing.'

'There was that Robin Williams film a while back,' said Will.

'*Patch Adams*,' his wife, Molly, filled in, 'but he was actually a bona fide doctor.'

'I picked up a leaflet,' Zac said. 'It's a charity – they fund specially trained clowns to work in hospitals all over the world. It made a difference to Tom, that's for sure.'

'How is he?' Molly asked.

'So so,' Zac said, but with a note of hope to his voice. 'That's the cruelty of eczema – when it fades, so does your memory of it; when it suddenly comes back with a vengeance, you have to deal with the physical and mental affliction anew. Tom seems to be coping this time around. He's not being teased at school, thank God, but it breaks my heart, it really does.' He looked to the middle distance. 'He's too young to have to be so brave.'

They ate in contemplative silence awhile. 'June?' Molly asked.

'She's fine,' Zac referred to the mother of his child, 'getting married in – well – June!'

'Same bloke?'

'Yup,' said Zac, 'it's cool – he's great.'

Molly picked spinach from her teeth. 'You must meet my friend Juliana – you'd really get along. She's gorgeous.'

Zac replenished the wineglasses. 'Sure,' he said. His friends were always setting him up – not because they wanted to see him matched and hitched, not because they were remotely concerned about him being single in his mid-thirties; in fact, they didn't do it for his sake or benefit at all. Zac was so universally liked, famous amongst his friends for being well-adjusted and fun to be with, that they introduced eligible women to benefit from his company. Zac, they felt, had such a heart that it couldn't be broken.

'Great,' said Molly. 'I'll fix up drinks or something for the weekend. She's over in London from South Africa for about six months on some project. Tall, very tall. She's a babe.'

Zac didn't enquire further. He trusted his friends' judgement. They always presented him with lovely women to play with. And what made the game such fun was that when it was inevitably over, there never seemed to be winners or losers. It seemed to him (and hitherto thankfully to *them*) that it was the taking part that was the point.

'I hated clowns,' Zac mused, 'when I was young. They frightened the fuck out of me.'

'Isn't it a risk, then, putting them in hospitals with sick kids?' asked Will, who had been far too engrossed in his lamb to participate in the conversation thus far.

Zac thought back to St Bea's. 'I think the hospital clowns obviously tone down their make-up and slapstick and tricks. Their faces weren't lurid at all – just a bit of white here and there, rosy cheeks, neat little red nose, funny pigtails.'

'Weird job to choose, though, don't you think?' Molly pondered. 'You know, literally making a clown of yourself every day. Having to look daft and behave like a fool.'

Zac considered this. 'I suppose,' he shrugged, 'but the one who spent time with Tom was bloody good. And, obviously, she could judge her success immediately so it must be pretty rewarding.' He poked around the couscous with his fork for crunchy bits. 'She didn't look daft at all, really.'

Quite beguiling, actually, if I think about it. Which I have been, for some bizarre reason I can't fathom.

Plates were cleared, puddings were chosen and the subject changed. Molly and Will were hiring a villa in Sardinia over the summer and did Zac want to join them at all? And then Will started talking about work and his nightmare boss. And Molly started telling Zac about Juliana.

'She was young,' Zac said, slightly absent-mindedly, 'late twenties? Something like that. You could see how hard she was working; how she was tuning herself totally to the needs and quirks of each kid she sat with. She was great.'

'Who? Juliana?' Molly asked, very confused and a little drunk by now.

'No, the clown,' Zac said, 'the one who treated Tom today.'

'Clowns give me the creeps,' said Will, asking for the bill.

'I've never found them particularly funny,' Molly said.

'I found them pretty scary,' Zac repeated, 'when I was a boy.'

Zac dreamt of Dr Pippity a couple of nights later, which he found odd, having not thought about her since the day at St

Bea's. The dream oddly disturbed him, though it was completely out of context – no Tom, no hospital. Dr Pippity had no make-up, no clothes defining her as a clown. In fact, she had no clothes on at all. She didn't speak with a zany voice, she didn't speak at all. But she did perform the most amazing trick on Zac. Her mouth, his balls. Zac awoke with a hard-on that required urgent attention. He went to his bathroom to clean up and caught sight of himself, sleep bleary, in the mirror.

'For fuck's sake,' he chastised himself, 'I thought clowns scared me – they're not supposed to seduce me!'

I must need a shag or something. About time. Ah well, the luscious Juliana, considerately lined up for me by Molly.

He couldn't get back to sleep so he went through to the living-room, flicked on the television and lounged in his banana chair, zapping channels and settling on MTV. Soon enough, the vacuous pop tunes irritated him, though the volume was low. He went to the kitchen for a glass of water and was momentarily bemused by the sight of the fridge. Dr Pippity, meticulously coloured in by Tom with his new crayons, grinned back at him.

He wanted to see her again. And he knew how simple that could be.

'Billy's party! I just phone and ask my sister-in-law for the entertainer's number. Pretend it's for Tom or one of his friends.'

Momentarily, he was quite excited about how easy this would be but soon enough, this disconcerted him. So he turned his back on the picture and took his briefcase to the bedroom.

Why on earth am I still thinking about her – let alone dreaming of her? She's a bloody clown – she probably hides behind her make-up and is a total social imbecile underneath it. Or irritatingly zany. Or just plain weird.

You liked her legs and can see that she's pretty even in preposterous pigtails and pan stick.

God, all she did was visit me in a wet dream and now I'm

telling myself I want to see her again. I must be overdue a shag, that's what it is.

Zac fell asleep, sitting up in bed, the lights on, papers strewn all over the duvet.

Zac met Molly's friend Juliana. She was sexy in a sophisticated, cool way. Zac decided he could forgo a sense of humour for such seductive eye contact. However, before he called her, there was something he needed to qualify first. The next Thursday, Zac told June he'd take Tom to hospital for his creams. June was pleased – she could have her wedding-dress fitting in peace, she told him. The clowns were there, but this time both were male. They were great and lifted Tom's spirits. It helped him enormously, his mind was taken away from his physical discomfort and he had a balloon in the shape of a parrot to take home. Though Zac knew all along that was the point – the clown doctors were not for *his* benefit but Tom's, of course – he couldn't help but be slightly disappointed not to see Dr Pippity.

His disappointment did, however, make him feel a little foolish. He sat Tom down with a drink and a biscuit when they arrived back in Hampstead.

'I'm just going to make a quick call,' he told his son. Tom was happy to munch and sip.

'Juliana? Hi there, this is Zac. We met at— Oh! Sure. I'm fine. Are you well? Great. I was wondering if you had plans tomorrow night? Shall we go out to play? Cool. Super.'

The lovely Juliana. Why on earth I was disappointed not to see Clowngirl again, I don't know. Hot date tomorrow – what could be better?

SEVEN

Zac has had no further dreams, wet or otherwise, featuring Pip. Which is just as well, really. Firstly, it wouldn't have been fair on Juliana, who Zac has been seeing for a good few weeks now. Secondly, it would have made it just a little more awkward and loaded when, the next time they *did* meet, Pip was to run her fingers through his hair, fondling his ears in the process.

Dr Pippity frequently ruffles the hair or tweaks the ears of patients' parents and siblings. She's been trained to. It's part of her job. It serves a twofold purpose. It's another way of eliciting laughter from the sick child, plus an important part of a clown doctor's work is to treat the family of the patients because they're often suffering, too. Clown doctors aim to lighten the load; to help diminish the burden carried by patients and their families in some small way, however temporarily. A minute spent grinning, laughing even, is a veritable tonic. It is also a minute when pain subsides and worry is sidetracked.

However, Pip has never had her handling of a parent backfire. Sure, sometimes her jokes and tricks have fallen flat – the parent perhaps feels awkward or reluctant due to desperately concealed stress and worry. But the patient has always enjoyed the tomfoolery and Pip knows, and the parent knows, that that's what matters. For Pip, though, to be hit on by the father of a patient, in front of the mother, too, is a situation wholly unexpected and for which she's had no specific training.

* * *

June, Tom's mother, hadn't intended to come to the hospital that day. She was up to her eyes preparing for her wedding that weekend and Zac had said he'd take Tom for his appointment.

'It's guilt,' Zac had teased her gently, when she had phoned to say that she'd come to the hospital. 'You running off on some glorious Caribbean honeymoon, leaving your son behind to fend for himself.'

'Bastard!' June had cursed in her defence, but fondly. 'He's not fending for himself, he's staying with you!'

Zac gave a sharp intake of breath. 'Dicey,' he warned, 'leaving him with me – well, that'll be fending for himself, all right.'

'You are a sod,' June laughed, 'and anyway, you cad – it's not as if you ever took me on a sumptuous honeymoon.'

'Well,' said Zac, 'that's because I never married you.'

'Bastard in capital letters,' June jested. 'I'd've declined even if you had asked me on bended knee with a rose between your teeth and a fuck-off diamond ring. I'm late. We'll see you in Out-patients at 3.00.'

I didn't ask her to marry me. It didn't cross my mind. Or hers. And, if I had, she'd have said 'no' anyway and thought me insane. It wasn't an issue. The only issue was to be good parents to a child born to two people who were strong friends and had been having good sex for quite a while.

Zac, wouldn't most people define the ultimate relationship to be one where friendship and good sex prevail?

Now, yes. At my age now – yes. Though the two never seem to go hand in hand nowadays – not that I'm complaining.

Juliana is fabulous in bed, but neither of us is pursuing this
even for friendship, let alone intimacy. And lovely lovely Lisa
– one of my closest friends but the thought of screwing her
verges on incest. Or take Pru – the two occasions we've been
to bed were pretty nondescript, yet we have a great laugh
together, getting drunk, talking rubbish. So that's why my life
wants for nothing. I have great friends. And I have fantastic
sex. But it's horses for courses in my book. I'd rather have an
enviable stable of different steeds and a choice of, er, mount,
than only the one horse, just the one all-rounder.

You're talking a string of spirited fillies versus just the one
old nag?

No. I'm not. That makes me sound a cynic and a cad and
I'm neither. June and I were young and impetuous and full of
those ideologies that, in your twenties, you formulate and
think are the answer to life itself. We had an on-off relation-
ship for a long time. She actually fell pregnant during a time
we weren't officially seeing each other. It was a casual one-
nighter, like we were prone to have in those days. But our
philosophy – then as now – was that we could be awesome
parents and great friends and simply not live together as Man
and Wife, or Girlfriend and Boyfriend, or He and She, full stop.

And it works?

You ask Tom. Just you ask him.

Out-patients. June and Zac sat with Tom, looking like a
very normal family. Except for the fact that the topic of
conversation between the three of them was June's
imminent wedding.

'Mum is worried in case I drop the ring,' Tom said,
looking to his father for camaraderie and perhaps one of his
inimitable one-liners.

'We'll sellotape it to your hand,' Zac said, 'and I'll carry a
couple of spares in my pocket. In fact, we'll do a swap, Tom.
You give me the real ones – I'll give you cheap imitations.
Your mother won't know the difference – and I doubt Rob-
Dad would realize, him having more money than sense, your
second dad.'

'I'll be sure to tell him you said so,' June chided with a chuckle.

'So'll I,' Tom said, with glee. Zac, though, had already teased Rob along these lines in the pub recently and Rob had quite ably sparred back.

'Anyway,' Zac continued, 'you and I will flog the jewels at the pawn shop in Camden and we'll bugger off to the Caribbean on the proceeds. Which hotel did you say you're staying in?'

'Daddy said "bugger",' Tom remarked.

'The Jalousie in St Lucia,' said June, 'and don't swear in front of the children.'

'But you said "shit" this morning, Mummy,' Tom said artlessly, 'when you dropped that glass.'

'I said "shoot",' June fibbed feebly. Tom was about to protest when a commotion caught their attention.

'Look, Tom!' said his father.

'The clowns are here!' said his mother.

Dr Pippity recognized the little boy with the eczema though she couldn't remember his name. She'd seen him upstairs and down. Up and down. It was good to see him in Out-patients again. She remembered seeing him on the ward once, swathed in dressings and looking like a mummy. Eye contact, on that occasion, had really been all she could use. So, in Out-patients, it really was a pleasure for her to use what she referred to as her Princess Diana approach – to touch and hold what others' prejudices would recoil from. She did 'round and round the garden' for Tom, and the 'tickle you under there' part produced a Harry Potter key-ring from behind his neck that he was most chuffed to be allowed to keep. Pip had bought a job lot from a dodgy stall at Camden Lock – unlicensed merchandise about which she had no qualms, confident that most children wouldn't notice the lack of a surreptitiously stamped TM.

'Are you still in love with Hermione?' Dr Pippity asked the boy, because though she couldn't remember his name, she did recall that he wasn't into Kylie. That Britney wasn't his kind of girl.

'Sort of,' Tom said, because it was the truth – he quite likes Natalie Portman now, too.

'Does that mean I have to wait for you to marry me?' Dr Pippity pouted. Tom looked slightly embarrassed. 'Well, I can wait for about, hmmm, twelve and a quarter minutes,' Dr Pippity continued, taking out a huge toy clock from her pocket. Tom laughed. As did his mother. As did his father. She'd seen him before, too. Probably right here in Outpatients or perhaps upstairs on the wards. The boy's father was looking at her almost imploringly. She misread his gaze. She thought perhaps he needed treatment by the clown doctor.

So she ran her fingers through his hair.

Pip ran her fingers through Zac's hair.

She's running her fingers through my hair.

'Yuck! Yuckkity yuck!' she declared whilst Tom laughed, June giggled and Zac was showered with the paper bits from a hole-punch. 'I don't think Head & Shoulders will get rid of that dandruff. That's *terrible*. Have you come to see the doctors? On account of that horrid dandruff? Are you here for a head and shoulders transplant?'

'No,' Tom interjected, a little seriously, 'it's me. We're here for me. For my eczema. Not my daddy.'

'Well, I think I can fix your daddy's Dandruff Disaster,' said Dr Pippity, producing an oversized pair of green plastic scissors the size of gardening shears. She hummed and sang and worked the toy all over the father's head whilst his son and the mother grinned. 'Oops!' Dr Pippity declared. 'I have cut off his ear.' She held a hand over Zac's left ear and made a theatrical display of searching high and low. Balancing the scissors precariously on his head, she produced a large, false ear from her pocket. 'Ear you are, dear,' she said, 'ear you go, ear's another one.' Her jokes were so corny that the adults had to laugh and to Tom, not quite six, her puns were extraordinarily brilliant and the cause of much mirth.

Undivided attention for just five minutes seemed to have a value lasting much longer – but soon enough, Dr Pippity was on her rounds, with her scissors and her hole-punch clippings and her spirits and her skill. Tom remained animated right up until he was called. June went with him. Zac stayed in the waiting area. And when Dr Pippity yodelled a heartfelt goodbye to everyone, that she was off on her rounds, Zac followed at a discreet distance.

What Zac didn't know – how could he – was that when clowns are in slap and motley, they are locked into their clown personae until the moment of make-up remover and cotton wool. It's not dressing up. It's not acting. It's a dignified art and profession. It's a very serious business. Who would ever accuse Superman of being Clark Kent in fancy dress? Clowns never drop their guise. Not even when they are on their own. And so it was Dr Pippity, not Pip McCabe, who was alone in the small washroom the clown doctors use to sterilize their props, wash their hands with antiseptic and compose themselves between ward rounds. Though the door was open, she was unaware of having an audience. Zac loitered out in the corridor, glimpsing her now and then as she larked about with the bin, treading on the pedal so that the lid opened and shut like a mouth – and a very good conversationalist it made, too.

'Excuse me,' Zac said, when she emerged. 'I just wanted to say "thanks".'

Momentarily, Dr Pippity couldn't quite place him – her mind was on the cancer ward she was about to visit. Then she caught sight of a few stray hole-punch pieces. 'That's okey-dokey,' she said, in her clown voice.

'I saw you at my nephew's party,' Zac said, wanting to keep her there for a moment, wanting her to be herself, wanting her to himself; not wanting to follow her towards the ward. 'Billy?'

'Dr Pippity doesn't do parties,' she said, needing to be on her way and slightly disconcerted by this man's attentions.

Weren't his wife and child downstairs?

'In Holloway? A couple of months ago,' Zac persisted. 'You gave me your card, not Dr Pippity, the other one. Mad Molly or someone. I had a headache.'

'That'll be the dandruff,' Dr Pippity jested, inwardly slightly insulted that Merry Martha could be thought of as Mad Molly.

I knew a Mad Molly once – she was barking mad and pretty unpleasant.

'I lost your card. Can I have another?' the man asked. 'I mean, do you get a coffee break on this job? Can I buy you a coffee? Or a drink – what about a drink after work? I live in Hampstead – where do you live?'

What the fuck am I doing? June is downstairs. And Juliana is this evening.

What the fuck is he doing? His wife and kid are downstairs and he's asking me out for a drink and wanting to know where I live?

'I only drink orangey-lemony-blackcurrant squash,' Dr Pippity declared, initially irritating Zac until he saw that she spoke mainly to a young patient who walked slowly past them, 'and *that* yummy stuff,' the clown continued, pointing to the drip the child was trundling and managing to raise a hint of a grin from the patient in the process. 'I have to be on my way,' Dr Pippity told the man, adding *sotto voce*, 'it's good to see your son in Out-patients rather than the ward. I'm pleased for him. For you, for your wife.'

'She's not my wife!' Zac declared, immediately regretting the urgency and defensiveness in his voice.

That's as may be, thought Pip as she made her way towards the ward, *but whoever she is or whatever she isn't, she is the mother of your child and she and he are just downstairs.*

'Idiot!' Zac cursed himself, as he returned to Out-patients.

'Weirdo,' Dr Pippity said to herself as she entered the ward. 'I don't think I'll ruffle the hair of grown men for the time being.'

EIGHT

'*G*old is ill!' Tom chanted. 'Please? Gold. Is. *Ill*!'

Zac never tired of his child's propensity to pronounce a word the way he heard it, even if the meaning became skewed. Tom was a master of this. He thought his grandpa was ill with Old-timers because he was seventy-five, after all. For Zac, Old-timers seemed to sum up June's father's affliction much more astutely and more sensitively than Alzheimer's. And now, this Saturday afternoon, Tom was saying that gold is ill with great conviction and joy.

'Golders Hill it is,' Zac granted and was rewarded with a hug that turned into a full-on rough-and-tumble. Zac loved the park at Golders Hill, an annexe to the heath extension at Hampstead. Flamingos and wallabies and rhea birds and deer, not to mention excellent home-made ice-cream, too, were all on offer. Families commandeered this section of the heath; mums and dads with Mamas&Papas prams and Bebecar buggies and every Fisher Price toy ever produced. There was a delightfully old-fashioned feel to Golders Hill Park; it had none of the pretensions of nearby Hampstead High Street. The Barbour brigade, with their designer labradors and under-retrieving retrievers and aesthetically muddied Range Rovers parked in the pay-and-display in

Downshire Hill, never ventured to this enclave of the heath near Golders Green. And the gays who cottaged and rummaged and flirted and felched in gloomy areas of the heath nearer Whitestone Pond also left Golders Hill untouched.

'Do you think Mummy and Rob-Dad are having ice-creams too?' Tom asked as he and his father strolled and licked their way over to the paddock to gaze at some goats.

'Probably,' Zac said. 'Hey! This time last week you were performing your ring thing.'

Tom looked at his toy watch which permanently read 3.30. 'You're right,' he said, 'and I didn't need sellotape.'

'You were brilliant,' Zac said earnestly, 'and you made their day. You made *everyone*'s day.'

'I hope that Mummy and Rob-Dad are having ice-cream at this very very very minute,' said Tom, pulling his father towards the deer. Zac, who thought that the concept of time zones might be just beyond his son's grasp, assured him that they most certainly were. The deer were Disney delightful; the goats, however, were pungent enough to make their ice-cream unpalatable so they meandered back towards the rolling lawns.

'Good God,' Zac said under his breath at the very same moment that Tom declared 'A clown! A clown!' The child stopped. 'It's *the* clown!' He looked at Zac and beamed. 'Quick! Let's go! Come on, Dad.'

Shit. It's only bloody Her. Clowngirl. She'll think I'm stalking her. It's not like I have a pair of sunglasses to hide behind. I'll keep an eye on Tom from a discreet distance and bury my nose in the paper. But that'll make me look like a comedy spy, of course. Anyway, Tom's not even six years old. He has ice-cream dribbling down his wrist in high wasp season. I must accompany him, I'm his father.

'Daddy, look!' Tom went charging back to Zac, standing on the periphery of parents near the stage. 'It's Dr Pippity, isn't it – but she's got funny clothes on, and much more *stuff* on her face than at St Bea's.' He scampered back to the throng of children and heckled with the best of them.

Oh dear, what have we here? Pip said to herself whilst she made an expert mess of bendy balloons. *It's that bloke with the dandruff. Looks like I have my own personal stalker. Look at him, loitering behind his paper. I can't see the wife anywhere. Well, he can look – but I hope he doesn't linger.*

'See! Spaghetti!' Merry Martha declared, holding aloft a scramble of balloons to much laughter from her young audience. 'Blast and bootlaces! I've forgotten the magic words – does anyone know any?' From the audience came shrieks of 'abracadabra' and 'open sesame'. A girl at the front in an immaculate dress with matching hair ribbons was sitting patiently, cross-legged, with her hand held aloft.

'Magic word?' Martha asked her gently.

'Please,' the girl revealed.

Martha performed a cartwheel to signify her approval. 'The best magic word of all,' she declared with a nod to the cordon of parents, 'a very pretty please from a very pretty young lady.' Her hands worked this way and that, whilst her face contorted into a display of entertaining grimaces and pouts. 'Voilà! No more spaghetti – a sausage dog instead! Oh! And another. Ah! And one more!' She distributed the balloons carefully to the quieter children in her audience, thanked everyone for coming and gave a genuflection of prodigious proportions. 'Time for you all to have a drink or a wee-wee,' she proclaimed, crossing her legs as if that was what she needed to do, 'before the puppet show. Ta-ta, ta-ra, toot-toot.' Two flic-flacs and she was off the stage.

Tom made his way back to his father. 'Did you see? Dr Pippity?' Zac nodded and suggested they return to the goats now that there was no ice-cream to spoil. 'No,' said Tom firmly, 'I want to go and say "hullo" to Dr Pippity.' Zac tried to say she was going home, that she was only half Dr Pippity today. 'No!' Tom declared. 'You can't be a half. Let's go and say "hullo". She's better than stinky goats. Come on, Dad, please?'

Why can't she just bugger off quickly instead of meandering her way through the park, chatting and jesting with every child she passes?

'We don't have time,' Zac tried to reason with Tom.

'We only just got here,' Tom protested.

'She's busy,' Zac said, not looking at her, not looking at Tom.

'She *snot*,' Tom sulked. 'All the other children get to talk to her – look. It's not fair, it *snot*.'

You're right. And why do I even care what she thinks of me? And why do I appear to care about it more than I care about Tom?

'Go on, then,' Zac said, 'run. I'll tell you how fast you are. Just say a quick "hullo". I'll catch up with you.' Tom belted off. Dutifully, Zac timed him, to the fraction of a second. He'd never fob his son off with an estimate.

Pip was trying to extricate herself from a thuggish nine-year-old boy and his sidekick who were trying to pickpocket her for balloons.

'Dr Pippity?' Tom greeted her shyly.

'Shove off!' snarled the larger boy, pushing him. But then as he stared at Tom a look of horror crept across his face. 'Yuck, look at him!' His friend did. 'His skin's coming off – and I touched him!'

'Flaky boy!' his friend joined in. 'I could puke!'

The larger boy wiped his hands with desperation on the grass. Pip was appalled. She'd worked with children with all manner of disabilities and afflictions for so long, frequently she no longer saw the physical manifestation of their illnesses. The boys were haranguing Tom whose eyes were smarting.

Don't cry, little guy, Pip thought, *it's what they want*.

Tom's bottom lip quivered. The older boy suddenly pushed his friend against Tom. 'Ha, ha, you'll catch his manky skin!'

The younger boy burst into tears, genuinely distressed, rubbing his arm furiously, as if his sleeve was contaminated with germs. He was no longer actively attempting to tease and hurt Tom. He was now fearful for his welfare. 'Mummy!' he sobbed, running off.

'You horrible little boy,' Pip said in her own voice, the sound of which completely took the bully aback. 'Go away or I'll phone the police.'

'I'll tell my dad on you,' he said, backing off nevertheless.

'And I'll tell your dad on *you*,' Pip threatened, 'picking on littler boys, trying to steal balloons. Who do you think you are? Sod off right now or I'll start yelling.' Standing there, hands on hips, multicolourful and made up to the nines, Pip still cut an imposing figure to the child who sauntered off, kicking turf and grumbling. 'Horrible child,' Pip reiterated. She turned back to Tom who was trying to wipe his tears away before she saw. With her thumb, Pip stroked the last of the wet off his cheek. And then she licked her thumb and smacked her lips. 'Yum, yum!' she cooed, in her clown persona once again. 'You have the most delicious tears in London The World The Universe.'

Tom managed a smile. 'You are Dr Pippity,' he declared.

'Sort of – I'm actually also Merry Martha today. Are you all right?' Tom nodded. 'Boys like him,' Pip said, in a gentler voice, with a cursory nod of her head in the direction of the other children, 'they're just silly bullies. I bet he wets his pants and has no proper friends.' Tom's smile broadened. Pip glanced towards the entrance to the park. She had a party to do in a couple of hours. She really should be on her way. But then she glanced at Tom.

God. I can't just leave him. Little mite.

'Where are your parents?' Pip asked.

'My mum's in the St Lucy Jalousie,' Tom said, wondering if he had the word order correct, 'in the Caribbean. But my dad's over there.'

'Come on, let's go over there, then,' Pip said – though giving her stalker the wrong idea, or the slightest encouragement for his perversion, was something she'd really rather not do. 'I hope you don't let idiots like that stupid boy upset you,' Pip said as they walked.

'I try not to,' said Tom with a weariness Pip felt no child his age should know. 'I just say "sticks and stones" to myself.'

'"Sticks and stones may break my bones but words will never hurt me",' Pip quoted back to him.

'That's right!' Tom said, feeling he had a true ally. 'My dad says it's what's on the inside that counts.'

'Beauty comes from within,' said Pip. Tom loved her even more.

'And anyway, the doctor says I will grow out of my eczema when I'm older. And it isn't catching at all,' he continued, almost pleadingly.

'Of course not,' said Pip, taking his hand and walking on. 'Why aren't you and your dad in St Lucia, too, in the Caribbean?' she asked conversationally, on their way over to the trees. Aware of the yarns children could spin, Pip had presumed the boy's mother wasn't truly away.

Mummy's probably making all sorts of North London organic stuff for the kid's tea. In a kitchen more suited to a Cotswold cottage, no doubt – Aga and gingham and scrubbed wood units.

'My mum's on honeymoon,' Tom explained, 'with Rob-Dad.'

Pip decided it was time to give the child's imagination a break so she changed the subject to balloons instead. 'If you could have a balloon that looked like anything you wanted it to, what would it be?'

And please God choose a cat, dog, parrot or tortoise.

Luckily, Tom procrastinated for so long that Pip had blown a balloon and twisted it into a parrot by the time he said 'Giant anteater, actually'.

'Will a parrot do?'

'It's brill! Thanks, Dr Pippity.'

'Martha.'

'Martha, then.'

'Actually, you can call me Pip.'
'Who?'

Zac, unaware of his son's altercation with the bully, did not know where to look, let alone what to expect, on observing the clown and his son making their way towards him. So he pretended he was engrossed in his newspaper. But that seemed rude. So he watched them approach. But that seemed ruder. So he decided to meet them halfway.

'Look at my parrot, Daddy.'

'It's lovely,' Zac told Tom, thanking the clown without looking at her. Pip thought the man spent an inordinate amount of time displaying a bizarre level of interest in her balloon sculpture but it gave her a chance, however fleetingly, and however quickly she dismissed it, to see that, in the sunlight, away from the hospital, no matter how peculiar he was on the inside, he was clad in a most appealing exterior. Eyes the colour of slate. Handsome face with neat features. Dark hair, short and neat. Trim physique clad in nicely cut clothes. Though a slight preponderance of navy, Pip felt, considering the balmy weather.

I don't know why I'm even noticing. He's not my type.

Oh? What's your type, then, Pip?

Don't have one.

So how do you know this chap isn't for you?

Because he's not. He's nuts, for starters, plus he has a kid. A child, for heaven's sake. Anyway, there's Caleb to consider.

I thought you weren't considering Caleb at all?

'She's got lots of tricks,' Tom was telling his father, 'and lots of names, too.'

'I have,' said Pip in Martha's voice. 'It means never a dull moment for me. If I'm boring myself, I just become Martha. If Martha's getting on my nerves, I summon up Dr Pippity. If Dr Pippity is tired, then I'm just plain old me.'

See! Zac thought, with a degree of relief. *She is an utter weirdo. With what is probably a sectionable personality disorder, too.*

Yet he couldn't help but think that she wasn't 'plain' in the slightest, whatever she might protest to the contrary. And however lurid her clothing and daft her make-up.

'Most people are locked up if they have as many personalities as me!' Pip said, right on cue, but to Tom and not Zac.

See, Zac thought, vindicated, *she's barking.*

'I must be off,' said Pip. Then she looked at Tom and took a sniff at her arm. She wrinkled her nose: 'Yeuch, I *am* off – past my sell-by date!' Tom giggled, Zac tried not to. She stopped herself from saying 'not really' to the bloke lest he thought she actually did smell, though why she cared what he thought she didn't know.

'Watch how fast I can run!' Tom boasted. Watching him belt off towards the deer enclosure, Pip marvelled how quickly children could bounce back from a knock. She was also quite charmed to see how his father timed him.

'Two revolting kids were picking on him,' Pip told his father when Tom was out of earshot, 'little sods.'

Zac nodded gravely, keeping an eye on the second hand of his watch. 'I bet he bore up OK,' he said.

'Yes,' Pip confirmed, 'but they were vile.'

'Poor old Tom,' said Zac. 'It's awful to say he's used to it – but he is. And for the most part, it doesn't happen often.'

'Well, I'm off,' said Pip, despite a perceptible loiter to the contrary which infuriated her.

'Yeah, good idea,' Zac said, with a derisory sniff in her direction, 'you do whiff a bit.'

Why did you say that?
Why did he say that?
Why the fuck did I say that?
Your sense of humour is so dry it's positively parched, Zac. Backtrack.

But he's standing there, an unfortunate and involuntary smirk stuck to his face while he racks his brain for a way to minimize the insult without drawing more attention to it. It's taking him too long. See, Pip is smiling cursorily but she's backing off.

She must think I am an absolute arse, now. I was only trying to pick up on her own joke.

Pip didn't see it that way. Why should she? After all, look what she's had to go by from Zac before.

What a dick. And whether it's a lack of manners or a warped sense of humour on his part, I can't say I really care.

'How fast?' said Tom, panting.

'There and back?' Zac asked. 'Two minutes forty in all.'

'Where's my clown?'

'Gone home, little 'un.'

Tom wasn't too upset. He now felt sure he'd see her again. Dr Pippity. Or the Martha one with more make-up and fewer clothes. Zac reckoned so, too. And didn't quite know how he felt about it, now that he'd made a prat of himself for the second, even third, time. Hastily, he reminded himself she was a clown, and wasn't that an odd thing to choose to be? And hadn't clowns frightened him when he was young? He thought of Juliana; her long legs and no holds barred. Then he considered Clowngirl with her stripy tights and daft voices.

Well, not that he's to know, but the next time Zac sees Pip, he simply won't recognize her at all.

NINE

'How was your visit today?'

'It was good, thanks – tiring as ever, but rewarding.'

Bloody hell! Caleb's managed it! Pip has granted him – or, rather, allowed *herself* – a couple of drinks after work. She's chosen a Sea Breeze and she's sipping it demurely. Ironically, today's one Tuesday when Pip needn't have worried about being on her own – the messages left on her mobile during her hospital rounds had Cat clamouring for Pip to cook dinner (and she'd provide plenty of wine), Fen imploring her to come and see the new Julia Roberts film (and she'd buy the popcorn) and Megan begging her to come and meet Dominic (and thus advise her whether to proceed). All three presumed Pip would be free for them.

`sorry, already have plans` she texts back to each of them, adding a few more kisses for Cat than the others. They'd just have to manage without her – now there was a novel notion! Cat was depressed about this, Fen was slightly pissed off and Megan was downright devastated, but Pip turned her phone off. Good job, really. One call taken from a friend or sibling in need and she'd have left the pub and Caleb without a second thought. But she's happily ensconced in an old Windsor chair, sitting by the window with the slow sun of the early evening drifting in and bestowing aesthetic merit on all it glances off. Pip watches Caleb as he returns from the bar with peanuts and crisps. The light is catching his features, accentuating his cheekbones and strong jaw line, spinning a little gold from his chocolate eyes. Pip feels content with her decision to have him for company.

'Anything to forgo rush hour on the Misery line,' she had said nonchalantly half an hour ago in answer to his suggestion of a quick drink. He'd been ready and keen to head off right there and then. Pip had laughed. 'Would you mind awfully if I changed and took my slap off? We might not get served otherwise.' Caleb had regarded her with the sober contemplation he bestowed on his patients. 'Nah,' he said dismissively, at length, 'you look fab and funky as you are. Let's go.' And with that, he had forcibly marched her down the stairs to the ground floor, out through the foyer, past the ambulance bay, through the courtyard where the more able-bodied patients took fresh air, beyond the hospital perimeters and out into the world. She did, however, manage to remove her false nose and slip it, sleight of hand, up her sleeve and then into her pocket.

And now she's sitting in the Windsor chair, across from Dr Caleb Simmons who is straddling a stool and presenting her with peanuts and crisps to accompany her Sea Breeze. He's drinking down a pint of lager. She can see that paediatrics is thirsty work. He's tucking into the snacks, too. 'I hardly ever find the time to even grab a sandwich on the hoof,' he explains, almost apologetically. Because for the next few minutes his mouth is full of peanuts, all that's possible is small talk – but it relaxes Pip and she's pleased to find out minutiae like his age (thirty-four), how long he's worked at St Bea's (three years), where he lives (Hoxton) and that he's going on holiday in a month to Belize (with a friend). He doesn't like to speak with his mouth full so he answers Pip economically and doesn't ask her anything. Much to her relief.

'Would you like another drink?' Pip asks, because she would certainly like another Sea Breeze. When she returns to the table, the snacks are finished and the packets have been meticulously folded into compact triangular pockets. A finicky process that strikes her as being at odds with Caleb's easygoing personality. She doesn't dwell on it. Actually, she is rather enjoying his company and would be happy for them to make an entire evening of it.

Caleb buys the next round.

'Here's to the clown doctors,' he toasts, 'and all that you do for the hospital.'

Pip is touched. She raises her glass and chinks his. 'Do you feel we make a difference – truly?' she asks. 'We've only been at St Bea's six months.'

'Absolutely,' Caleb replies. 'You have to remember that though the kids know we are here to make them better, they also associate us with discomfort and pain what with the procedures and operations and drugs we administer. You lot provide fun and relief – you're the spoonful of sugar that helps the medicine go down.'

'That's great to hear,' says Pip, chinking glasses. 'The Renee Foundation is placing clown doctors in Manchester and Glasgow this autumn – that'll be seven hospitals in the UK.'

'How did you get into it?' Caleb asked, because he'd never really thought about it and it now struck him as rather intriguing.

'I was working as a clown already,' Pip explained.

'Odd,' Caleb mused, 'but interesting. How did you get into clowning?'

'Oh,' said Pip breezily, 'I think I was possibly born one. No,' she corrected, 'necessity dictated I become one very early on – family traumas and all that, so creating laughter and distractions became my responsibility and, soon enough, my forte.'

There wasn't a lot Caleb could say to that, so he nodded in what he hoped, by virtue of his bedside-manner physiognomy, was an understanding way.

'Plus,' Pip continued, quite proud of her c.v., 'when I was little, a retired clown lived nearby and he used to paint my face for me. I've barely modified it since then.'

They were suddenly aware that Pip was still in her slap and that the other drinkers were casting inquisitive glances in her direction. Pip didn't mind that she was the centre of some quiet attention; for once, she quite liked it. 'I have my own egg, you know,' she announced proudly. 'Clowns register their clown faces by painting the design on an egg shell,' she explained, 'so if you want to check whether I'm kosher, you can visit the Clowns Gallery in Hackney where my egg is displayed alongside hundreds of others.'

'So there's a whole clown community?' Caleb asked.

'There's even a clowns' church,' Pip informed him, 'with a service of thanksgiving for the gift of laughter and the life of Joseph Grimaldi on the first Sunday of February. If I was more God-fearing, I'd go,' she added almost apologetically.

'I had no idea,' Caleb mused. 'I guess I just thought of clowns nowadays as being slightly dodgy entertainers – perhaps comics who aren't funny enough or acrobats who aren't accomplished enough or actors who aren't skilled enough. I imagined you all worked in isolation, leading odd lives, generally hiding behind your masks.'

'I'm a very capable acrobat,' Pip proclaimed, 'and I turned down drama college for circus school. I trained under a brilliant French clown called Manouche. I'm also pretty good at trapeze. Clowning is an art, you know,' she continued earnestly. 'It requires physical skill, dramatic ability, imagination with a sense of the comic and, perhaps most importantly, an understanding of human nature.'

'Did you run away to the circus?' Caleb asked.

'No.'

'Have you seen Cirque du Soleil?'

'A billion times.'

'Do you smoke?' Caleb asked, offering her a cigarette and lighting one for himself.

'Not if I'm sober,' Pip replied, feeling on the way to woozy but thankfully still at the stage of refusing cigarettes. 'Look at you, Doctor!' she remarked. 'Don't you know fags'll kill you?'

'Totally,' Caleb said darkly, 'that's why I do it.'

Pip took a sip of her drink and thought that she really shouldn't think he looked sexy the way he drew on the cigarette.

'Ever eaten fire?' Caleb asked, taking a deep drag.

'No,' said Pip, 'but I've played with it.' She was rather pleased with that answer.

'So have I,' Caleb said somewhat gravely. 'Do you juggle?'

'Yes.'

'So do I,' said Caleb, rather darkly. Pip decided swiftly not to read into this so she suggested they go for food.

'What do you like?' Caleb wondered.

'I don't know,' Pip said. 'What do you fancy?'

He drew on his cigarette and regarded her levelly. 'I fancy *you*,' he said, with intense eye contact. Pip giggled though she cursed herself immediately for doing so. She felt nervous – and it irked her.

'I want to get out of these clothes,' she said, not intending innuendo but quite enjoying Caleb's raised eyebrow and sly smile.

Back at St Bea's, Pip changed and then they had sushi in a place off Liverpool Street. It probably wasn't a good idea to mix sake with the Sea Breezes she'd had earlier. Certainly not a good idea for it to lead to her happily accepting cigarettes from her date. Though the second made her feel quite queasy, being in the company of a doctor put her at ease. So she had a few puffs of a third but politely declined the suggestion of a nightcap.

'I'm doing face painting in Brent Cross shopping centre tomorrow – I'll need a steady hand,' she justified, 'and then I have a birthday party to do in Hampstead Garden Suburb at tea-time – and I'll need a clear head if I'm going to do a handstand and God knows what else.'

'Another time?' Dr Simmons proposed.

'Sure,' Pip heard herself saying with no pause for thought, 'why not?'

What a gent – hailing a black cab and escorting her halfway across London, telling the cabby to wait, please, as he took Pip to her front door.

'Great evening,' Pip thanked him, wondering in her somewhat boozy and brazen state if he might kiss her; hoping that he would, thinking she really ought to maintain eye contact to encourage this to happen. She looked up from her bag, from pretending to fumble for keys. Lovely eyes, she thought, hers darting away from his; at first shyly, soon enough coquettishly.

'Good-night, then,' he said, luring her eyes back to his as his face came close to hers. He kissed her gently on the cheek, his lips lightly brushing the corner of her mouth.

'Night,' Pip all but whispered, keys in her hand, her eyes locked on to his. She lifted her chin and parted her lips and immediately, Caleb's mouth was on hers and swiftly, his tongue was flickering at her lips. And suddenly, her tongue was in his mouth. The kiss slowed and intensified. He tasted of soy sauce and lager. He tasted of being a man, a doctor called Caleb Simmons. When their mouths separated, suddenly the sound of the taxi's chuntering diesel engine seemed very loud, very near, somewhat impatient.

'Shall I send the cab away?' Caleb murmured, using his little finger to lift a lick of hair from the corner of her mouth, using his thumb to smooth it behind her ear. 'Shall I come in?'

Pip wanted more kissing. In fact, she wanted a lot more. All of him. All over her. Rude sex would be very nice, thank you very much. They could begin in the cramped porch, start ripping at each other's clothing in the sitting-room, be down to underwear, dry humping against the wall of the corridor, then arrive at her bed buck naked and raring, even roaring, to go. She had the desire. She had the imagination. Thanks to the Sea Breezes and sake, she had the confidence. And in her bedside drawer, she even had the condoms. The sex would be tantalizingly urgent and over quickly. A fuck. But they'd rest up a little and then do it again, more languid, lasting longer, going further, going deeper, coming to the same conclusion (simultaneously, if they could synchronize).

Caleb was fondling her breasts through her clothing and Pip, with his thigh between hers, was rubbing herself rhythmically against his leg as they continued to kiss. The cab's engine was clicketing, the meter running. Sex was an imminent possibility. A pricey one, thought Caleb, estimating the cab fare whilst continuing to tongue Pip. Perhaps too costly, thought Pip, pulling away though it took some strength, mental and physical.

Pip sent Caleb on his way. 'Another time,' she said, placing her finger on the tip of his nose, then kissing him softly there.

'Sure,' said Caleb with his easy smile. 'Good-night, Pip.'

'Night, Dr Simmons,' Pip said, waiting till he'd climbed the basement stairwell and was up on the street, smiling down at her, before she opened her front door and let herself in.

Of course she wasn't going to let him in – not physically, certainly not metaphysically. And it didn't really have much to do with her busy schedule the following day. There hadn't been a man in her house, let alone her bed, to say nothing of her *life*, for months. And even then, she didn't truly let that one *in*. While Caleb's osculation had made her horny as hell, her pride and her privacy had kept him at bay. Anyway, as she often proclaimed to her friends and sisters, there were always vibrators. So, as Caleb headed for Hoxton in the cab, his hand lolling over his hard-on, Pip went to bed with a rather peculiar-looking contraption which made strange whirring sounds at inopportune moments. It did do, however, exactly what it said on the packaging.

The only thing about having an orgasm with a battery-operated device is that post-coitally one is hugely aware of one's solitude. I guess sometimes having a bloke in your bed is preferable, even if he does roll over, fart and fall dead asleep.

But Pip makes light of this. Even to herself. She sits up in bed and takes two Nurofen with three glasses of water. She cannot afford to be remotely hungover when she awakes. Tomorrow is a very full day but one when she'll see off most of this month's mortgage payment. She switches off the light but stays sitting up. She's spared no thought for Fen or Cat or Megan, hasn't a clue how their evenings turned out. Though she tries to conjure up an image of Caleb, strangely enough it is that odd stalker bloke who slopes across her mind's eye. Vividly. She's slightly taken aback that he should accost her so.

But there again, she thinks to herself, *he* is *my stalker*.

Nevertheless, she wonders why she's conjured him up.

I guess his presence serves to emphasize just what a nice chap, by contrast, Caleb appears to be. Well-adjusted. Quite conventional. Nice manners. No kids. Little baggage. Friendly.

'Pretty normal, really,' Pip whispers into the darkness, slipping down under her duvet. And, of course, Pip is very earnest about the importance of being normal.

TEN

When Pip isn't working hard earning her wage by making people laugh, she spends much of her spare time looking after her sisters and caring for her friends. Invariably, this requires making them laugh, too. For free. Regardless of overtime and weekends. And then there's Django; Pip feels compelled to lighten his load. He's worried about Cat and it is to Pip whom he turns for updates and reassurances. Her phone bill is huge. As is her supermarket bill on account of all the soup she makes for Cat's freezer and the luxurious treats she buys to cajole her youngest sister's appetite.

Pip has grown up believing that she is her sisters' keeper. For one who spends an inordinate amount of her day falling about and fooling about, her duties as clown and eldest sister are responsibilities she takes very seriously. She's the Great Looker-After. It's not that her friends and family forget that sometimes perhaps she, too, would benefit from some TLC, actually it wouldn't cross their minds that she'd ever need any. Good Lord, Philippa McCabe is never blue! She's never had a crisis in her life! She's so capable, so happy-go-lucky, she orders her life beautifully, she's totally in control! However, there is small print to such compliments and it reads that actually Pip McCabe is never *allowed* to be anything other than happy herself, therefore available for others unconditionally whensoever she's needed. The world would stop turning if Pip cried 'help'. What would Cat do? Or Fen? Or Django? They wouldn't know what to do and, quite frankly, they wouldn't like it. Pip's needs would be their loss. They'd be at a loss; utterly.

For the most part, Pip doesn't feel used or hard done by. Quietly, we can surmise that her eagerness to be the Great Looker-After and Dispenser of Laughter in some way guards against any enquiries into her own welfare. Pip wants everyone to be safe and happy, but she is also aware that, for as long as they are the ones in need, they won't have the wherewithal to probe or pry into *her* well-being.

Consequently, she hasn't told anyone about Caleb. She'll argue that there's nothing to tell. Perhaps, though, it's to avoid being questioned. Pip doesn't have any answers. And she doesn't like to be questioned. Nor has she told them about Zac – what on earth is there to tell? After all, she doesn't yet know even his name – and she can't very well refer to him as Stalker Bloke. Anyway, quietly she's aware that she's elaborated to herself, for her own amusement, the extent of his interest in her. Deep down she knows he's not a stalker, just a bloke who keeps bumping into her, whose social graces are clumsy. Pip believes it is preferable to keep Caleb and Zac to herself, so she can indulge in imaginative tangents whilst she's having a bath or travelling to work; sneak in a little day-dream whilst Megan or Cat or Fen discuss this grave matter or that. Fundamentally, though, Pip knows that to expose the bare facts surrounding either man would reveal that there's not much there at all, really.

There's been little development between Caleb and Pip since their late-night doorstep embrace. Dr Pippity's visits to St Bea's don't always coincide with Dr Simmons's ward rounds and when they are on the same ward at the same time, both clown and doctor are too focused on their patients and their jobs to sneak away for even a quick hi-how's-it-going, let alone consult diaries and arrange dates or steal a kiss, for goodness' sake. Yesterday, he pinched her bottom just before she changed wards. She was quite taken aback. She felt compromised – believed his behaviour to be unprofessional. Fortunately, she was just about to go into the washroom to disinfect her props and wash her hands, so the symbolic wiping of a paper towel against her posterior restored her composure and enabled her to continue with her ward rounds in fine style.

'I'd rather you didn't pinch my bottom again,' she warned, somewhat prissily, when she came across him having a cigarette in the ambulance bay as she made her way to the tube.

He looked crestfallen. 'What, never ever again? But it's so damn *pinchable*, Pip.' He stood up and came close. 'In fact, I'm glad I have a fag in one hand and the *Telegraph* in the other or I'd be in full fondle of your buttocks right now.'

Don't bloody laugh at his lousy rubbish joke. He's incorrigible. Don't even bloody smile.

'You're incorrigible!' Pip protested, frustrated that she was so easily flattered and praying she wasn't blushing.

'You're blushing,' Caleb said. 'And I'll be happy to bet dinner that you're not blushing on *those* cheeks alone,' he remarked, kissing them for emphasis, 'or that it's merely *these* lips that are moist right now,' he whispered, kissing her mouth.

Pip McCabe was truly stuck for words. His blatancy, his lewdness, was an unexpected turn-on. What was she meant to say? Should she admit that, yes, she really did want to go to bed with him, and judging by the state of her knickers, why didn't they just forget the whole dinner-wager thing and cab it back to one of their flats right now? Or should she act all demure? Or should she play hard to get but flirtatious with it?

For Christ's bloody sake, this is the kind of advice I dispense to my sisters and friends the whole time. I'm forever helping them to compose fabulous soliloquies. And now I'm standing here like a lemon, gawping and speech-less, flushed, drooling and damp. I can't practise what I preach because I can't remember what on earth it is I advocate.

'Cat got your tongue?' Caleb asked slyly, raising one side of his mouth into a sly smile.

Pip McCabe regarded him. Momentarily, her thoughts wandered to her sister, Cat. She ought to call her. She really ought. Later.

Now, however, she tilted her head and placed her hands on her hips. 'Actually,' she heard herself say, 'there's a pussy who'll have your tongue in a flash.'

Jesus, Pip! Was that you? You minx!

God knows where that came from! How can I switch from pissed off with him for pinching my bum to suggesting cunnilingus? I should go. I really should. I have no idea whether this is a good idea – and that is the point precisely. I'll go. I'll go and see Cat.

'Dinner, then?' said Caleb. Now it was his turn to hope that his excitement wasn't too obvious and he nonchalantly held his *Telegraph* against his bulging groin as a precaution.

She's speaking my language. And it's an invitation beyond my expectations at this stage.

Though Pip's mind was flooded with half-sentences of 'I should . . .' and 'I'll phone Cat to . . .' and 'For God's sake, I really . . .' and 'Django won't be . . .', her voice had a mind of its own. 'Your place or mine?' Pip asked. 'And let's not bother with dinner.'

Time will tell whether it was a good thing or bad that a seamless, Hollywoodesque scene-change straight to the bedroom – to humping, writhing, sighing, happy, glistening bodies – was denied them. Caleb was on a late shift that night. And the next night, Pip had promised to accompany Fen to the birthday party of the editor at her work who she was furtively starting to see. So Caleb suggested Saturday night and Pip accepted as demurely as she could.

However, the verbal acceptance of carnal relations

between the two of them – the acknowledgement of the imminence of this – took Pip a good few strides on from her senseless celibacy. Her attitude changed and with it, her demeanour. Quite possibly, the subtle but significant shift altered the potency of her pheromones. Or at the least, simply bestowed an allure of availability and willingness.

Little did she know that before Caleb would get her into bed, she'd have been bought drinks by Zac and would have accepted a date from him.

ELEVEN

When Pip saw Zac across a crowded bar, she was hardly going to tell her sisters 'Oh look, there's my stalker, yes, I suppose he *is quite* handsome but don't be fooled by good looks because actually he's rude and odd, to say nothing of the baggage he lugs around, brimming with an ex-wife and sick son.'

There again, nor was Pip likely to reveal that, in the next twenty-four hours, there was a strong possibility that she'd be in bed with a doctor from St Bea's with whom she'd already had great aural sex.

But Zac *was* there that night and Pip was quite taken aback that she should be amused rather than disconcerted, perhaps just a little excited rather than unnerved, that she had a certain pride rather than horror that the man over there, yes, the good-looking one in the navy jeans and navy shirt and spectacles that used to be free on the NHS but no doubt now cost a small fortune, was her own personal stalker.

Perhaps there was a part of her that would quite like to say 'See that bloke? I can't get away from him.' Not because she sought her sisters' protection – because she didn't really fear him at all and of course she could look after herself well enough, thank you very much – but because actually, she

66

was rather proud that her so-called stalker was so easy on the eye. However, duty called and decreed that the only blokes who warranted her focus were the one Fen was considering sleeping with, and the one Cat was deludedly desperate to have back. Tonight was about encouraging Fen to go for it and persuading Cat to leave well alone.

No. Pip wouldn't be saying a word to her sisters. She couldn't possibly. What – have the focus on Pip McCabe? Put herself in the hot seat and under the spotlight? Good God, no. No, thank you. Pip's a great believer in there being a Time and a Place; frequently she uses the unsuitability of one or the other as a prophetic sign or else a perfect excuse. Soho, in the hurl of her sister's potential boyfriend's birthday party, provided her with neither the time for Zac nor the place to mention him to anyone. Ah, but there again, Pip, nor would a quiet night at your flat, or Fen's or Cat's. And a weekend up in Derbyshire wouldn't be the right forum either, would it? Over the phone wouldn't do. Nor would the grapevine. The time and place are rarely aligned in Pip's eye.

So, Pip sipped champagne in Soho, providing morale support for one sister (Fen's morals were, for the most part, in good shape) and utter support for the other (Cat had had a bad day after quite a good week, and the champagne was making her slightly unsteady on her feet). It had taken all manner of cajoling – including Pip walking on her hands at Cat's flat earlier – to persuade the youngest McCabe to come out with them. And now look at her, bedecked in Whistles, partaking of champagne *and* eliciting a few appreciative glances from present company. Pip was well aware that champagne could be a dangerous thing. A little was a very good idea, too much could be disastrous, the distinction between the two could be perilously indistinct.

'What do you think of the Holden guy then?' Cat whispered, nudging Pip and giving a surreptitious nod in Fen's direction.

'Well, he's well-spoken,' Pip analysed, 'charming, too.

Obviously fairly well-to-do, not that it should count for a jot. I've been watching him and he gazes at Fen at any opportunity. That's good. She's not one to waste time on someone who feels anything less than absolutely smitten by her. I think he could well be worth her while. Good luck to her.'

'I like champagne,' giggled Cat, who simply thought Matt hunky, Fen lucky and that they should go for it, 'and I like those dingle-dangle things.'

'Looks like Fen's on her way to Matt's dingle-dangle thing,' said Pip.

Cat whooped with laughter. 'I meant the lights here!' Pip knew perfectly well what her sister had been alluding to, but she also knew that her misinterpretation would cause merriment. Which it did. Pip raised her glass to the lighting – interestingly constructed multifaceted cubes of coloured Perspex floating with no visible means of support, diffusing light into colour and mood. Cat chinked glasses with Pip, her very own visible means of support.

'I like the padded walls,' Pip remarked and, to test her theory, Cat gently nodded her body against them. Pip sat down and patted the space next to her: 'But Jesus, these seats are uncomfortable.'

Cat snuggled against her sister. 'Is there any more champagne?' she wondered out loud. 'I *love* champagne.' She paused, looking temporarily alarmed. 'I think I might be having fun.' She looked at Pip with her brow concertinaed. 'Am I? Is that OK?'

'Why don't we discuss it over more champers – I'll go and find some,' said Pip, delighted that her sister had found something that she loved and was halfway on the road to having fun.

'What do you think?' Fen hissed, catching Pip's arm as she embarked on her champagne quest.

'I think free champagne is a fabulous idea but I think it's all gone,' Pip said. 'Certainly it's gone to Cat's head.'

'I mean about *him*. About *Matt*?' Fen asked wide-eyed and close to, eagerly awaiting her sister's response.

'I think any man who has a party in a room with padded walls is very considerate indeed,' Pip colluded, 'and any man who stands all those bottles of champagne must be worth keeping.' She observed her sister. 'And I think any man who sets his attentions on my sister has impeccable taste. And he'd better treat you very nicely or the dingle-dangles will get it.' Pip winked at Fen and wandered off in search of champagne.

'Dingle-dangles?' Fen murmured to herself.

There is no more free champagne. Pip decides, though, that champagne is what Cat must drink. Not because Cat loves the stuff, but because Pip won't have her mix her drinks; she's mixed up enough as it is. If it's champagne that's giving her joy, champagne she shall have. To the bar she goes.

And that's when she comes across Zac.

She takes her place along the counter right next to him. Their elbows touch. But it is only when the barman allows her to queue-jump that she's aware of him. Zac stares at her, irritated. Pip glowers back. Then she quickly looks away.

Fuck! It's my stalker.

It is indeed. And he's pissed off. He's been brandishing a twenty-pound note in the direction of the barman for ages without success.

'What's a guy gotta do to get a drink round here? Sport a cleavage?' he grumbles with a touch of wit that the noise of the bar renders inaudible.

Grumpy sod, Pip thinks. 'Sorry,' she says, establishing eye contact, 'you were here first.'

'Whatever,' he says brusquely, 'go ahead.'

He doesn't recognize me. He hasn't a clue who I am.

Pip can't order and pay quickly enough and she weaves and shimmies her way back to Cat who is chatting amiably to Fen and Matt. A side of her wants to go, wants to avoid confrontation, doesn't want Zac to suddenly recognize her, to approach, let alone converse. A side of her, however, newly unleashed thanks in no small part to Caleb, wants to play, wants to rile Zac and surprise him. A side to her is amused that he doesn't recognize her and a side to her is slightly irked. So she stays, with half an eye on Fen, half an ear for Cat who is now drunkenly verbose, and half a mind to search Zac out and perform a magic trick on him.

Luck puts Zac directly in her path a short while later when she returns to the bar for yet more champagne for Cat. This time Pip smiles directly at him and he smiles back. That pretty girl who audaciously pushed in at the bar, he observes. The one who looks vaguely familiar.

At the heaving bar Pip waits an indecently short while to be served.

I haven't a clue how I can feel insulted by him in Holloway, offended by him at the hospital, disconcerted by him on Hampstead Heath – and yet now rather taken with him in Soho.

Especially as you have Caleb keen and he comes with no added complications of children and stalking tendencies.

'Champagne, please.'

Ask yourself which bloke your sisters would deem the more suitable.

'Two glasses, thanks.'

I'm not telling Cat and Fen a thing – much less asking them anything of the sort.

When Pip turns from the bar, drinks in hand, she tries to catch Zac's eye but he appears to look straight through her. She feels oddly rejected. Rejecting her feelings, however, she returns to the other side of the club where Cat is actually allowing herself to be chatted up by one of Matt's mates and barely senses her sister's return. Fen, meanwhile, has her lips a centimetre from Matt's and she plants the first of many birthday kisses. Pip averts her gaze and busies herself tracing the rim of the wineglass. It feels as though her work is done. She feels like a spare part. She feels she is no longer needed. She wonders if she could just slip away.

'Look, I know this sounds corny – and I swear it really isn't my style – but maybe I could buy you a drink?'

Stalker Bloke!

She hadn't seen him approach. She hadn't expected him to. She's unprepared. It's not a state she is familiar with or one that she likes.

Shit.

For God's sake, why not just say 'yes', Pip, with a 'please'. Flicker your eyelashes and have a flirt. He's only offering to buy you a drink and you don't currently have one, Cat having just swiped it. Nor do you have anyone to talk to. This might pass the time. This might be amusing.

'Oh, I don't know,' Pip all but cautions, 'I'm here with my sisters.'

'Well, I'll get them drinks, too, if they'd like?' he suggests. 'Or is it more that you need their seal of approval?' He's ingenuous but momentarily, Pip wonders whether he's mocking. Then, however, she observes that his face is open and his eyes are soft and he's tilting his head in an acquiescent way. He shrugs: 'I don't have sisters,' he explains, 'I wouldn't know.' He redeems himself with that.

He still doesn't recognize me. I don't know whether to be offended or entertained.

He's tired, Pip. A little pissed, too. And the bar is atmospherically lit or downright dim. And you look pretty different out of slap and motley.

'Look,' says Zac, 'can I buy you a drink, or shall I just dig a hole right here and dive headfirst into it?' He's never before resorted to chatting women up in bars but he's elicited a laugh from the girl and he rather feels he's done quite well. Friendly without being smarmy, witty not corny, self-deprecating not self-satisfied.

'Sure,' says Pip, 'why not.' Her sisters are occupied. Their glasses are full. They won't need her for the time being.

'What'll you have?'

Pip licks her lips and appears to think about it, her index finger raised for emphasis. 'May I have,' she ponders and pauses and then regards him with direct eye contact and a lascivious twitch of her mouth, 'may I have orangey-lemony-blackcurrant squash?' Zac stares at her because, what with the pervasive chatter, the ambient music playing a little too loudly and the good few beers in his system already, combined with the trippy dingle-dangle lighting, he thinks Pip has asked for a cocktail he hasn't heard of but that he probably should know. 'Orangey-lemony-blackcurrant squash.' she repeats.

'Right,' he says, trying to remember the precise order.

Pip repeats her request, once more, in Dr Pippity's voice. And she raises her eyebrow and gives him a sly grin. And it is then that the penny drops.

'Bloody Jesus bloody Christ,' he murmurs. Pip can't hear him but she can certainly lip-read. 'Clowngirl?' Zac exclaims. 'Dr Whatsit or Merry Thingy?'

'Pip McCabe,' Pip says cordially, extending her hand most demurely, slightly concerned that he looks just a little alarmed.

'Crikey,' he says, and is immediately concerned that his vocabulary and the fact that he's ruffling his hair excessively is all a bit too Hugh Grant.

I won't say 'I didn't recognize you with your clothes on', *then.*

'What's a nice clown like you doing in a circus like this?' Zac asks instead.

There's a pause but fortunately Pip breaks it with a laugh.

'We have to slip out of our slap and motley sometimes,' she explains.

'Is that what it's called?' Zac asks, vaguely interested, eyeing the queue at the bar.

'Sometimes, it's more slop and mutley,' Pip says.

'Now, tell me slowly what it is you drink,' he says, quite wanting a trip to the bar to restore his composure.

Pip laughs: 'They wouldn't mix it correctly here, I fear,' she says, 'so make mine a glass of red.'

'Coming up,' he says, relieved. 'My name's Zac Holmes, by the way.'

'Good to put a name to the face,' says Pip drily, 'after all this time.'

Zac sets off for the bar but returns almost immediately. 'I'd just like you to know,' he shouts above the music, 'that I'm not some crazy bloody stalker.'

'I know,' Pip says to him, 'you're Zac Bloody Holmes.' He nods, relieved, and heads for the bar. Pip watches him.

He has a pretty winning smile – for a stalker. But he also looks a little like my friend Susie's ex. And God, did that guy screw her up by screwing her over and screwing her sister.

Don't tar him with the same brush. Don't tar him, full stop. You hardly know him.

But I ought to remember that he's been insolent to me before. And he started chatting me up – In A Bar. And didn't realize it was me. He's probably on the pull. This is probably his style. If so, it clashes with mine.

And of course you mustn't forget that you have your big date with Caleb tomorrow night.

Exactly.

'Wait till I tell Tom,' Zac says, returning with drinks. 'You know – my little boy?' His face lights up. 'Of course you do.'

'How is he?' Pip asks, and is told he's doing OK. Zac starts talking about him, the usual anecdotes laced with paternal pride, which of course run on and on. After a while, with her drink almost empty, Pip wishes the subject would change.

And I also wish I didn't find him attractive. I mustn't. It must be the alcohol. After all, this is the bloke who has stalked me in hospitals, been rude to me at children's parties, behaved oddly in public parks and has been making passes at me in a bar. And he has a kid and an ex and he's odd. So what if he's good-looking? Distortion by drink!

'We're not talking baggage as in a small backpack,' Pip says into her wineglass a little later when Zac has gone to the bar to replenish their drinks, 'we're talking excess baggage – on such a scale that he'd be fined heavily if he tried to check it in at the airport.'

Zac returns and confirms Pip's misgivings when he starts regaling her with Tom's Harry Potter obsession. He's just about to ask her what sort of a name Pip is and what sort of a career clowning is, when two girls approach. They flank her like bodyguards and eye him with some suspicion.

'Zac,' Pip interrupts, glad for a chance to move on from Tom and J.K. Rowling but bemused that it is the arrival of her sisters expediting it, 'these are my sisters, Cat and Fen.' Privately, Zac is almost irritated by their eccentric names, but he greets them politely and hopes they'll go away.

The sisters don't go away. Cat and Fen hang around because they are unused to seeing their sister in male company, a stranger's company. So they loiter.

Oddly, Pip wishes they'd go away. Of course, she blames the wine.

Why else would I quite like this Zac Holmes odd sod to myself for a little longer?

Fen whispers to Pip that Cat is pretty pissed and should they all go? Pip can see that Cat really should leave now but should not return home unescorted. Fen, with sudden nerves over Matt, wants them all to leave together. Go back to hers and make popcorn, she suggests. Have a chat, she proposes. For a split second, Pip is exasperated and just wishes her sisters could take some initiative and take care of themselves. Even if just for half an hour longer. However, she says nothing of the sort. She tells Fen not to be stupid, she'll take Cat home, Matt will no doubt take her home. 'It's his birthday,' she spells out. 'You're his number one present.'

Pip returns her attention to Zac who is being stared at by Cat, not for any reason other than that she's at that stage of inebriation when whatever her gaze falls upon is fixed. Fen kisses Cat and nods at Zac. Then Pip nods at Cat and gives

Zac a quick peck on the cheek. 'Ta for the drink, Zac,' she says, 'but I have to go. My sister here is lovelorn and pissed. It's a fatal combination.'

'Sure,' Zac says almost eagerly, because the sad drunk sister looks as though she may well burst into tears or throw up. Or do both, in whichever order, rather soon. Pip guides her out. Zac watches her go. She has a nice bottom.

Let her go. Odd sisters with stupid names. Come on! Not my type. To say nothing of the fact that she's a frigging clown, for Christ's sake.

However, when Pip returned unexpectedly a few minutes later, he was surprised how pleased he was to see her. Her drunk sister was looking ominously green around the gills and Pip gave him an apologetic raise of her eyebrows as she guided Cat towards the toilets.

'My sisterly duties do have limits,' she said, standing by his side moments later. 'Accompanying Cat right *into* the loo goes beyond them.'

'Look, can I perhaps buy you a drink sometime when you're not surrounded by sisters and we don't have to yell above dippy-trippy music and the bar staff aren't fascists?' Zac felt uncharacteristically nervous but the beer in his system encouraged him to ramble on. 'I mean, I know it appears I've been rude to you in parks and hospitals and kids' parties but it's been unintentional – just unfortunate. I'm not rude by nature, honestly. Nor do I chat up girls in bars, or anywhere really, for that matter. And I've never met a clown who isn't male and elderly and scary.' He paused for breath, wondering how to follow that. 'And I'd like to buy you a drink because you seem interesting and you've meant a lot to my son.' He stopped and scratched his head. 'But I don't want to buy you a drink as a grateful parent-type,' he rattled on, 'but actually simply because you. Are. Really. Quite. Pretty.'

Oh, fuck. What am I saying?

God – what is he saying?

Pip hadn't yet said a word in response. And the lighting had been momentarily dimmed to such a level that Zac could barely make out her features, let alone judge her expression.

'Well, Pip, I've made a fool of myself.'

However, just the slightest shake of her head, just the glimmer of a smile, bolstered Zac. 'Look,' he said, laying a hand lightly on her shoulder, 'I just think maybe it might be a laugh to get together for a quick drink sometime.'

'Sure,' Pip shrugged. Though she had the time, she suddenly found she did not have the inclination to give accepting his offer a second thought. 'Why not!'

'Cool,' he nodded, so surprised at her equanimity that all he could do was say 'cool' again into his beer glass.

'I'm in the *Thomson's* directory,' she said, extending her hand to shake his. 'Well, Merry Martha is.'

'Cool,' Zac said one final time.

Then there was a Cat amongst them, looking grey and sheepish. Pip started to guide her out. She turned around and nodded at Zac. He made a telephone motion with his hand. She nodded again. He watched her put her arm protectively around her sister and then they were gone.

Zac hadn't spared a thought for Juliana. He didn't mind in the least that she wasn't with him that night. She had prior arrangements. Not that he'd invited her, anyway. After all, they were only simply *seeing* each other – fairly regularly, yes, but with no stipulation of exclusivity. They weren't an 'item' and this was underlined by the fact that when they went to bed – which was the purpose of each time they met – they did so to have sex, not to make love to each other or sleep together.

Zac rejoined his friends in the club and brushed off their questions about who was the girl he'd been chatting to as 'just someone I've bumped into a couple of times'.

I'm not sure why I want to pursue this Pip McCabe, he mused as he headed home by cab a couple of hours later. *But*

I do know I'd like to pursue her – so I guess I'll find out why when I do.

I haven't spared a thought for Caleb.

Pip considers this fact as she tucks up Cat in bed, bucket at the ready, before making a bed for herself on her sister's sofa.

Does that mean I'm an old slapper? Or is it like having two job offers and initiating second interviews before deciding which one to plump for?

'Hang on,' she says quietly into the darkness, 'I already have two jobs.'

For a girl who has proclaimed that she isn't remotely in need of one man, let alone two, she nevertheless goes to sleep wondering whether Stalker Bloke will call, and how her date with Dashing Doc will turn out tomorrow. She hopes to see the former again soon. And she's looking forward to seeing the latter sooner than that.

TWELVE

*S*he'd never admit to it, but Pip was actually quite looking forward to *not* spending a Saturday night on her own. (Though she has oft proclaimed that Saturday nights are overrated and are a great opportunity to catch up on ironing.) And she was looking forward to *not* having sex on her own, too. (Though, as we well know, she is a great advocator of the merits of vibrators.) She was hopeful that, this time tomorrow, she wouldn't be reading the Sunday papers on her own, either. (Though she has never revealed to family or friends that it is only ever on Sunday mornings that she is prone to feeling just on the lonely side of alone rather than happy to be on her own.) She felt it was fair to suppose that this time tomorrow, she might be snuggled up in Caleb's bed (which she'd envisaged to be a mahogany *bateau lit,* billowing extravagantly with white Egyptian cotton); papers and croissants and fresh fruit all in a scatter around them. She could almost smell the coffee. Perhaps they'd wander off to Petticoat Lane or Spitalfields or buy bagels in Brick Lane for brunch.

Just then, waking on Cat's uncomfortable sofa at the crack of Saturday dawn in noisy Camden, the notion of East London on a Sunday seemed romantic, even exotic. Pip felt as though she was off on a mini-break. For a tryst. Breakfast in bed. Hand in hand, strolling around places she'd never been. Silently and quickly, she dressed, tidied away the bedding and popped her head round Cat's bedroom door. Her sister was sleeping very deeply. Pip wrote her a note saying she hoped the hangover wouldn't be too tenacious – recommended Nurofen and regular Coca-Cola stirred to flatten the fizz – and then left to stroll, a spring to her step, back to her own flat a mile away.

Once home, she ironed. She ironed because, of course, she would be otherwise occupied that Saturday night. She ironed whilst trying *not* to wait for Caleb to call and to distract herself from checking the time too frequently. She allowed herself to check the time only after ironing every four items. She ironed everything that needed it, as well as a fair few items that didn't.

She sat down, bemused and unnerved. Not because Caleb hadn't yet called, but in acknowledgement of her own anxiety. It was this which perturbed her. She read into it. She was anxious as to when exactly he would call, and she was anxious that there again, he mightn't. It unnerved her that actually, she *did* care one way or the other; that what Caleb did or didn't do, might or might not do, was affecting her mood. He had control and he didn't know it but she knew that he had; it worried her that she seemed unable to redress the balance. She couldn't do the mind-over-matter thing which she had so frequently extolled, and which she had exhorted her friends to do – and she minded because it mattered.

She told herself that if Caleb hadn't called by 11.30, he wasn't worth it; but it was approaching that time now and it made her anxious. Ten minutes later, she told herself that if he didn't call by noon, it meant he wouldn't be calling at all. She told herself that the fact that he hadn't yet called must mean he wasn't that keen. She asked herself if he was worth being bothered about. Why did she care? Why couldn't she just take it or leave it? Have him or have not? Happy-go-lucky – that was what she was famous for. Instead, alone, she was angry with herself. Silly stupid cow. All it had taken was one snog in her stairwell, and one flirtatious conversation in the ambulance bay, to turn her into any one of the number of her girlfriends who'd turned to her frequently over the years fretting whilst waiting for phone calls.

Of course he'll phone, she'd say to them. Don't read anything into it, she'd say. And when those phone calls never came, Pip would successfully reassure her girlfriends that *he* wasn't worth it anyway, *he* wasn't worthy of *them*. It appalled Pip that today she was unable to practise what she preached.

Her phone rang at 11.52. Before she answered it, she tried to recall the deep meaning she'd allocated to post-11.30, pre-12.00. He hadn't called by 11.30 so, oh yes, that's right, of *course*, it meant he wasn't worth it. She felt the ball was in her court when she picked up the receiver. She lost the serve, however, when she heard Cat's voice at the other end, thanking her for looking after her. Pip felt deflated. And irritated with Cat, to whom she gave short shrift.

Bugger. If Caleb bloody calls now, I'll just pretend I've completely forgotten and I have other plans and I'm terribly busy and I had such a late night in Soho last night so maybe another time, Dr Simmons.

The phone rang. Pip refused to acknowledge the shot of adrenalin, the hit of hope, as she answered it.

'Hiya, Pip, Caleb here.'

She said 'hullo' demurely, whilst inside her head, the voices of the London Philharmonic Chorus were belting out a triumphant 'Hallelujah!'. It was 12.05. What had that meant? Well, it didn't matter any more, did it, because here he was, chatty as you like, phoning her and arranging their date.

'Still free?' he asked. 'What shall we do?'

Well, Pip, aren't you going to have *completely forgotten*? Aren't you going to enforce a rain check in your pursuit of the hard-to-get line?

'Well,' said Pip, pretending to think about it.

'I could come over – I know where you live,' Caleb suggested lightly.

'Or I could come to you – because I don't know where you live,' Pip riposted. 'We could browse Petticoat Lane and Spitalfields and buy bagels from Brick Lane. It's all new territory to me.'

Yes, Pip – why not divulge your Egyptian cotton fantasy too and, while you're at it, go ahead and order your Sunday papers as well?

There was a pause at the other end. 'It's just – well, sorry – but I'm needed. I'm on call tonight,' Caleb apologized.

Do not sound disappointed, Philippa.

'Oh,' said Pip, sounding disappointed.

There was another pause.

Why not implement your rain-check theorem? If there isn't going to be a Sunday morning, is a Saturday afternoon really worth it?

'Hey, I don't have to leave till 7.00-ish,' Caleb was saying with detectable eagerness. 'It's only noon now.'

It was settled. He gave Pip his address and though he gave her directions from Old Street underground station, she called for a cab instead and dismissed the fifteen-pound fare.

This was the stage that her friends would text her. In cab – wish me luck! Or perhaps hot date – think of me! Or even off 4 rampant sex. Call u l8r! Though Pip would text them back a mixture of enthusiasm and advice, she'd also chide them for jumping into cabs, at some man's command, with such haste and eagerness. But of course, as she headed east by cab, there was no one for her to text because no one knew of her plans. Indeed, no one even knew of a Dr Caleb Simmons.

Caleb's flat was smaller than she'd imagined and she had to be stern with herself not to be disappointed. She hadn't considered that it might be in a modern block. She'd been thinking loft apartment in quite some detail. And there was no *bateau lit*. Just a smallish divan without a headboard and with a navy blue duvet set. She checked it out on a surreptitious snoop after asking for the toilet. The bathroom was too cramped for a bath. She noted the *Psycho* shower curtain with the silhouette of Norman Bates's mother brandishing the knife. She swiftly decided it must have been a Christmas present from some younger brother. She observed that the lid was on the toothpaste, the soap was not soggy in the dish and the toilet seat had been down when she entered. The flat was clean, uncluttered and tidy, the walls were white and the flooring was wood laminate throughout. She'd have decorated pretty similarly if she had lived here, she thought, and quietly congratulated herself and Caleb on their compatibility when it came to décor. However, the apartment was not remotely soundproofed from downstairs's television or the blazing row being conducted upstairs in a mixture of Anglo-Saxon expletives and patois.

'I've had to tend to a broken nose in the past,' Caleb told her, motioning to the flat upstairs. '*She* whacked *him*.'

'Well,' Pip said lightly, pleasantly surprised by cornflowers in a vase, 'I suppose it means you don't have to resort to the telly for soap opera.'

I'm sure Cosmo would say a vase of flowers shows a strong man at ease with his feminine side! Good.

'What are your neighbours like?' Caleb asked with genuine interest and slightly wistfully.

'Elderly,' Pip said. 'The one directly above me makes the best apple crumble in the world.'

I bet his cooking skills are quite good, too – I bet he sits at that table over there and eats properly, not propping a ready-meal on his lap in front of the TV.

'Lucky!' said Caleb (who often ate ready-meals, occasionally at the table but usually while watching TV). 'Talking of apple crumble, I'm hungry – shall we go out and grab lunch?'

They ate Greek, ordering every *meze* on the menu and a couple of items off it, too. The staff greeted Caleb with familiarity and warmth and Pip was delighted. Mr Popular.

Mr House Proud. Mr Flower-arranger. Mr Normal. Dr Simmons.

Mr *Psycho* Shower Curtain, Pip?

I told you, I reckon that was a gift from some dodgy brother.

Does he have a brother – dodgy or otherwise?

I don't know. I haven't yet asked. And if he doesn't, so what – Mr Post-modern Sense of Humour it is!

Pip made sure that she matched Caleb in the garlic stakes and she also made sure that she surreptitiously limited how much pitta she ate. She'd read in one women's glossy or other that Bread Brings Bloat. Garlic breath was one thing, a pot belly quite another. She couldn't believe that a dodgy diet tip was dictating her lunch. The pitta was lovely – slightly charred – and she was only allowing herself one slice. Ridiculous. She would surely direct such a word to any of her friends who eschewed pitta for the same reason.

After lunch, they strolled around and looked at the buildings and chatted idly about what they usually did at weekends. Pip didn't say 'ironing' – she said, ever so casually, 'I tend just to hang out – if I'm not working.' Caleb said he was on call more often than not. Pip told herself she ought to lodge this fact for future musing. She could well have Caleb *and* continue her routine of Saturday night ironing. She even thought about the following weekend, hoping Caleb wasn't on call, hopeful that he'd try to change shifts if he was.

'I love shops like these,' Pip enthused in front of an All A Quid emporium. 'I buy lots of stuff for Dr Pippity in such places.'

'Let's go in then,' Caleb suggested, holding the door for Pip and earning points by doing so. (*Mr Manners*, she added to her list.) They spent a happy and lucrative half hour there, Caleb insisting on paying for the treasure that filled Pip's basket. 'See it as a twenty-quid donation to the Renee

Foundation,' he said, brushing away her effusive thanks. She kissed him with gratitude. And he kissed her back. With lust. And then they kissed each other desirously though they were blocking the doorway. Only the shopkeeper clearing his throat, and an elderly passer-by tut-tutting, decided them to walk briskly back to his flat and continue their kissing there. It was late afternoon, after all. And, after all, he was on call that evening.

The fact that his flat was even more noisy than before lunch put Pip at her ease. It lent a certain ambiguity to her sudden giggling – because the woman upstairs yelled 'You're a fucking pathetic bastard cunt!' at much the same time as Caleb grunted involuntarily on lifting her T-shirt to feast his gaze on her breasts presented pertly in a broderie anglaise bra. And for similar reasons, Caleb hummed the theme of *Grandstand* drifting up from the flat below when Pip unbuttoned his jeans and eased them down his legs. Pip could bite her lip and raise her eyebrows as much for catching sight of the impressive bulge in his Calvins, as for hearing the woman upstairs yell 'Fuck off and get out of my fucking life, you twatting tosser!' By the time that Caleb and Pip were naked, the television had been turned off and the twatting tosser had obviously fucked off. Yet they stood, in stillness and silence on a Saturday tea-time, admiring each other's nudity and their very good fortune. They were relaxed and raring to go.

It had been a long time since Pip's last sexual encounter. And that had been a nondescript and slightly perfunctory session with Mike, the sweet bloke she'd never been in love with, many months ago. She'd known Mike for quite a while. He had treated her to many dates before asking, with great reverence, if he might take her to bed. Caleb, by comparison, she hardly knew, yet she was happy for him to do all manner of things to her that afternoon. And she found she genuinely wanted to reciprocate. Not so much you scratch my back, I'll scratch yours; but more, you do that flickery thing with your tongue tip on my clit and I'll do something feathery with my lips against your balls. And look, we can do so simultaneously! Pip and Caleb silently congratulated themselves on bedding such capable, imaginative and exciting partners. Caleb attributed Pip's athleticism and inventiveness to her grounding in acrobatics and skill as a performer. Pip credited Caleb's consummate knowledge of her body and his gentle but confident handiness and finger work to his demanding medical training. He seemed to her to be an intelligent, considerate and mature person. Coupled with the fact that she found him immensely attractive, she was utterly at ease and their coupling was intense and enjoyable.

Of course he used a condom.

Pip was home by 7.30. She was physically tired and emotionally exhausted and wouldn't have had the inclination to do the ironing anyway, had there been any. She watched whatever was on the television, smiling to herself that, in all probability, Caleb's downstairs neighbour was watching the same programmes.

*　*　*

'Ruth?'

'Hi, Zac! What are you doing *in* on a Saturday night?'

'Just catching up on stuff – making a few calls, paying a few bills, watching a few vids I've recorded recently,' Zac said nonchalantly, if a little defensively.

'I thought you'd be wining and dining and sixty-nining.'

'Well, you have a dirty mind and my brother can only have married you for that, not for your looks,' he sparred back.

'Fuck off!' Ruth laughed. 'Well, it's good to hear from you – do you want to speak to your bro? He's burping pleasantly, having polished off a take-away curry.'

'Jim always was the one with manners – I'll have him in a

mo'. I just wondered if you have the phone number of that clown girl who did Billy's party?'

'Merry Martha? Sure, hold on. Hang on. Ah. Here. She's good – quite pricey, but the kids love her. Are you planning for Tom?'

'Perhaps. Maybe. I just thought I'd give her a call and find out what's what.'

Zac never lied though he did Ambiguity and Issue-skirting very well. He thanked his sister-in-law, had a brief conversation with his brother who burped down the phone at him, and then ended the call to phone Pip.

I said I would. It's just I didn't want to obtain her number from the Thomson*'s directory.*

However, her answering machine was on. It wasn't even her voice but a slightly computerized polite recording from BT. Zac was undeterred.

'This is Zac Holmes – from last night. Just phoning about that drink and wondering if you fancied a civilized cup of tea tomorrow? At some posh hotel, perhaps? Crumpet and cream? Innuendo unintentional. Anyway, I'll try again later. Bye.'

Pip's hand had hovered over the receiver throughout. She told herself she'd talk to him later when he called back. If she felt like chatting. But no one phoned Pip that Saturday night. She instructed herself to savour a Saturday evening all to herself, musing that if things progressed with Caleb, they might soon be in short supply – depending on whether he was on call, of course.

No chores outstanding. She wasn't hungry. There was nothing to watch on TV. She'd recently finished an Anne Tyler novel and would pick up a new paperback in a day or two. Neither Fen, Cat nor Megan needed her. There were no more household chores. So she could just settle back in her sofa, hugging the cushions she'd made the covers for, sipping a Rioja she'd been saving for a special occasion. She could just relax and indulge in recalling her afternoon with Caleb.

And yet she replayed Zac's message, too.

I want to contemplate how it is that suddenly I have two men on my trail. I want to wonder why it is I'm finding it rather amusing rather than faintly irritating or remotely unnerving. It's weird, I feel somewhat brazen – attractive – the centre of attention. What's weirder is that I actually like it! Could I develop a taste for it? Where would that take me? Should I look before I leap?

'I don't need a man,' she says, switching off the television having absent-mindedly channel-hopped for the last hour because there really is nothing worth watching, 'of that I'm sure.' She takes her tray of picked-at supper things through to the kitchen, washes and dries everything. 'I don't need one man let alone two, but you know what – and I can't believe I'm thinking this, let alone saying it out loud – it just might be fun, for a little while, to be wooed and pursued.'

THIRTEEN

*W*ell, it's lucky that neither the accountant nor the clown is superstitious – if they were, they wouldn't be agreeing to meet in this chapter. Mind you, does it say much about their morality, or lack of it, that they are meeting without the knowledge of the people they're sleeping with? No doubt they can justify that they have no immoral intent – no intent whatsoever – other than plain curiosity and having something to eat, something to do on a Sunday afternoon.

Pip's mobile phone beeped a text message while her land-line was ringing. She had the 'Style' section of the *Sunday Times* in her hand and was looking forward to skimming it before settling down to the broadsheet itself. She presumed her phones would be Cat and Fen – with news to tell and advice to ask. Pip had temporarily forgotten that it was much more likely to be the two men.

u tired me out! i'll b struck off . . . cs x

'Hullo? Is that Pip? Well, it's Zac here – morning.'

Is this what they mean by double dating? Pip wondered as she read the text message from one man and said 'good morning' to the other.

'Do you fancy fruit cake and tea later, then?' Zac asked.

Pip thought for a moment and wondered if she oughtn't to keep her day free, in case Caleb should be around. But she was appalled at herself – knowing how she'd give any of her girlfriends short shrift for dithering in such a way. Zac wasn't asking if she fancied a fuck, just fruit cake.

I don't like raisins.

For God's sake, Pip, there'll probably be Victoria sponge, too.

'Sure,' Pip heard herself say, before she'd truly considered whether it was a good idea or not.

'Good.' Zac was both pleased and surprised. 'Be sure to skip lunch!'

Pip was testing out texts to return to Caleb while Zac was asking her whether she'd like him to pick her up or meet him there. She agreed to meet Zac at Green Park underground later that afternoon. 'God, I hope he's not taking me to the Ritz,' she muttered whilst texting Caleb to say that she was walking like John Wayne thanks to him.

However, when it was time to start getting ready, she considered at length what to wear, trying on three or four combinations before settling for a pistachio linen shift dress she bought in last summer's sales and a vanilla-coloured cardigan from Agnès B she'd paid full price for. (When Zac saw her, he'd think she looked good enough to lick.) She thought kitten heels would be overkill, but she was pleased with the way that soft blue suede Adidas pumps completed the ensemble in an informal but quirky way. She took care with her make-up and decided to leave her hair loose.

Zac noticed. 'You've let your hair down, Miss McCabe,' he said, greeting her with a kiss which both flattered and surprised her. He didn't, however, go on to tell her that in her soft colours she looked as lickable as ice-cream. He bit his tongue instead and guided her down Piccadilly.

Zac is not taking Pip to the Ritz for tea. She presumes they're headed for Fortnum's. No. He's keeping her on the opposite side of the road. The Royal Academy, then? But he guides her left, well before those hallowed portals. Albemarle Street. Brown's Hotel. If there are two things that Pip will learn very quickly about this man, they are that he is not flash, nor is he predictable. She's never been to Brown's before; actually, she's never even heard of the place. But immediately, she wishes she was staying for a night or two.

Well, I'm not sure what it says about Caleb's effect on Pip and I'm not sure what it says about Zac's effect on her and I'm not sure what it says about Pip herself, but for all her abstemiousness when it came to the pitta bread yesterday, she's gorging herself to the gills today. She doesn't leave one crumb of delightful finger sandwich; in fact, she even dabs up a stray strand of cress from the plate. She tells Zac she couldn't choose which variety was the nicest – egg and cress, cucumber or salmon – but that she could eat them all again.

'Save yourself,' he says, delighted that he's going to get his money's worth. Juliana, by comparison, insists on expensive restaurants where she reads the menu as if it's an exam paper for which her revision is lacking, invariably prodding the food around the plate into interesting configurations but ingesting only a sparrow's portion in the process. So it's refreshing for Zac, therefore, to tuck into tea with the clown – even if she picks out every sultana from her scone. She does this so daintily, however, that it can almost be seen as a vagary of tea-taking etiquette.

And she's sucking great globs of crusty clotted cream direct from a teaspoon now that the scone's gone.

Pip, however, has both room and desire for the gorgeous miniature gateaux and selects a *millefeuille and* a coffee éclair *and* a strawberry tart. She takes rapid sips of her Lapsang and leans across to Zac. 'If I wasn't in such genteel surroundings,' she confides in a sprightly whisper, 'I'd do a great big belch.' It's the first thing she's said since talking about the sandwiches and Zac snorts involuntarily into his tea, splattering himself. He's wearing navy from top to toe so it doesn't show. 'Mr Holmes!' she chastises. 'Manners maketh man! Please respect your genteel surroundings.'

God, I think I'm in love with her.

Don't be daft, you hardly know her.

Zac sweetly enquires after Cat, and whether the other sister (he can't remember her name, he thinks it's Finty or Ffion or something) bedded the birthday boy. Pip realizes that the particulars of Cat's chronic hangover are as inappropriate over such a fine tea, as the details of what Fen and Matt got up to after the party. She says her sisters are fine and she asks about Tom. She'd like to hear that he's well, but she doesn't want minutiae.

I mean, he's a sweet little boy – but he is this man's little boy. The chap with whom I'm taking tea and having a laugh has a young son and ex-wife. Remember, I really, truly, cannot be doing single-parent baggage handling.

Not that you have any intentions towards this man, of course.

Of course.

Just as well, because Zac could chirp on for hours about Tom and their visit to HMS *Belfast* yesterday.

'What do you do,' Pip interrupts, 'for a living?'

Zac sips his tea and tips his head. 'I'm an accountant,' he says without apology or embarrassment, 'actually.'

Pip thinks he must be joking. He'd apologize or be embarrassed if it were true, surely? Then she wonders if he's lying – and if so, what a strange fib and what a peculiar job to choose. She hopes he's not a liar, but she also hopes he's joking. She knows she mustn't exclaim 'You're joking!'

I suppose an accountant is better than an estate agent or bailiff or undertaker. Slightly.

She nods and thinks another change of subject would be good. But not back to children.

Look at me. Out to tea with an accountant who's a single parent. I think I'd rather be in Hoxton with Dr Simmons. Anyway, I ought not to be here, even if I'm not there.

Come on, Pip, you're having fun. Tea is delicious and conversation flows.

But he's an accountant.

So what, you're a sodding clown.

'I've never met an accountant before,' Pip says, as if he's from a planet far beyond our solar system. 'I'd never have guessed it.'

'I've never met a clown before,' Zac shrugs, as if he's pleased that he has, anyway. 'How about a stroll through the park?'

They took a leisurely walk through Green Park and over into St James's Park. Pip realized how full she was and was grateful to walk off some of her indulgence.

'Did you know the Queen owns all the swans in the UK?' Zac told her. 'And that if you kill one, you can be put to death?'

Pip regarded him. She stopped walking and looked at her feet, shuffling them a little (and observing a little jam on her right pump). 'Damn,' she said, all forlorn, 'I'm just *so* partial to killing swans. Whenever I have the chance, really.' Zac gave her a nudge and told her to piss off. She laughed.

'How did you get into clowning, then?' he asked with genuine interest. 'I mean, it's not the most *usual* of careers, is it? Is it lucrative?'

'God,' Pip raised her eyes heavenwards, 'you're not going to suggest doing my tax, are you?' Privately, she thought that might be a very useful thing and she should develop this friendship. After all, Django had impressed upon each niece when they left home the importance of befriending a doctor, a dentist, a lawyer and an accountant in their lives. Fen had managed all four at university. Ten years on, this weekend Pip could finally count a doctor and an accountant. Which meant poor Cat was the only sister with no useful friends. 'Well, I make what I call a tidy living. I've been a clown for as long as I can remember,' she told Zac. 'I doubt whether I'd be much good at anything else.'

'But why clowning?' Zac probed. 'Are you hiding behind

some mask? Is there some tragedy in your life that you are overcompensating for?'

Pip laughed so effusively that she started coughing. It gave her a chance to collect herself. It gave Zac the chance to pat her on the back. And give her shoulder a quick squeeze. And a gentle rub. She surprised herself by not flinching, though she feared she blushed a little. 'Simply put, I love making people laugh,' she declared, breezily as you like to contradict her blush, 'and I discovered very early on that not only did I enjoy it, I'm pretty good at it, too.'

'It must be quite an art,' Zac said thoughtfully, 'and hard work, too, I imagine.' Pip was flattered. 'I mean, your hospital work must take it out of you.'

'It does,' Pip confirmed, 'which is why the Renee Foundation who fund me regulate our hours carefully. And trained us rigorously. But, basically, by Tuesday and Thursday evenings I'm spent.'

'I bet,' said Zac quietly. 'You must see things you hope you'll never see again.'

Pip nodded. 'I've seen children who don't look like children. I've seen children die. I've seen parents of children who have died. It haunts me.'

Zac didn't know what to say. 'God, we're lucky with our Tom,' he said to himself as much as to her, 'it could be so much worse.'

Suddenly, Pip felt a little tired. Instead of talking about tax with her accountant, she was talking about the taxing side to her job. She'd rather not. It was the weekend, after all, a pretty momentous one at that.

'Let's change the subject, hey,' Zac suggested, taking a seat beside her on a bench dedicated to Elsie Who Loved This Spot. They watched the swans. Pip was still glad to have eaten every crumb of her tea, though it meant they had nothing to feed to the birds.

'They can be vicious buggers, swans,' Pip remarked. 'Say one attacked you and, in self-defence, you killed it, would you still be sent to the Tower?'

Zac thought about it. 'I'm not sure,' he said with great deliberation, 'but I'll be sure to ask Her Majesty next time I see her.'

Pip stifled a laugh and continued very earnestly: 'Oh, and do you see her often?'

'Three or four times a year,' Zac shrugged, 'you know, when she needs help with her VAT and tax returns.'

Pip gave him such a hearty shove that he nearly fell off Elsie's bench.

'I met her once,' Pip recalled, 'no doubt it's etched in her memory.' She looked to Zac to see if he was remotely interested. It appeared, from his penetrating gaze, that he was. She hadn't noticed until then that behind his trendy specs, his eyes were such an unusual slate-grey. 'I gave her a posy when she visited Bakewell. I was seven. My uncle Django told me I'd forgotten to curtsy. I told him in no uncertain terms how *actually*, thank you very much, I'd "lowered myself" instead – as if it were a far more deferential genuflection.'

'What were you doing up in Bakewell?' Zac asked, enjoying a very clear picture of a young Pip lowering herself to her Queen, posy at the ready.

'Oh,' said Pip, surprised. They'd been chatting so easily that she'd forgotten how little he knew about her. 'It's where I grew up.'

'Do your parents still live there? In Bakewell?' Zac asked, building a very different picture from the free-love family, chickens-in-the-garden image he'd had before.

'My father died,' Pip told him, 'and my mum has since moved away,' she continued, omitting Denver and the cowboy and abandonment in general, 'but my uncle Django still lives in Farleymoor, at the house where I spent my childhood.'

'Are you close as a family?' Zac asked.

'God, yes, very,' Pip enthused. 'Mum's like an older sister. Django – my late father's brother – is wonderful. We're a great family. Christmas and birthdays are just the *best*.'

*

Pip?
  Pip!
  Philippa McCabe?
  What on earth made you say all that?

'Sounds blissful,' Zac said wistfully. 'My folks are definitive expats – I hardly see them. I think they're currently in Dubai. Or there again, perhaps it's Hong Kong. I honestly would have to consult my address book to verify. I have a brother, though,' he added, in case she was remotely interested, 'we're quite close. You did his son's birthday party – Billy, in Holloway. The first time we met.'

  'Oh, yes,' Pip said, hastily adding 'dysfunctional childhood' to her list of negatives regarding Zac.

Pot. Kettle. Black. Pip?

She can't hear me. She's on a roll with her imaginary family.

'Mummy always says if I had been a boy, I'd've been called Billy.'
  Is that true?
  Whatever.
  I mean, not just the 'Billy' bit. Did you *ever* call her *Mummy*?

  'Tom,' Zac declared, 'is just *Tom* – not Thomas or anything. Little blighter doesn't even have a middle name. He just seemed so *complete* when he was born – and Tom seemed to be the name he came with.'

  'I really ought to be going,' Pip said, because she wanted to change the subject but didn't know what to.

  'Sure,' said Zac, 'me too. Share my cab?'

  'Oh, that's OK,' said Pip, 'I'll hop on the tube.'

  'You sure?' Zac asked. 'It's no problem.'

  'Honestly,' Pip assured him. He walked her to Green Park underground. 'I had a really lovely afternoon,' Pip told him, touching his arm. 'Tea was gorgeous. It was fun. Thank you.'

'Any time,' Zac said. And he meant it.

Pip smiled a little shyly. Looked at her pumps, the jam splodge. Shuffled a little.

'How about it?' said Zac, biting the bullet. 'Another time? We could dine on roasted swan or something.'

Pip laughed. 'Perhaps,' she said.

'Can I call you?' Zac asked.

'If you like,' Pip answered, with some more soft shoe shuffling.

'Good,' said Zac, 'good.'

And it does seem good to him. He would like to see her again. She's far more normal than he'd previously thought. She's really rather sweet. Pretty. And sexy, somehow. And her sense of humour is close to his own.

FOURTEEN

Zac has called Pip a few times. Though his offer of roasted swan still stands, a second date has yet to materialize. It's not that Pip has actively avoided setting a day and time; she's just had other things to prioritize. She's been busy at work and play and, as usual, doing a lot of looking-after. Cat worries *Will he or won't he*, Megan wonders *Should I or shouldn't I* and Fen is thinking *Does he or doesn't he*.

However, though the premise of Zac's calls is invariably to try and find a time and place to meet again ('If it's treason you're worrying about,' he said recently, 'we can always eat curry instead – I don't think there's such a thing as swan *jalfrezi*'), he and Pip chat easily for a good twenty minutes each time. She's always pleased to hear from him. And she will get around to seeing him again – it just might not be soon.

Caleb, by contrast, seems only ever to call her on the spur of the moment. Or, as Pip interprets it, he calls the moment he knows he's free. And though Pip is a fine one for telling her girlfriends and sisters never to be readily available for dates, she herself has so far indulged Caleb by coming at the click of his fingers. In a cab, by tube, and in bed with him, too – such is his manual dexterity. So, when she heads to his flat fifteen minutes after a summons by text or phone, she reminds herself to understand that his heavy shift-work means it is difficult for him to operate within a relationship any other way. He's a gentleman, she says to herself, he doesn't want to make arrangements he can't keep. 'And remember,' she tells herself sternly, 'as soon as he knows he's free, he calls me.' She feels quite flattered, really. And the time when she was halfway to Hoxton but he called to say he was needed, she didn't mind. She felt proud that her doctor was in demand. And he'd apologized with a saucy little text message very late that night. And he'd sent flowers the next day.

It's something about the very urgency of her dates with Caleb which Pip finds so intoxicating. He wants her to come as quickly as she is able. Directly to his flat, straight into his bed. Once there, however, coming quickly is the furthest thing from his mind. He explores her body with intense relish, bringing her teetering to the edge of orgasm but demanding that she holds it, controls it, lets it subside. Then he takes her there again. And again. Finally, her climax is explosive. The sex is very good. She's never slept with anyone for whom sex is so carnal and rude.

Her previous boyfriends had been courteous to the point of being bland in bed. 'Let me make love to you,' Rupert used to murmur with a soft transatlantic twang utterly at odds with his regular Edinburgh accent, thus turning Pip quite cold in the process. 'That was beautiful,' Mike would always say gently after their ten-minute couplings; Pip stifled giggles at first, but was soon biting down yells of annoyance. Harry, with whom she had but a short dalliance, actually used to ask 'How was it for you?' and Pip found that however nice it had been, such a question diminished it immediately.

'Nice fuck,' Caleb tends to say, withdrawing from her almost as soon as he's come. His baseness turns Pip on so much that she's ready and keen to fuck again, however exhausted the first bout has left her.

It's refreshing, she thinks.

I've never been one for small talk, for love and all its panoply. It's a massive ego boost that this man desires me so. I love it that having sex with me absorbs him so totally, that he keeps his eyes shut tight throughout – savouring every thrust, in every position – rather than gazing into my eyes in a cringingly deep and pseudo-meaningful way.

So, you are having fun?

You bet.

But what do you do when you're not in bed together?

Why waste time on not being in bed together!

But do you chat?

We talk dirty.

But does he make you laugh?

He certainly knows how to tickle my fancy. He's the first man I haven't had to show where it is!

But does he make you feel cared for?

He desires me. Ravenously. And for God's sake, I can take care of myself.

No one at St Bea's knows that there's anything going on between them. And the secrecy of it all is titillating for them both. Anyway, it would be unprofessional, they justify. It is unnecessary, they decide. What's the point of broadcasting it, they agree. St Bea's is business and their time there is busy; the patients are their priority and nothing must distract or detract from the fact.

And what of Zac and Juliana? Same as before, really. Zac is nothing if not consistent. So, they meet fairly often and have pretty good sex. Not unlike Caleb and Pip. However, Zac usually treats Juliana to a post-coital meal in Hampstead, or some courteous foreplay by taking her to a movie or for a few drinks first. It's a very balanced arrangement, both people are gaining the same degree of satisfaction. Neither wants for more. Both are sated sexually and intellectually. It's perfect. Juliana has a handsome, amusing and considerate escort for the duration of her stay in London. Zac has little need to wank or turn up to friends' parties on his own.

Where does Pip fit in? Does he think of Pip? What does he think of Pip? What does he think of, when he thinks of Pip? Has he told Juliana that he calls her, that he's trying to see her again? If he pursued Pip, could it be construed as infidelity? Would he give up the one if the other was even a possibility? Zac Holmes is pretty *au fait* with his morality, though he sees keeping a couple of irons in the fire as a wise precaution. Zac is in no hurry to do anything about either woman. Time will tell, he tells himself.

He does look forward to speaking to Pip – the calls in themselves are energetic and fun and it's become irrelevant that a date has yet to be set. There's always laughter between them, and they've started teasing each other, with wit and a touch of familiarity. Zac likes it when Pip insults him. Like when she told him to fuck off and go play with his calculator. He had the last word, though. Much to Pip's delight, he told her to ensure she put on plenty of slap or else she'd frighten the children.

Things don't have to be going on for things to be going on. And yet, Zac and Pip have said nothing to their nearest and dearest. 'What's there to tell?' they tell themselves.

Honestly, Philippa, you're sleeping with one man and taking tea and long phone calls with another, yet the very existence of both is not known by anyone who knows you. You justify that Caleb is just casual fun and frolics, but if that's the case then longevity won't play a part. So, what will happen when it ends? You tell yourself Zac is just a friendly bloke but you feel yourself come alive during your conversations with him. He's hardly of no consequence. He's someone new in your life as much as Caleb is. You may not need people, you may feel you are totally self-sufficient, you may tell yourself there's nothing to tell, but wouldn't you quite like to be able to confide, discuss, reminisce, work through? Simply have the fun of a good girlie gossip?

And you, Zac – you are sleeping with a glamorous woman who doesn't make you laugh and who is hardly value for money at the Orrery or whichever fancy restaurant you take her to. Yet you chuckle like a teenager over the phone with a girl who's a clown and who has a penchant for cream teas. You can justify that you have plenty of platonic friendships with women and Pip is a welcome addition to this list. That she's not your type if you care to compare dress sense and general deportment with a woman like Juliana. But you look forward to your phone calls with Pip more than you do to actually seeing Juliana. And admit it, it's not often that you *haven't* managed to take a girl out on a date. So, nothing is going on with Pip, that's true. But it's not for want of trying, is it?

It's a Thursday in mid-June. Pip has been sleeping with Caleb for almost a month and so it's also been nearly a month since she last saw Zac. Though they spoke last night, Zac hasn't told Pip that he'll be accompanying his son to St Bea's today. He's decided to surprise her, to relive his stalking days of old. He's happy for Dr Pippity to be a surprise for Tom, too, because his son hasn't needed treatment for over a month and is miserable about having to return.

'Dr Pippity!' Tom's face lit up and despite it being sore to smile, he displayed a grin of prodigious proportions. Dr Pippity bounded over and ruffled Tom's hair, and his father's hair, too. 'Young man!' she declared in her funny voice, winking at the boy and winking at his father, 'you've made my day! I was feeling poorly and grumpy and now you're here I feel better!' Tom felt most proud. He was so glad he'd come to hospital to make the clown doctor feel better. Another child ambled over, legs in callipers and tongue going this way and that. 'Hullo,' Dr Pippity said to her, 'you've made my day too! What a lucky clown am I to be surrounded by such silly sausages. See, you're making me laugh till my sides split and there are tears in my eyes.' On cue and unseen, Dr Pippity ripped a small piece of material for a gruesome sound effect, then squeezed a bulb attached to a thin pipe tucked behind her ears which sent water dribbling down her cheeks. Tom and the girl were wet and delighted – only a clown doctor could get away with calling them funny or silly and yet still make them feel normal and altogether better.

Pip performed her dandruff joke on the girl's mother who joined in admirably. Then she shook and shook Zac's hand with squeaks and parps and toots going off every second. More children in Out-patients gathered round and Dr Pippity liberally dispersed stickers and colouring-in drawings and lousy jokes. She teased parents, tweaking their hair with a giant red comb into various unflattering configurations. She mimicked the nurses as they passed. She appeared to sneeze all over a consultant, sonorously blowing her nose on his white coat-tails. She took sips of patients' water and ran off with a packet of crisps that belonged to a very scrawny-looking boy. She returned them untouched, of course, but the child still held out the packet to her.

'Crisps?' Dr Simmons proclaimed. 'Can I have one?'

It took but a moment for Zac to realize that something was going on between Clowngirl and the fantastically handsome doctor. Merely glimpsing the glance that shot between them was enough.

He felt numb. He felt stupid.

She was skipping away. Off to her ward rounds. Her operatic 'bye-bye, ta-ra, ta-ta, toot-toot' was general, she made eye contact with no one. She was going and Zac was just going to have to let her go.

Tom was called.

Forget it, Zac said to himself, holding his son's hand and following the nurse, *just fucking forget her.*

There'd be no second date, let alone roasted swan. Not even a curry. Zac was struck by a wave of disappointment. And a surge of some other emotion he hadn't the time or inclination to analyse now.

FIFTEEN

Zac really screwed Juliana that night. He'd been uncharacteristically monosyllabic when she'd phoned earlier and had been resistant to her suggestion of meeting for Thai first. At his flat, Zac fixed her a drink and poured himself a large brandy on ice. Watching her sip her Semillon, he thought how little they knew each other. He swirled the liquor around the glass, spun himself a half revolution this way, then that, in the Eames. He regarded her levelly; he wasn't sure just then if he wanted her to stay or go. But then she slipped her beautifully pedicured feet out of her Gina sandals and padded across the lounge to the banana chair. To straddle it necessitated hitching up her straight skirt a little. She could have managed this with her hands alone but he was well aware that for good measure and maximum impact, she undulated her hips from side to side as well. It was choreographed, contrived, not that it bothered him.

She licked her lips, sucked her fingertip, then used it to trace the rim of her glass. 'I'm going back to South Africa,' she announced, now flicking her tongue around the rim. She scrutinized Zac for a reaction. He didn't appear to have one. 'A few debriefings,' she elaborated, 'but I'll return to the UK for a short while before going home for good.'

Zac wondered whether Juliana was expecting him to respond in a certain way and whether sex tonight would depend on that response. Going to bed with this woman was suddenly very important to him. He wanted to be naked, eyes closed, humping hard. He wanted to fuck her so that the image of Pip and the dry feeling in his throat would fuck off. He looked at Juliana and nodded and shrugged. His erection was caught at an odd angle behind his trousers. He shifted his position. He felt pent up but horny, too. Being aware of his basic desire had actually given him what he believed to be definitive insight.

Juliana is so much more my type than that other one. Sassy and long-legged and beautifully turned out. She makes good money, she's independent and sussed. She doesn't just look her age, she acts it, too. She's experienced – in bed, in business. I like that. I mean, look at her legs – lean and tanned. Not clad in stupid stripy tights. Her hair is scraped back into a neat fold – whatever it's called – and her face is without blemish. Gorgeous haughty eyebrows, expensive but subtle make-up, teeth courtesy of three thousand pounds' worth of re-enamelling. She's so not Pip – thank God. She's so much more what I like, what I'm after, what I'm used to.

'Bon voyage,' Zac raised his glass to Juliana who sipped sultrily at her wine. He downed his brandy and poured himself another measure; the bottle was to hand at the side of his chair. He couldn't be bothered to fetch ice. He'd have it straight. Neat. It scorched. He could handle it. He stared over to Juliana. Her glass was nearly empty. He couldn't be bothered to replenish it. She knew where the fridge was. He was in a dark mood. As beautiful as she was, this woman irritated him tonight. He'd fuck her, certainly, but not from direct desire; more from an oblique need to get something out of his system – and not merely an ejaculation of sperm. 'Did you want to go out and eat?' Zac asked out of politeness alone.

'No, babe,' Juliana said, 'got to watch my weight.' She'd made similar remarks for as long as Zac had known her, fishing for compliments, but today for the first time he couldn't be bothered to flatter her.

'A top-up?' he offered, hoping she'd go to the fridge herself, if so. She gave a lascivious smirk. She walked over to him, her sinuous body slinking towards him like a Siamese cat on the prowl. She was silent. She sat on her heels at the foot of his Eames lounger and slowly travelled her fingers up his legs, massaging his musculature through Gap cotton twill. She took her eyes away from his only temporarily, to admire the twitching bulge behind his flies. She traced her fingers along the length of his shaft. The buttons were practically popping themselves open and his cock sprang to attention through the gap in his boxers. Zac caught his breath as Juliana slowly, lightly, drew her hands over the length of him. There was something incredibly titillating about seeing long manicured fingernails, varnished the colour of damson, trace the dimensions of his cock. She could just as well dig in and hurt him as be gentle and feather light in her fondle. Just like when she took him in her mouth (and she had this great way of taking all of him all the way down), she could so easily bite him. When he was in her mouth, he could gently stroke her head, or he could enmesh his fingers in her hair and thrust her head down deep. Spearing her throat. Making her gag. Making him gasp. God, her blow-jobs were good. She was either a natural or she'd watched a glut of porn movies and learned the moves brilliantly.

Usually he'd ask. Usually, Zac would wait to be invited. Not tonight. Tonight, he went ahead and came in Juliana's mouth with no warning, no words, not even an anticipatory quickening of his breathing. Just one long exhalation. Usually she'd swallow. Follow it up with some seductive lip licking and a sated glaze to her eyes. Tonight, she spat out his spunk into her wineglass. He wasn't offended. It wasn't as if she'd wasted good wine – her glass was empty – and it wasn't as if he'd offered to refill it for her.

*

Pip phoned Zac a couple of days later and left a message on his answering machine. 'Hullo, Zac, it's Pip here. Just to say it was great to see you and Tom last Thursday – sorry I couldn't spend more time with you both but a clown doctor's duties come first. Anyway, speak to you soon, hey? Ta-ra.'

He listened to it once more, decided there was nothing to pick up on between the lines, nothing to listen to again, nothing to reply to. So he didn't. He deleted it. It seemed to him to be an appropriate reaction. Not least because it counteracted the ridiculous softening effect that her voice alone appeared to spin through him.

Pip hadn't phoned Zac for any other reason than to say 'hullo'. She didn't expect him to reply – there was nothing to respond to. Simply, she had thought of him, Tom too, as she headed east to Caleb's on a Saturday afternoon. And that was the only reason for her call.

God – life is really quite sussed at the moment! she mused, showering at Caleb's an hour or so later; her cab already waiting outside his apartment block.

Molly phoned Zac. He picked up the call midway through her message. She wanted to arrange farewell drinks for Juliana – or did he have something special planned just for the two of them? No, nothing, he said, giving her the go-ahead to organize an evening.

Zac phoned his brother. Not that he needed to or even really wanted to. They'd had beers last week which had been good and lively. Actually, though he wouldn't admit it, Zac was hoping that his sister-in-law Ruth would answer the phone. His wish was granted, yet he was stuck for words. What on earth was he going to say? Why had he phoned? What was it, exactly, that he wanted to say?

'Hiya!'

That'll do for starters, Zac.

'Zac, how are you? Thank you for returning your brother in such a sorry state the other night. I slept in the spare room. He slept with a bucket. Which, I hasten to add, he forgot about the next morning – but which I found. Though of course he'd already left for work.'

'Never could take his drink,' Zac laughed.

'Grounds for divorce,' Ruth muttered, 'or a trip to Emporio at the very least.'

'I'm sorry,' Zac said with heart.

'Actually,' said his sister-in-law, 'any time – if it happens again, sod Emporio, it's Prada here I come.'

'My dear,' Zac joshed in passable plummy tones, 'if you want to do Prada, you'll have to change postcodes.'

'Perhaps changing husbands would be less hassle,' Ruth mused.

'There's always that,' Zac agreed, having often thought this woman was actually too good for his errant brother. 'Listen, I was phoning because Tom's been a bit down and I thought it's been ages since he and Billy hung out.'

'Great idea,' Ruth enthused. 'How about tomorrow – for once it's a Sunday with no parties to go to. But Jim is playing in some golf tournament with the blokes.'

'How about kite flying on Parliament Hill, weather permitting?' suggested Zac who, though fond of his brother and 'the blokes', was useless at golf.

'Only if I can have a 99 ice-cream,' Ruth said, 'weather permitting.'

'Permission dependent on whether you behave yourself,' Zac laughed.

Zac's kite wasn't the only thing he tied in knots the next day. Ruth rather enjoyed the spectacle of her brother-in-law tripping over his words as much as over the twine. She had never entertained the notion of Zac Holmes becoming tongue-tied. She was tempted to tease, but actually his vulnerability was really quite touching and she was flattered it was to her that he was turning.

'It's just – I don't know – whatever,' said Zac, forcing the words out whilst tugging at the line as Billy and Tom craned their gaze skywards. 'You know?'

'Of course,' Ruth responded, 'you're making perfect sense, dearest.' She spied the ice-cream van and wondered if it was unseemly to head for it less than fifteen minutes after arriving at the park, less than an hour since a hearty lunch at Giraffe in Hampstead. She'd wait, she decided, until Zac had got off his chest whatever was currently clogging it.

The kite was airborne and momentarily steady so Zac gave one section of string to Billy to hold, the other to Tom. The children stood as still as the kite would let them, tugging gently every now and then on their respective ends, grinning at each other and their parents. Zac came close to Ruth. 'I think I'm interested in someone,' he announced, 'and it pisses me off.'

Ruth tried not to grin, or look surprised, or make it obvious that she was racking her brains wondering who. 'Blimey, Zachary,' she grinned, 'I'd never have guessed!' Her irony was lost on him. 'Who who who?' This seemed a more conducive approach. Zac grinned in a slightly embarrassed way, unable to maintain his pissed-off demeanour. The kite remained helpfully aloft and Zac was quite encouraged by Ruth's enthusiasm. 'Actually, you know her,' he said rather portentously. Still Ruth racked and grinned and asked who, who, who. 'It's just,' Zac almost whines, not answering, 'I don't know what to do. Truly I don't. Me, of all people. I don't bloody *know* what to bloody *do.*'

Because Ruth had such scant information, she couldn't comment, so she nodded sagely and waited. Despite being desperate for details, she knew better than to press her brother-in-law for the woman's identity. 'I mean,' Zac continued, bolstered by Ruth being all ears and much nodding, 'what would *you* do? If you were me?' They watched the boys concentrating on the kite. 'The thing is,' Zac pushed on, 'it's all a bit odd for a number of reasons.'

'I'll say,' Ruth agreed vigorously, thinking that all of this really was a bit odd for a number of reasons. Zac Holmes! In a tangle over a woman! Uncharted territory! What on earth *could* she advise? Who on earth *was* the woman?

'I don't even think she's my type,' Zac confided forlornly, 'and it all started off badly anyway – with it appearing I was stalking her or being rude to her,' he continued. He paused. Then smiled. 'But then we went out for tea and had fun. And ate loads. And chatted easily, about swans and stuff. And she looked pretty and I wanted her to share my cab. I'd really have liked that.'

'And?' Ruth prompted, when Zac broke off to apologize to a father and son whose rather plain kite had just been dive-bombed by Billy and Tom's.

'We speak on the phone a fair bit,' Zac shrugged, 'but I don't know if I'm flogging a dead horse, barking up the wrong tree, putting my eggs into one basket, getting the wrong end of the stick – and any other cliché along those lines you care to come up with.' He flopped down on the grass. Ruth didn't know whether to laugh or pinch him or embrace him.

'What you mean is,' she said in tactfully hushed tones, 'you're interested in her but you don't know if it's reciprocated and you are therefore unsure – perhaps apprehensive – about attempting to pursue her?'

Zac shrugged.

'Fear of rejection?' Ruth suggested. Zac snorted in a somewhat derisory manner, though Ruth was spot on.

'She already has a sodding boyfriend,' he grumbled, offering the essential missing link.

'Aha,' said Ruth, who had to bite back the urge to comment on how many fish there were in the sea, 'the desirability of unavailability.'

'Anyway, to be frank, she's *so* not my type!' he declared to Ruth and looked at her imploringly, as if wanting her to agree and thus release him from even thinking about her ever again; or, better, disagree and come up with a plan.

'If she didn't have the boyfriend,' Ruth pondered, 'would you be more forthright?'

Zac thought for a while and then shrugged . 'If I buy you an ice-cream, will you tell me what to do?' he said.

'Sounds like a fair trade to me,' said Ruth.

Zac returned with 99 cones all round and the four of them sat on Parliament Hill, licking and cooing. Ruth and Billy wolfed down their Flakes before touching the ice-cream and then tried to steal Zac and Tom's. They failed. Zac had no idea Tom knew such vocabulary and was far too shocked and much too amused to reprimand him. The kite was hoisted aloft once more, steadied and handed to the children. Zac returned Ruth to his conundrum.

'At the end of the day,' he sighed, 'I don't know what to do. She's involved with someone so I don't know why I'm wasting my time even *thinking* about her. As I've said, she's not really my type anyway, for Christ's sake.'

'Your *type*?' Ruth posed, not as a genuine question but with a tone of incredulity instead. It was lost on Zac who just nodded sulkily. 'Your type,' Ruth said astutely, 'is women you don't have much in common with. Women you don't need to get involved with.' Zac lifted his shoulders to insinuate that wasn't that the best way? 'Now you've gone and met someone different,' she defined, 'who happens to be spoken for,' she continued, 'and you're pissed off.'

'S'pose,' Zac admitted, slightly petulantly.

'I think you'll just have to be disappointed,' said Ruth. 'Sounds like it's no go. It's probably due to the fact that she *is* fun and chatty and all the other stuff, that counts for *you* liking her and that *she* has a boyfriend already.'

'I guess,' said Zac.

'Who is she, then?' Ruth asked softly. 'You say I know her?'

'That clown,' Zac replied.

Ruth didn't realize he was talking of the girl's actual vocation. She thought perhaps he was insulting her boyfriend. 'Who, though?' she persisted.

'That *clown*,' Zac stressed, 'the one at Billy's party.'

Ruth had been stunned into silence three times in her life: when she passed all her A levels with top grades after minimal revision and glandular fever; when Jim proposed midway through a curry; and when the pregnancy test went blue with Billy. Now she was silent for the fourth time – the day when Zac said he'd fallen for the clown she'd found in the *Ham and High*. 'You know,' said Zac, 'she calls herself Merry Bloody Martha though her name is, in fact, Philippa McCabe – only ever known as Pip. She also clowns for sick children in hospitals. She's pretty intelligent. She's pretty, full stop. And lively. And funny. And eats like a horse. Fuck it all.'

'Mum, why's your mouth open like that?' Billy interrupted, having come over to ask for a drink of juice.

'I'm fine, darling,' Ruth replied, sending him off with a carton and one for Tom, too. 'Zac, I had no idea,' she marvelled, turning to her brother-in-law who raised his eyebrows and plucked at snatches of grass. 'Have you seen much of her? Have you slept together? Bloody hell – am I the matchmaker? Am I to blame? To credit? Do you pay me? Does she? How much?'

'I told you, we went out for tea – and I haven't kissed her, let alone shagged her,' Zac informed his sister-in-law, feeling finally at ease. 'It's just we seem to get on well – laugh and tease and chat. Easily.'

'But she has a boyf, you think?'

'Yes. I saw him, some bloody doctor at the frigging hospital.'

'She wasn't just having an innocent flirt, like one tends to, with colleagues? Like one *does*, with dishy docs?'

'That,' Zac proclaimed, 'was the give-away. She caught his gaze, looked away and didn't say a word. That's how I knew. She was chatty and tactile with everyone else.'

'Maybe she hates his guts?' Ruth suggested feebly. Zac raised his eyebrows, faintly annoyed. 'You weren't there,' he said, almost resentfully. 'When she said "hullo" to him, she did so in her own voice, not Dr Pippity's.'

'Oh,' Ruth said quietly, not fully aware of the significance.

'Her nose didn't light up when he said something,' Zac sighed, 'nor did she mimic him in any way.'

112

'Ah,' said Ruth in what she hoped was the appropriate tone.

'Instead, she simply took one of the little boys' crisps,' Zac said, 'and then she turned away from the doctor as if she hadn't even noticed he was there.'

'Well,' Ruth declared though she now had no idea what to advise. She wanted to encourage her brother-in-law because it was the first time she'd seen him interested, let alone smitten; but how could she when the facts of the situation seemed clear and the situation seemed futile indeed? 'Maybe just nurture your friendship with her,' she suggested feebly, 'and perhaps it'll finish with Dr Kildare?'

'That's what's so strange,' said Zac. 'I adore having friends who are female — but with Pip, it won't do.'

Ruth couldn't add anything to that. All or nothing. Zac would just have to continue dating gorgeous women who meant nothing emotionally.

'Shame really,' Ruth said later that night. Her husband looked up briefly and supposed she was talking to herself again so buried his nose in the dregs of the Sunday papers. 'There's a lot to Zac, and it would be quite nice, really, to have him settled.' Jim just made affirmative noises in his throat, having not heard a word.

Later, Ruth couldn't sleep. She crept out of her bedroom and phoned Zac. It was almost one in the morning.

'It's me,' she whispered.

'Hullo,' he whispered back; Tom was staying over and had insisted on sharing his bed.

'I think you should tell her how you feel,' Ruth imparted. 'You have nothing to lose in doing so. If she's really into this guy, then you're no further away from where you are right now. If she isn't, then you're paving the way.'

'Yes?' said Zac. 'Maybe.'

Ruth's plan of action sounded quite good at such an ungodly hour.

In the cold light of the next day, however, Zac rejected it as totally unfeasible.

SIXTEEN

*I*t wasn't long before Zac was wondering whether to loiter. He decided against it, but only because Kentish Town tube, which was Pip's nearest station, really was not a particularly pleasant location to frequent unless he was to develop a taste for Special Brew in earnest. Furthermore, he couldn't very well traipse Tom down to St Bea's in the City without an appointment; that was unthinkable. He did momentarily consider shoving his arm into a sling or casually hobbling around the ambulance bay evincing a limp, before reminding himself that St Bea's was a hospital for children. He then wondered about phone tag – phoning until it was Pip, not the voice mail, who answered the call. However, both these approaches – by foot or by phone – seemed to him to be those a stalker would make. No. Neither would do. And letter writing was far too Jane Austen, totally un-him, very un-twenty-first-century and anyway, it would hardly be taken seriously. E-mail? Did a clown have much use for e-mail? Text message? Too teenage. Telepathy? As if. Messenger? Who – like Cupid? Yeah, right.

But Zac simply couldn't banish the image of Pip from his mind's eye and he felt his impotence was twofold. There was nothing he could do. So nothing was going to happen. He was incapable of forcing his mind over the matter.

Whether it was Cupid or Puck or Fate or Coincidence, Zac didn't have time to ponder or care. All he knew, midway through the next week, was that he was queuing for the same movie with Juliana as Pip was with one of her sisters. The lovelorn one. Kit. Cat. Something like that. Good job Pip was taking her to see the new Austin Powers and not the weepie with Helen Hunt.

What a daft question, of course Juliana didn't want popcorn or ice-cream or family-size bags of confectionery. Nor did Zac really, but he could see Pip procrastinating over the various foodstuffs and he took it as a golden opportunity to approach. As much as he wanted to talk to her, he was also quite content just to look (her bottom appeared very pert in lightweight cargo pants) and to listen (she was ordering large nachos with extra everything, plus Maltesers, a small sweet popcorn and a Pepsi). He was also keen to touch (her hair was loose and she was wearing a flattering white vest top) but of course he didn't.

The sales assistant, apparently incapable of speech *per se*, slightly modified a gormless expression by raising an eyebrow and widening an already gawping mouth to encourage Zac to place his order.

'I'll have orangey-lemony-blackcurranty squash, please. A big 'un. Ta.'

Zac was staggered that the sales assistant lolloped away, no questions asked. And he was delighted that Pip spun on her heels and greeted him.

'You!'

'You.'

'Are you here to see a movie?' Pip asked. Zac noticed she was wearing mascara. She didn't need to, but it suited her anyway.

'Nah,' Zac replied, 'I like hanging out here. It's my favourite bar for a gourmet snack and a delicious drink.'

Pip laughed. 'Don't make me laugh,' she pleaded, 'my

mascara will run. I thought we were going to see the Helen Hunt weepie – hence the eye make-up as a precaution against crying.'

'Ain't got the drink what you wanted,' the sales assistant announced robotically and resumed the gawp to await Zac's alternative.

'Mineral water and Minstrels. No! M&Ms. Wait! I've changed my mind – Revels,' Zac ordered, earning Brownie points from Pip in the process. The sales person trudged away. 'How are you?'

'Fine,' said Pip, trying to balance the nachos and the popcorn whilst tucking the chocolate into her bag. 'And you? I left a message last week. Would you like a nacho?'

'No, thanks,' Zac smiled.

How shall I just drop the boyfriend into the conversation? How the fuck do I do that? Ruth! What would you suggest? Something like 'Are you here with your bloke?'

'Popcorn?' Pip offered.

'Thanks, but no,' Zac declined.

How about 'Does your bloke like weepie movies, too?' God, that's rubbish. Shall I just shoot straight and ask her on a date? 'I say, Pip – fancy a drink tomorrow night?' Or should it be 'I say, Pip, fancy a drink some time – if your chap doesn't object'?

'Sip of coke?'

'No, ta,' said Zac.

Or perhaps 'Look, Pip, we get on pretty well – why don't we give it a go?' I mean, I'd get full marks for directness with that one. My honesty might just sway her.

'Malteser?'

Zac shook his head.

Fuck it. Who am I trying to kid? No point.

'Are you on a diet?' Pip accused. 'Was the cream tea too much for you?'

Zac laughed.

It wasn't enough, Philippa McCabe, it merely whetted my appetite and has had me salivating for more.

The Revels were unceremoniously plonked down before him and, to solicit further approval from Pip, Zac added a high-class choc-ice, encrusted with almonds and stuffed with cookie dough, to his order.

'That's my boy!' Pip proclaimed, who was tempted to order one of those for herself.

I wish, thought Zac.

'I'd better go,' Pip said, 'I want to make an inroad into these nachos and I can't possibly miss the trailers.'

'Enjoy the movie,' Zac said, 'and the nosh.'

'Anyway,' smiled Pip, backing away, 'your girlfriend is probably dying for a Revel.'

Fuck fuck fuck.
She's not my girlfriend!

Zac was horrified that Pip had even noticed Juliana, let alone come to the conclusion that they were an item.

'See you soon,' said Pip, walking off, bending her head to lick up a popcorn or two as she went. Cat hadn't noticed Zac, she hadn't really noticed how long her sister had been gone. She was in a world of her own, wondering whether she really felt like seeing a film that would make her laugh and forget about her woes for ninety minutes. Was that the right thing to do? She was unsure. Feeling miserable had become almost the norm to her, cathartic even; wouldn't the Helen Hunt weepie thus be more appropriate? She could really have a good cry; unlike her eldest sister, she purposefully hadn't put mascara on that evening.

Pip linked arms with Cat, having given her the popcorn to hold. 'Tuck in!' she said. 'I bought it all to share. I could never scoff the lot by myself.' Actually, Pip could very well demolish every last mouthful. But it was a pleasure to share. 'Austin Powers!' she marvelled to Cat who was gingerly picking at the popcorn and was secretly quite tempted by the synthetic aroma of the nachos. The lights dimmed and the trailers began.

Zac didn't really give the movie his full attention as he was powerless not to surreptitiously scour the forest of heads in front of him. He couldn't find Pip. If Zac knew that Pip liked to remain in her seat, waiting for the credits for Best Boy, Key Grip and Gaffer, sitting there right until the disclaimer about no animals being ill-treated during filming, he'd have asked her then and there to marry him. Unfortunately but significantly, Juliana liked to go just as soon as the end credits started to roll. So he left as soon as Juliana decreed and they went back to her serviced apartment in Marble Arch where she serviced Zac very well indeed. There was little point abstaining because there was no point pursuing Pip. Not with her having a boyfriend already and now presuming that he had a girlfriend.

* * *

However, taking a cab home at midnight, Zac decides to text Pip. However teenagery this approach had seemed previously, text messaging now seems to be the most concise, even intimate, method to approach Pip and broach the subject of her boyfriend. He justifies that Ruth insisted he be upfront and forthright so he is merely obeying orders.

`mike myers = total fucking genius.`

He may not have given the film the appropriate attention, but instinct tells him that such a proclamation will strike a chord with Pip.

`yup!! he brill!!!`

The reply is almost immediate. He's pleased. But what should he write next? What's the best way to incorporate his girlfriendless status into a text? How can he verify the status of Pip's doctor, too? And, most importantly, do as Ruth told him and actually tell her how he feels?

'Christ,' he fulminates, not caring that the cab driver glances back at him, 'why should any of this bloody matter?'

`u free 2moro?`

Should he send that? He does.

sorry nope.

Damn. Aha! Here's an opening, though.

hot date? Zac sends back.

praps!!! Pip replies, the ambiguity frustrating Zac, the excessive use of exclamation marks simultaneously charming, irritating and demoralizing.

lucky dr kildare? Zac texts brazenly, telling himself that putting 'lucky' will also serve to reveal, albeit indirectly, how he feels.

dr who? Pip responds.

Shit. What to write now?

st b's. Zac pauses. He looks at the screen till the illumination switches off. What the hell. your boyf, methinks he adds and he sends it without a question mark. The wait seems interminable. Finally, his phone beeps. He accesses Pip's reply.

yup - dr caleb simmons.

'I didn't ask his stupid fucking name!' Zac shouts. The cab driver does not look around. He's near the punter's destination anyway. The midnight hour, in his twenty years' experience, always brings out the emotional, the irrational, the deluded.

'Ta,' Zac mumbles, thrusting a tenner at the driver. 'Keep the change.'

'Thirteen forty, mate,' the cab driver says diplomatically. Zac hands him an extra fiver and mumbles for him to keep the change. He goes into his flat. Shuts the door, presses his back against it and shuts his eyes, banging his head gently; two three four.

Fuck. Fuck. Fuck.

It suddenly seems strategically crucial to phone Ruth.

'I just saw her at the cinema. She thinks Juliana is my girlfriend. Then I texted her and asked her outright about the boyfriend. I was right. He is. Not only that, Ruth, he's called fucking Caleb.'

It took the first two sentences for Ruth to realize who it was talking hoarsely down the phone at her so late at night.

'Bad luck,' she says, trying to sound sympathetic. She feels that tonight isn't the time to talk about all the fish in the sea. 'If it makes you feel better,' she adds, 'she obviously has a penchant for biblical boys.'

'It doesn't,' Zac says morosely, 'but ta anyway. Goodnight.'

'Zac?' Ruth interrupts. 'Did you tell her how you feel? Not just ascertain the doctor's status? Did you *tell* her?'

Zac thinks about it, knowing well how the female opinion and standard on this matter probably differ from the male. 'Sort of,' he says, 'I mean, not by poetry or full-on serenading, of course.'

'Good,' says Ruth, 'glad you did. It's important.'

He tries to go to sleep. He chants 'fuck fuck fuck' to himself, though fucking is far from his mind. And the possibility of fucking Pip is so far off that it doesn't register even *beyond* the foreseeable horizon. He sends one final text an hour later.

'Blimey,' Pip says aloud softly, about to brush her teeth and turn in for the night. She slips between the sheets. 'I referred to Caleb as my boyfriend!' This certainly requires the exclamation mark. It's a statement that Pip finds extraordinary. 'I guess I *do* have a boyfriend. I suppose Caleb and I, a good six weeks down the line, *are* beyond the stage of just "seeing" one another.' She tries a couple of sentences out loud to see how they sound, to see if they roll off her tongue in a natural way.

'Caleb? Oh, he's my boyfriend.'

That was easy enough.

'I was just saying the guy I'm going out with is a doctor.'

That sounds quite good, too.

Pip giggles. Is it really time to go public?

Sure.

Why not?

What has she to hide? And, with Caleb, doesn't she have rather a lot to be proud of and actually show off?

Just before she falls asleep, she wonders to herself if Caleb himself has been referring to her as his girlfriend. If so, it must follow that he thinks of himself as her boyfriend, too. She wonders about this. And then she drifts off.

Pip doesn't retrieve Zac's last text until the next morning.

lucky bugger.

She doesn't get it. She hasn't saved his texts of the previous night and she can't really remember them anyway.

'Lucky bugger?' She presumes it's something to do with Austin Powers but she can't think what. She locks her front door and heads for the bus.

* * *

So Juliana returned to South Africa, temporarily at least and, for the time being, Zac felt Pip might as well be in Timbuktu, so remote was the possibility of anything developing there. The accountant threw himself into his work and immersed himself in socializing with his friends, devoting his weekends to being the best father in the world. He invested as much energy into his free time as into his work so that he simply didn't have any spare time to become thinking time. He didn't have time to think of Pip. Therefore he didn't. And it was easy enough. He was thus at an utter loss about what to do, how to react, what exactly to feel, when he came across her crying her eyes out a week later, and when the reason for her tears became clear.

SEVENTEEN

*P*ip was toying with inviting Fen and Matt, Megan and Dominic over for dinner. She'd been pontificating for some time. Not so much because she was miserly with her personal space, possessive of her spare time and somewhat obsessive about spills and stains, but because she was considering inviting Caleb, too. How cosy would that be? How frighteningly grown-up? Moreover, Caleb would actually be the point of the gathering. How significant was that? How bloody symbolic? After all, she hadn't yet told anyone of his existence. Apart from Zac, of course. But no one knew of Zac's existence either. And yet dinner for six seemed somehow presumptuous. Though she'd been with Caleb two months now, she'd let him in to her flat on just a couple of occasions and that was only because he'd all but begged. One time he said he'd been spending too much time in the East End and that he craved a change of scene; on another, he said the neighbours were madder than ever and he needed refuge. Oddly, Pip didn't enjoy sex as much in her own bed as at Caleb's flat. Both times, she had hoped he would not presume to stay the night and yet when he didn't even ask to, calling a cab ten minutes post-coitally, she was a little taken aback.

If I organize a dinner thing, would he want to stay over

afterwards? Will I want that? Whether he does or doesn't, can you imagine how often my phone will go the following day with Megan and Fen desperate for details? Then, of course, Cat will be told and will want to hear it all anew.

She looked at her calendar. Cat would be going off to the Tour de France soon enough.

'It's not like I actively want to keep information away from her,' Pip muttered, 'but that's how it will seem because I doubt I can fix something up before she leaves. But to do so once she's gone won't seem right, either.'

So, no dinner party?

No.

No opportunity for friends and relations to meet your boyfriend?

No. Not at the moment. Anyway, it's not as if he's been brandishing me around his own social circle.

Hasn't he?

No, thank God!

No one at all?

Not a soul.

Anyway, isn't Caleb going away himself fairly soon? It might well seem affected to organize a meet and greet before he leaves.

I'd forgotten about that! But of course. That settles it, then, and what a relief!

It was a Thursday. Caleb was aware that Pip liked company and specific things to do in the evening and it was his pleasure to assist.

'Why don't I come home with you?' he suggested, having nipped in to the glorified cupboard at the hospital where she was mid-metamorphosis between Dr Pippity and Pip. 'Can you hang around half an hour? Or shall I meet you later?'

Pip looked at him in the mirror, then glanced at herself with half her make-up off, the remainder smeared grotesquely. 'Sure,' she said, 'but don't rush. Come later. I want my well-earned luxuriate in the bath first, anyway.'

'Lovely,' he said softly, coming close behind her and sliding his hands gently along her collar-bones to the base of her throat. 'The sternoclavicular dip,' he marvelled, using his fingertips to touch her there. 'For me, it's the most feminine, alluring part of a woman.' He slipped his hands lower until they cupped her breasts. 'Not that these aren't your finest assets,' he said. Coquettishly, Pip spread her legs a little and led his hand down to the gusset of her spotty tights, while she looked up at him, all wide-eyed and winsome. Caleb swallowed. 'I stand corrected,' he said, kneading his fingers gently but insistently at her crotch. 'This is perhaps my favourite part of you.'

'Dr Simmons,' Pip remonstrated, though she moved her pelvis to rub herself against his hand, 'are you actually off duty?'

'Fuck,' he sighed, though he intensified his touch.

'*When* you're off duty,' Pip said with glee, picking his hand up and flinging it away theatrically, 'I'll consider whether to grant you entry. Now sod off.'

Caleb smiled and gazed and saw beyond the smear of face paint and the hair tied back any old how. He would have been happy for Pip to have rubbed off all her remaining make-up over his bare body. He wanted to ravish her right now. But, as she said, he was on duty. Later. Later.

'You clowns,' he sulked in jest, 'you're no bloody fun, you're all mouth and no trousers.'

Pip regarded him squarely. 'I assure you,' she said, 'a smile isn't the only thing I'll raise in you later on. I'll be all mouth and you'll be no trousers.'

She walked to the tube with a spring to her step. Caleb. He was such an attractive mix of manners and mischief. Maybe a dinner party *would* be a laugh. She knew that Megan and her sisters – anyone, really – would like him very much. Being with him made her feel feisty. She was truly enjoying the fun of it all. It was lovely to be involved with someone she respected, but who she could be so playful with, too. She was quite surprised how, quite early on, she was turned on

124

and flattered that he referred to her genitalia as her 'gorgeous cunt'. Previously, she'd hated the word and would never have countenanced a man who used it – whether as expletive or anatomically. Pip didn't really have a word for her nether regions. Mike had called it her 'fanny' which she'd hated as soppy and childish. Rupert had referred to it only the once as her 'privates' and she'd ended the relationship soon after. Harry had been most reverential towards her 'vagina' which made Pip think of her doctor and smear tests. But Caleb tells her that her cunt is gorgeous and Pip is happy to share its mysteries with him.

The following Tuesday, she was back at St Bea's, spinning laughs and weaving smiles, distributing respite and little gifts, lifting the mood by lowering the tone. It was a good session. One of the nurses told her she had brought into the ward the glorious sunshine and warmth of the high June day. Pip was full of energy and decided to stay an extra hour to tell some lousy jokes and perform skilfully clumsy acrobatics in Out-patients. She'd take a quick break first. She paged Caleb. He joined her in the ambulance bay. It was nearing tea-time but still hot. He looked harassed. He looked as though he felt the opposite of Pip. It appeared his day was as bad as hers had been good. The sunshine had no positive effect on him. What could she do to help? She touched his brow and ran her hand down his cheek, over his neck to his arm. She squeezed him fondly. 'You OK?'

'Sure,' he said, lighting a cigarette and sucking on it as if he was starving, 'just a few hassles.' He looked at her and frowned. 'You know,' he clarified, 'the stuff of headaches.'

Pip nodded. 'Sometimes this place can be like that – and I'm only here a few hours a week,' she said sympathetically, giving him a supportive rub between the shoulder-blades.

'You're a sweet, sweet thing,' he said affectionately, ruffling her hair. Momentarily, she didn't like it. She wanted him to only ever think of her as the vamp with the gorgeous cunt, not a sweet thing he could pet. But she let it pass.

Those were her own self-doubts surfacing, she chastised, nothing to do with Caleb. She should feel flattered and heartened that he appeared to be so fond of her, that she seemed to be all things to him.

'You know I'm away next week,' he stated, out of context but with emphasis.

'That's right,' Pip said. 'Shame – I was going to suggest dinner at mine, or a weekend away, perhaps. Maybe when you're back.'

Caleb didn't say anything but he looked down at her fondly. 'You'll come back all tanned and gorgeous and I won't be able to keep my hands off you!' she said, hoping to lift his mood. 'I'll bet you can't wait to go – just steer clear of the local dusky maidens, if you please!' He looked down further, engrossed in his shoes. 'Shiny,' Pip said, looking too, thinking it sounded a bit daft but so what. 'Is your friend looking forward to it?' she asked.

'Friend?'

'The mate you're going on holiday with?' Pip said.

'Sure,' said Caleb, lighting another cigarette immediately.

'Which mate?' she asked. 'The one you play squash with? I haven't even asked you!'

'Jo,' said Caleb.

'Joe,' Pip repeated, it didn't ring a bell.

'Correct,' said Caleb.

'I don't know if you've mentioned Joe?' she said, trying to remember if he had.

'No,' said Caleb, 'I haven't. Andy's the bloke I play squash with.'

'Of course. Andy – that's right!' she nodded as if she knew Andy well. 'So which one's Joe?'

'Jo,' said Caleb, 'is my girlfriend.'

EIGHTEEN

*O*h, how you kick yourself when, months later, you think of the perfect retaliatory quip for a situation which so desperately warranted one at the time. Would you not endure the torment of the whole event again if it meant you could deliver that definitive killer rejoinder? No matter how eloquent a person, it is rare, unless you are a reincarnation of Oscar Wilde, to have the perfect retort at your disposal. A *coup de grâce* on the tip of your tongue. Unless you have a brilliant scribe working on your behalf, you are unlikely to deliver a soliloquy worthy of an Oscar, let alone Oscar W himself. The ultimate means to reassert your dignity and walk away, head high, with the satisfaction of the moral high ground *and* the last word is, unfortunately, a talent which eludes most.

Our heroine is not related to Oscar Wilde, nor does she have any Hollywood connections. Anyway, this isn't fiction. It's the here and now and she's a clown and she's just standing there. It's a glorious summer day but a chill has coursed through her making her shudder quite violently. Her heart is thudding, her mouth is agape, her brain is short-circuiting. Disbelief churning with nausea and mixed with a sickening quota of humiliation renders her utterly incapable of any sound, never mind an air-punching speech with a rousing soundtrack and spontaneous audience ovation.

'Shit!' Caleb is saying, on account of her expression. 'Pip – I honestly thought you realized.'

Hit him, Pip!

'Fuck!' he's continuing. 'I feel so bad! You must think I've led you on?'

Don't you let him talk himself out of his guilt!

'I truly thought you were cool about things,' he's saying with a look of deep concern. Actually, it's more of a mask than Pip can ever paint. Caleb's expression – a beguiling blend of care, sympathy, sensitivity – is not natural to his personality, nor is it spontaneous to the situation in hand. It's not an honest reflection of how he feels, it's not sincere in the slightest. But it is pretty convincing. He learned how to manipulate his face during his medical training. At the same time as studying physiology and swotting up on anatomy. When he was also practising illegible handwriting for prescriptions and the most meaningful way to say 'hmmm'.

'God, I'm so sorry, Pip. I *so* didn't mean to hurt you.'

This isn't remorse, it's contrived and it's bullshit, Pip. If you still can't speak, belt him!

'Are you OK?' he asks. 'Hmmm?'

The clown with the gorgeous cunt nods her head meekly and prays a tear won't splash on the doctor's shiny sodding shoes. Go on! Stamp on them!

'I feel dreadful,' says the doctor who doesn't, 'I really thought you were on my wavelength.'

Pip looks up sharply, as if *he's* accusing *her*. Kick him on the shin, Pip!

'I mean,' Caleb continues, feeling slightly appeased, 'I really thought you were into the whole no-strings-sex thing? You know, friends who fuck?'

Is Pip clearing her throat? Or is she swallowing down tears? Or is she about to throw up?

'I got you wrong and I'm mortified,' Caleb says with fairly credible solemnity. 'Damn!'

Pip clears her throat. 'No, Dr Simmons,' she says quietly. She stares at his stethoscope because she just can't drag her eyes up to his and she doesn't want to look at his stupid shiny shoes any longer. 'I had *you* wrong.'

Away she walks. Beyond the ambulances, past the patients taking fresh air, past the visitors steadying themselves with cigarettes, past the staff on breaks chatting on their mobiles or wolfing down snacks. Pip strides out beyond the hospital perimeter. In her slap and motley, her braided hair sticking out at jaunty angles, her pockets aflap with the toy tools of her trade.

She's not looking where she's going, she doesn't know where she's headed, but she doesn't look back, not even a glance. Her eyes are smarting, her vision is impaired, but she doesn't slow up. Forward. Onward. It's as if the further she can be from the hospital, the further she will be from the past. She needs to keep walking in the opposite direction and, logically, into the future.

Dr Caleb Simmons is still in the ambulance bay. He stubs out his cigarette and returns to the wards. He thinks that didn't go too badly. At least there hadn't been a scene. He does like Pip and she's great in bed. But he's fond of Jo, too, who isn't that exciting in the sack. And he very much likes Alice, the nurse on Hogarth ward; she comes as a pair (sometimes literally) with her friend the dental nurse from Dalston.

It isn't about open-mindedness versus being prudish, modern versus old-fashioned. It isn't about strength of feeling or depth of love. It certainly isn't about what is right or what isn't. It is not a question of ethics. Caleb, actually, doesn't believe he has done anything wrong. Pip is upset and he is sorry that she is. That was never his intention. He reasons how morality is a highly subjective issue. Sure, Pip is hurting but, he justifies, he didn't wilfully cause it. Far from it. If only he had known. Anyway, he's said sorry, after all.

*

Still Pip walked. She went through Liverpool Street station, circumnavigated Broadgate Circle twice (completely oblivious to the flamenco group providing complimentary entertainment in the ring), meandered until she found herself on Moorgate and then walked aimlessly around every floor in M&S. Outside, she window-shopped all the '3 for 2' books on offer in Books Etc. and almost felt like crying when she saw Pret A Manger was closed though she was incapable of eating a thing. Finally, she found comfort in the Edwardian grace and greenery of Finsbury Circus. She walked around it a couple of times, steering clear of the City bucks already drinking at the Pavilions bar. Suddenly, gazing at the perfectly manicured bowling green, Pip realized how tired she was, how sore her feet were and how she desperately needed to sit down and take stock. She chose a bench and sat on pigeon shit without caring. A litter bin nearby smelt unpleasant with a lunch-hour's worth of leftovers fermenting in the sun.

She sat there for some time, feeling confused more than sorry for herself, though sorry for herself she certainly soon felt. 'I thought he was *normal*,' she whispered out loud. God, she felt such a fool. She cried. Then she felt even more of a fool. But she couldn't help sobbing afresh when she thought how she'd never have sex with Caleb again, and that was certainly something to mourn. The rampant fling had been flung away. And not by her choosing. And that didn't seem fair.

People were starting to stream out of their offices for the day. Pip didn't notice. She wasn't aware of what the time was, nor did she care how she looked, sitting there. A splash of colour amidst all the navy and grey sensible work suits. Actually, not so much a splash, more a splodge – her make-up was smeared and streaked from her tears. People stared; some slowed down, others hurried past. Some wondered initially if the clown was providing some form of street entertainment. But there was no begging bowl. And there was nothing particularly funny about her. Just odd.

Only one person actually stopped. Sat down right next to the clown, on some pigeon shit, too. Sat beside her and put a comforting arm gently across her shoulders.

'Are you OK?' he asked. He was on his way to the pub for a swift half or two with a couple of colleagues. They loitered. He motioned for them to go on ahead.

Her face was striated with rivulets of murky green, streaks of inky blue and smudges of red. Most of her clown white was now a miserable grey. Most of her lipstick had smeared around her mouth, like someone who'd gorged at Pick Your Own berries. Or had been in a fight. Well, in a way, Pip has been in a fight with a pick your own. She picked on someone not of her own calibre. And just then, she believed, she'd lost.

'Are you OK?' the good Samaritan asked again.

She wiped her nose sonorously against the back of her hand, transferring a bruise-like welt of make-up in the process.

'Pip?'

She looked up. Bloody hell, it was Zac Holmes. She stared at him. His face was creased with an expression of utter concern and he was doing the caring shoulder squeezing and 'hey hey'ing with great commitment. He was so solemn that, momentarily, Pip wanted to giggle. However, the abiding emotion was one of gratitude and a feeling of safety and, accordingly, she laid her head against his arm and let her tears subside. Zac didn't intrude. He allowed there to be silence. And if the passers-by wanted to speculate as to his relationship with the crying clown, let them. And if his colleagues took the piss later, or didn't bother to wait for him at the pub, then so what. They were only work associates, merely the least dull amongst those he worked with.

For Pip, sitting in the middle of an area of London alien to her; sitting on bird shit in her clown doctor's uniform, her face a disaster area that could frighten children, her life a far cry from the control she so arrogantly assumed she'd instilled; it all seemed suddenly to make perfect sense. She hadn't told a soul about Dr Simmons. But one person knew of his existence. That person, Zac Holmes, was the very person sitting next to her, in pigeon poo, too, being liberal with his maternal clucking and sympathetic back rubbing. The back rubbing was soothing. Rhythmic, steady; just the right amount of pressure. She felt lulled and her breathing regulated.

'Oh dear,' she sighed, 'bollocks.'

'Are you all right?' Zac asked. Pip looked up at him and nodded. 'Look, my office is that building just over there – why not go in and take five. Or rip up a newspaper. Or make a phone call. Or have a good yell. Or just wash your face?' Pip nodded and let Zac lead her away.

'Welcome to Hell-hole,' Zac said of his office with a hint of embarrassment. 'They're mostly the same around here – beautiful buildings buggered up by hanging ceilings and truly diabolical lighting, space subdivided into as many work pods as possible. If it's not liquid lunches giving me a headache, it's the sodding ambience here. I have a headache most days. See?' He pulled out a packet of Nurofen from his pocket to verify. 'Anyway, Clowngirl, second left for the ladies' loo. Off you go. Shall I get you a drink? Would you like the strange liquid from our machine which might be tea, or there again coffee? Or a plastic cup of plasticky water? It's from that world-renowned well of purity – the Dell Valley Spring. Not that I can find Dell Valley on the map. Or the Internet. Not that I'm a sad bastard for researching it. Anyway, what'll it be?'

'I'm OK,' said Pip croakily. Zac felt that was a matter for some conjecture but diplomatically, he said nothing. She went to the ladies', he looked around his floor. There was no one around. Just as well, really. The company was threatening a batch of redundancies soon and Zac's derisory comments concerning their vending machines and office ergonomics could surely amount to something sackable.

It is not an easy task to remove stage paint with water

alone. In fact, water alone actually is not recommended. Cold cream is the best antidote; Simple Soap will do, but it's a lengthier process. Water doesn't really work. Pip, however, had more sense and respect for her skin's sensitivity, than to resort to the industrial pink liquid soap in the wall-mounted dispenser. She'd winced on seeing her reflection and had momentarily cringed at the thought of the spectacle she must have provided to everyone she passed from St Bea's to the bench. Oddly, though, she wasn't mortified that Zac had seen her so; when she saw the state of her face, she was extremely glad he had come across her and laid his company's facilities at her disposal. When Pip emerged, she looked something akin to an art teacher at the end of the school day. If it wasn't for her clothing, she might not attract even a second glance.

She approached Zac a little shyly. 'Thanks,' she said, with a coy dip of her head against her shoulder, which wasn't wholly unintentional.

'No problem,' he replied. 'I wouldn't take you to meet the Queen looking like that, but I will escort you wherever it was you were headed.'

'That's precisely it,' Pip confessed. 'I had no idea where I was going – just where I was coming from.'

Zac nodded sagely, slightly confused at the solemnity of Pip's tone but feeling it was rude to pry. 'Hot liquid?' he offered. 'Plastic water from the Dell Valley?'

'Perhaps the plastic water,' Pip said gratefully, 'and a couple of painkillers.' She looked around her. How could people work productively in such an oppressive and cramped environment? 'Which is your desk?' she asked Zac when he returned, surveying Pod-land.

He looked a little embarrassed. 'Well, it's over there actually.' Pip looked 'over there' and to a side of the floor where there were three or four single offices with smoked glass doors and not a pod in sight. 'In one of them.'

'One of those,' Pip corrected automatically. 'Are you the boss?' she asked, almost accusatorily.

'No no!' Zac denied breezily.

'But you *are* a bit of a hot shot?' Pip pressed. 'You're *not* one of the proletariat working in Pod-land with no natural light?'

'I do have an office to myself,' Zac conceded, 'and a window.'

'May I see?' Pip asked. It seemed preferable to stay here than to be outside, having to decide which direction to take. It was much better to be with Zac than to be on her own. It was good not to have the time to think about Caleb. She was going to change the subject in her mind and soul. Forget all about it. About *him*. For a while, at least.

'If you really want to,' Zac said with a perceptible shuffle. 'It's just a boring old office, though.'

Pip had to nudge him to lead on. 'You lucky sod!' she exclaimed. 'You have two sash windows, a high ceiling, ornamental coving, corporate art *and* a coffee percolator!'

'I work hard,' Zac shrugged, thinking that Pip probably didn't know a Herman Miller *Aeron* chair even when she was swivelling on it; certainly not that it cost a thousand pounds.

Pip noted the photos of Tom at various ages on the window-sills and Zac's desk. And then she noticed the clock above the door. It was nearing 7.00. She'd left the hospital almost three hours ago. And her stuff was still there. It was one thing taking the tube home looking like an art teacher at the end of the day, albeit one dressed as a clown; it was quite another to have to break into one's flat because the house keys had been voluntarily left at work. And, of course, there was no way she could turn up at either of her sisters', or Megan's, because they would want to know why. And who.

'Are you all right, Pip?' Zac asked, discerning that she wasn't actually looking at his magnetic paper-clip pyramid but was simply staring, deep in thought, probably to the nub of the matter – whatever the matter was.

'Yes,' she said, unconvincingly. She was as unlikely to tell Zac all that had happened that afternoon, as she was to ask him if she could perhaps take refuge in his flat for the night so that she didn't have to return to St Bea's.

'Finished snooping?' he asked, thinking he'd quite like a pint now, either with dull colleagues or the paint-stained clown. The pint was the point and he was thirsting for one. It had been a long day. Awkward clients with complex accounts. And then Clowngirl turning up, quite literally on his doorstep, sobbing as if she couldn't stop. Well, she had stopped now. In fact, she'd brightened up discernibly. 'You can rummage through my drawers, if you like,' he said, 'or join me for a pint? Or that lemony-blackcurrant stuff.'

'That sounds like a fine idea,' Pip said. Zac opened his drawers. Pip laughed. 'I meant the pint,' she explained. Zac had hoped that's what she'd meant – but hadn't wanted to tempt fate. Having a drink with Zac, thought Pip, would give her more time not to have to think about keys and St Bea's and the bloody doc and his roving cock.

Zac took her to a pub near Leadenhall Market – not because it was a good stroll away and therefore unlikely to be frequented by his colleagues, but because it was historical with a great atmosphere and he thought Pip might like it. Drinking on a system that had churned so violently with adrenalin was akin to drinking on an empty stomach. Two glasses of Rioja and Pip was burying her head in her hands, wailing. She looked up at Zac, tears prickling her eyes, and whispered 'Bastard!'

'Me?' Zac whispered back.

'Of course not you,' said Pip. She wouldn't be drawn further until another glass of Rioja had lubricated her vocal cords.

'Boyfriend giving you gyp?' Zac asked, on chinking empty glasses.

'Gyp!' Pip smiled. 'You're funny, you are. Bit old-fashioned, aren't you?' He noticed she was starting to slur her words slightly. She noticed that, occasionally, there appeared to be two of him.

'I also say "crikey", sometimes,' Zac confessed.

'My boyfriend,' Pip said, banging her fist on the table for emphasis, though it landed in a puddle of Rioja that subsequently splashed on her white coat and Zac's shirt (it was navy, it didn't show), 'my so-called *boyfriend* has a *girlfriend*, I learn today. And she's *not* me.'

'Bloody hell, Pip,' said Zac, 'how ghastly for you.'

'*Ghastly*,' Pip repeated, holding her index finger aloft for emphasis, 'is an understatement. It's a downright fucking nightmare.'

'You had no idea?' Zac said, his concern etched across a very furrowed brow. How on earth could she have had no idea? Momentarily, they both pondered this. Then Pip shook her head. 'No clues in his flat?' Pip thought of the *Psycho* shower curtain. No matter how much she wanted to hate Jo and presume her to be a complete cow, she just couldn't credit any woman with buying that comedy shower curtain. So she shook her head. What about the fresh flowers, Pip?

I took those as an indication of Caleb being in touch with his feminine side.

'I was a bit on the side,' she shrugged, looking up at Zac, humiliated and hurt.

'Poor Pip,' said Zac.

'Fucking bastard wanker,' Pip proclaimed, histrionically.

Zac wanted to laugh but of course didn't. Pip was deadly serious. 'You found out today and left the hospital on the double?' he asked.

'On the double,' Pip mimicked, Zac's occasional, trademark quaintness making her smile. 'Yes,' she confirmed, looking tearful, 'he told me today. Then made this big thing about how he thought I knew. How he thought that I was a friend who fucked. How he thought I was cool about *that*.'

Zac registered the hurt on Pip's face and decided now was not the time to say that he had fucked a fair few of his friends, too. And in this day and age, perhaps it was a genuine misunderstanding for the doctor to have made. He didn't tell her because it would have been tactless, but also

136

because there was something about her wide-eyed hurt that in an instant made him review his own behaviour. Though he didn't think his lax sexual predilections immoral, certainly not reprehensible; but he thought he had perhaps been a little louche of late. More then than now, though. Pip's outrage made her seem all the more artless and it made him smile and soften.

'Thing is, my keys, my bag – everything is at St Bea's,' she said, starting to sob.

'It's no problem,' Zac said, squeezing her arm, 'we'll go together – I'll go in, if you like. I'm good at bullshit – I have to deal with Customs and Excise the whole time, remember!'

Zac left Pip lurking in the taxi outside St Bea's. He went into the hospital, smiled charmingly at the women behind the Reception desk and explained that his good friend Philippa McCabe, one of their clown doctors, had left suddenly that afternoon – family emergency – and he'd come with her authority to collect her belongings. One of the women accompanied Zac to the small cupboard-room. He then escorted her back to the front desk. He thanked both women profusely.

'Family emergency?' smirked one to the other.

'Another casualty on Dr Simmons's ward,' the other sniggered back.

NINETEEN

'*L*ook, you're sharing my cab and that's that,' Zac informs Pip. 'It's too late and too hot for public transport.' Zac observes her: though she's pouting intentionally, she's swaying without meaning to. 'Anyway,' he says, 'I'm a gentleman and you're pissed. So I'll escort you home and not hear another word.' Pip giggles. Zac's right. She is drunk and he is a gent. Fine. Whatever. Taxi. There's one. Let's go.

She hugs her bag and gazes out of the window.

'What do you have tomorrow?' Zac asks. 'Can you take some time off? Treat yourself to a massage or have a swim or meet a girlfriend for lunch?' Pip is vaguely aware that the concern and common sense he is bestowing on her are similar to those which she'd dispense to any of her girlfriends in a comparable situation. 'A splurge of retail therapy?' Zac suggests.

'Are you gay?' she asks artlessly, tactlessly, but with no malice.

'What?' Zac, however, is visibly disturbed. 'Fuck off.'

'It's a compliment,' Pip says, head nodding sincerely.

'No, I'm bloody not gay,' Zac chides defensively. Far from homophobic, he is nevertheless somewhat offended. 'What the fuck made you think that?' He's starting to regret the cab, the mercy dash to St Bea's, the loan of his office. He reminds himself he always thought Pip was weird.

'It's a compliment,' Pip hurries yet again, embarrassed that she's obviously hurt him. 'I only meant because you're such a good listener and the advice you give is like a girl would give a girl.'

Zac looks out of the window. God, Camden is grim. Someone is puking by a lamppost. A mangy mongrel with three legs lollops across the road, followed by its equally dishevelled and limping owner. A disturbingly respectable-looking middle-aged man emerges from the sex shop, adjusts his spectacles and hails a cab. The smell of kebab and pizza seep into the taxi though the windows are shut.

'A strong feminine side is a *gift*,' Pip is tapping his arm. 'Gays and women have it – men rarely do.' Zac looks at her and glances away. 'I'm sorry,' she says, 'I meant no offence, I just meant that for a hetero boy you are –' she pauses, 'nice.'

'Don't worry about it,' Zac says with equanimity though he's still smarting a little.

'Your girlfriend,' Pip tells him, 'is a lucky, lucky girlfriend.'

'I don't have a girlfriend,' Zac says.

'The cinema,' Pip frowns.

'She's just a friend,' Zac says nonchalantly.

'Friends who fuck,' Pip says sadly with a heavy sigh. Zac doesn't correct her; they've passed Kentish Town tube, which she's told him is her nearest, there seems little point in initiating a heart-to-heart or an in-depth analysis at this point. 'Right,' Pip directs the cabby, 'left! Left again! Second lamppost on the left.'

She gets out, a little unsteadily. Zac remains seated.

'Can I use your loo?' Zac asks. 'I'm bursting.'

'Of course you can,' Pip says without a second thought. It's only Zac, after all. The boy so nice and so sensitive he might as well be gay. She pays the cabby, though Zac protests.

*

Because Pip has always been at the helm of previous relationships, because her previous boyfriends were all keener on her than she was on them, she has no concept of what the rebound is. She understands the theory and she's warned many a girlfriend about it. But the signs and urges are unintelligible to her. By the same token, Zac has no ulterior motive on entering her flat. The girl is drunk; he's been told he's as good as gay; it's been a long day. Hardly the ingredients for a *frisson* to simmer. He's asked to come in to her flat because he's desperate for a pee, that's all. Pip has let him in because he's desperate for a pee, that's all.

The sound of a man taking a pee in her bathroom, combined with the effect of a long drink of chilled mineral water in the familiar and comforting environment of her home, sobers Pip up quite markedly. Zac emerges and she smiles a little sheepishly at him.

'I feel better now,' she says, brandishing the Badoit bottle.

'So do I,' says Zac. 'Great bathroom – the mosaic is divine.' He winces. 'You're right, I *do* sound gay.'

'Don't!' Pip pleads as if the mistaken notion now pains her far more than it can possibly irk him. 'The mosaic is actually an easy-to-follow kit from Homebase,' she confides, hoping that to put herself down might make Zac feel better, 'it wasn't expensive.'

'Very industrious,' he praises.

'Would you like some water?' Pip offers.

'Sure,' he shrugs. She passes him the bottle of Badoit and he takes a good swig. He looks around her sitting-room. It's very similar to what he saw of her bedroom. 'Have you recently moved in?' he asks, noting the ubiquitous calico blinds, the lack of personal trinkets, undercoat everywhere, the total absence of colour.

'No no,' Pip says, taking it as a compliment that it all must appear so pristine, 'I've been here years.'

'Are you redecorating, then?' he asks. She frowns. 'The undercoat,' he waves his hand around, 'and, I mean, all your furniture is without covers.' She glowers. 'You seem to have hidden all your stuff away,' he continues.

'Actually,' she says, quite icily, 'this is how I choose to live.' Zac falls silent. He looks around again, perhaps he's drunker than he thought, perhaps he needs to blink. He blinks. He's relatively sober. And it all looks as he thought it had. 'But there's no colour,' he says quietly.

'You're too much of a bloke to discern the subtle gradations of tone,' Pip says primly, despite the contradiction to her previous supposition of homosexuality, 'too much of a lad to appreciate the fullness of minimal clutter.'

Zac the pacifist pulls on a guilty face though he'd still maintain that Pip's flat is lonely rather than peaceful, sad rather than serene and cold rather than calm. 'Don't mind me,' he says, 'I'm a bit of a philistine.' He takes another thirsty pull at the Badoit bottle. And observing him do so — the way he slants and then closes his eyes, the fullness of his lips, his neck pulsating with every gulp, his physical presence in her space — does something unexpected but intense to Pip McCabe.

Her heartbeat quickens and her mouth goes dry. She's gone all light-headed and knows it isn't from alcohol. It's due to desire. She feels damn horny. Her body is buzzing and her mind is whirring. She's always appreciated that Zac is easy on the eye but, right now, she actively fancies him.

Genius! The ultimate way to close her ghastly day and put distance between her and the reprehensible Caleb Simmons, is standing a few feet in front of her! She holds out her hand for the bottle. She makes sure her fingers brush his when she takes it. The touch sends an electric impulse surging through her. She keeps her eyes on him as she drinks. She licks her lips when she's finished.

'I'd better make a move,' Zac says because, for a split second, he's just felt a rush of lust for Pip but he warns himself that, despite weeks of desire, tonight is not the right time for consummation. Or even a snog.

*

141

Now, I know Zac is our hero and he really is a hero — gentlemanly, sensitive, amusing, handsome. And Caleb, by comparison, is a downright cad. And our heroine has been wronged today and is hurt and confused. And although she is a clown and he is an accountant and one would have thought that never the twain would meet let alone mix, there *is* something nicely compatible about these two. But not yet, surely? Tonight wouldn't be right. Though Pip is sobering up, there's still enough alcohol and adrenalin in her system both to dictate and skew her inclination. And though Zac is relatively sober, he's still had a knock, however slight, to his masculinity. They'd have sex for all the wrong reasons and would very probably jeopardize sex for the right reasons in the future. No. They oughtn't to come together — in any sense — tonight. The timing would be awry. There's half a book to go, anyway.

'Mind if I call a cab?' Zac asks.

'Sure,' says Pip, 'I'll call one for you.' She dials. 'Kentish Town to Hampstead, please. Soon as you like. Forty-five minutes? Jesus!' She turns to Zac, the receiver cupped under her chin. 'Forty-five minutes,' she repeats though of course he's already heard that.

'Jesus,' he says. 'Don't worry, I'll find a black cab — there'll be plenty.'

'Shall I try another cab company?' Pip suggests, hovering her hand over the phone.

'It's OK,' Zac says, 'as I said, I'll catch a black cab, no problem.'

But Zac doesn't move.

Pip offers him the bottle of water and he takes it. He isn't thirsty. But he drinks. He offers it back. She takes it. She drinks.

'You're still in your uniform,' Zac observes. She does look daft, pigtails jutting out, face grimy, wearing a doctor's coat emblazoned with patterns and pockets dripping with

142

fantastic plastic. Spotty tights. She's taken off her shoes. He notices how neat her feet seem.

'You're right,' Pip says, 'I'd better go and change.' But she doesn't. She flops next to him on her sofa. Zac doesn't leave to take a taxi home and Pip doesn't change out of her work gear. They both just sit there, wondering how they're going to do what they know they're going to do. She knows if he makes a move to leave, she'll grab him. He knows if she goes next door to change, he'll follow. So they sit in stillness and silence, wondering who's going to do what to whom and when.

Pip sighs and stretches her legs out. 'Do you like my tights?'

Now, in all the come-ons that Zac has had in his sexually active life, no one has coquettishly presented him with a pair of spotty tights for his delectation. The tights are horrendous. But the legs beneath are shapely.

'They're awful,' he says.

She laughs and jiggles her legs. 'Tools of the trade,' she says.

'Nice pair of pins, though,' Zac says. His hand automatically hovers above her knee. He must make a move – a move to leave, catch a cab, not to touch her. Lightly, Pip places her hand over his and guides it to rest on her knee. She must get out of her tights. Go to sleep. Their breathing is audible and quickening.

'I must go to sleep,' she whispers, glancing at his eyes, suddenly unable to look anywhere else. They're slate-grey. They're gorgeous and they're swallowing her whole.

'I must catch a cab,' says Zac. He can't keep his gaze still. It darts from her eyes to her lips to her legs and back again. To her lips once more. They're moist. Her knee fits into the palm of his hand. It turns him on as much as if he was cupping her breast.

'Would you like another drink of water?' she whispers.

'No, thanks,' he murmurs back, 'I must be going.' He

stands up and walks to the door. Pip follows him. 'Night, Pip,' he says.

'Night, Zac,' she says. He opens the door and steps outside. She closes the door and goes back into her flat. They both breathe a sigh of relief yet kick themselves, too.

Zac easily hails a black cab on Kentish Town Road. He settles himself inside and gives his address. But he tells himself if the next set of lights is red he'll jump out. It's green. 'Stop the cab,' he says. He gives the driver a tenner. And jogs back to Pip's.

She's half-expecting the bell when it rings. She wonders whether it's advisable to answer the door in spotty tights, her hands providing an impromptu bra. But that's precisely what she does.

They don't bother with chit-chat about a dearth of cabs or a drink of water or needing the loo or having to get out of one's work clothes. Zac steps inside, scoops Pip in his arms and starts kissing her on the lips. The cheeks. Her left eye. Her right ear. That gorgeous dip at the base of her neck between her collar-bones, whatever it's called. Pip is weaving his hair through her fingers, tickling his neck up and down, running her hands over his shoulders, grasping his biceps, unable to hush her desirous gasping. They're kissing deeply, tonguing each other, exploring each other's mouth for taste and sensation.

Lips are bitten and sucked, necks are grazed by teeth, ear lobes are nibbled, tongues dance. They haven't made it beyond the living-room. Pip has pulled Zac against her and he has her up against the wall; she's pressing her body so insistently against his that he hasn't had the chance to see her bare breasts, to admire them, let alone fondle them, though he's sure they must be gorgeous. He pulls away, with some effort. And feasts his eyes on her torso. Fabulous. He grunts and stoops so he can take her nipple in his mouth, his fingers kneading, his hands cupping. Pip walks to her bedroom and he follows. She peels off her tights, slips out of her knickers, opens her bedside drawer and passes him a condom. He unbuttons his trousers and he pulls down his boxers. His cock springs to attention and attention is precisely what Pip lavishes on it. He's so hard, his cock seems to be straining within the skin, his balls tight in their sack, twitching. She kisses each in turn. Kisses the tip of his cock and then lays back on the bed, spreads her legs and watches him roll on the condom.

After such a lengthy prelude, they dispense with further foreplay and head straight for hasty, straightforward penetration. Missionary position all the way. He comes before she's quite ready but for her, an orgasm wasn't the point. Her satisfaction is complete – she was desired and she desired.

Caleb, you can fuck off. I'll be fine. No damage done. I am unscathed.

Zac withdraws and they lie there, panting. Pip is exhausted. He's at that delicious post-coital state of physical depletion and heady drowsiness. With her eyes closed, Pip reaches for the bedside light and switches it off. She can't remember drifting off to sleep. But she is certainly aware of waking up.

TWENTY

*P*ip knew something was amiss when an itchiness woke her. Something was prickling her cheek and spiking at the corner of her mouth. Though drowsy, she brushed the back of her hand against her face with panic, assuming it was a spider or an earwig or some other creature from a dream, come to life. It wasn't. it was her hair. It was her hair braided into a pigtail. Her clown's hair. What on earth! Slowly, she opened an eye and tried to focus and define a strange configuration on the floor by her bedroom door. What was *that*? Was there something under it? The fog of reverie and fug of hangover began to lift and her gaze alighted on Dr Pippity's white coat. First the plaits, now the coat. Honestly! Over there, her knickers. What's this under the sheets? Tights? Pip McCabe never *ever* leaves clothing strewn around her room like this. Pip McCabe *always* puts her clown away as soon as she's home from work. Someone, it seems, took the clown to bed.

Oh
bloody
bloody
hell.

Pip turned over very very slowly. The man in her bed was sleeping soundly. Turned away from her. His breathing was as rhythmic and un-intrusive as the steady phut-phutting of her quartz clock. In her head, however, alarm bells were ringing cacophonously. Not only had she had sex, she'd let the man sleep with her the whole night through. In her bed. She didn't remember him asking. She didn't remember offering. But here he was. It struck her – how on earth could she have slept so well? A man in her bed the whole night through. How could that have happened? Yet she'd slept fine. Undisturbed. That in itself was disturbing enough. And he was still there. She had a slight headache. Not too bad.

Badoit.

Bottles of it.

She remembered.

He turned over, yawned. Pip was somewhat surprised that she wasn't repulsed by the sight of him. He looked quite nice, actually, in a cosy, crumpled, morningish sort of way. A tiny speck of spittle had collected in the corner of his mouth and stripes and furrows from the pillow's creases were indented on his cheek. She had no idea what on earth she was meant to do next. She lay as still as she could without actually holding her breath. She wanted nothing to rouse him until she had a plan of action. She contemplated the best way forward, staring hard at a spidery crack in the ceiling for focus.

Zac watched her for a good few minutes. Her face was still smudged here and there with blurs of slap. Her hair was bristling out of the pigtails and, having been slept on, they were twisted this way and that like broken ribs. She looked like a discarded doll. She was almost motionless, staring with great intensity at her ceiling. The sheets nearly covered her. She obviously didn't realize that the areola of her left nipple was just visible. Zac, though, was very aware of it; he would really rather like to kiss it. The thought of a lazy morning hump was very appealing. For Zac, there was something fantastically slovenly and decadent about sex in

147

the morning before showering, coming just hours after sex at night without showering. His cock was certainly wide awake. But a part of him, the softer side – the gay side, as Pip had so guilessly defined it – was actually happy just to observe the girl; to think how pretty she was, how peaceful he felt in her bed, how nice it was to wake up to her make-up-stained face and starched fuzzy hairdo. Yin and yang. His cock appreciated her for the one, his head and heart for the other. He closed his eyes and with a hastily contrived sleepy sigh, rolled over so he was nearer to her. She didn't seem to react, she was still scrutinizing her ceiling. If he puckered his lips, he could reach her bare shoulder to kiss it. So he did.

'Morning,' Zac said.

'Oh, hi,' Pip replied as if she'd been so deep in thought that she'd been completely unaware of his presence, and that his presence was no big deal.

Actually, Pip wanted the day to be well under way. She wanted to leap out of bed with a clichéd cry of 'Goodness, is that the time?' For the first time ever, Pip McCabe wanted the excuse of a proper job – an office, a commute, a contractual 9.00 to 5.00 – to rush off to. She wanted a long hot shower, to use classic Nivea to cleanse and treat her face, Neutrogena products for her neglected hair and itchy scalp. Now, most of all, she wanted to curl up on her sofa with a cup of camomile tea. All on her own.

But she just lay there. She couldn't leave the bed because she was acutely aware that she was naked. Laid bare. She didn't want to be observed. Though Pip actually has commendably few self-indulgent body complexes, that morning she felt intensely shy about revealing her nudity. She was aware of her niggling headache, but was unsure whether this was a hangover or the pressure of her anxieties. She'd rather not think about it. It was difficult to think of much else. And she hadn't even let her mind venture to Caleb.

Zac stretched his arms above his head, exposing a swatch of dark underarm hair and a good line of muscle along his torso. He turned to her again, kissed her shoulder a second time.

'God,' he murmured, 'is that the time?' He scrambled out of bed, his bum and balls and semi-stiff cock all on display, and padded naked across her bedroom, turning to face her at the door to the bathroom. 'Have you a towel?' She nodded, not quite knowing where to look, slightly startled that he seemed so at ease while she felt somewhat out of her depth – in her own home. 'Mind if I borrow your toothbrush?' She shrugged and focused her gaze on the door handle to the bathroom, just left of Zac's groin. 'Are you a tea or coffee person? Either'll do me,' he said cheerfully with a grin and a wink and disappeared into the bathroom. She glanced at his bottom before he closed the door. Shapely. She wanted to giggle. Of course, she didn't. There was something about his ease – though it startled her, she wasn't actually taken aback. She had the feeling that if the venue had been his home, he'd have offered her toothbrush and tea – without her having to ask.

She listened to him pee. Heard him fart. Again, she wanted to giggle. Of course, she didn't. She heard the taps being turned on, blasting at first, then quickly moderated. She listened to him brushing his teeth. With her toothbrush. Then the shower started. Should she tell him how temperamental the hot tap was? No, he could figure it out. She could hear the shower curtain being adjusted and the change of the watercourse as it hit his body.

'Ouch! Fuck!'

He can figure it out, Pip thought, leaving her bed. He'd started to whistle. She knew the tune but couldn't place it. Damn. What was it? She hummed it softly as she went through to the kitchen to boil the kettle. It was a song from the sixties but the version she knew best was a cover in the early eighties. Bugger – what *was* it?

Zac had appeared, dripping water in her kitchen, his modesty concealed by a towel secured sarong-style around his waist. Pip was too full of thought to fancy him though she did take note, somewhere in her subconscious, that physically he was what she'd acknowledge appreciatively as 'buff'.

'Great,' he said when she handed him a mug of herbal tea. He took a sip and looked as if he was going to cry or throw up. 'Jesus, what is *that*?'

'Morning Refresher,' she said with a faint frown, 'orange and lemon zest, ginger, green tea and meadow herbs.'

'It's –' Zac took another sip as if he were at a wine-tasting. He spat into her sink. 'It's utterly vile. Meadow herbs? More like motorway grass verge or farmyard dung heap. Haven't you any Darjeeling?'

'It's in the cupboard,' said Pip, pointing. 'Help yourself. I'm going to have a shower.' Off she went, our house-proud, personal-space-protective, secrecy-guarding girl – leaving a half-naked, damp man with the run of her flat.

She locked herself in her bathroom. Pip was as ill at ease in her own home as Zac was comfortable, mooching around and helping himself. She wished she was miles away. Anywhere. Just not here. Somewhere else. Just alone. Zac wished she'd hurry up. It would be nice to have breakfast together before he left for work.

Zac discovered she was out of Darjeeling, but there was some Earl Grey and English Breakfast. 'Please God let there be more than soya milk in her fridge,' he murmured, stooping low to see inside. Marks & Spencer organic semi-skimmed. And a packet, already opened, of Dairylea processed cheese triangles. He laughed. He had a little search of her cupboard when he put the tea bags back and was comforted by the presence of KitKats and salt-and-vinegar Hula Hoops nestling furtively behind all the biodegradable organic herbal righteousness at the front.

He took his tea and a KitKat through to her sitting-room. He sat but momentarily, soon enough wandering over to the shelves and looking at the few framed photos. There were the sisters. And some old chap – possibly the cranky uncle or the late father. A Derbyshire stone farmhouse. A small dog with a ragged ear. He couldn't see any of the mother – there were probably volumes of photo albums in those low, flush cupboards though. He spied a copy of *Heat* magazine tucked into the beechwood newspaper rack alongside *Vanity Fair* and *Traveller*. He flipped through it and was soon engrossed in a double-page spread of particularly scurrilous goings-on in the celebrity world. Much as he'd like to continue nosing, much as he fancied intruding on Pip's shower and having sex with her again – perhaps up against her bathroom wall or dripping wet on her bedroom floor – he really needed to head off. Meetings and spreadsheets and office politics all awaited him. He gathered his clothes, sniffed each item briefly, and dressed. He hovered by the bathroom door. The shower was finished. He knocked politely and waited. 'Pip?' he called. 'I'm off to work now.'

'OK,' she called back politely, sparsely. He was slightly taken aback.

'Have fun,' he said to the door, gently.

'You too,' she replied, with contrived lightness, through the wall.

'Bye,' he called a final time, her front door open.

She didn't reply, she assumed he wouldn't be able to hear her from there, with her still barricading herself in her bathroom. And Pip McCabe doesn't raise her voice.

Pip emerged from the bathroom, somewhat tentatively, once she was sure he had gone for good. She was struck immediately by the state of her bedroom. Her bed had been made. The decorative cushions had been arranged almost exactly to her very precise specifications. Dr Pippity's coat and tights were draped neatly over the back of the bedroom chair. Last night's knickers were placed discreetly beneath them. Pip dried herself and dressed. Her initial reaction was praise; that here was a man as anal as herself. Her second thought played upon the anal: 'He *must* be gay,' she decided. 'How many straight men can there be with innate design savvy for cushion display?' She thought of Caleb. Though he might obsessively fold his crisp packets into neat triangles, his pillows were always annoyingly unplumped. Lumpy. He merely straightened the edges of his duvet. 'Well, *that* was all about surface appearance,' she concluded stroppily and started humming the tune Zac had been whistling but which she still couldn't place.

In lieu of a conventional job and bustling office to rush off to, she turned to that camomile tea and meditative snuggle on her sofa that she'd been craving since waking. Oddly, Zac's derision of 'farmyard dung heap' did make her laugh and think fleetingly of grubby grass verges on motorways. So she had coffee instead. Instant. With sugar. And a KitKat to dunk. She noted that the photo frames had been moved, however fractionally. She saw the copy of *Heat* magazine. Though she had a brimming conscience to unravel and analyse, she found herself flipping through the magazine instead, gladly switching off her mind and putting her soul on hold. How on earth would she know where to start with her scampering thoughts? Much better to put a pause on the lot for half an hour and look instead at pictures of young actresses-models-whatevers falling out of a succession of London bars.

She read the magazine from cover to cover. She wished she didn't have a day off. She was desperate to be Merry Martha, even Dr Pippity, so that she had a reason not just to sit there and be Pip McCabe with all this thinking time on her hands and all this weighty contemplation to undertake.

Zac's day was so busy it really should have precluded even a couple of seconds' focusing on anything other than planning meetings, dealing with office politics and checking spreadsheets. His mind, however, kept darting back to Pip, swivelling in his chair, commenting on the Scottish Colourist lithograph, marvelling at his coffee percolator. He could still sense her presence. If he closed his eyes, he could conjure her scent. If he listened carefully, beyond the phones and the clatter of the office, he could hear her voice. He opened his eyes and could see her so vividly, staring at her bedroom ceiling with her grubby face and ridiculous hairstyle. He felt good and yet just a little uneasy, too. There had been no open arms that morning, just a closed bathroom door. There had been no gentle joking or affectionate 'see-you-later's. Just a brief instruction to have a good day. In fact, she'd merely been politely replying to him. She'd instigated nothing. Zac refused to countenance that maybe he'd been no more than a one-night stand to her.

He left work on the dot of 6.00. The tube was there for him and he was home within forty minutes. He took a chilled Budvar from the fridge, picked up his cordless Bang & Olufsen phone, and settled into his banana chair. No. Not right. He tried the Eames. Oddly, it really wasn't as comfortable as it usually was. He went through to the bedroom and sipped his lager whilst looking out over downstairs's garden. He put the beer bottle on the window-sill and dialled Pip. He was nervous. It both amused and baffled him.

The phone's ringing, Pip. Aren't you going to answer it?

'Hey,' says Zac.
'Hullo,' says Pip because it's too late to turn her voice into a hastily disguised answering machine message.
'Good day?' he asks. 'Did you have some me-time?'
'I did,' Pip says. She's hardly used her voice all day. It sounds odd and feels strange.
'And your hangover?' he enquires.
'Nothing one of your Nurofen couldn't fix,' she says.
They both sigh into an awkward silence.
'Good day?' Pip asks.
'Great but manic,' Zac says, racking his mind for what it was he was phoning to say and how he was going to phrase it.
'Cool,' says Pip, 'well,' she says, 'yep – great.' She notes how quickly the conversation has become so stilted.

'Anyway,' Zac says, 'I'd better go. Just thought I'd give you a quick call, you know?'

'Ta,' says Pip, 'good.'

'Bye then,' says Zac, at once regretting the entire call.

'Ta-ta,' says Pip.

'Bye then. How do you feel today?' Zac suddenly launches, 'About – stuff?' Could he really have been just a drunken one-night stand to her? What about the cream tea? And daft conversations about swans?

Pip is flummoxed. She has no idea how to answer because she's spent the entire day trying to avoid wondering how on earth she feels about 'stuff'.

'Pip?' Zac interjects into her silence. 'It's just – well – I was wondering if you wanted to do something tomorrow night – it being a Thursday.'

'I'll get back to you,' she says, after a lengthy pause. 'I think I'm seeing my sisters, you see,' she adds slowly after some time.

'Sure,' says Zac with an easygoing vocal shrug that belies the discomfort he feels. However, perhaps it's his attuned feminine side that tells him to give her the kind of space a bloke would need. Not to push, not to pry. 'No probs.'

'How was your day? In your fancy chair presiding over Pod-land?' Pip hurries because, although she doesn't think she wants to see Zac tomorrow night, she also doesn't want to be on her own just yet.

'Fine,' Zac replies, 'as I say, rather manic.'

It's all gone cringingly stilted. Both Zac and Pip are aware that the awkwardness is really quite inappropriate for two people who have traded bodily fluids and shared the sanctity of a deep sleep together, but it is probably symptomatic of it all anyway.

'Um,' Pip murmurs, 'well, I ought to let you go now. Thanks, though, for calling. And thanks for the offer – you know, about tomorrow.'

'Sure,' says Zac with his trademark equanimity, 'pleasure. Thanks for last night.'

'Yes,' says Pip.

'If not tomorrow,' Zac presses courageously, though he tells himself to shut up, 'perhaps soon enough?'

Pip makes a noise in her throat that, for five minutes after the call, Zac thinks was mostly affirmative. Soon enough, though, he's convinced he was merely a shag for a pissed girl on the rebound.

Pip had managed to pass the entire day without interruption from her inner thoughts. Whether this is a commendable achievement, is open to debate. However, once she had soaked the day away in the bath with new fizzing bath tablets from Space NK, hung out the washing and triple-checked that all was spic and span in her flat, it really was time to tidy below the surface.

She wanted to go to bed and fall straight asleep. However, when she slipped between her sheets, she could vividly sense the man who'd been in her bed, in her body. His sleep-crumpled face, funny specks of spittle, his peaceful soft breathing. The smell of him. She remembered, with a pronounced twitch of desire, how he'd stretched across her to see her clock. His armpit. How she'd felt his skin, sensed his strength and drawn in his scent, and been turned on by his masculinity. She looked over to her bathroom door and could conjure him facing her, buck naked and full frontal, asking about towels and toothbrushes.

What is it about Zac? Is it that he's so at ease with everything: himself, me, my world? I mean, I had him to stay the night with no second thought, without even being asked, with no shadow of doubt. He's seen me looking my worst. I can't even remember much about the sex per se, but I am well aware of the desire that drove it.

You've never met anyone quite like him.

Perhaps not.

Many people never will.

Perhaps.

Think of your friends, your sisters, who fall for men with none of his qualities.

Exactly.

But?

For Christ's sake, think about it! Zac's plus points are that he's mild-mannered, handsome and makes me laugh. But remember, my first impression was one of mistrust. Not to mention the fact that he's an accountant. He's mid-thirties and single. To top it all, he has a kid. Can you imagine the weight of his bloody baggage?

I'd like to tell her that the baggage she thinks Zac shoulders is far more weighty to her than it is to him. But there's no way she'll hear that just yet.

'I like him,' she murmurs out loud, 'I really do. But deep down I think I oughtn't to go further.'

And Caleb? Just a day ago you were planning dinner parties and to reveal your coupledom to family and friends. You almost loved him, or at least you felt very strongly for him on account of him being so 'normal'.

'Is that why I slept with Zac?' she asks out loud. 'To get back at Caleb? To get over him? Was it simply just the drink influencing me? Or that I was feeling vulnerable? Perhaps vindictive – wanting to even the score?'

That's what we'd like to know.

'Perhaps a little of all those things,' she decides, but now in a whisper. 'Whatever the reason and however comforting and timely, Zac Holmes is *not* relationship material. And neither am *I*.'

Pip isn't going to think about Caleb or consider his 'normality', or lack of it, just now. She's humming, instead. Suddenly, she has remembered the tune Zac was whistling in her shower that morning.

'Smokey Robinson,' she says, relieved, '"Tears of a Clown".'

She can only remember one line and she falls asleep,

singing it over and again, feeling blank and refusing to think about Caleb or Zac.

> But in my lonely room I cry
> the tears of a clown
> when there's no one around

It was past midnight. Without considering the time, Zac phones his sister-in-law Ruth.

'Yes?' she answered the phone, hushed tones not concealing alarm.

'Shit,' Zac whispered back, 'it's only Zac. Is it too late?'

'Zac,' Ruth said, dropping the whisper for a quiet voice, 'these late-night calls are becoming a habit!'

'I shagged Clowngirl,' he said, hating himself for dumbing it down, wishing he'd been brave enough, truthful enough, to say, 'Pip and I had sex last night but I don't think I was more than a one-night stand to her.'

Ruth, however, could hear very clearly between the lines. Fundamentally, if it had just been a shag, why was Zac phoning at this hour? After all, if it had been just a shag, why confide in her rather than brag to his brother? No, Ruth realized, it had been more than a shag; Zac and Pip had slept together.

'Hold on,' she said, 'your brother is sleeping. I'll take the call in the other room.'

If only Pip could have eavesdropped on what Zac said, how he phrased it and the tone of voice he used.

'I found her crying her eyes out,' Zac said. 'Appears that her dashing doc was actually a bit of a wanker with a steady girlfriend. Anyway, I cheered her up – as did a bottle of Rioja. And I took her home and one thing led to another.'

'You shagged.'

'It was passionate,' Zac qualified almost defensively, to Ruth's silent approval, 'but it felt like it had been a long time

157

coming. Like there's been some unspoken build-up. An inevitability.'

'Congratulations,' said Ruth, wondering why Zac sounded less than triumphant.

'I don't know where to go from here,' he confessed. 'I really like her – as more than a potential fling. But you know what – I can't believe I'm going to say this – I'm a bit anxious.'

'Why?' Ruth asked, knowing she could easily fill in Zac's gaps but knowing, too, that it was better for him to voice them out loud.

'Two things, really,' he said after a pause. 'One: what am I about to get myself into? Is it worth it? Am I really ready for romance now, over and above simply sex which has been so simple over the last few years?'

'Number two?' Ruth pressed.

'Two,' Zac obliged, 'nervousness. Are my feelings reciprocated? Or is she just on the rebound? I think I may be nothing but a one-nighter to her.'

'There's only one way to ascertain both,' Ruth defined. 'Broach number two first and then, if the answer is favourable, just relax into number one and see where it takes you.' Ruth could sense Zac nodding. She could almost hear his brain charging over his concerns. 'You could be pleasantly surprised,' she said sweetly, 'you might have found a very good thing indeed.' Still he was quiet. 'Zac?'

'She's on the rebound,' he suddenly announced, with a complete change of tone, 'and anyway, she was drunk, too.'

'Zac Holmes,' Ruth said, 'I think you're only going with that strand so that you don't have to actually ask the girl how she feels. You're plonking the onus on her so you don't have to take risks.' Zac didn't reply.

'God, for a beefy bloke you're a bloody wimp,' said Ruth, knowing it sounded harsh but confident it was the right thing to say. 'Good-night, Zac. Good luck.'

*

Zac hung up and hummed softly the tune that had been on his brain all day. It was almost getting on his nerves.

> Now there's some sad things known to man
> but ain't too much sadder than
> the tears of a clown

There *was* something about Pip, behind her slap and motley, her carefree zest and energy. Zac didn't want to give too much credit to clichés of hiding behind a mask. But the truth was that he'd seen her in despair; vulnerable and hurt. The truth was, he felt for her. He really felt for her. But the truth was also that though the notion was certainly intriguing, the encumbrance of it was not. It was all starting to get on his nerves as much as Smokey's tune. It would be better to get both out of his mind.

Think of a different song.

How about Marvin Gaye, 'Sexual Healing'? How about focusing on the fact that Juliana would be back from South Africa in a week or so?

TWENTY-ONE

*C*onveniently, if deludedly,
Pip reckoned she could levy against Fen the way she
decided to feel about and deal with Zac. She wouldn't have
been able to have seen Zac that Thursday night anyway,
even if she'd wanted to. A phone call from a distressed
Django revealed that the middle McCabe girl, whom everyone thought so sensible and soft and centred, had actually
been seeing two men at the same time. Lovely Matthew
Holden, the urbane and generous young magazine editor
with his own flat in Islington, who already had Pip and Cat's
seals of approval. And now, it seemed, some other chap as
well, a bloke called Someone or Other Caulfield, twenty
years Fen's senior. An impoverished landscape gardener in
Derbyshire, apparently. That's how Django knew. When Fen
was allegedly assessing sculpture in a private collection in
Derbyshire. They'd been seen. In broad daylight. In a local
pub, good God.

Pip and Cat were horrified, not just at the perceived
wantonness of it all, but more at Fen's secrecy. They'd had
no idea and that, to them, was far more shocking, much more
insulting and hurtful, than the notion that their middle sister
was a morally inept slapper. Fen, upset but not defensive,
went to great lengths to attempt to explain to Cat and Pip

that she wasn't playing one man off against the other. She tried to reveal how each man satisfied the two strongest strands in her life – town and country – and the myriad associations of each. She implored her sisters to believe how deeply she felt for both men, that she herself felt both fine *and* capable about keeping them apart. That, quite simply, at this juncture, she couldn't choose between them, nor even see that she had to or ought to. No one was going to be hurt, she proclaimed, she would ensure that personally. She had never been in love but now she was, and twice over. She felt privileged. She wanted her sisters' support, even if she had to bide her time for their approval.

However, Fen's situation is a whole different story. Suffice it to say, that night, alone in her flat and believing herself to be at her most level-headed, Pip took Fen's situation and manipulated it to her own ends. Thus Pip now stacked upon the baggage she presumed Zac to be burdened by, a clump of her own negative theories about love itself. Her hastily contrived conclusion was that love was not worth the effort. In her eyes, neither her sisters, nor her friends, were better off for the presence of a man (or men) in their lives. She reasoned that she'd been happy enough when single – indeed, considerably happier than at present – and that all her current worries and insecurities and her tears had come only when men had been involved or, rather, when she'd been involved with men.

It was thus with a liberating sense of relief that Pip concluded Zac to be a great bloke she'd had sex with the once, and Caleb simply a bloke she'd had great sex with for a couple of months. Swiftly and decisively, she relegated both men to her past and put both down to experience, because for her present and her future, she decided that neither was a good idea. Neither provided the answer because, actually, she had no questions. She'd tried them both out. One naughty. One nice. Neither necessary. After all, she had already decided that she needed to keep herself stable and available for her two sisters: Cat was heading off to the Tour de France in little over a week and Fen was no doubt going to spin out of control pretty soon, too. Thank goodness June was fast heading for July and soon she'd be able to think in terms of 'That was a month ago'. Thank goodness for the approaching weekend in Derbyshire. The sisters were to travel up together tomorrow evening, once Fen had finished work, Cat had filed copy, and Merry Martha had done a seven-year-old's birthday party in Maida Vale.

* * *

Of course I'm going to give Pip something other than her sisters to think about up in Derbyshire! The conclusions she's sketchily drawn in her bid to tidy her life are far too hasty, poorly composed and irritatingly nebulous. So, guess who's going to seven-year-old Benji's birthday party in Maida Vale? Billy is. With his cousin, Tom Holmes. And though Tom's Auntie Ruthie is taking them and is due to collect them, too, once she's seen who the entertainer is, she'll phone Tom's father and ask him to pick the children up instead.

* * *

'Would you mind, Zac?' Ruth says softly with a very passable impression of someone with a chronic headache. 'My head is *killing* me.'

'Let me call June,' Zac says, 'I have a stack of bollocks to wade through before I can leave.'

'June's away with Rob,' Ruth reminds him in a flimsy voice, 'that's why Tom's staying with us tonight.'

'Bugger,' says Zac, 'I forgot.'

'Don't worry,' Ruth says with a wince worthy of a medal for martyrdom, 'I'll take a couple of painkillers and try to nap in the car for a few hours. I'll be fine. Honestly. Don't worry. Please.'

'Don't be daft,' Zac says gently with an edge of guilt, 'it's no problem – I'll just bring the work home and do it over the weekend. You go home directly. It's no big deal. Not at all.'

'No, honestly,' Ruth says meekly, knowing it's important for Zac to actively want to collect the boys, not just do it as a favour to her, 'I shouldn't have asked.'

'Stop it,' he chides. 'I won't hear another word, there's no issue. Nothing comes before my son. Go home, Ruth, rest.'

'Oh Zac,' she all but whispers, 'thanks so much.'

'Are you OK to drive?' he asks. 'Why not leave your keys and take a cab?'

'I think so,' she replies with a credible quiver to her voice. 'I should be OK. If I head off now. If I take it slowly.'

Ruth revs her engine with some triumph. She embarks on the mother of all detours: from Maida Vale to Holloway via Westbourne Grove. The circuitous route is totally unnecessary but a sublime pleasure. Two hours' quality shopping time is a luxury Ruth seldom has nowadays. She can't remember when she last browsed around Agnès B and Paul Smith and APC without Billy tugging her sleeve, whining to go. It must be even longer since she treated herself to tea and cake at Tom's Deli rather than burger and coke in McDonald's. Momentarily, she feels just slightly wicked about her white lie. Will she be tempting fate by faking it? Might a monster migraine tomorrow be her comeuppance? No. Rubbish. She is doing a very good deed indeed, match-making the clown and the accountant. She is well deserving of the wodge of cake, plus the Hepburnesque A-line dress. Oh, and the Diptique candles and the armful of cornflowers and delphiniums. After all, she *had* resisted the divine bag at Paul Smith.

Initially, Zac was irritated to turn up in Maida Vale so early when he'd left work harassed and in such a rush. Soon enough, though, he couldn't believe his eyes, his luck or how fantastic it was that Ruth should have a migraine on a day when the traffic was so light. For a split second, he felt guilty at the degree of his pleasure in Ruth's malady. But his sister-in-law's headache was an absolute blessing. In fact, he was downright delighted that she felt too poorly to collect the kids, that he'd turned up so damn early. Because – well, what do you know! – three guesses who's entertaining the children at Benji's seventh birthday party! Just then, despite being one of life's most down-to-earth non-believers, Zac worshipped the gods of fate and fortune for having smitten Ruth with the headache. He even took a moment to send vibes of thanksgiving heavenwards.

Because there was his clown. Over there. Doing a precarious handstand as proficiently as Les Dawson used to play the piano in an expertly bad way. Her shapely legs akimbo, one clad in red and green stripes, the other in blue and yellow spots. Her body swaying this way and that, threatening to topple at any moment. She was yodelling 'Heads, Shoulders, Knees and Toes' at breakneck speed. Oh, the skill of it!

There was Pip, mid-handstand, mid-song when, from her upside-down vantage point, she spied at the back of the room a pair of legs in chinos, feet in suede slip-ons, that could only belong to one person.

She forgot the words.

She forgot how to maintain a handstand.

She forgot what she was meant to feel about Zac.

She was acutely aware that she was upside down with her legs splayed, her body tilted at a gravity-defying angle.

Silence.

'Eyes-and-ears-and-mouth-and-nose,' she suddenly sang shrilly, flic-flaccing herself upright and taking a deep bow. 'Heads, shoulders, beans-on-toast, beans-on-toast.'

'*Knees-and-toes!*' the children shrieked back the correction. '*Knees-and-toes!*'

Merry Martha, looking flushed and very jolly, put her hands on her hips and frowned: 'That's what I said, diddle-eye?' She sang again: 'Heads, shoulders, beans-on-toast, beans-on-toast!' Again, the children protested 'knees-and-toes' and again Merry Martha got the song wrong.

Zac was laughing. Not because she was Perrier Award-winningly funny, but because her antics and energy infused the room with infectious daft jollity. The skill of her magic was to weave such apparently simple and unconditional fun in and around the children. And by the looks on their faces, she was achieving this in abundance.

'Where is Bendy?' Merry Martha asked, though she now spied Tom for the first time and gave him a grin. 'Where is Bendy?'

'Who?' the children chorused.

'Bendy!' the clown declared, as if they were stupid. 'The Burp-day Boy – *Bendy*!'

'Benji!' Benji proclaimed, his hand held aloft. 'It's *Benji* and I'm him. It's my *birth*day.'

'Come here, Bendy Burp-day Boy,' the clown ordered, to much mirth. 'I am going to create for you – cos it be your Burp-day – a balloon in the shape of a, um, a, um – *balloon*!'

Benji looked vaguely disappointed when the clown blew a long thin balloon and presented it to him. 'Thank you,' he said anyway.

'Can I have it back, if you please?' Merry Martha asked, grabbing the balloon before the child had a chance to hand it over, let alone protest. 'Thanking you kindly, Burp-day Boy.' With a twist and a stretch and a knot and a mutter and a whistle and a daubing of marker pen, the clown returned the balloon as a sausage dog. There were appreciative gasps all around. She made more animal forms and distributed them amongst the throng. She established eye contact with Zac. 'Dearie me, dearie me,' she squawked, 'there is a great big kid at the back with no balloon.' Twenty pairs of eyes fixed on Zac. Followed by nineteen sniggers (Tom was the exception).

'He's not a kid,' Tom protested with his hand up, 'he's my dad.'

'Oh well, then,' Merry Martha declared all sulkily, 'if he's only an old mad dad, no balloon for *him*!'

'But I think he could have one,' Tom said, suddenly concerned that he'd deprived his dad of Merry Martha's highly collectible latex sculpture (Tom had kept Dr Pippity's balloons until they'd wrinkled and deflated and stuck dustily to themselves). 'Even if he is just an old mad dad. I think he might *like* one, anyway.'

'Righty-ho,' the clown trilled, wrestling with three long balloons and then wielding her marker with gay abandon. 'Come on up, old mad dad.' Zac approached, holding her eye contact and twitching his mouth, raising his eyebrows in an 'I'm warning you, bitch!' kind of way. 'You're right,' the clown marvelled to Tom, 'he's *too* big to be one of you. He *is* an old mad dad.' She turned to Zac, eyes a-sparkle. 'Would you like this balloon? It is a balloon in the shape of a bunny rabbit. It is a delectable collectible.'

Zac grinned at her and said 'Yes, please' in an animated way.

'Firstly, you must stand on one leg,' the clown decreed. He did so. 'Now you must place your hand in front of your mouth,' she ordered. And he did so. 'Now you must place your other hand behind your back, please, like this.' She demonstrated. He did so. 'Now,' she said, winking at the children, 'you must hop around the room like a Red Indian who has trodden on a wasp, making loud Red Indian-style noises to ward off evil spirits and praise the balloon gods.'

Zac looked at her as if she were mad and well on the way to a jolly good hiding. But, with an 'I'll get my own back later' kind of smirk, he did as he was told. The children fell about laughing. Even Merry Martha momentarily laughed like Pip McCabe. 'Well done, old mad dad,' she said, 'here is your prize.' Zac collected his trophy and returned to the back of the room, with most of the children wishing their dads were even half as mad. While Merry Martha involved the children in a mass, tuneless rendition of 'Happy Burp-day Dear Bendy', Zac admired his balloon rabbit. On its belly she'd written 'Bunny Girl xx'. It gave him as much of a sudden thrill as if she'd taken his cock and deep-throated him there and then. His conscience tried to remind him to focus on Marvin Gaye and Juliana. But he told himself to shut the fuck up. She didn't think of him as a one-night stand. How could he have worried that she was merely on the rebound? She liked him. She wanted him. That was all that mattered.

As soon as Merry Martha took off her motley and Pip put on her clothes, her confidence evaporated. Every swipe of cold-cream-clotted cotton wool took off a layer of her effervescent self-confidence along with a layer of slap. She brushed her hair with the repetitive vigour of a sufferer from obsessive compulsive disorder, not because she wanted to comb out the kinks from the pigtails, but because she needed more thinking time. Actually, she just needed to think. The trouble was, she couldn't focus. The trouble was, she really would have to emerge from Benji Richardson's bathroom sooner rather than later. Why had she written on the balloon? Why was she still standing in the bathroom in W9 when she should be hurrying home, wolfing down a bowl of soup and heading out of London to the Peak District with her sisters? Fundamentally, why was she excited to see Zac, wilfully flirting with him, when until she'd seen him upside down half an hour ago she'd successfully convinced herself that he was unsuitable and that she had no interest in him? Why did she think that closing Benji's bathroom door behind her as quietly as possible, that tiptoeing along the corridor, would make any difference to the inevitable posse awaiting her downstairs?

Tom threw his arms around her waist. Benji's mother shook her hand with gratitude. The birthday boy himself looked sorely disappointed that in real life, she was not particularly exotic nor appeared to have anything in her pockets. Zac simply winked at her and smiled in his inimitable, attractively lopsided way.

'Cash OK?' Benji's mum asked, handing her an envelope

addressed to Ms Martha. 'There's a little extra for you. Marvellous! Thanks so much.'

'Thank you,' Pip said. 'I must dash.'

A couple of meters to the front door. A quick walk to the tube. You can do it! You can do it because you must. Go on! Go.

'Can we give you a lift?' Zac offered, holding the front door open for her. 'We're headed north as it is.'

Pip told herself, *implored* herself, to decline.

You're meant to be heading north yourself, you silly cow. True north. North as in Derbyshire. In the next hour or so. Cat! Fen! Django! Do your duty! Go north.

'Thanks,' Pip was horrified to hear herself accept, 'that would be great.'

Zac held the car door open for her and in she climbed. Billy and Tom fired questions at her, non-stop, from the back seat. It meant nothing to them that Kentish Town was on the way to Holloway. Thus, they didn't notice that Zac made no effort to drop her off there, nor that Pip made no request to be dropped off there, or even thereabouts, either.

Ruth was well aware that Zac's passenger seat was occupied despite his commendable efforts to distract her on the doorstep by blocking her view and asking about the state of her headache. The boys had scampered into the house, manic in the final throes of hyperactivity due in part to the additives in the luridly iced birthday cake.

'Do come in for a drink,' Ruth said, with a scheming glint to her eye which Zac mistook as a symptom of her headache.

'No no,' he declined, 'I ought to head home.'

'Of course – you have work to do,' Ruth reasoned, with a nod of her head towards his car which Zac misread as a headachy twitch.

'Yes, yes,' he said, thinking that his sister-in-law was really bearing her headache bravely to be so chatty and attentive.

'See you tomorrow,' Ruth said, smiling commendably for one suffering so. 'We'll expect you around lunch-time.'

'Sure,' said Zac. 'Bye, Tom. See you.' He waited for Ruth to close the front door before he headed back to his car. Ruth, however, darted to the study and peeked through the venetian blinds.

Zac and Pip sat there for a while, looking directly ahead. 'Your place or mine?' Pip asked.

'My turn to play host,' Zac replied. He started the car and they headed off.

While he drove, Pip made a call from her mobile phone. 'Fen? Hiya, it's me. Listen, I think I'll come home tomorrow. That kids' party has given me a sodding headache. I'm going to go directly to bed.'

They snogged like teenagers, did Zac and Pip. Though how many teenagers own an Audi Quattro and have a residents' permit bay outside a beautifully maintained conversion in Hampstead is open to question. They snogged like teenagers who had snuck into a parent's car. Zac had nosed into his parking space and the ensuing silence in the car was louder and more loaded than when the engine had been running and the radio on. Zac cleared his throat in a bid not to voice 'Home sweet home!' which was on the tip of his tongue. Pip turned to him as if she was about to say something, too. Nothing. So they stared intensely at one another momentarily before instinctively grappling each other close and thrusting tongues into each other's mouths.

They necked with the voracious hunger of adolescents; none of the fancy lip work, the refined nibbling and sensuous tongue-flickering they'd perfected over the years. They simply gorged on each other, slurping and sucking and gobbling each other's gobs. Like a lust-soaked youngster, Zac pawed at Pip's breasts through her shirt. He wasn't so much fondling as grabbing and kneading. On her part, Pip had one hand locked around the belt-loops of Zac's trousers while the other scuttled up and down his torso. If Pip's jeans hadn't been so tight and if the pitch of the car's seat hadn't been just so, Pip and Zac would have delved down to Base 3. As a somewhat poor second, Pip travelled her hand over the bulge surging sideways and twitching behind Zac's trousers. It was nearing 7.00 and people heading for the Well's Tavern enjoyed the spectacle in the Audi.

I'm that age, some thought enviously, *and I haven't snogged like that since I was a teenager!*

God, thought others, *when was the last time I made out like that – let alone in a car!*

'Not much more we can do in here,' Zac panted.

'Let's go inside,' Pip panted back.

'Not much I can do about that for a few minutes,' Zac rued, looking reflectively at the lopsided marquee his straining cock had made of his trousers.

'Well, if I don't get out soon,' Pip parried, 'I won't be able to move – I'm starting to stick to my knickers as it is.'

They giggled, felt as flushed as they looked.

'Come on,' Zac said once his trousers were hanging more decorously, 'let's go inside and get squelching.'

Pip didn't know whether to giggle or gasp on entering Zac's apartment. She didn't know whether she was in the midst of some post-modernist joke or merely standing in a flat that had been disastrously decorated by a previous and colour-blind tenant.

'Home sweet home,' said Zac; Pip stifled a chuckle.

'It's very, um –' she faltered, not wanting to make a fool of herself nor offend him, 'zany.'

Zac regarded her. 'Are you taking the piss?'

'God, no!' Pip protested. 'But it's certainly a blaze, a *bombardment* of colour in here,' she defined.

'Compared to your place, sure,' Zac said tartly. 'Remember – I'm an accountant. I have to have some colour in my life or else the greyness of it all would consume me.'

Pip looked around quietly and considered the surroundings.

It's certainly different.

It's quite good.

It could grow on me.

Mind you, I don't think I could live with it myself.

'Drink?' Zac suggested.

'Whatever you're having,' said Pip.

He handed her a Budvar. 'Doritos?' he offered.

'If you're having,' Pip said. Zac opened a bumper-sized packet and they stood in the middle of his sitting-room, sipping lager, munching corn chips and contemplating an intensity of colour that would have had Matisse rapturous.

'It's very neat and tidy,' Pip said, looking further afield.

'God!' Zac exclaimed, clutching his brow. 'Not another sign of my latent gayness? I have a cleaner twice a week — there!'

Pip laughed and slapped his arm, leaving salty finger marks. 'I rather think I have it on good authority,' she said with a lick of her lips and some coy eye contact, 'that you're rampantly heterosexual.'

'Actually, Pip,' Zac said gravely, quite startling her momentarily, 'I'm rampant, full stop, just now.' He came close and took her ear lobe into his mouth. 'Sex first,' he murmured, 'we can do the guided tour later.' With that, he took the Dorito which was approaching her mouth, took her beer bottle, and placed both on the window-sill. He then led the way through to his bedroom. Pip was so focused on satisfying her lust, she didn't even notice the bright orange rug.

They stripped each other of clothing and inhibitions; the curtains remained wide open, the sash window up. And when they took to Zac's bed, after a lengthy prelude of vertical foreplay, they fell on top of the covers, their feet at the pillow end. Pip was aware of her nakedness and his. The light, the lightness; the breeze and breeziness. It excited her. It was very different from Caleb's flat. That had been more of a den – enclosed and darkened and secret. In contrast to Hoxton, Pip was aware of fresh air and height in Hampstead. It was filtering in through the open window, licking at her body. It was light outside and in. She felt comfortable, all topsy-turvy on Zac's bed, just three days after first having sex with him.

The foreplay had been good but the snogging in the car had been better and, similar to the sex at Pip's flat, the penetrative element was more the end of the means than the point of it all.

'A good fit,' Zac had murmured on pushing up deep into her. He didn't so much desire to make love to her just then, more he had a basic need to release the pent-up orgasm that had been looming since their frolicking in the car.

'Feels good,' Pip whispered back, thinking that if Zac kept that angle and pace, she could come quite easily, quite soon.

'Are you close?' he whispered, his skin prickling with sweat, his breathing pacy.

'Yes,' she gasped, placing open lips against his shoulders and tasting salt.

Fuck! Not that close, Zac. Slow down! Wait up a little longer! Damn.

Zac bucked against her, groaning; pinned himself as high up as he could penetrate and closed his eyes to appreciate every spasm. Finally, he gave a long, appreciative soft whistle. 'Fuck!' he marvelled, looking at her with triumph and gratitude.

Though it turned her on greatly to feel his orgasm so precisely, because this was only the second time they'd had sex, Pip didn't feel comfortable enough to continue to hump and grind against Zac's spent cock to reach her own climax. However, as her body calmed down, she found her mind drifting back over the whole afternoon. Back to the party, the charged atmosphere after dropping off Tom and Billy, the frantic nooky in the car, having sex on top of the covers in a room with the windows and curtains open. Here she was, lying diagonally on a bed, as sweaty as the man next to her, a man who made her laugh and made her gasp and made her a day late for a visit home to Derbyshire.

What price an orgasm, she pondered? In some ways, sex

with Zac had begun on spying his legs upside down through her handstand. It had continued in Benji's hallway, they were still at it in traffic on Junction Road, even with Billy and Tom in the back of the car; there was a momentary pause to drop the boys off in Holloway, resuming it when driving back to Hampstead and, of course, at it like rabbits when stationary outside Zac's flat. Perhaps they were still having the same sex from two days ago, when her hair was in plaits and her make-up was smudged. Maybe that's what it's about, Pip. Perhaps you shouldn't see sex as unique, distinct encounters, with a beginning, a middle and an orgasm. Maybe the best sex is a continuous session, sometimes lasting a lifetime, replete with interruptions and variations, friendliness and franticness, coming, going, hot passages and cold, colourful moments and noisy interjections amidst a pervasive sense of give-and-take pleasure. Maybe that's what making love's about. Is that how you make love? How love is made?

Pip looked over to Zac. He looked sleepy.

'It was fun,' she confirmed, 'a good fit. God, I'm hungry.'

After a sushi dinner and a stroll around Hampstead, they returned to Zac's and chatted about personal trivia into the early hours. Pip curled up in his Eames chair, he sat relaxed on the ample matching footstool. They talked about school and college and losing their virginity and what drugs they'd tried and how if it wasn't for the Stone Roses there could have been no Oasis. Zac had been to Reading Festival a couple of times and Pip had juggled at Glastonbury. However, neither fancied doing the tent-and-mud-and-spliff thing again. Pip confided that she didn't even much enjoy gigs any more, too much heaving, too noisy to hear, the floor too sticky with spilt beer.

'I'm a bit of a limbo lad, I guess,' Zac defined. 'I've grown out of it, too – but I'm simply not a classical-concert type of bloke. If truth be told,' he whispered as if deep in confession, 'I actively dislike opera. It's not that I don't "get" it. I just don't like it at all.'

'As for me,' Pip declared in low tones, 'I don't care for the theatre – I prefer the movies.' Her voice became stronger on seeing Zac nod. 'Theatre is bloody expensive, uncomfortable, too, and I simply don't like the artifice of it all. Curtain calls infuriate me – I feel ripped off, like I've been *had*. I thought I was meant to believe in the character, not applaud some actress smugly taking a bow for faking it. No, for me, film is far more compelling.'

'You can't beat a good John Grisham,' Zac proclaimed.

'Nor a classic Jilly Cooper,' Pip laughed.

'Do you remember a band called China Crisis?' Zac suddenly asked, sure that she would.

'Oh God!' Pip exclaimed. 'Bloody marvellous song they had, "African and White" – tell me you have a copy!'

He did. Zac had an awesome collection of vinyl and a sleek, state-of-the-art Linn hi-fi system appropriately and amusingly called the Klimax 500. After China Crisis, they played A Flock of Seagulls, and then they pranced around the sitting-room to 'The Safety Dance' and sang along to the Go-Gos and Pip did a passable impression of Clare Grogan on whom, Zac revealed, he still had something of a crush. Then, as they chilled out to Pink Floyd, they reminisced their way through all the *Watch with Mother* programmes they could remember, often impersonating the characters, too. Pip could do the mice from *Bagpuss* perfectly. Zac could remember practically every plot line from *Mr Benn*. All at three in the morning. Maybe it *was* all part of the same thing. Pip confessed to having had a penchant for, and a sizeable collection of, puff-ball skirts; Zac admitted to a mullet hairstyle with extravagant highlights and even had a photo to prove it. If sex earlier had been fun, all of this was too, maybe even more so.

Eventually, they shuffled back into the bedroom and folded into one another in Zac's bed, sleeping soundly with inner smiles coating their dreams. As she drifted off, Pip knew she wouldn't have forsaken this for Derbyshire, in fact she wouldn't have missed this for anything.

When she awoke the next morning, however, Pip McCabe had a complete change of heart and mind. As soon as her slumber had lifted and she was aware of the here and now – the orange rug, Budvar on the window-sill, the fact that it was Saturday morning – she modified her attitude drastically. She disregarded all the qualities of the situation, overlooked the many merits of the man and disparaged the glow of contentment she'd experienced so positively the previous night.

She swiftly decided to be appalled at waking up in Hampstead, in Zac's bed, bombarded by garish walls, furniture shaped like giant fruit and rugs the colour of kids' poster paint. The flock of seagulls had flown off and she was desperate to go-go.

Jesus, she concluded to herself, as if closing the deal on the whole disastrous idea of it all, *even sex with my vibrator is better – at least I climax.*

She was desperate for Derbyshire. She'd shower there. She'd buy breakfast at St Pancras. It would do – she wasn't that hungry. Her priority wasn't food or personal hygiene or even, truthfully, to get to Derbyshire. The most pressing need in Pip's life that Saturday morning was to get out of Zac's flat as fast as she could and flee the memories altogether.

Unfortunately, creeping away was not going to be possible. Zac wasn't in bed; he could be heard humming Soul II Soul from the kitchen whilst operating a noisy gadget. The scent of warm croissants drifted through. Pip chanted to herself that she wasn't hungry, she rebuked herself for already missing the first train to Chesterfield. She hurled back the duvet and at that moment, Zac entered his bedroom, proffering a tray of breakfast.

'Oh, I *do* like to start the morning with split beaver,' he remarked deadpan, while Pip lay there stark naked, spread-eagled, horrified. She whipped the duvet back over herself.

'I'm late,' she said, 'I really need to go.'

'Sure,' Zac shrugged amiably. He'd woken charmed by the presence of Pip and the memories of the previous night. 'Breakfast?'

'Not hungry,' Pip all but barked, though she eyed the croissants and the jug of whatever it was that Zac had been so sonorously juicing. Zac wafted the basket of pastries beneath her nose and she found herself unable to resist. She was famished. Sushi is all very well in that one never goes to bed afterwards feeling bloated or stuffed, but it hardly tides a person over for very long. So Pip had a croissant. And a long drink of juice (pink grapefruit, passion fruit, kiwi and banana).

'Wake up and smell the coffee?' Zac joshed, pouring Jamaican Blue Mountain from a gorgeous Alessi cafetière. Pip sipped. She felt physically revived but emotionally still in free fall.

'I have to go,' she told Zac.

'When are you back?' he asked.

'Tomorrow evening or Monday morning, I'm not sure yet.'

'Shall we do things next week, then?' he asked. Pip looked nonplussed. 'You know, *things*,' Zac said, 'heavy petting, break-dancing, go to the movies, not listen to any opera?'

Pip couldn't answer. She was out of her depth utterly. She observed a twitch of bemusement flicker across his face. Somewhere, lurking deep inside her, a very quiet voice that she couldn't quite hear, asked her if she wasn't slightly mad.

Look at him!

Remember it all!

Kind and lovely and fun and compatible!

Zac filled her coffee cup again. She didn't want to be charmed by the fact that he'd decanted the milk into a ceramic jug. 'Nothing heavy,' he attempted. 'You know – just hang out together a bit. A bit more. A bit more often.'

'I can't,' she suddenly declared. 'Timing – everything. I just can't, Zac. Please understand.'

Zac regarded her directly. Her brow was twitching this

way and that in a rather unbecoming manner. Her gaze seemed shifty but dulled. She was all closed off and her body seemed spiky and hard – a far cry from the soft and welcoming haven it had been just hours before.

Not again, he thought.

'Understand what?' he asked.

'You're great, sex was good,' Pip said in a rather patronizing tone she didn't really mean but simply couldn't help, 'but I was in love with Caleb.' Zac analysed his fingernails while she spoke. Pip couldn't begin to analyse her bizarre declaration. Zac hadn't expected the twinge of jealousy, the pang of insecurity. He hoped it didn't register on his face. Fingernails. Keep looking. 'I mean, maybe we should just be friends.' Pip was staggered that she should use a clichéd phrase she had always loathed. Zac had stretched out his fingers and was tracing the veins on his left hand. 'Friends who fucked,' Pip dared, demonstratively using the past tense. 'No hard feelings, hey?' She put her hand on his arm.

He knew her words well, he'd used them himself on a fair few occasions. They didn't have a very nice ring to them. There was an ugliness to the sound of it all, a pervasive ugliness smearing grubbiness over last night, over waking this morning; a sudden and surprising ugliness to Pip which contradicted all he'd believed her to be.

'You know what,' Zac said, standing suddenly though it caused juice to splash over the linen and the milk to spill over the tray, 'that's just cool with me.' Pip was still beneath the duvet and wondered whether she should make a move to clear up the mess. After all, directly or otherwise, the mess was of her making. 'In fact, I should be the one to apologize. I guess *I* took advantage of *you*,' Zac declared, hands on hips, eyes dark, 'when I found you in tears and then got you hammered the other night.' Pip glanced up at him. This she wasn't expecting. 'And I guess it's only logical that you'd be on the rebound yourself,' he persisted, his voice and gaze cool. Her lips parted. She'd really quite like to defend herself. 'So sure, let's be friends – whatever,' Zac shrugged. 'It's great that you're cool about the sex thing,' he reasoned, his slate-grey eyes flat but penetrating. 'As you say, no big deal.'

Pip nodded, feeling she might well burst into tears with the weight of it all; instead, she swallowed and quickly declared to herself, 'Well! What a bastard!'

It felt as though there was a tangle of cold, wet spaghetti muddling her mind and clogging her conscience. Her intestines felt knotted and twisted and seething, like a can of worms. 'May I take a shower?' she asked.

'Sure,' Zac shrugged, already making his way out of the bedroom.

No *Psycho* shower curtain. Just a scarlet and violet striped panel protecting the sunshine yellow lino flooring from the oversized, ceiling-mounted shower rose. It was gorgeous, like being in a tropical downpour. Aveda body cleanser and a loofah. Thick towels the colour of lemon meringue pie. It seemed a travesty to put on her knickers from last night, despite turning them inside out in a bid for added freshness. Momentarily, Pip was saddened by the symmetry of using Zac's toothbrush. The bristles were hard and her gums bled.

Fully dressed, she hovered in Zac's bathroom. She wanted to go. She wished none of this had happened – not the fun nor the frolics, nor her misgivings, nor her stupid declaration of indifference, certainly not her feelings otherwise. She felt rooted to the spot, scared to face him again, dreading returning to the outside world; to her beloved Derbyshire where she'd be helpless not to confront the meaning of her actions and, of course, the neuroses that instigated them. To say nothing of the energy required to sort out Cat, sort out Fen, sort out Django.

She had to go. It must be appearing odd that she'd spent so much time in the bathroom long after she'd had a shower and cleaned her teeth. Gingerly, she opened the door. Zac's linen had been changed. There wasn't a crumb to be seen. She walked softly through to his living-room. Immaculate.

No sign of the beer bottles or scrunched-up Doritos packets or the stacks of 45s and piles of 33s. In fact, no sign of Zac either. She glanced over to the galley kitchen. Clean and sparkling. No one there.

'Zac?' she called quietly. Silence. Then she saw a note on the footstool of the Eames.

> *Gone to pick up Tom.*
> *Have fun with your mum.*
> *See you around. ZH*

It was the worst confrontation of all. Far worse than if Zac had still been there. She didn't reread it. She hurried from the flat. Rushed to the tube, and belted home. Packed. Hurtled back to the tube and headed for King's Cross St Pancras. The train was at the platform. She jumped on and ran through the carriages. She felt sick from the physical exertion, but at least it took her mind off feeling sick from all the bullshit. All the while, racketing round her head she was yelling at herself.

'My mum? My fucking *mum*?'

TWENTY-TWO

Zac was really quite taken aback. Bloody offended, actually. If truth be told, it *hurt*. He felt a fool. He had been taken advantage of. There was no denying it. He stopped momentarily to contemplate whether this was how those four or five girls (How many had there been? How awful not to quite remember) had felt who'd been no more than one-night stands to him. Well, he wasn't going to compromise his self-respect. It wasn't as if he actually needed Pip in his life, anyway. And right from the start, if he was honest, hadn't he thought her a little on the odd side of eccentric? Sure, all was fun and feisty at the moment, but the likelihood was that if anything *had* developed beyond a fling, she'd soon have irritated him supremely. Wouldn't she? She and he were hardly the stuff of a worthwhile relationship or potential long-term couple.

Anyway, he had so much else in his life, he really had no need of Pip McCabe; he'd hardly notice her absence. No question about it. Nothing more to discuss. Nothing to rue or misconstrue. Certainly nothing to regret. Nor even much to remember, actually, come to think of it. Not that he was going to expend any further time or energy thinking of it. Nothing to think about.

*

When Zac saw his little boy, he hugged him very close and breathed in the incomparable scent emanating from the top of his head. Zac believed it to be a secret bar-code of sorts, a gift to a parent.

'Legoland?' Tom whispered, expectation dancing across his eyes.

'Yes, please!' Zac responded.

'Bye, Billy,' Tom waved from the pavement, 'bye, Auntie Ruthie – thanks for having me.'

Billy and his mum waved. Tom and Zac waved back.

Ruth went through to the kitchen and rustled up lunch for her son and husband.

'Zac not coming in?' his brother asked, putting his hands at his wife's waist and nuzzling her neck.

'Off to Legoland,' Ruth said.

'Wonder how his hot date went,' Jim mused, not that he was particularly interested in his wife's in-depth analysis on such subjects, nor really in his brother's love life itself.

'I wonder,' was all Ruth said. Jim wandered off to play PlayStation with Billy.

Ruth dried her hands and folded and re-folded the tea towel. It had been odd. Zac certainly hadn't emanated the glow of a well-laid man. No sparkle, no depth to his surface smile.

He might as well have painted it on, Ruth thought.

TWENTY-THREE

'*I* know that your mother ran off with a cowboy from Denver,' Django McCabe reasons with his youngest niece, 'but you chasing through France after a bunch of boys on bikes – well, isn't that taking the family tradition to new extremes?'

The McCabe sisters are back home in Derbyshire once more. Though they don't mean to undermine their uncle, Pip and Fen are persuading Cat, for the umpteenth time, that a coveted position in the press corps of the Tour de France will provide a fantastic chance both to heal her broken heart and further her budding career as a sports journalist. The girls and their uncle are in the garden, a haven of neat lawn, mature shrubbery and a veritable arboretum on the edge of untamed Farleymoor. They are lolling about being a family – an unconventional one, perhaps, but solid, close and open. Fen is lounging under the cedar tree, day-dreaming, as is her wont. A tyre on a rope still dangles from the sturdy old branches, though it is only ever Pip who swings from it now. Cat prefers her tyres by the pair and nicely balanced on a titanium bike. Usually, she's hurling her mountain bike over the moors, but today, she's opting for a sedentary afternoon in the garden. While Fen prefers to use the garden to sit and think, or lounge and listen, Pip is usually flic-flaccing its breadth, cartwheeling its length or scaling its heights by squirming up the rope and dangling upside down by just one limb before leaping effortlessly to the ground, landing with a somersault, then righting herself to hold a pose, motionless and triumphant. Just as her training on the trapeze had taught her. Just as watching Olga Korbut when she was young had inspired her.

Today, though, with Fen reclining peacefully under the boughs, Pip allows her sister safety and space and perfects a run of flic-flacs across the lawn instead.

'I don't know, Django,' she protests in Cat's defence, slightly breathless. 'Think of all that Lycra,' she says, as if it is a concept universally appealing, 'lashings of it! And a squadron of shiny thighs!' It is an image that does little for Pip but she knows that her lovelorn sister needs all possible bolstering if she is going to cope in France for a month, fighting for scoops in the press corps. Pip is happy to provide support. She does it so well. It's her self-imposed duty. It's her role. It takes her mind off things. She has responsibilities, thank God. After all, their mother *did* run off with a cowboy from Denver when they were small.

Django and Pip stay up after Fen and Cat have gone to bed. They're sipping Cointreau and eating After Eights which have passed their sell-by date but still taste good enough. They are happily ensconced in the main sitting-room – a room whose name the family changes according to time of day or season. This afternoon, they would have referred to it as the Library. Once the weather is cold enough for a fire to be lit, it becomes the Snug. On summer afternoons, it is the Quiet Room. In mornings, it is the Morning Room. When the girls were young and naughty, it was Downstairs. At the moment, it is the Drawing-room, on account of it serving as an excellent backdrop to conversation, After Eights and Cointreau.

'I'm worried about Fenella *and* Catriona,' Django confides, using their names in full for emphasis, though the twitching of his eyebrows and lowering of his voice would have sufficed.

'Oh, you needn't be,' Pip says breezily, both to mask her own concerns for both sisters and to hide the fact that her personal life, too, is in a state of chaos. She doesn't want Django to worry. In stature and personality he may well appear robust, and his demeanour is as colourful as his original Pucci print shirts and paisley neckerchiefs, but Pip is also aware that he is approaching his sixty-ninth birthday, after all, and feels it her duty to allay his fears. She seeks to reassure him by making light of it all. 'You leave it to me, old man,' she laughs. 'I'll make sure there's laughter in their lives and food in their fridges.'

'Of course, Cat is better off without him,' Django reasons, instantly comforted by Pip's assurances, 'but she is just so miserable. It pains me to see her hurting so. Can she truly cope in France?'

'She'll bounce back,' Pip says, nudging her shoulder against Django's. 'France is a good idea.'

Django raises his eyes heavenwards. 'If anything, I'm slightly more concerned about Fen.' He strokes his side-burns, thinking quietly to himself that he must remember to dye them to match his hair, which he did himself last week with a preparation appetizingly called 'Fingerlickin' Fudge'. 'Cat rids herself of one knave, and Fen takes on two at once,' he ponders, silently reminding himself to tint his eyebrows, too. 'Where's the sense in that? The logic?' He glugs his Cointreau. 'The morality?' He's suddenly aware how his consternation might seem hypocritical in the light of his well-publicized and colourful past.

'You can talk!' Pip protests, right on cue. 'O Squire of the Swinging Sixties and High Priest of Hippydom!'

'But you see,' Django says, because the liqueur has suddenly made him lucid and alert to the situation, 'although I did most certainly gad about during the 1960s – and a fair part of the 1970s, too – it was all conducted *in context*. It was what people did. We had no hindsight to guide us. It was, we thought, the way to go – burn the bras, ban the bomb, smoke the weed, take the trip, share the love. But you see, our mistakes, the diseases we contracted, the brain cells we damaged, the emotional price we paid – and some are still paying off – this is the legacy we hand down to you.'

'You mean the "been there, seen it, done it" mentality?' Pip interjects. 'That we should learn from your findings?'

'Yes,' says Django. 'Fenella oughtn't to fiddle with two chaps at the same time. It'll end in tears. It's just not wholesome.' Django looks forlorn.

'Django, you misunderstand – we're not talking gang-bangs here,' Pip says, trying to lighten the tone by lowering it. Django gives her a disparaging look but replenishes her Cointreau anyway. 'Fen simply can't decide between two men – one's rich, one's poor; one's town, one's country; one's young and one's old.'

'Old?' Django barks, as if he'll challenge the cad to a duel.

Pip says she thinks he's fiftyish. She can see that her uncle is relieved to retain ultimate seniority – that if needs be, Fen's older beau is still young enough for Django to scold.

Though Pip feels it wise to reserve her judgement in front of Django, deep down she finds Fen's situation somewhat distasteful and Cat's circumstance truly upsetting.

I fear that it won't be long before I see Fen in the kind of state Cat is in now.

'If Fenella isn't careful,' Django warns, 'she'll be in Cat's current pickle.'

Pip just sips her liqueur. She doesn't want to respond.

The whole thing is giving me a headache. Though I think I understand their situations, it doesn't mean I have to empathize. Yet it's not like either sister is particularly wayward or morally inept. Cat is sweet and kind and had the terrible misfortune to pick a bad card – none of us saw it coming. Fen is quite refined and reserved in many ways, hadn't had a boyfriend in years and – I don't know – two came along at once. She has high standards; I guess she wants to make sure she chooses the very best.

'And you, Philippa, anyone on your horizon?' Django enquires, offering After Eights to facilitate revelations.

Pip settles back into the sofa. It seems to have an innate recollection of her shape and weight, appearing to both suck her in and support her. She sips her Cointreau and fixes a demure half-smile across her lips; pretending, relatively convincingly, that she's relaxed and content and happy to savour another chocolate, thank you very much, before answering.

Anyone on my horizon? A shit who took me for a ride – and a great bloke who I've treated shittily. I guess you could say Cat doesn't have the monopoly on shits. And it isn't just Fen who's been juggling two blokes. I oughtn't to be quite so quick to judge if I haven't practised what I preach.

'God, no!' Pip responds casually instead, having licked her lips and neatly folded the After Eight wrappers. 'You know how I don't need a man in my life,' she waves her hands as if wafting away the issue. 'Everything's cool. Hunky-dory. Fine and dandy. A-OK. All is well.' In the light of Django's reaction to her sisters' state of affairs, she's quite unnerved to see by his brow rubbing that her answer isn't satisfactory. 'You needn't worry about me!' she perseveres, a little too keenly. Still he looks perplexed. 'There's no way I'll give you and my sisters any cause for concern, any excuse for gossip over too much Cointreau and half a box of After Eights late at night! I'm perfectly happy and very healthy – I don't need a man and I don't need money.'

'But Philippa, my dear, it's not what you *need* that is the issue. Wouldn't you rather *like* a little of each?'

It's on the tip of Pip's tongue to tell her uncle in no uncertain terms of her pension and savings plan and her vibrator, so as to silence him. She'd quite like to stomp from the room muttering 'Give me a fucking break.' But of course she does nothing of the sort, nor says anything that comes close. Far too risky to reveal even a glimpse of her recent past. No point anyway, it is her *past*, after all.

'I'm not bothered,' Pip says instead, very lightly.

'Beware complacency!' Django warns.

'I'm not complacent,' Pip assures him, 'I'm happy as I am. Honestly. Anyway, I'm far too busy. Life is good.' She doesn't want to talk any more. She's gone from defending her sisters, so her uncle doesn't worry, to justifying her own choices so her uncle doesn't worry. She pretends the drink has gone to her head and she tells Django she'll take some fresh air before turning in. He lets her go. He has no choice, really.

'There's more to that girl than meets the eye,' he says to himself as he polishes off the After Eights. 'I'll have to wait for her to introduce me to her inner quirks – and qualms.' He creaks himself out of the sofa, with which he has a love-hate relationship because, though he thinks it looks the part, he's always found it so damned uncomfortable. He pads over to the window and spies Pip kicking at the turf and slumping down beneath the cedar. Her preoccupation makes him acutely aware that she craves space, peace and privacy. Even if he's unseen, he's still fundamentally intruding, and as he respects his niece he turns away. One thing is for sure, the inner calm he depends on her exuding, that he's always been so proud of, is missing.

Pip knows it's both churlish and childish to boot the poor lawn. But it's quite satisfying and she's doing it nimble-footedly and half-heartedly enough so that no clods are actually despatched. She's softly chanting her mantra, 'Don't need a man, don't need money', kicking the grass for emphasis on 'man' and 'money'. The rhythm of the words is satisfying. But deep down she knows that the fact that they roll off the tongue so gratifyingly is irrelevant. In all honesty, she admits that her phrase would be far better suited to the soulful voice of some jazz diva, than declared histrionically by a young clown to friends, family and herself. Tonight, Pip can hear how stupid it sounds. The stillness of the Derbyshire air, the darkness of the night, the ageless calm of the landscape, the familiarity of her childhood home, cause her words to reverberate and force her to listen to them. She can kid herself in London, but she can't do so here.

What on earth does her mantra mean? What does it mean that she has held so steadfastly on to it all these years? Though she may not want to listen, if she is honest – and up in Derbyshire, alone and outdoors, she cannot be otherwise – she'll have to admit that a little more money would be pretty useful. She may be a great advocate of calico and raw cotton, but she did see a skein of linen and silk the colour of a labrador puppy. She touched it with her fingertips, let it brush against her cheek, wafted it around. But she was already in the red that month and the council tax, water rates and final demand for gas and electricity had yet to be paid.

So a little more money wouldn't go amiss.

And might not a man be quite nice, Pip? Especially if he was quite a nice man?

Unfortunately, her long-held position as mentor and therapist to the womenfolk around her has given her indirect exposure to all manner of unsuitable men. Those who have toyed with her friends, and the ones who've dared screw with her sisters. To say nothing of Dr Caleb Simmons. Pip's loyalty to her sex and siblings will not permit acknowledgement that, just sometimes, those men might not be quite as bad as they are mercilessly made out to be. That, perhaps, innocent issues of simple incompatibility or love having run its course may have been at the root of her friends' and sisters' traumas. Plus, her friends and sisters themselves were hardly blameless – feisty can also be demanding; loyalty can sometimes be claustrophobic; possessiveness can be a by-product of a passionate personality.

The fact that Pip has been single for some time, along with the fact that she's never been in love, have resulted in her demands becoming more stringent and her expectations being more unrealistic. She has set her bizarre standard concerning baggage, against which no human who has lived a little can ever really measure up. Therefore, in Pip's eyes, all men do fall short and must be avoided. And, therefore, she can declare with a sense of relief that of course life is easier without them. It is far simpler to be dismissive of all men than even to hint that sometimes, occasionally, she might want just the one.

She's still kicking the ground in time to her chant. But now her foot makes impact on the word 'need'.

I don't. I really don't. I don't need more money. I don't need a bloke. I don't need the hassle.

She's caught up in generalizations because if she referred to specifics, she'd have to turn her mind to Zac Holmes. She knows she hasn't treated him very well, that she hasn't been honest. Not only has she been rude, she's also lied to him. What on earth was all that bullshit about being a friend happy to fuck? About being in love with Caleb? And, most unfathomable of all, about a close mummy–daughter relationship?

Surely, the truth will out, as it always does. And then won't it be Pip herself who appears as one utterly weighed down by baggage accumulated from many provenances? Her behaviour could quite turn a man off. For all you know, Pip, he's chanting himself to sleep thinking, 'I don't need Pip McCabe. I don't even want to see her again.' He probably thinks you're more hassle than you're worth. Anyway, you don't need him or want him, do you? And the way you've treated him will certainly have made reconciliation so burdensome that it will be more trouble than it's worth. Is that why you did it? Break something before it had the chance to break you? Are you that fragile?

She can't hear me. Would she even listen if she could? See, she's swinging on the tyre-rope, like an ape on acid. It's nearing one in the morning. She's hanging from one foot, her arms outstretched. She is saying something. But I can't quite hear. She's moving too fast, slicing the air, she's upside down. She's slightly breathless – acrobatics uses much adrenalin, hanging upside down, travelling at speed, takes the breath away. What is it that she's saying?

'I've fucked up.'

She whooshes through the air.

'Sure – now he'll never fuck me up. But would he ever have? He wasn't the type to. He was lovely. But I've fucked up.'

Swing. Swoosh back and forth. Over and over and over again.

'I've fucked up. I've fucked up. I've fucked up.'

Even when she's upside down; even when her life is topsy-turvy; she knows herself inside out, does Miss McCabe.

TWENTY-FOUR

*S*o the accountant and the clown set about forgetting each other. Juliana had come back from South Africa and was once more amusing Zac after hours – and often *for* hours. Once or twice he told himself how good it was to have a woman who made his body feel absolutely spent but in no way taxed his mind. Soon enough, he stopped theorizing altogether and just lay back and enjoyed himself.

Work for Merry Martha picked up now that the school summer holidays were under way. There was face painting to be done, and open-air shows at Golders Hill and Parliament Hill. A friend even set up a weekend's work in Brighton. Pip was far too busy balancing things on her head, or balancing on her head, to wonder if little Tom might ever be in her audience, his father, too.

Dr Pippity continued to dispense her therapeutic skills at St Bea's. She was relieved and happy that she never saw Tom – it must mean that his eczema was doing well. Dr Simmons had returned from his holiday and Pip was pleasantly surprised to see how a tan did not become him. He looked a little broiled and somewhat leathery. She also found it quite satisfying that he seemed much more ill at ease in her company than she was in his. She didn't see him that often anyway, and outside the hospital grounds, she never gave him a second thought. That was the power of her mind over matter; she no longer minded and had swiftly decided that he didn't matter at all. She'd managed to delete all memories when she deleted his text messages.

Fen continued to dither between her two men and maintained her parallel lives in town and country. She didn't ask Pip for advice or support, nor did she offer details or anecdotes. Megan and Dominic were at that sickly stage of courtship where verbal and physical declarations of love are far too frequent and cloying for public consumption. Soon enough, they were spending their time together alone together. Even on Tuesday and Thursday evenings.

Cat had made it to the Tour de France and was now heading for the Alps. Pip and Fen often watched the TV highlights together; soon enough they could recognize specific riders in the peloton, understand certain aspects of strategy and even master the correct pronunciation of cyclists' names and bike components. Cat revealed that she had fallen for a doctor on an American team. Her older sisters had only to read between the lines of her race reports for the *Guardian* newspaper, to detect the enormous uplift in her spirits.

Pip and Fen were, however, realistically cautious on Cat's behalf. Both felt an overwhelming urge to verify her welfare and authenticate the intentions of this doctor, firsthand. It seemed like a very sensible idea to journey to France for a surprise visit that weekend. Django provided funds and a blessing.

'Believe me,' Pip had murmured ominously to Fen, 'doctors can be perilously seductive.' Fen didn't think to pry. It would never have crossed her mind that her sister spoke from anything other than encyclopedic knowledge, certainly not from personal experience, on such matters.

Pip was trying to pack. Fen was sitting on her sofa, flicking through a copy of *Procycling* magazine.

'Listen, I'll take a couple of fleeces,' Pip was calling from the bedroom. 'I'm sure it'll be chilly on the mountains and I'll bet you've only packed flimsy stuff.'

''Kay,' Fen said, somewhat preoccupied by a photograph of the thighs of an Italian sprinter called Stefano Sassetta.

'And I've bought some bumper packs of Mars Bars and KitKats for Cat. It sounds like her diet thus far has consisted of baguette, garlic and complimentary portions of stuff on offer from the sponsors each morning,' Pip called through, this time from the bathroom.

''Kay,' Fen replied, now distracted by the bulging, Lycra-clad crotch of a rider called Fabian Ducasse.

'And there's only so many freebie sweets or chunks of cheese that a journalist can eat, surely,' Pip remarked, coming into the lounge to set the video, 'or that are good for one's health.'

''Kay,' said Fen. Pip went over to see what was absorbing her so. And she spent a reflective moment or two appreciating the dimensions and supreme glossiness of a Spanish rider's physique.

'I'll pack her some Colgate, too,' Pip said, and returned to the bathroom to fetch a new tube of toothpaste. She reappeared with a rucksack packed perfectly and hoisted on to her shoulders. '*Vive le Tour! Allez!*'

Fen laughed. The phone started to ring. Pip checked her watch. They were in good time and their cab hadn't yet arrived. 'I'd better take it,' she said, 'it could be Django with a last-minute worry, I suppose.' She answered the phone, her rucksack still aloft.

'Hullo?' said a woman. 'I'm after Merry Martha?'

'Speaking,' said Pip, changing her voice and demeanour for professional purposes.

'Oh! Great! I wanted to book you for a birthday party.'

'Hold on,' said Pip, 'I'll just check the diary.'

'The first Sunday in August is the date my husband and I are hoping for.'

Pip checked. She was free. And the Tour de France would have finished the previous week so she wouldn't be bound to the television. 'Yup,' she confirmed, 'I'll just take your details today and nearer the time, we'll discuss what kind of a show would be appropriate. So we have the date. What sort of time?'

'Mid-afternoon?'

'Perfect. Now,' said Pip, 'name?'

'June Price,' the woman replied.

'And how old will June be?' Pip asked.

The woman laughed. 'Well,' she said, 'between you and me, thirty-four next birthday. Actually, the party is for my son, he'll be six,' June Price elaborated.

'His name?' Pip asked, nodding to Fen that she'd be wrapping the call up imminently.

'Tom,' Mrs Price replied.

'It's in the book,' Pip told her new client. 'We'll speak nearer the time.'

'Wonderful!'

'Goodbye now.'

The cab had arrived. Fen was heading out for the street. Pip unfurled the blinds and checked that certain lights were on, others off. She double-locked the door and she and Fen headed for Waterloo and the Eurostar to France. Her baggage was starting to nag.

I'll redress the load, shift the balance, when I have the chance.

TWENTY-FIVE

*P*ip certainly shifted the balance whilst she was away, though it might take some time to see whether she added to her baggage or lightened her load. Far from home, she did something she'd never done, something she thought she'd never want to do, something she certainly wasn't setting out to do, something she probably wouldn't do again. If anyone had told her she would have a one-night stand even once in her life, let alone on the lumpy mattress of a bunk bed in a hostel on a French mountain top, she'd probably laugh in their face and privately feel somewhat disturbed. The thought of it wasn't remotely titillating to Pip. After all, if she wasn't bothered about having a man in her life, then a quick one-off shag, devoid of home comforts, must be far down on her list of priorities. Nevertheless, she found herself sneaking away from the bed she was sharing with Fen, for a fumble with a lanky lad called Alex. In a bunk bed. In a hostel. At the summit of a French Alp.

Of course, Pip didn't leap straight from train to bunk bed. On arrival in Grenoble, her priority was to locate Cat and assess the doctor. Tracking down Cat was not easy – even glimpsing a flash of the race was tough, with the huge crowds lining the route and many areas permitting no access whatsoever without some laminated pass or other. Pip and Fen eventually found Cat and they found her in fine form, too. She was staggered and delighted by their surprise visit, and supremely grateful for the chocolate and toothpaste. She introduced her sisters to her colleagues in the press corps and, of course, to her doctor. Though both older sisters attempted to maintain a certain circumspect aloofness from him, they found Ben York to be genuine and exuding all-important wholesome affection for Cat. The girls were relieved and pleased, not least because they were also secretly hoping for an introduction (though they'd settle for an autograph) to any of his glorious Team Megapac cyclists.

For three weeks in July, the French are obsessed with the thrills, spills, scandal and skulduggery that underscore the Tour de France. If the Tour de France is a soap opera of sorts, the landscape for the race is as much a colourful character as any of the cyclists themselves. Fortuitously, Pip and Fen's impromptu visit coincided with the race's high point of theatre, the stage to L'Alpe D'Huez, cycling's Mecca — twenty-one hairpin bends and gruesome gradients. It is a mountain that most sensible folk ski down rather than cycle up; the riders having tackled a staircase of mountains immediately beforehand. As they did yesterday, and will do again tomorrow. Not to mention having ridden up and over the Pyrenees last week. Oh, and with well over 1,000 km left to ride to Paris.

Pip and Fen's first full day in France started at 5.00 a.m., with their seasoned hack of a sister driving them to the awesome mountain so they could stake a good vantage point for the race which would reach them late that afternoon. The stage Pip and Fen were to witness was 189 km long, would take the winner just under six hours but would see ten riders quit the race and four others ignominiously disqualified for limping over the line outside the time-limit. With no pause for rest, no chance for mistakes, the cyclists might have to piss, eat, even shit and puke, whilst in the saddle. There were 200,000 fans on L'Alpe D'Huez. Some had camped there days in advance in relative luxury in RVs, others had slept a couple of nights under the stars in sleeping-bags that did little to combat the surprising cold. Some fans had simply partied last night away and would continue to do so until well after the race had finished and the riders were having their massages in the hotels in the next valley.

The atmosphere was of a carnival; Pip and Fen were delighted. They'd only come to France to check up on their sister; now they felt as though they were enjoying a mini-break with entertainment thrown in for free. Spectators had their countries' flags painted on their faces, some wore ludicrous wigs, others dressed in costumes ranging from angels to the devil. Euro-pop of questionable quality blared from boomboxes. Some people had guitars. A group of six, clad in cycling gear, formed a veritable brass band. Regardless of the ungodly hour, booze flowed and spirits soared. Pip wished she'd brought Merry Martha's outfits, something to juggle with, a little slap at the very least. Still, she was glad she'd thought to bring fleeces. It may have been July, but up the Alp, at that hour, it was freezing. However, a friendly Dutch crowd brewed the sisters tea and topped it off with schnapps. And some Belgian blokes with alarming moustaches gave them brushes and whitewash so Pip and Fen could partake of the tradition of painting riders' names along the tarmac for encouragement.

The rain came well before the riders. Fen and Pip were drenched but kept warm by the atmosphere and a considerable amount of schnapps. Though the action of the race and the drama of its cast is a whole other story, suffice it to say that the McCabe girls witnessed the most gut-wrenching but also uplifting sights of sporting prowess, of man against mountain, of triumph over adversity. The riders' tortured pace as they passed by – still stunning despite the severity of the climb – meant their pain-scorched faces were wincingly visible, their laboured breathing horribly audible, as their lactic-acid-addled muscles struggled to make sense of the final mountain of the day. One rider even slogged past with the added humiliation of an upset stomach coursing down his legs in rivulets mixed with sweat and rain. All the heroes Pip and Fen had come to know from television coverage and magazine photos were within touching distance. It was awe-inspiring. The girls were soon hoarse from cheering. Their brief sojourn in France was turning out to be humbling, entertaining and memorable in equal measures. England seemed far away. That was no bad thing for each of the McCabe sisters.

Pip and Fen were able to see Cat and witness firsthand her change in spirits, her growing confidence, the certain glint that Dr York had sparked.

Fen was afforded time out from the two loves of her life and all the incumbent contemplation and management that this required.

Pip grasped the opportunity for a one-night stand to provide distance and a diversion from the perceived mess of the previous weeks.

Pip would like us to believe that it had a lot to do with altitude. The air being thin. Being so high. She'd rather not level too much responsibility against the many swigs of schnapps followed by a boozy fondue, for blurring her vision or influencing her actions. Would she have found Cat's colleague Alex attractive if she hadn't been wearing rose-tinted beer goggles? Or if her day hadn't been so multicoloured by the dramas of the race and the high spirits (and bottled spirits) of all those around her? Would she have found Alex attractive enough to accept even a second date if she'd met him back home? In the mundane light of everyday life, would she have had a one-night stand with him in London? Would she even *want* to see him again?

However, up there, back then, on top of a mountain, thawing out over a steaming cauldron of kirsch-drenched fondue, Pip thought Alex charming and attractive and a pleasure to match, flirt for flirt. She justified the fact that he smelt rather strongly of garlic as a pitfall of the limitations of the press buffets. Not his fault. Not a reflection of his personality. It wasn't as if it was something he *couldn't* help, like smelly feet. Garlic was simply an occupational hazard for the journalists, she decided.

'You don't half stink of garlic!' Pip said to him with a glint in her eye, nevertheless, as they were strolling back from the restaurant.

'The Alps,' he shrugged his broad shoulders, 'a breeding ground for vampires. With my hot blood, I need to take every precaution to keep them at bay.' His retort made Pip laugh and even like the garlicky wafts seeping from his skin and breath. 'Have you any vampire tendencies?' he asked her. 'Any links with Transylvania, however tenuous?'

'Derbyshire,' Pip told him, 'via Sutton Coldfield, originally,' she elaborated, pulling her hands into the sleeves of her fleece. It was cold up there in the thin air of the mountain top. 'And I can't say blood is among my favourite tipples.' Momentarily, Alex looked crestfallen. Pip couldn't think what she'd said that could have upset him so. 'Sutton Coldfield's not that bad – there are some quite nice parts,' she rushed, hoping to soften whatever blow it was she had unwittingly delivered, 'and Derbyshire is divine.' She unfurled the fingers of one hand from the fleece and touched his elbow.

'Huh?' Alex said. 'Oh. No. I was just sad that you are not even a fraction vampire.' He rubbed his brow and looked thoroughly perplexed. 'How am I going to get you to suck anything of mine now?'

Fen, Cat, Ben and the gang kept walking. Pip stopped dead in her tracks, gobsmacked and motionless in the theatrical throes of a long, silent, outraged laugh. Alex stopped too, all wide-eyed and winsome, or as much so as his lumbering six-foot-two-inch frame would allow. Once she was breathing again, clasping her chest for dramatic emphasis, Pip regarded Alex with mock shock horror delineating her features, sending added sparkle to her eyes, her mouth agape. Before she knew what was happening, but long before her sisters turned around to see where she was, Alex had plugged Pip's mouth with his tongue and given her right buttock an enthusiastic squeeze.

'My bed – bottom bunk – 2.00 a.m.,' he whispered, licking his lips and winking at her.

'Dream on!' Pip remonstrated. Though the fleece sleeves covered her fingers, she put her hands on her hips and held her head high in mock outrage. Alex's plan was, of course, one she planned to carry out, but she wasn't going to pamper his ego with even a quick 'OK'. She stomped past Alex in contrived indignation, but with a concerted wiggle nevertheless. She linked arms with her two sisters and the three McCabe girls walked jauntily to the apartment. Each had a spring to her step. Each felt a growing sense of liberation and *joie de vivre* that none had felt for some time. Too much altitude? Too little oxygen? Too much alcohol? Too little sleep? So what! Who cares! The combination was obviously a rather good one. The three McCabe girls went to bed that night with smiles on their faces and minds full of larky memories.

Pip wakes with a start. It's 4.00 a.m. How can that be? She's two hours late for her bunk bonk. How and when did she fall asleep in the first place? Never mind that she's only had three hours' sleep in almost twenty-four hours. She's bemused – she went to bed wide awake, willing Fen to fall asleep, watching the clock and imagining Alex yards away preparing a boudoir of debauchery for her. Instead, somehow, she fell dead asleep. Damn!

She lies in the bed she's sharing with Fen and listens to the lulled, rhythmic breathing of her sister sound asleep. Her heart is thuddering excitedly. The walls are thin. She can detect snoring from another room. Is it Alex? If so, isn't that a turn-off? And if it is him, doesn't it mean he's fast asleep? And if so, should she not wake him? After all, he has to go to work tomorrow. Say he wasn't serious in the first place? About 2.00 a.m.? About a bonk in his bunk? Dare she verify?

Which would benefit her more, sleep or sex? Pip pontificates at length until she wonders why on earth she's wasting time. It's now almost 4.15 a.m. Fen is still sound asleep. And whoever it is, is still snoring. Pip sidles from the bed and slips out of the bedroom. She's relieved to deduce that the snoring is not Alex's. His door is ajar. She eases it open, a breath of light coursing into the room and catching on his shoulders. He's in the bottom bunk. Facing away from her. His shoulders are masculine. He looks too big for the bed. The duvet is half on the floor, managing to cover his modesty whilst presenting a muscled back tapering to a neat waist.

Pip fights to suppress a giggle and a snort. She feels extremely naughty, all this tiptoeing and lip biting in the silent watches of the night. Will the floor creak? Will someone hear? Will someone catch them at it? She is holding her breath because she doesn't know if she wants to wake Alex or not, or whether or not he wants to be woken. She's well inside his room now; so far, so silent. She eases the door to almost closed. The room is plunged into darkness. Her eyes aren't adjusting but she knows the vague direction and distance to Alex. She pads across the floor. It's disturbingly gritty under her bare feet. Never mind. It's irrelevant. Really, *all* of this is somehow irrelevant – being so far from home, in a world as surreal as the entourage of the Tour de France.

For such a big bloke, Alex sleeps very delicately, his breathing less audible even than Fen's. Pip is chewing her lip, clenching and unclenching her fists, swallowing giggles, telling her heart to hush up – surely people in the valley below can hear it pounding excitedly against her chest. She can make out Alex's form without actually seeing him. She can sense the body heat emanating from the bunk. She thinks she can detect garlic. She bends down over him. The pattern of his breathing remains unchanged. Yes, she can smell garlic. She's so fired up she refuses to think of it as an unpleasant aroma. She stays motionless, trying to compose a rhyme or pun on 'vamp and vampire', on 'bunks and bonks', on 'better late than never'.

'Psst,' she hisses instead. 'Oi!' she whispers. 'Alex?'

He rolls over and reaches a sleep-hot hand up to her cheek. He shunts over and holds the sheets open. She can smell man – all pheromones and sweat and garlic. It's heady and thick and intoxicating and she's keen to be skin close. She slips between the sheets. The bed is narrow and though they manoeuvre themselves this way and that, no matter how they entwine their limbs, lying side by side is simply not possible. By the time they have found a comfortable configuration, Pip is actually lying on top of Alex, and they are snogging with such intensity that the position seems entirely appropriate anyway.

He's wearing pants – she knows they're not boxer shorts because in the dark her hands have figured out a great deal about his body. He appears to be clad in rather scanty briefs. She fleetingly thinks how, if the light was on, such a sight would surely be a turn-off. They may even be patterned! God forbid they were brown. Didn't all blokes do the boxer thing nowadays? At that ungodly hour, however, in the dark, on the top of L'Alpe D'Huez, it really didn't matter and Pip wouldn't have cared if Alex was wearing a lacy G-string. In brown.

They dry hump while they kiss. Alex's hands travel and explore her body energetically and hungrily. Pip uses her fingertips to determine him – the quality of his skin, the tone of his muscles, the hair on his stomach, the length and thickness of his cock straining against the elastic of his underwear. She eases his pants down, trying to banish the term 'posing pouch' which keeps goading her.

He's already done away with her T-shirt, and she wasn't wearing knickers, anyway. His hands sweep up and down over her outer thighs and then fondle her inner thighs more slowly. Grasping and feeling and kneading. She bucks her body and spreads her legs. She knows she is wet and ready and she rather wants his hands and his fingers to cut the courteous detours and head straight for the playground. Alex obliges and his manual dexterity makes Pip gasp. Do that again! It's still too dark to see, though as he touches her (God, do *that* again), she marvels at his long fingers. Longer than she remembers. Actually, she can't remember how his hands look in reality. She can't conjure a picture of them. She knows he doesn't bite his nails but she can't recollect any specific details. Just that his hands weren't really worth noticing, for one reason or another. Anyway, they're making a great impact on her now and surely that's the point of them.

She's thinking she ought to return the favour and pay his cock some attention. She'd be happy to. A tantalizing blow-job perhaps, with her body swung round so that he can feast on her simultaneously. A position she's never been hugely comfortable with, on account of it leaving everything open to the elements and to scrutiny. But that's with the light on. Or curtains open. On the bottom bunk on the top of the mountain, it's pitch black, remember. So Pip straddles him, facing his feet. She sucks his cock down deep until she's at risk of gagging. She thrusts her sex against his mouth, her bottom against his nose. He's groaning. She sucks and licks and tongues him with energy and imagination. He groans and pants. She feels rather proud. She rotates her pelvis and pushes against his face. He's moving vigorously, flinching, moaning, jerking. She all but suctions her nether regions against his face. He places his hands on her buttocks and shoves her away. 'Can't breathe!' he gasps, with an audible exclamation mark. 'Let's just shag, hey?'

Alex stumbles from the bed, muttering 'condoms' under his breath, heading off into the dark void of the room to try and locate them. Pip lies stock-still and silent. Alex bumps into something. 'Fuck!' He trips over something else. 'Wank!' He makes a terrible noise as he rummages around in some bag or other. 'Bugger, where are the sodding bloody things?' Pip is on the bottom bunk. Suddenly, she's all but blinded. Alex has switched the light on. It's a moment of blaring reality. He squints at her, she blinks back. His hair is all over the place. The neon light is brash and it buzzes. The room is horrible. Alex's stuff is everywhere. His bottom is hairy. His feet are huge. Pip sees it all in an instant and swiftly stares instead at the springs of the upper-level bunk. She's concentrating on not letting the moment go. She wants to come. He's searching through his bags, tossing out a fortnight's worth of dirty laundry.

'Bingo!' he mutters on retrieving a bashed packet of prophylactics of a brand Pip doesn't recognize.

Get on with it, Pip thinks. 'Switch the light off,' she whispers instead, as if it's a kinky idea, rather than absolutely crucial. Alex does so and clomps his way back to the bunk.

'Ouch! Wank!' he exclaims hoarsely, having first bumped his head, then scraped his shoulder, on the cold metal frame of the upper bunk. For Pip, the moment has now all but gone. She could so easily give him a peck on the cheek and crawl back to bed with Fen and fall asleep for a welcome few hours. But suddenly it's supremely important to bring to fruition what she set out to do. She wants to finish it with a full stop, not a comma. She'll just come. Then she'll go.

With a rustle and a jiggle and a snap or two, plus further fulminations, Alex is covered and ready for action. Penetration takes but one attempt and because of the height and width restrictions of the bed, they adopt a position that is deep and intense. They buck and hump. The mattress is lumpy but mercifully, the bed doesn't creak. Both Alex and Pip opt to keep as quiet as they can. It adds to the intensity. It's furtive and desperate and he drills into her while she grinds against him. She feels as though she's sucking him up high, he feels as though he's spearing her deep. Why is it called 'missionary'? There's nothing remotely pious about what they're doing.

'I'm close,' Pip murmurs, 'oh God!' Despite his uncouthness, the garlic, the swearing, the clumsiness, right at the right moment Alex reveals expert knowledge and sensitivity on how to intensify Pip's orgasm. He slows his pace right down and subtly changes the angle of thrust. As he senses her spasms subside, he picks up his own pace, rams into her and spurts. The fact that his cock jumps wildly, causes Pip's orgasm to reprise. The feeling is fantastic and intense. She's forgotten that the lights were ever on. That there's grit on the floor. That Alex is messy and scruffy and has huge ungainly feet and a hairy backside. What she can't deny is that he really does reek of garlic. She's suddenly very tired, aware that it's been a long day and there's another to follow. She kisses Alex on the cheek. 'That was rather nice!' she whispers.

'Night, Pip,' he replies sleepily, with gratitude. He's happy that she's off. The bed is far too small to accommodate two, even for the briefest post-coital cuddle.

'Goodbye, Alex,' Pip says quietly, with intent.

TWENTY-SIX

*S*o far, we've seen Pip with three very different men. In the East End. In her own bed. On top of a mountain. Although she would say that Caleb probably leads purely in terms of consistent erotic value, the orgasm with Alex actually ranks the highest. Though she'd currently dispute the final analysis, we can see that there is no contest with whom she has the best overall fit. Though she and Zac might just about recognize this, even if it is lurking in some far-flung region of their subconscious at present, the point is whether the accountant and the clown can digest humble pie and come together again to walk hand in hand into the sunset for us. Unfortunately, at this juncture, both have convinced themselves that they're not remotely bothered about seeing each other again. Neither actually thinks that there's even a future for a friendship now, let alone the potential for a relationship in the offing.

Currently, there's no way they'd even have a one-off, no-strings shag again. Pip has quite put Zac off her. And she's made her mountain-top shenanigans with Alex pale Zac into an insignificant slot in her past. Sexual sorbet. She had a bad taste in her mouth. She tells herself that the shag with Alex has cleared it and shoved Zac unceremoniously to the back of her mind. Or so she likes to think. If she thought otherwise, as indeed she did all too briefly in Derbyshire, she'd have to admit that the mess is of her own making – as are the amends. No. It's much easier to put the baggage into storage. And that's what she thinks she's done.

'Oh, hullo, is that Merry Martha the clown?'

'Speaking!'

'Hi there, this is June Price – we spoke a couple of weeks ago about my son's party?'

'Hold on a tick, I'll just fetch my diary.'

'This coming Sunday?'

'Sunday, Sunday. Ah yes! Tom.'

'Yup. Smashing – just to confirm a few details.'

'Absolutely – fire away!'

Pip has always enjoyed August for work. It might not be the most lucrative month, but it's certainly the most civilized. She detests December though she can easily double her normal wage. In August, there's as much outdoor work for a clown as indoor. Plus, by then the children are well relaxed into the pace of their summer holiday from school. Behaviour is usually very good. Energy levels have been managed by plenty of exercise and fresh air. Parks and clubs lay on special activities that are godsends for parents and treats for children. Being with friends becomes special and something to look forward to, rather than run-of-the-mill as in term-time. The beginning of August is a time long before boredom. Parents are usually revitalized by the proximity of a gorgeous vacation abroad. Moods are generally good throughout the households.

Pip has every reason to look forward to working on the first Sunday in August. The party is local. Swiss Cottage. She's not even needed till 3.30 p.m. There'll be only fifteen children. Thus she needn't be abstemious at the party Megan's throwing the night before. She can have a good lie-in *and* a leisurely time with the Sunday papers. She'll go to Covent Garden on Wednesday – she has no other appoint-ments that day. She'll buy something frivolous to wear (so what if it's just the once) to Megan's party. And she needs to replenish her supplies of slap. She's working Tuesday and Thursday as Dr Pippity, of course. Friday morning she'll be at Brent Cross shopping centre, hired by a children's boutique to pull in the punters. No problem.

'Oh, hi, this is a message for Merry Martha. Hullo, it's June Price here – about the party on Sunday. Can you give me a quick ring at some point? Just want to discuss a few more details. Thanks so much. Oh, it's now Thursday. Tea-time. Thanks. Bye.'

Pip returned Mrs Price's call on Friday afternoon. Brent Cross had been frantic but fun and she'd been paid cash there and then.

'Mrs Price? Merry Martha here.' Pip had the telephone tucked under her chin whilst she wound tissues between her toes. She was giving herself a pedicure. After she'd finished clowning in Brent Cross, she'd popped into the branch of Fenwick's there. With all that cash in hand, she'd treated herself to some Chanel nail polish. Rouge Noir. Reassuringly expensive. Now, with phone secured between ear and shoulder, Pip was gliding the varnish on in slicks the consistency of crude oil and the luscious hue of aubergine.

'Ah,' said Mrs Price, who envisaged Merry Martha taking the call dressed as Merry Martha, 'thanks for getting back to me.'

'Is everything OK for Sunday?' Pip asked, neatening up her little toenail by removing a tiny fleck of stray nail polish with her thumbnail. 'I've bought new batteries for my light-up nose!'

'Wonderful!' Mrs Price laughed. 'My son – Tom, the birthday boy, of course – wanted me to ask you if you'd be doing balloons.'

'Of course! No birthday is complete without balloons.'

Mrs Price sighed with relief. 'He always keeps them –

even when they're flat and squidgy. Your parrot is his favourite. He's had a couple of them.'

'Oh?' Pip said. 'Has he seen me before, then?'

'Gosh, yes!' Mrs Price enthused. 'You're his best birthday wish come true!'

'How lovely,' Pip smiled, three toes done, seven to go. Maybe she'd do her fingernails, too. 'I'll make sure it's a party to remember.'

'On a personal level,' Mrs Price confided, 'I'm so looking forward to him having a clown at home rather than hospital.'

Pip paused, varnish brush loaded, hovering. 'Hospital?' she asked.

'Yes,' said Mrs Price, 'Tom knows you foremost as Dr Pippity.'

'Tom?'

'I mean, I doubt whether you'd know him – you must see so many kids,' Mrs Price continued almost apologetically. 'My son Tom has treatment at St Bea's,' she explained, 'for eczema.'

A glob of nail polish fell in slow motion from the brush. It hit the sofa. It was followed by another drip. Which fell on the carpet. Two drops. Darker and thicker than blood. As a stain, even more difficult to remove.

'Tom,' Pip repeated, unable to make sense of the spilt polish, or the identity of the child; the word 'eczema' echoing cacophonously around her head.

'As I said,' Mrs Price repeated warmly, 'you must see so many children, I doubt whether you'd remember him. Though you might when you see him. He's so gorgeous, even if I do say so myself. Proud mum and all that!'

'Actually, I *do* know Tom,' Pip said distractedly, absent-mindedly coating an expanse of toe, almost down to the joint, with nail varnish. 'Hermione from Harry Potter. He like Hermione.'

'Yes!' Mrs Price exclaimed, exuding gratitude. 'Hermione! That'll be Tom. He's so excited about his party – I can't tell you.'

'Tell him I'll see him on his birthday,' Pip said in a monotone voice she couldn't help. 'Tell Tom I'm looking forward to it, too.'

No, she wasn't. Pip wasn't looking forward to the party at all. If there was any way she could get out of it, she would. She regarded her six painted toes, three of which were horrendously smudged and messy. She stared at the spilt polish. She didn't have the energy or inclination to finish her pedicure or set to work on the stains on her sofa and carpet. She sat there, the brush out of the bottle, drying out, wondering if there was any way she could cancel her Sunday booking. In fact, there were plenty of ways – she simply had to choose one, and quickly. She could phone in with fictitious flu or a made-up migraine or an imaginary sprained ankle. She could call Fizzie Lizzie and ask her if she'd like the job instead. And if Fizzie Lizzie, ever busy and popular, couldn't help, Pip could try Bo Jingles – she was local. As was Betty Brown Clumsy Clown. She was great with balloons. There were many possibilities. But Pip knew that none would do. If she hadn't heard firsthand that Tom himself was so excited, if she hadn't been asked on Tom's behalf about the sodding balloons, cancelling would have been no problem. But the boy was looking forward to Merry Martha making his day. So how on earth could Pip McCabe refuse?

Pip observed the entry for Sunday in her diary: 'Price Party, 3.30 p.m. Swiss Cott. (Tom / 6 yrs).'

Was there any way she really could have put two and two together? No. No clues at all. The surname Holmes hadn't been mentioned; the location was Swiss Cottage, not Hampstead. It was Tom's mother who was organizing it. Mrs Price had mentioned her husband; however, the father of her child had not come up in conversation by name or status. There had been no opportunity for Pip to have even an inkling of anything untoward or unconventional. Let alone that this woman had borne the child of the man Pip herself had bedded.

Momentarily, Pip harboured a faint hope that maybe Tom's broken home was just that – dysfunctional parents divvying up alternate birthdays, alternate Christmases, weekends, bank holidays, whatevers. That this year it was the mother's turn. Hopefully, Zac was *persona non grata* and had no invitation, let alone access, to his son's sixth birthday party. But Pip swiftly cursed herself. That wasn't wishful thinking, it was utterly unpleasant and cruel. She was ashamed. Even if they weren't together, Tom's parents provided him with a stable and loving childhood, surely.

Pip thought back to that time in the hospital – the first time when Zac had asked her out, having stalked her through Out-patients and up to the renal ward. Asked her out for a drink. Orangey-lemony-blackcurrant squash. Hadn't both parents been with Tom then? She'd had no idea they were anything other than a conventional happy family. Which was precisely why Zac's approach and overture back then had appeared so unsavoury to Pip. Pip let her gaze fall on the sorry state of her half-varnished toes. What a bloody mess. The simplest fact was the most logical – June Price, with whom the child lived, had organized his sixth birthday party at home. You wouldn't fit fifteen children in Zac's sitting-room, after all. The Eames lounger wouldn't cope. It wouldn't be fair on the banana chair. Parking was a nightmare. There was only the one bay and that was for his Audi.

Pip replaced the brush in the bottle of nail polish. She placed it in the waste-paper basket. Again, she scrutinized the booking as it was written in her appointments diary. It was glaringly obvious from the phone calls that Tom's mother had no idea that the clown she'd hired for her son's sixth birthday, the very clown who had brought him so much pleasure and comfort, had in fact had sex with her ex-partner, Tom's father. Twice. Pip realized that June Price, therefore, wouldn't have a clue that now the clown and the ex-partner were both harbouring a strong desire never to see each other again. Mrs Price would never have given Merry Martha the gig, had she known.

And, had she known, she certainly wouldn't have told Zac to bring his South African 'friend' along with him.

Fuck fuck fuck. I can't cancel now. Bugger bollocks. Of course Zac will be there. Shit shit shit. There's nail varnish everywhere.

TWENTY-SEVEN

And what does Zac know of the birthday festivities for his son? Nothing at all. Just that June has devoted her life, or the past month at the very least, to organizing everything. What luxury to leave it all in his ex-partner's capable hands. Trips to Waitrose, Tesco, Asda, M&S and Sainsbury's. Cake ordering. Entertainment organizing. Goody-bag stuffing. Invites and chase-ups. Bulk purchasing of wet wipes. Not to mention the post-party-fall-out clean-up operation. June has seen to it all, and done so with aplomb, good grace, boundless energy and great results.

'Just turn up, Zac,' she's told him, 'and bring that new one – Julietta-ana – by all means.'

Juliana is happy to attend the party – she had nothing else planned and, with London in August being so dead, it seemed unlikely that any viable alternatives would materialize. Anyway, she could check out Zac's ex-partner and wish his son a happy birthday in one fell swoop. However, she had no desire to traipse around Toys "R" Us. That was well beyond the call of duty. She'll meet Zac later on. She'll go and have a massage first. La Stone therapy.

Zac is spending his Sunday morning alone in the toy superstore wondering how many automated model dumper trucks a six-year-old can have. Wouldn't he like Lego? A jigsaw? No, Tom wants dumper trucks. He already has a veritable fleet.

'Maybe he's going into business,' Zac laughs out loud. 'My son Tom, the Eddie Stobart of model trucks and tractors!'

Actually, Zac is standing in the middle of the dolls aisle, staring absent-mindedly at a doll that the packaging proclaims 'Makes pee pee. Cries. Says Mamma. Realistically. Requires 2 AA batteries'. The doll isn't remotely realistic. It's quite frightening, really, with a pug-ugly face, staring eyes and a granny's hairdo. But Zac is preoccupied with the image of Tom as a truckie and he's enjoying another hearty chuckle. A mother standing nearby fixes him with a look of mistrust and ushers her young daughter away. Zac doesn't notice. He heads for the model cars and finds a smorgasbord crammed with them. After great deliberation, he chooses a green machine. He's fairly sure there's not one similar – in hue, form or multifunctions – in his son's collection. It requires four AA batteries, which can only be a good thing. Zac feels he's found the ultimate present and he's proud. He heads for Hampstead, spending ages in a variety of shops en route in pursuit of the perfect birthday card. It's almost lunch-time. He told June he'd arrive just after lunch. So he could have some quality one-to-one time with his son, the brand new six-year-old, before the party begins.

June Price's front doorbell goes.

'Can someone get that?' she shouts through from her kitchen. 'I'm having an icing crisis!'

'I'll go,' Zac offers, leaving Tom enthralled with his shiny green dumper truck while his stepfather Rob-Dad is engrossed in constructing impressive garaging from empty present boxes. Zac goes to the front door.

There stands Juliana.

There stands Pip.

Pip and Juliana are stood on the doorstep.

Pip and Juliana are standing there, side by side, right in

front of Zac. Though he blinks hard, it doesn't make a blind bit of sense.

Where are you going to look, Zac? What are you going to say?

Fuck me.

Luckily, he says that to himself.

Pip and Juliana. Juliana and Pip. Pip in jeans and a T-shirt. Juliana in Joseph.

'Hi,' he says, not looking at either woman, staring over both their heads instead, 'come on in.'

The three of them hovered in the hallway until June came through from the kitchen. For a woman emerging from the midst of intricate icing issues, she looked remarkably composed – and clean. Mahogany hair swishing around her face in a meticulous bob, radiant skin, eyes sparkling behind fashionably frameless spectacles, a genuine smile subtly enhanced by just a lick of lipstick.

'Hullo,' June greeted them cordially, 'hullo.' She shook Juliana's hand first, then Pip's. 'Nice to meet you,' she told the former, 'fantastic to see you,' she told the latter. 'Zac, you settle Juliana – I'll take Martha up to change.'

'Pip,' Zac said. June didn't say 'pardon' because she was used to Zac's quirky expressions and presumed that to be one.

'My name is Pip when I'm like *this*,' said Pip, patting her T-shirt. Zac stared at her, June regarded her thoughtfully, Juliana wasn't remotely interested. 'Merry Martha, like Dr Pippity, is my clown,' Pip explained, holding up her bag, brimming with props and costume, for emphasis.

June nodded. 'What's your real name, then?' she asked, because she didn't think that 'Pip' could be a real name. Actually, she's right, in a way.

'Philippa,' Pip said with a weary sigh. She suddenly felt too fuddled to explain or justify. She was acutely aware of Zac's proximity. How deluded must she have been, she wondered, to presume that she'd never have to see him again? She might well be allowed to disappear and change and reappear in her wacky alter ego, but she'd still have to share the same orbit for the rest of the afternoon. She felt as tired as if she'd just performed and done an encore for forty children. 'Philippa McCabe,' she said to June, hoping that would be enough.

It satisfied June. 'Come on, Ms McCabe, let's get you settled.'

As Zac led Juliana through to the sitting-room, he thought how he had never heard Pip refer to herself by her full name. It sounded odd. Too many syllables or something. Too mature or sophisticated, somehow. Out of sorts with the girl he knew. Philippa. It sounded so rounded, feminine. But Pip suited her better. It was punchy and bright and complemented her personality, rhyming with 'zip' and 'flip' and 'hip' – all of which defined her. As well as 'blip', which Zac tells himself sternly is all she'd been.

Now, take Juliana – there, even more syllables. And undeniably more mature, indisputably more sophisticated, ultimately less complex. Who cared that nothing seemed to rhyme with her name – neither she nor he had any delusions of poetry between them. Zac took Juliana through to see the birthday boy, whom she greeted in the same demure manner she'd employ to greet a forty-year-old. Friend, colleague, stranger, lover, child – she gave each her beautifully manicured hand to hold. Zac was slightly disappointed that she chose to sit by the window and flip through one of June's glossy magazines. She expressed no interest in the truck, the day, the garaging. Rob-Dad seemed to catch her eye temporarily, though he remained far more engrossed in his cardboard architecture. Tom, however, didn't seem to notice, let alone care – and that, thought Zac, was the main thing, surely.

June was so open and friendly towards Pip, taking her to the kitchen for a cup of coffee, nattering away as she led her up to the spare room, that Pip felt almost obliged to inform her of the history with Zac to save any future embarrassment. Of course, she did no such thing. But she immediately warmed to June and half wondered why Zac and she were not together. To Pip, they seemed to have all the attributes of a very good couple.

It's a bit sad, isn't it – but something of a phenomenon, too, I think – that you often see a couple who seem so well suited but who just can't keep it together.

Yes, Pip, or even get it together in the first place.

'This is the spare room,' June announced, 'though it's hardly spare – it is an essential rather than surplus space where we unceremoniously dump all our stuff.' She took Pip into the room almost proudly. 'Actually, it's one of my favourite places in the house. It's the contents that make it so. I spend hours in here, mooching and reminiscing. I can't work out whether it's cathartic or a bit pathetic.' She gestured to a wall stacked to the ceiling with boxes. 'Books, photo albums, baby clothes, all my university English files and essays, Rob's collection of model cars, mine of wooden ducks.' June rubbed her brow. 'My grandmother's wedding dress is in that trunk. Moiré taffeta and stunning. I suppose I should be ruthless and unsentimental and chuck the lot. But would you?'

Pip shook her head vehemently. 'Luckily, I have my childhood home in Derbyshire to amass all the stuff I wouldn't dream of chucking out – which is basically everything I've ever owned.'

June laughed. 'I mean, I'll put money on my husband never using that sodding windsurf board again – he has no sense of balance, let alone sea legs, or much affinity with the water at all!' Pip leant her back against something – a cot. 'I guarantee you, that will never be used again!' June proclaimed. Pip looked a little startled until June made a scissors-snipping gesture with her fingers and winked at her. 'Do you have children?' she asked Pip.

'No,' Pip confirmed, a pregnant pause causing her to wonder whether she ought to justify or explain.

'I just have the one,' June said, 'but not with my husband – with the bloke who let you in. My ex.'

Pip nodded as if she was only vaguely interested and far more concerned with slurping her tea. Suddenly, though, she wondered how June and Zac's relationship *did* work; logistically, emotionally. Also, why it *hadn't* worked. And the fact that they weren't together – but obviously remained fond of each other and in constant contact – how on earth did *that* work? How was so little visible damage possible? Pip knew this was probably a perfect time to probe – before any details were revealed about herself and Zac. Yet there seemed little point. There was nothing between them. And that, she had to concede, was the point. Just a coincidence that she was there today. That Zac was the father of the kid. Yet still Pip felt awkward.

'It's cool,' shrugged June, who had warmed immediately to Philippa far more than she had to the willowy South African. 'Zac – Tom's dad – and my husband get along fine and always have. I think I'm lucky that the only two men I've ever been serious about are so well-balanced and sorted within themselves. Plus that my son has two fantastic fathers – the lucky little bugger!'

Please don't ask me if I'm involved with anyone.

Pip desperately searched the room in a glance for some interesting possession or other that would serve to change the topic of conversation. And distract her from considering the words 'well-balanced' and 'sorted' being used in conjunction with Zac.

'Are you involved with anyone?' June asked.

'No, no,' Pip said breezily, physically brushing the question away with a swipe of her hand, 'haven't really had the time or the inclination recently.'

'Mind you,' June said, wistful, even gently jealous, 'I half envy you all that peace and quiet. The fact that you need answer to no one but yourself – you need *think* of no one but yourself. Just the thought of luxuriating in a bath every single bloody day! It's an in-and-out job for me,' she bemoaned. 'Rather like sex once you're married,' she continued, with good comic timing and a facial expression to match. 'I ought to let you transform yourself into Merry Martha,' June apologized. 'The bathroom's next door along. Are you sure you have everything? There's loads of cotton wool and all manner of potions and lotions – just help yourself.'

Pip assured her she was well stocked. She liked June instantly; she could well imagine her easily fitting into girls' nights with her sisters and pals. Pip swiftly decided to blame Zac for spoiling this potential.

'Thanks,' Pip said, 'thanks for the coffee. And the chat. Sometimes, I'm ignored – shoved into a broom cupboard and just as soon shoved out the front door.'

'Nightmare,' June murmured with genuine concern. 'You can stay for tea, if you like. Now I'm going down to scrutinize Juliana – that woman you came in with? She's my ex – Zac's – new squeeze and I'm intrigued. Gorgeous shoes and amazing legs – the cow. But that's all I've clocked so far. I'm hoping she has unfortunate teeth. Or no personality.' With that, she grinned at Pip and turned for the door. 'It's odd, isn't it – I mean, I have no desires, latent or otherwise, for Zac. No way! Not in the slightest. In fact, I'd love to see him happily settled.' June was then momentarily distracted by some forgotten possession or other peeking out of a storage box. She shook her head to restore her to the present. Pip would have shaken her otherwise for the same effect – she was hanging on her every word. 'Yes, I'd love Zac to find – or at least embrace – the kind of stability and life I've found,' June theorized, 'and yet there will always be something just a little galling about him having glamorous girlfriends.' She bit her lip as if she'd revealed some deplorable side of her personality. 'Actually,' she continued, 'it probably comes down to me being a bitch. I'm sure Aesop has a suitable fable! Dog in a manger? I don't know – more like, I'm happy for him to feast all he likes, as long as it's bland!'

Pip McCabe feels horribly, disastrously, helplessly bland. She wants to slump herself down in a self-pitying heap.

Unfortunately, she chooses an old Space Hopper and thus has to do a fair bit of precarious balancing which makes her feel all the more ungainly. Lovely, attractive, bubbly June. A child. A fulfilling marriage. A mature relationship with an ex. A three-bedroom house. A spare room with memories she's not embarrassed by. A skill with cake icing. Suddenly, Pip wants to be June.

Juli-bloody-ana. Pip had no idea. She'd've analysed her painstakingly had she known. She had assumed the slightly aloof, fabulously coutured slender woman was a mother of a party-goer. It hadn't crossed Pip's mind that she was in any way attached to Zac. She didn't recognize Juliana as the woman Zac was with at the cinema that time. Not that she'd taken much notice. She hadn't once stopped to wonder if Zac was seeing someone else more recently. Since they'd slept together. She hadn't actually stopped to wonder what he was up to. If he was even happy or in good health. She'd confined him to a closed moment in time, locked him in a dim part of her mind – and hadn't presumed reality to treat him any differently. She hadn't bothered to consider that he might not be at the party on his own. That his life might well be a party. She hadn't stopped to think that he'd be utterly capable of moving on, of inviting other women into his bed. Of forgetting all about Pip. Had Juliana been treated to cream tea and A Flock of Seagulls? A rather private teenagery side of Pip suddenly wondered petulantly whether Zac actually liked Juliana more than he'd ever liked her.

Sitting up there, she tried to stabilize herself on the Space Hopper whilst trying to kid herself she was stable in herself. To maintain a brooding melancholy was no mean feat, but her acrobatic abilities helped. Somehow, she felt diminished; in her mind's eye she elongated, elevated and further beautified Juliana. She was sure, if she ventured downstairs, she'd confront a vamp of proportions to rival Elle MacPherson. No doubt embroiled with Zac in erotic kissing imbued with a healthy, rare mix of tenderness and desire. Pip even looked out of the window to see if there was a flat roof to jump on to, or a fire-escape to make her exit by. But she could hear the doorbell ringing, and the squawks and falsetto chattering of a growing number of six-year-olds.

I feel horribly uneasy. Like a child who does not want to perform. I feel very alone and rather small, by myself in this room, in this house. With all of them downstairs. I don't want to be here! I want to go home! I want to do a disappearing act, not clown around in front of Zac. June. And Juli-bloody-ana.

If you weren't so fiercely private, you could be on the phone now, to any of your friends and sisters. For comfort and support. Advice and a game plan. But they have no idea of your situation because you've fastidiously locked them out.

Zac and I ended badly. Things like that happen. All the time. But we can't change that.

Yes, you can.

Whatever. Never mind. It doesn't matter. Look at the time. This is work. And with a bit of slap and a change of clothes, I can let Merry Martha take over for the afternoon and give myself a break.

Actually, Pip, you need to give yourself a hard time before you've earned a break.

Pip prevaricated over walking downstairs, finally making a very slow passage indeed towards her audience. She walked with the deliberation of someone trying not to damage eggshells, or of someone trying not to be damaged by a carpet of broken glass; as if every step had the potential to turn into a stumble, as if she was wearing incredibly high heels with a restrictive gown. Pip, however, was in motley and clumpy shoes. Every step, however slow or tiny, was bringing her nearer to a place she'd rather be far from, closer to a man she didn't want to see again, to his new girlfriend who high-lighted all her own inadequacies, to his ex-partner who symbolized all that she didn't have and most likely never would have. For the first time in her professional life, Pip was dreading taking centre stage. She felt sure she was to be the laughing stock. It felt as though she was falling, falling flat and flailing and fast.

She'd applied her slap as meticulously as ever. Dressed herself carefully and festooned herself with the tricks of her trade. But for the first time in her career, Pip knew she had merely painted on a clown mask. She was simply wearing fancy dress. The notion was appalling.

Merry Martha hadn't come through that afternoon. Pip was on her own. Surely, everyone would be able to see behind the painted smile. June wouldn't have her money's worth. Tom's expectations and memories would be dashed. Only Juli-bloody-ana would be satisfied. This, however, was on the assumption that Pip had been important enough to Zac to be known of by his new girlfriend. Pip then supposed Zac probably didn't give a shit. That she hadn't been important enough for him to mention to his current girlfriend. Please God, then, let him not even care to watch her act. Pip was resigned to feeling lousy. For the next hour or so in a full house. As well as home alone later. And for God knows how long after that.

* * *

It's interesting how one party, in one location, can mean so many different things to those who are there.

Without exception (apart from perhaps a small boy who threw up after one marshmallow too many), the children had a ball that afternoon; a stupendous, overexcited time of it.

Pip, though, loathed every moment. Pretending to be Merry Martha was as difficult as if she had chosen any other existing clown to impersonate. Usually, Martha simply took over Pip and the act tumbled along naturally. This afternoon, every joke, each trick, the lilt of her voice, every song and whistle, required immense strength of character combined with ten years of experience to pull off.

Zac felt supremely irritated – he felt denied the chance just to enjoy the festivities for Tom's sake and on Tom's level. He resented the fact that he had to consciously think about where he was looking. He really didn't want to catch Pip's eye. But he felt obliged to catch Juliana's though he had no desire to do so. He didn't want to answer when his ex-partner sidled up to him and said, 'Cool clown – look how delighted Tom is!' Ruth's wink-wink-nudge-nudging was near-unbearable. When she elbowed him during an elaborate part of Pip's act, he felt like shoving her back. Halfway across the room and out into the hallway. He hated himself for frequently checking his watch. He shouldn't be wishing his son's sixth birthday party would be over.

Juliana was plain bored. She found the noise level intolerable and the food stomach-turning. She found June disappointingly mumsy and her new husband good-looking but gormless. These people were not her type. Their life was not one she coveted. She was slightly put off Zac because of his inextricable links here. Tom didn't interest her at all. She felt nothing towards him, really. He was a kid. What could you add to that?

June was exhausted and delighted – her happiness directly proportionate to the breadth and longevity of the youngsters' smiles. She craved no acknowledgement for her organizational skills. She just wanted to witness their smiles and the excitable yacking. She wanted Tom to proclaim this day the best in his life.

Rob-Dad simply thought it was all rather jolly. He even managed to sneak off unnoticed every now and then to catch up on some lap or other of the Grand Prix.

Tom was in seventh heaven. Or sixth, rather. It was his special day and everyone was ensuring he didn't forget it for a moment. The presents were fantastic! And look at all this stuff Mum's done to eat! And almost best of all, the clown – his clown – in his own front room, with balloons and songs and brilliantly stupid tricks. Tom threw himself into the vortex of his party, letting the action and the affection revolve around him. It was the best day of his life. No, the very best day was the one when the bandages came off. This, then, was the second-best day of his life. And anyway, he was six now, near enough a big boy, he'd be growing out of his eczema soon, wouldn't he.

Out of all the guests, of any age, it was perhaps Ruth who was enjoying the party the most because it delighted her on so many different levels. She adored her nephew, Tom, and it was wonderful to see him so bright-eyed and his skin so good. She adored his father – her brother-in-law. And loved the house. And June's cooking. And June. And what icing on the cake Juliana provided! Ample fodder for Ruth and June to nip off to the kitchen later for furtive bouts of analysis and general deconstruction. And if there was a cherry on the top, then the clown girl was it. Ruth didn't know whether to watch Merry Martha perform, or to observe Billy and Tom's pleasure in her act, or to scrutinize Zac's reaction to her, or assess how much Juliana knew. Or should she just grab June's elbow, haul her out to the kitchen and reveal all? Once she'd seen Billy and Tom's jaw-dropped delight in the entertainer and had observed Zac shuffle uneasily, checking his watch for the umpteenth time; once she'd seen Juliana stifle yet another yawn and smirk at some of the soft furnishings in the house, Ruth grabbed June and mouthed, 'Kitchen! Now!'

June couldn't quite believe what she was hearing.

'Backtrack, backtrack!' she demanded, rooting through a drawer for a bottle opener while tearing off the collar on a bottle of Semillon with her teeth. 'You're telling me that the clown and Zac have had some kind of fling?'

Ruth nodded.

'Like, with dates?' June tried to make sense.

Ruth nodded vigorously, grateful for a good glug of wine.

'And sex?' June asked, taking a swig direct from the bottle before filling a glass.

Ruth was wide-eyed, her head bobbing as though she was utterly drunk already.

'My *ex*? Tom's *clown*?' June tried to fathom, downing wine as if it were juice. 'Have had *sex*?'

Ruth grinned. 'Yup, a couple of times, I think.'

'How?' June marvelled.

Ruth cocked an eyebrow. 'I guess he put his willy in her—'

'Yes, yes!' June laughed. 'But how on earth did my ex get it together with a clown? *This* clown. Or how in hell's name did the clown come by my ex?'

Ruth shrugged. 'I think it's been quite some story,' she said reflectively.

June paused for a moment. 'Sounds like it.' She took a contemplative sip. 'Actually, I instinctively really like the clown,' she said, 'even more so now I've met Juliana. The Willowy One seems to me to be on the patronizing side of aloof – I can't imagine sharing chocolate, wine and gossip with her. But I have a hunch Pip is much more on our wavelength.'

'Snap,' said Ruth. 'Actually, I've watched Juliana cast all sorts of withering looks over your fixtures and fittings. Like she disapproves.'

'There again,' said June, ever the diplomat, 'maybe she just has an awkward manner. Maybe she's just shy? I mean, perhaps Zac really likes her. Though I can't see what he sees in her – apart from the obvious!'

The two women looked at each other and then laughed.

'But,' June continued, 'unfortunately, it seems that Pip is in Zac's past tense.'

'And he does seem incredibly tense,' Ruth mused.

'Right, thinking hats on,' June said. 'God, poor Philippa – she'll be mortified when she finds out that I know. I was giving her all sorts of gory details upstairs.'

'A clown and an accountant,' Ruth declared. 'Doesn't look particularly promising on paper, does it?'

June considered this. 'Agreed. Plus the fact that something has obviously gone awry,' she reasoned. 'Any ideas or info?'

'I don't know,' Ruth replied, 'I mean, Zac doesn't really "do" details, does he?'

June chinked glasses with Ruth and they sipped their wine while they set their minds to scheming.

'Well, for starters,' June said with a sly lick of her lips, 'we need to throw them together – I could always pretend not to have any cash and could my ex possibly pay the clown for services rendered?'

'But wouldn't they both be mortified?' Ruth gasped.

June meant no malice. 'My thinking is that if it's an outside party making them feel awkward, then they'll seek some kind of solace in each other,' June revealed. 'Perhaps. Sort of. I hope. You never know.'

'Well, it's worth a try,' Ruth conceded, 'it'll get them alone and talking at any rate.' They returned to the mêlée. Merry Martha was doing a handstand. June and Ruth looked at each other in triumph. They were on the right track. It wasn't just the children who were trying to look up her skirt. Or was it down, from that angle? Ruth and June observed that the father of the birthday boy, whether subconsciously or otherwise, appeared to be gazing at her gusset, too.

'Zac,' June whispered, sidling up to him, 'would you mind awfully paying the clown? Rob and I are out of cash – we spent it all at Sainsbury's.' Zac regarded June. Utter horror zigzagged across his brow and made a gaping aperture of his mouth. 'Thanks so much,' June said artlessly, squeezing his arm, 'much appreciated.' Still Zac looked appalled. 'You do have cash, don't you?' June asked with contrived innocence. Zac baulked and frowned and couldn't say a word but he checked his wallet and there were obviously enough twenty-pound notes for the fee. 'You're a star,' June said. 'I'll pay you back. I've asked the clown to stay for tea, too.'

TWENTY-EIGHT

*P**lease please please don't let her stay for tea.*

Zac was practically choking on birthday cake.

Please please please let me be able to leave without bumping into him.

Pip was taking her make-up off as quickly, if not as thoroughly, as she could. Stay for tea? Not likely!

She descended the stairs to the hallway as noiselessly as possible. Which was a stupid thing to do, really, as it meant that no one heard her and therefore no one knew she wanted to go and needed to be paid. She gave a little cough. But the racket coming from the kitchen was such that even a fully voiced 'hullo' from the hallway would have gone unheard. Pip felt down and defeated.

If I had less pride and more dignity, maybe I'd just go without being paid. Fuck it, they can send a cheque in the post.

But wouldn't you be more noticeable by your disappearance? Wouldn't they wonder why?

Oh great. Just great. Fucking marvellous. This is all I need.

'Hi,' says the Willowy One, emerging from the guest WC in the hall.

The One in Jeans, with hair jutting this way and that, traces of make-up clinging here and there, simply raises her hand in a humble wave.

Juliana looks a little puzzled. 'You OK?'

'Just dandy,' Pip replies flatly, trying not to notice the extraordinary length of the woman's legs, nor how flawless her complexion or fine her bust, trying to turn deaf ears to the description 'sultry vamp' which is in her mind. 'Just getting ready to go home,' Pip says. This is good enough for Juliana who returns to the party. It is of some consolation to Pip, however puerile, that Juliana has left a noticeable smell in the guest cloakroom.

'That clown is hovering by the front door,' Juliana tells June.

'Tell Zac, will you?' June asks Juliana.

'That clown is hovering by the front door,' Juliana tells Zac.

Zac tries to catch June's eye but his ex-partner is deep in conversation with Ruth. He looks at Juliana. She looks bored. Suddenly, he feels strongly that even if she is bored, she shouldn't show it. It is Tom's birthday, for Christ's sake. His son, after all. Zac leaves the kitchen.

Pip is standing by the front door, taking an inordinate interest in a fairly nondescript brass finger-plate. Zac clears his throat. She turns and stares before her eyes dart this way and that. He looks pissed off and she feels uncomfortable.

'You all right?' he asks perfunctorily. 'Juliana said you looked like you were loitering.'

'I'm fine!' Pip says. 'Juliana was coming out of the loo as I came downstairs.'

An awkward silence ensues. It saddens Pip who suddenly remembers vividly the daft phone calls she's shared with this man. The ease at which they've bantered late at night or over tea. How kind he was when she was sobbing on the bench near his office. The delight he's taken in her work. Snogging in his car. The fact that he does breakfast in bed. Of his own accord. With excellent coffee. That he decants milk from carton to china. She glances across at him, a sensation welling inside her that could very well spill into an audible apology if only she'd let it. But she sees that he's fidgeting and so she finds it easier to tell herself that he'd rather she bugger off than do declarations.

'I'm just going,' she says, tipping her head and trying to smile in a gentle way. 'Please say "goodbye" to Tom. He looks so well – his skin has improved dramatically since I last saw him. And thank June – she's great.'

Zac nods – his son and ex-partner *are* great. He leans against the wall, hands in pockets, one leg bent nonchalantly. But his easy posture belies his discomfort. He hasn't made eye contact with Pip. He's spoken to the top of her head, the middle of her T-shirt, her shoes, a dent in the front door just to the right of her. He takes out his wallet. 'June's out of cash,' he says quietly.

'A cheque will do!' Pip declares, not wanting Zac to pay her, cash or otherwise. The concept is horrendous. It's not just that she feels suddenly dirty, or cheap – but more that she believes if she accepts money from Zac a formality will then exist which will supersede any vestige of friendship. They'll become little more than business acquaintances.

'It's cool,' Zac shrugs, thumbing through the notes.

'Honestly! Please!' Pip pleads, though an image of that month's red bills looms large in her mind's eye. 'Tell June to pop a cheque in the post.'

'She likes to honour her debts,' Zac explains.

'I trust her!' Pip cries.

'She's insisting,' Zac says firmly, approaching Pip with the money. Pip can't back away because she's pressed against the door as it is. 'Here,' says Zac, 'take it. Tom's had a brilliant party. Thank you.'

Reluctantly, Pip takes the money and shoves it in her back pocket. 'Pleasure,' she says quietly.

Zac backs away. He passes the guest WC and wrinkles his nose, shutting the door firmly. Temporarily, Pip experiences an odd sense of satisfaction, of one-upmanship over Juliana. But it's only fleeting. Why should it be otherwise – Juliana is with Zac and Pip is heading home on her own. 'See you around, then,' Zac says, turning.

'Bye,' Pip mumbles because there's no opening for small talk, let alone a chat. She tries to open the door but she's all thumbs. Zac does it for her. The afternoon sunlight hits them, rendering them momentarily blind. Pip descends the short flight of steps to the street jerkily, blinking. She glances back at Zac. He's hovering at the door. Good, she thinks, good. Hovering could well be the first step to wavering. She raises her hand to wave and puts a smile on her face. 'Ta-ta,' she says.

'Cheerio,' he replies, hands in pockets but shoulders relaxed. She feels her spirits lift.

That's such a Zac thing to say – 'cheerio'.

She turns back to say something else. She's not sure what. Anything. Whatever. But the door has been closed and Zac has gone.

TWENTY-NINE

*P*ip is back at her flat again. Slumped down on her sofa, emotionally and physically exhausted; grateful for the tranquillity and thankful for solitude. She sits and stares at nothing in particular, unable to prevent a barrage of images from her recent past from rampaging across her mind's eye. Caleb, Zac, Alex. London, Derbyshire, France. Fen, Cat, Django. Megan, Dominic. Dr Pippity, Merry Martha. Tom, Billy. Hoxton, Hampstead. Lights off, curtains open. Hospital wards, accountancy offices. Text messages, tea for two. Cheesy music and cheesy Doritos. Laughing, crying. Shower curtains, bunk beds. It's been a funny few months; colourful, for sure. The look and feel. The smells and sounds. The different tastes. A matter of taste. What matters. What is it that matters? What's the matter?

Dragging her gaze outwards, Pip is suddenly struck by the monotony and bland beigeness of her surroundings. She is aware of a bad taste now, lingering in her mouth. Over the years, she could have gone for colour but she has obsessively settled for neutrality. She's kidded herself it's classy and mature, won't date and will camouflage flaws. But now she thinks it's all a bit bloody boring. And slightly drab around the edges.

'True enough, it echoes my life.'

How on earth had she not made the connection before? That she doesn't date, specifically to camouflage flaws.

'Of course it *echoes* – because all is hollow and silent.'

She regards the blobs of nail varnish on the carpet and the sofa. Gradually, it is dawning on her that her long-held philosophy, and strictly adhered-to coda, are not just inherently flawed but somewhat deluded, too. She rummages around in the waste-paper basket. If only she could find the nail polish, she'd happily spatter it around the furnishings. But of course, as soon as Pip McCabe decides something is rubbish, she won't tolerate it being anywhere near her. So that nail polish isn't in the waste-paper basket, it's outside somewhere in the communal bins.

'Me being so bloody hasty,' she admits to herself with regret. 'It cost a small fortune. It was Chanel, after all. What a waste.'

What were you going to do with it if you still had it? Add a few more blobs on the sofa as a symbolic act of defiance against yourself? The thing is, Pip, a token splattering of nail polish here and there might not be quite enough. Nail varnish is not appropriate, anyway. It would indeed be hasty. It's time for something much more considered.

Apart from her commitment to St Bea's, Pip McCabe cancelled all appointments, though she could barely afford to, and laid low for the next five days. She tried not to check her mobile phone for the text messages Zac had no intention of sending. She tried not to hope that the answering machine would flash up a message that, in fact, it never crossed his mind to leave. She found it easy to ignore the messages and invitations left by her friends and sisters. One thing she did do, which dramatically broke with her self-protection insurance policy of old, was to think about her recent past, of Zac and Caleb and even Alex. Though she maintained affection for only one of the three, she knew they were all worth thinking about.

How different my life would have been, would be now, if I'd thought more about them at the time – even if such a process necessitated me confiding in my nearest and dearest.

It slowly dawned on her that Cat, Fen and Megan – even Django – could have altered the course of her life for the better, had she let them. She reckoned they would have seen through Caleb far more quickly than she had – because, of course, she'd have let them meet him. And they'd have seen Zac bedecked in his true colours much faster. Thus Alex's flirtations would have amounted to little more than flattery – perhaps a tinge of temptation – which they'd have ensured she quashed. And, very probably, she wouldn't be on her own now, avoiding their phone calls and wishing for calls that will never come.

And who can blame him? I fucked up. It's such a shame.

It's such a shame Pip hasn't quite reached that stage of awareness and courage that would have her lift the receiver, dial the number and say 'hullo'.

It's Friday evening. She's on her own. She lifts the receiver, dials the number, waits for an answer and then says 'hullo'.

'Hullo,' Fen replies, 'I've been trying you all week!'

'I know,' says Pip, 'sorry.'

'How's tricks?' Fen asks.

Pip pauses. 'Tricky,' she replies.

'You OK?' Fen asks, a note of concern discernible in her voice.

'Ish,' Pip confides. 'I've been better,' she says quietly, 'I could do better.' There's the truth! 'Listen, I was wondering if you and Cat might come round to mine tomorrow?' Pip pauses. 'I'd like your advice.' She pauses again. 'I need your help.'

Fen is taken aback. 'Would you like me to phone Cat?' she asks, wanting to be of some practical assistance.

'No, no,' Pip says, 'I'll phone.'

'Is everything OK?' Fen pushes, worried for her. 'Are you all right?'

'I hope I will be,' Pip reveals, having to clear her throat to strengthen her voice. 'I'll see you tomorrow, then?'

'Night,' says Fen softly, 'see you tomorrow.'

'Hi, Megan, it's me. You're probably out and about or in Dom's den of iniquity. Um. It's just. Fuck. Anyway, thanks for your messages – sorry I haven't phoned. It's just. God. Listen, might you come to mine tomorrow – I mean, if you're not busy? It's just. Shit. It's just. I don't know. I guess I'm a bit low. I'd love to see you. I need some advice, really. Can you come?'

Pip hopes her best friend can make it, too. She brushes her teeth and slips into bed. She looks around her bedroom. It would look fine as a photograph in *Livingetc*. But to live like this in reality is actually plain boring. Neat and tidy and bloody dull. It's nothingy. All of it is nothingy. It's been so for years.

'This isn't solitude. This is loneliness.'

THIRTY

*O*n Saturday morning, Cat and Fen arrived at Pip's at much the same time as Megan. They greeted each other on the doorstep with whispers of 'What are you doing here, too?' and 'Did she say anything else?' and 'Do you know what's wrong?' and 'When did you last see her?' and 'She's seemed absolutely fine – what on earth can it be?' and 'I've brought loads of chocolate to facilitate a thorough heart to heart.' Pip opened the door to them. They swept her through into her lounge on a tide of fond smiles and warm embraces and gifts of chocolate éclairs, Jaffa cakes and magazines. It was almost overwhelming for Pip. She had to bite her tongue to prevent herself from asking them all to leave so she could burrow back into bed, be on her own and forget that any of this ever seemed like a good idea.

Fen gestured to the sofa. 'Isn't that Django's old bedspread?' she exclaimed, privately thinking that using it as a throw was very un-Pip and really rather unpleasant, considering the stains and the holes and the indisputable fact that pea-green candlewick would simply never be in vogue.

'What's with the bin bags?' Megan asked, regarding a few scattered over the floor.

'Where's your *stuff*?' Cat asked, noticing that the shelves were utterly bare and that greasy outlines on the walls were all that was left of the mirror and the Rothko poster.

'I wanted you to help me,' Pip explained without actually answering any of their questions. They all regarded her expectantly. 'Cup of tea, anyone?'

'Coffee,' Cat requested, looking at her eldest sister quizzically, 'if you're making.'

'Tea,' Fen said, scrutinizing her sister for further clues, 'ta.'

'Tea,' Megan said quietly, glancing around her, 'please.'

Pip went through to the kitchen and returned with a laden tray. Her sisters and her best friend sipped their drinks politely. And waited.

'I thought you could help me,' Pip said at length, only after she'd eaten an éclair and had licked her fingers thoughtfully. 'It's all so dull and boring,' she said. 'I want to introduce a little colour into my life.' Three pairs of enquiring eyes burrowed into her. 'I've always eschewed it without ever actually trying it,' she continued with a shrug, 'but I thought it was about time to take some risks.'

The three girls nodded though their eyes revealed that they were none the wiser. 'And if it doesn't work out,' said Pip, 'perhaps you could advise me on an alternative plan.'

Her posse continued to nod but regard her blankly. *Them*? Advise *her*? How? While they attempted to fathom it all, Pip went into her bedroom and reappeared with a selection of trial-sized tins of paint. These she opened and, without further ado, she went from wall to wall, daubing great globs of colour in large random patches. Cat, Fen and Megan watched, open-mouthed. 'Help me,' Pip implored. 'Which do you think? What suits best?'

Why couldn't she say on the phone that she just wants us to help decorate? Fen wondered to herself, rather bemused.

Is that it? All she wants is for us to help choose bloody paint colours, Cat remarked to herself, somewhat disappointed.

I could have just bought her a copy of Livingetc. *and then spent the morning snuggled in bed with Dominic*, Megan thought to herself, a little annoyed.

Their irritation and disbelief were but momentary because the sight of Pip splodging colour willy-nilly was at once peculiar and endearing. Putting their grievances to one side, Fen, Cat and Megan entered into the spirit of the case in hand. They were unanimous and enthusiastic that the deep ochre was a gorgeous colour and would suit the living-room very well. They were agreed that the yellow was too acidic, the scarlet too garish and the violet just a little too suggestive of witchcraft. The ochre would do very well, it was rich and positive, classic yet fresh; it would enliven the room without overwhelming the dimensions. They weren't prepared for Pip to declare that the back wall ought to be a different shade altogether. And, though they didn't necessarily agree with her on the terracotta hue she favoured, her eagerness was so beguiling that they encouraged her with her choice.

'Tell me that Django's old bedspread goes!' Fen pleaded. 'It doesn't go with ochre or terracotta. It has to go!'

'It's only to protect the sofa whilst we redecorate,' Pip assured her.

'I'm not sure the carpet isn't going to look a little grubby,' Megan pointed out.

'Nothing that a great big colourful rug can't fix,' Pip proclaimed.

'Is Carol Smillie lurking in your bedroom?' Cat asked, peering out into the corridor. 'Or Lord Long Lacy Sleeves,' she wondered, 'that Llewelyn-Bowen bloke?'

'Nope,' Pip assured her, Fen and Megan. 'Just me. Ringing the changes.'

With colours and finishes agreed upon, Pip left her gang with rolls of masking tape, more bin bags and a long list of what to do to prep the room while she went out to the local DIY shop to buy paint and rollers. Her sisters and her best friend admitted to one another that they were slightly baffled by the fact that the help Pip required was of a purely practical nature. They were slightly taken aback by her choice of colours. By her choosing colour, full stop.

'It could work, though,' Fen said, looking around the sitting-room.

'It's time for a change,' Cat agreed, quite liking the deep claret colour but seeing Pip's point about the chosen shade of terracotta.

'It'll take some getting used to,' Megan remarked, 'for her as well as us.'

The women brushed and dabbed and rollered the cream walls away. Radio 2 provided innocuous background entertainment and the Jaffa Cakes provided sustenance. Before long, they all thought to themselves that it was a refreshing way to spend a Saturday.

'What about your bedroom, Pip?' Megan asked, sponging an ochre skid off the skirting-board.

'I think lilac's a great bedroom colour,' Fen said, 'very soothing and dreamy.'

'Your curtains and blinds,' Cat said, 'dye or die? Lord Long Lacy Sleeves did something very effective with a printing block made out of a potato.'

'The thing is –' said Pip. Then she paused. She put down her roller and regarded the three of them. Beloved Megan wearing a shower cap to protect her hair; dearest Cat with masking tape stuck to her elbow; cherished Fen with spatters of ochre freckling her face. Pip looked from one to the other and the next. She shrugged, sighed, picked up her roller and set at her patch of wall again. 'The thing is,' she said, 'I'm sort of in love with this bloke called Zac. I think.'

* * *

Pip carried on painting, the sticky clicketing squelch of loaded roller against wet wall providing the only sound. Fen, Cat and Megan were motionless, their jaws dropped to the limit of their hinges, their minds whirring and wondering if they'd heard right. Eventually, a goop of paint, dripping from Fen's brush noisily on to the plastic sheeting, caused Pip to look up from her task and the three of them to shut their mouths and swallow. Pedantically, Pip laid down her roller and turned to face them all.

'The thing is,' she said, 'I *am* in love with this bloke called Zac.' Her audience were hanging on her every word, not that the words 'love' and 'Zac' made much sense to them at all in the context of Pip's life. 'But the thing is,' Pip carried on, regardless, 'I've scuppered any chance of a relationship with him.' Her younger sisters and her best friend continued to regard her with incredulity. 'Not because of Caleb,' Pip said casually, by way of explanation that of course meant little to them, 'nor because of Alex,' she added in a nonchalant way, leaving them none the wiser. 'No,' Pip proclaimed defiantly, 'simply because of *me*.'

Pip had covered almost the entire wall before anyone spoke. Fen broke the silence. 'Caleb?' she asked, feeling almost virtuous that there was she with only two men on the go, while here was Pip suddenly revealing three.

'Caleb,' Pip confirmed, 'Dr Caleb Simmons – a paediatrician at St Bea's. I was sleeping with him for a couple of months, earlier in the summer.'

Fen, Cat and Megan tried not to gulp too noisily and attempted to retain some control over the extent to which their eyes ogled. Did they just hear that correctly? Pip? Philippa McCabe? Their friend and sister? Having casual sex with some doctor from work for a couple of *months*? How did that come about? When was this? Why hadn't they *known*?

'Alex?' Cat asked, thinking of her colleague on the Tour de France and thinking 'Surely not!'

'I had a one-night stand with Alex in the bunk bed up on L'Alpe D'Huez three weeks ago,' Pip confirmed. Megan wondered why on earth Pip hadn't divulged such fantastic gossip. Momentarily, she was quite taken aback. Fen and Cat wondered how the hell she could have had sex right under their noses without them knowing. Though they both felt somewhat offended, they didn't ask her. They didn't know how to. This Pip was so new they had no idea how to break into her outer packaging, for starters, to say nothing of fathoming what made her tick inside. So the three of them just stared at her. And wondered how she could continue to paint walls whilst making revelations of such magnitude.

'Zac?' Megan asked.

Immediately, Pip stopped painting and looked crest-fallen. 'Zac Holmes,' she said. She looked from best friend to sister to sister. 'He's a lovely bloke.' She shrugged.

'You've had a fling with him?' Megan pushed. The abbreviated dialogue which sufficed between the sisters was not enough for her. 'With this Zac Holmes person?'

'I've slept with him twice,' Pip said quietly, 'but given him a hard time for much longer.' No one quite knew if the *double entendre* was meant, let alone meant to lighten the tone or set the scene. 'Look, shall we just paint the terracotta wall now?' Pip was starting to feel out of her comfort zone, on the verge of regretting her disclosures. She was quietly asking herself what the fuck all the fuss was about, why on earth she had made public any of the three men. Caleb, Alex, Zac – they were simply part of her past, after all. Weren't they? Furthermore, they had hardly been in her life long enough to have been a part of her life, anyway. What was the point of deconstruction and analysis, of regrets and hopes? It was all destined to come to nothing. It already had. There was no future. 'Oh,' Pip barked, 'forget it all. I have. No point. Meant fuck all anyway. Let's just paint.'

'Sod the frigging terracotta,' Fen said sternly.

'Hear bloody hear,' Cat muttered, glowering at Pip.

'If you're in love with this Zac bloke,' Megan asked coolly, needing to temper the inflammatory tone between the sisters, 'why isn't he in love with you?'

If I'm in love with him, why isn't he in love with me?

*

A very fair question – and if Pip answers it astutely, all the reasons why he isn't will provide all the pointers to how he could be.

'Because,' said Pip, 'I have not treated him particularly well. I guess you could say I've led him on – led him to believe that I was up for it when I wasn't, that I was someone who I'm not, that I wanted something I don't.'

'"Up for it"?' probed Megan. 'Are you talking just sex?'

'More,' said Pip. 'You know – seeing each other. Hanging out. Spending time together. As well as sex. You know – do things. Stuff.'

'A relay-shun-ship,' Megan spelt out as if to a child.

Pip shrugged and nodded. 'I just didn't think him suitable.'

'Why not?' asked Cat who'd calmed down. She was intrigued. After all, her eldest sister was full of theories as to why *her* ex was so unsuitable.

'Because of his baggage,' Pip said with a defiant shrug that deep down she knew did Zac a disservice.

'Baggage?' Fen enquired.

'His life,' Pip said, sighing. 'So much to deal with.'

'Like what?' Fen asked, thinking of all the stuff she herself was dealing with in her life.

'Like he has a child,' Pip exclaimed as if that should be enough. There was silence. She dropped her head slightly, eventually looking up at the three women rather meekly. They were standing in a semicircle around her, brandishing their brushes and rollers like weapons. She wasn't sure whether they were standing guard around her, or closing in threateningly.

'Is that a problem for him?' Megan asked. She repeated herself because Pip's pause was too long. 'Doesn't he like his kid?'

Pip felt very bad. Zac adored Tom, loved being a father, he had no problem with it at all. He saw it as a blessing. 'He loves his child,' she practically whispered. 'Little boy. Six. Tom.'

'Has he an ex, then?' Cat asked, keen for clues. Pip nodded after another lengthy pause. 'Does she cause him grief?' Cat probed. 'Is he not over her? Is the split hideously acrimonious?'

Pip thought back to Tom's party on Sunday. She thought back to Zac and June sitting together in Out-patients. How he spoke about her. How she spoke about him. How Tom spoke about them. She shook her head. 'They get along brilliantly,' she mumbled.

'So what do you mean by "baggage"?' Fen asked to mutters of approval from Megan and Cat.

'He has a kid and an ex and a complex history!' Pip protested, stamping her foot. 'For fuck's sake!'

'For fuck's sake,' Fen retaliated coolly, 'it seems his history is *your* baggage, not his.'

Pip felt her eyes smart. Couldn't they all just fuck off and leave her alone! Go on – sod off, the lot of you! No. She'd invited them here. She'd confided in them. She'd asked them to help imbue her life with colour. Painting walls was only one aspect of it. Cat, Fen and Megan were merely being honest. Covered in ochre emulsion. Doing as she requested. Helping her. Time for Pip to peel off the masking tape.

Pip was mortified. Fen, Cat and Megan considered the facts so far as if discussing a particularly good BBC drama. The only thing that didn't make sense to them was why on earth the heroine hadn't snapped the hero up and taken him off the market immediately.

'He sounds a honey,' Megan said.

'He's a sodding *accountant*!' Pip remonstrated, as if brandishing the trump card. However, she was horrified that Megan, Cat and Fen should all nod approvingly rather than look dismayed.

'Must be fairly solvent, then,' Fen remarked.

'I'm a *clown*!' Pip cried, as if they were dense and missing the point altogether – though she no longer had any idea what the point was.

'Too bloody right,' Cat said firmly, 'and you've lost the last laugh.'

'Leave me alone,' Pip sobbed. 'Fuck off, the lot of you.'

'No,' said Fen, taking the paint roller from Pip's hands.

'No,' said Cat, leading her eldest sister to the sofa.

'No,' said Megan, going to the kitchen to make cups of tea because her best friend certainly looked as though she could do with one.

They let her sulk. They let her slurp her tea and bolt her biscuits. They let her sob. They let her sniff snottily. They let her sigh. They let her rub her eyes and bury her head in her hands. They let her proclaim half-sentences like 'and then of course' and 'but anyway, it's all so' and 'also, the fact remains that'. They let her sit still for as long as she wanted to. And she sat there, in a world of her own, for quite some time. They let her mind whirr and ruminate without them probing into what she was thinking. Ultimately, they simply let Pip be. But they held her hands and stroked her hair and patted her knees as she did so.

Eventually, she blinked. The tension in her shoulders subsided, her face softened and she looked around her, as if some fog had lifted.

'I like the colour,' she said. 'Good choice, girls.'

'Did you like Caleb?' Cat asked.

Pip looked for the answer in her lap, then at her socks, without success. She looked from Cat to the others, though she couldn't maintain eye contact for long. She gave a shrug. And then a sigh. 'In fact, you know what? I did,' she revealed. 'I tried to kid myself for ages that he was just a hot shag. But actually, I think I did like him – or the idea of winning him over. Maybe it was because he was a little enigmatic, slightly ambivalent, and that can be oddly seductive. I guess I had a fair few hopes pinned on him or on myself, rather. That he'd fall for me. Sounds a bit clichéd, deluded, arrogant even.'

'What happened?' Fen asked.

Pip smiled to herself. How differently she would have answered such a question in the past. 'You know what?' she said. 'It turned out that it was me who was just a shag to *him*. He had a girlfriend I didn't know about. He presumed I was up for some no-strings action. And the thing is, I thought I was – in theory. But in practice, I realized that I wasn't.'

'Bastard!' Megan spat, rallying to Pip's side.

'No,' Pip corrected her, 'no. You know what, Caleb is simply someone with a different outlook on love and sex than me.' Privately, Cat, Fen and Megan each wondered whether they could ever be as magnanimous in such a situation. 'His morals are on a different plane. Not incorrigible or cruel – just different. He's as at ease with his morality as I am with mine. Ultimately, I felt a fool – yet he never set out to make a fool of me.' Privately, Fen, Cat and Megan all thought Caleb sounded like a cocky wanker. But they respected the peace Pip had found in the situation and so said nothing.

'Alex?' Cat asked. 'What was all that about?'

Again, Pip smirked to herself. 'I was drunk,' she shrugged, 'and I'd just slept with Zac for the second time and run away from him for the second time. I thought Alex would take my mind off things. Prove to me that Zac was just a shag. That he wasn't worth pursuing, that relationships were too much like hard work and simply not preferable to a nice little gratuitous one-night stand.'

'And?' Cat asked.

'I was wrong,' Pip declared, 'once more.' She sighed. 'God, I don't mean to sound crude – but if pursuit of orgasm is what it boils down to, you're better off with a vibrator. Believe me.' How could such self-awareness and revelation make one feel as though a weight had been lifted and yet also so heavy with fatigue?

'And Zac?' Fen asked.

'Every time he's attempted closeness, I've fled,' Pip revealed quietly. 'He's been friendly and flirtatious in his unique oddball way for months. Way before Caleb. I resisted him, telling myself he was a weirdo. And when I found my fondness growing I told myself he was too complex and burdened to be worth my while. And when I slept with him and woke up next to him I told myself it was a bad idea and I ought to scarper.'

'Does he know about Caleb?' Megan asked.

'Yes,' said Pip, 'and he came to the rescue when it all fell apart.'

'Does he know about Alex?' Megan asked.

'No,' said Pip, 'no. We haven't really spoken since I left for France.'

'What do you mean "haven't really spoken"?' Fen asked.

'Last Sunday,' Pip informed them all, 'his ex booked me to perform at their son's sixth birthday.' She fiddled with a KitKat wrapper. 'Unbeknown to Zac, of course.'

'Jeez,' said Cat.

'Fuck,' said Megan.

'God,' said Fen.

'He paid me,' Pip said quietly. 'For my services,' she added. 'In cash.' It sounded as abhorrent as it had felt.

Cat, Megan and Fen repeated their expletives in hushed tones. They all sat on the pea-green candlewick bedspread, lulled by the soothing ochre surrounding them. They all wondered what to say. What could be done.

'Could you woo him?' Cat suggested.

'No,' said Pip, thinking of Juliana and ranking herself such a frumpy second place that even attempting a duel would be complete humiliation, and futile, anyway.

'Confide?' Fen said. 'You know, divulge your own fear of intimacy and stuff.'

It was only now Pip realized that to reveal how her own mother had run off with a cowboy from Denver when she was a child could be quite persuasive. But of course, she had already made up that whopping lie about her kith and kin being paragons of closeness and the last word in conventional family values. 'No,' said Pip.

'Could you just phone him to say "hullo"?' Megan asked. 'Text him to say how r u? E-mail? Snail mail? Simply say "sorry", and ask for another try?'

'Not much point,' Pip said darkly. She flicked the scrunched KitKat wrapper carelessly into the centre of the room. 'He now has a girlfriend six feet tall, glam and gorgeous. And he's simply not interested in me.'

'He has a girlfriend,' Fen repeats.

Cat says, 'Shit.'

Megan says, 'Damn and blast.'

'He has a girlfriend,' Pip confirms, 'and he's simply not interested in me.'

THIRTY-ONE

*P*hilippa McCabe feels as though she's at journey's end. Her baggage is heavy and uncomfortable. She needs to dump it, to move on. However, she has no idea in which direction she ought to travel next, or how to go about unpacking because it will mean choosing what she's happy to forsake, what she wants to carry with her. She has spent most of her adult life firmly in the driving seat, resolutely behind the steering-wheel, deciding precisely where she will allow Fate to take her and what she will permit Future to hold for her. For the time being, though, she'll just have to stand still awhile, surrounded by ochre and terracotta walls (and a fuchsia-coloured ceiling in the bedroom). For the time being, Fate and Future are simply not up to Pip. Though they could well be down to Ruth and June.

'The thing is, we can't tell him what to do,' said June late at night to Ruth over the phone, 'believe me! I tried it – and we split up, remember!'

'You're too right. Zac has to feel that *he*'s made the choice,' Ruth said. 'We can but sow the seeds of Suitability in his mind by planting the tiniest niggles in his conscience.'

'Ultimately, he has to feel *he*'s made some ground-breaking, life-altering decision,' June agreed wholeheartedly.

'I mean, you and I are undoubtedly High Priestesses of Manipulative Malarkey,' Ruth mused, 'but we'll have to use all our cunning to stay hidden in the wings while we pull the strings on this one.'

'I rather think it shouldn't come down to Zac making the *choice* between one and the other,' June said. 'He'd be so concerned about hurting the one or the other that he'd very probably decide to go without either.'

'You're right. First things first. We'll have to assist in giving Juliana a subtle shove in the direction of the exit,' Ruth said. 'She goes back to South Africa soon,' she elaborated, 'ish.'

'Agreed. But we'll have to act fast – we can't let geography provide an easy way out,' June said. 'Zac has to want to dump her.'

'Not just *want* to – he *has* to,' said Ruth.

'How?' June asked. 'I mean, he seems perfectly content with the way things are going.'

'I know,' Ruth admitted reluctantly. 'There must be a way. How indeed?'

June and Ruth barely knew Pip. And it wasn't as if they really knew Juliana either. But they did know Zac inside out, being his ex and his sister-in-law, after all. They cared about him supremely, being his ex and his sister-in-law, after all. Yet they couldn't truly say that Juliana was wrong for Zac. The point to Zac is his great consistency – his personality remains steady and untainted regardless of the woman he is with. Or women. Or lack of. You simply never know with Zac unless you ask, and sometimes he won't say, anyway. He's always good old Zac, whether he's single or spoken for, or spoken for by three women at once, or two women together.

Some people positively shine under the direct influence of another person being part of their lives. Some wither. Some become worryingly remote. Or upsettingly out of sorts. Or downright disagreeable.

Cat and her ex would put on a very good impression of

togetherness whenever they were in company. Lots of hand holding and declarations of future plans. Those around them cringed. It was depressing. It was so painfully transparent. Cat's eyes were dulled and her smile, when it was seen, was far more painted than any Pip gave Dr Pippity or Merry Martha. Friends soon stopped inviting them out as a couple. That their nothingness could be so visible was upsetting. Their façade was flimsy. The show they put on was upsetting for all. It was horribly obvious that before they arrived, or as soon as they left, they would succumb to either aggressive silence or full-on warfare.

Since Megan and Dominic have been together, however, Megan's bubbly personality has fizzed over into infectious effervescence. She's herself but even more so; as if Dominic has provided a luscious glossy top coat over her already colourful disposition. And Dom's friends give credit to Megan for the ease with which he now socializes. He was always part of the party, but invariably it depended on the number of pints. Now he chats and jests so energetically, he hasn't the time – or the inclination – for the volume of liquor he once leant on.

Zac, though, simply never seems to change. Which is why he's such a trustworthy and dependable mate. Which is why his friends often don't know if he's seeing someone or not. Which is why his friends feel confident in presenting their friends to him. He's so nice, he's so much fun, he's so sorted. He has manners and values and strength of character. You'll be safe with him.

However, Ruth and June weren't really thinking of how Pip might benefit from Zac – of course she'd be happy and fulfilled and treated with respect. Like all the others. No. Ruth and June's drive was Zac himself. Both women – and it surprised them – had an inkling, a drift, a hint, a taste, that Zac's life could be surprisingly enhanced by the presence of that weird and wiry girl who paints herself peculiar, does things with balloons for cash on a Sunday and makes sick children feel just a tiny bit better on Tuesdays and Thursdays.

'Juliana may well not be *wrong* for him,' Ruth said over coffee in the O2 centre where Tom and Billy were rampaging around the soft-play gym, 'though I'll admit that her svelte limbs and general gorgeousness cause vile sensations of spite in *me*! It's just that Pip might well be more *right*.'

June laughed. 'I so totally agree!' she said. She pondered, while she stirred and stirred the excessive foam on her coffee with the wooden stick given in lieu of a plastic spoon. 'Our reasons are wholesome, aren't they?' she asked. 'I mean, I have nothing *against* Juliana – apart from her afore-mentioned physical attributes which are more my problem than her achievement. It's just – I don't know – I do seem to have something *for* Pip.'

Ruth considered this whilst thinking to herself that recently Stardust's cappuccino had become all froth and no substance. Where was the coffee? Blimey! All the way down there. A bit weak, lukewarm. But it would do. Whatever. She'd rather settle for it than have the hassle of taking it back and making a fuss. The parallel with Zac and Juliana struck her. Juliana looked the part, but was there that much to her? Below-the-surface details? Did it really bother Zac? Knowing him, he'd avoid hassle, reason that she was fine. Whatever.

Ruth picked out a couple of blueberries from their stodgy muffin cladding. It suddenly struck her. 'Essentially, all we're doing is food combining, June,' she declared. 'Great chefs know which ingredients will work even better when brought together, than when taken on their own merits, however high.'

'Bagsy be Nigella Lawson, then,' June laughed, 'because you are so Gordon Ramsay!'

'Fuck off!'

'See!'

'Strawberries and cream,' mused Ruth.

'Sherbet and a lollipop,' June suggested.

'Roast potatoes and gravy,' Ruth added.

'Rocket and parmesan,' said June.

'Better plan a menu, then,' said Ruth. 'Here's to a recipe for success, and happy endings.' They chinked their coffee mugs. 'I'll give him a call.' She phoned Zac. 'Hullo, it's Ruth,' she said. 'Fine, fine. You? Great. Work? Cool, cool. Oh, he's fine. I'm out with the girls Thursday so I'm sure he'd be happy for some company. Yes. Sure. Cool. Listen – Friday night – do you have plans? No? Would you like to meet for dinner, then? You *and* Juliana? Deal's off, other-wise. No. Pardon? Not at all! Whatever gave you that impression? I think she seems really – nice. That's why I'd love to see her again. Great. Just let me know. Ta-ra.'

Ruth felt that the timing promised to be very good. All would be cooked to perfection. And, just then, the timing in the O2 centre was pretty spot on, too.

'Here she is,' whispered June excitedly, able now to scrunch up the leaflet she'd picked up in the O2 centre a couple of days ago and had kept in her bag ever since.

'Indeed she is,' said Ruth.

Right on cue, Merry Martha came clumping into view, holding a bunch of helium-filled balloons emblazoned with advertising from a local company – not that the children would mind, or even take note. Free balloons? Fantastic! Writing on them? So what! Almost instantly, the clown was mobbed by children. She began to sing in a ghastly falsetto, falling silent every now and then to bestow a maniacal grin on her young audience or to pepper pregnant pauses with burps and squeaks and honks and farts.

Ruth and June regarded each other, eyes asparkle. They appeared to have all the raw ingredients at their fingertips. They just needed to start cooking up something spectacular. No time like the present.

So what if their boys would have supper late? Ruth and June felt that quality time with their sons' favourite clown would beat any sticky, over-sweetened synthetic pudding they could rustle up, anyway, surpass even the treat of an extra half hour's television. The clown was finishing her slot by dispersing all the balloons and dispensing raucous fart noises as well. Still the children swarmed around her. Not for freebies, but simply for attention. Play a joke on *me*! Cover *my* hair with the paper bits from a hole-punch! Make my hand squeak when you shake it! Squirt *me* with water! Say something silly about *my* name! Suddenly, all that could be seen of the clown was a pair of stripy legs and clodhopping orange shoes swaying over a sea of children's awestruck faces. And that's how Merry Martha took her leave of her audience – by walking away on her hands singing a dodgy version of Diana Ross's 'Upside Down'.

June picked her moment and then approached. Merry Martha had upended herself, slightly breathless and probably quite flushed under all the pan stick.

'Hullo,' June greeted, 'remember me? June – Price? You gave Tom the party of his life.'

'Hullo,' said the clown, suddenly being poked, then hugged, by Tom and just poked by Billy. It was difficult for June to gauge her reaction because of the painted smile and ready-delineated eyes. But the clown was staying put and that was good. 'Fancy a cuppa?' June offered.

'Thanks – but I really ought to make tracks.'

Cue Tom and Billy. 'Please!' implored the one. 'Beg you!' pleaded the other. They tugged at her starched skirt and reached up, hoping to pull her pigtails, too.

'I really ought to go,' the clown apologized. June panicked to herself. But the boys came to the rescue again. Though they physically twisted her arms, it was ultimately their crestfallen expressions which worked wonders. 'Well,' the clown faltered, 'maybe just a very very quick one.'

'You can swig an espresso if you haven't got time to sip a cappuccino,' June suggested. The clown laughed and said that in fact she could murder a cup of Earl Grey.

Pip was led off by Tom and Billy who held tight on to her hands and brandished smiles of triumph and ownership at all the children they passed. The ex-partner of the man she was in love with but was trying to forget, walked a few steps ahead. Pip felt simultaneously terribly uncomfortable and yet also strangely privileged. A direct link to Zac. Contact, however indirect. Perhaps there'd be news of him. Even a mention would do. Maybe news would get back to him. Even a mention would do. Suddenly, Pip's walk slowed to a shuffle – the boys presumed this was purposeful and thought it hilarious. It now struck Pip that she was steps away from coffee with Zac's ex and kid and what the fuck was the point of *that*? Nothing but an acetic reminder of what had been, what went wrong and what would never ensue. And anyway, how on earth was she going to feel when she returned home alone later on? Tom and Billy dragged her along.

The sister-in-law was also there.

'Do we Martha you or are you Pip?' Ruth asked reverentially, whilst shaking her hand and smiling warmly. Little did Ruth know how she'd just delivered magic words.

This Ruth woman understands that clowns are people, too.

Very well then, Pip would stay for Earl Grey – the last half-hour had been thirsty work, after all. Adult company would be quite nice, too.

'Pip'll do,' Pip said.

June returned with tea and a slice of ginger cake. Gratefully, Pip partook of both.

They were thoroughly interested in her. Pip was flattered. They asked all about her training, about the highs and lows of such a unique career, what skin-care regime she used to combat all that slap, what fitness programme to maintain such impressive acrobatics. They marvelled at her answers and proclaimed themselves dowdy, unimaginative and unfit by comparison. They asked where she was from. How old was she? How long had she lived in London? And where did she live, did she own or rent? Alone? Pip found herself answering them in full, and soon enough slipping in details

253

that hadn't been required but were lapped up, anyway. The boys were bored and wandered off to stare at the tropical fish and the shooting water sculpture flanking the escalators.

'Your sisters,' June asked, 'what do they do?'

'Cat – she's the youngest – she's a sports journalist,' said Pip. 'Fen, the middle one, she's an art historian.'

'Are you close?' June probed, while realizing how easily they were chatting – so easily that she had completely overlooked the fact that she was sitting with a grown woman dressed as a clown. Who'd slept with her ex. Fleetingly, she wondered whether Pip had been in costume. She couldn't remember Zac having any kinks or quirks about dressing-up outfits.

'We are very close,' Pip said, with a smile that broadened the painstakingly painted one, 'because –' She paused. Was this a good idea? What was the point not telling the truth now? 'We're very close because there's only us and our uncle.'

'Django – in Derbyshire?' Ruth recalled from five minutes earlier.

'Yes,' said Pip.

'He sounds fabulous,' said Ruth, while quite admiring the design of Pip's clown face. Not garish. A white base. Rosy cheeks. Eyes delineated in black and embellished with a diamond shape here, a heart shape there. Nose tip neatly painted red. Ears, too. Pigtails meticulously zany. Clothing bright and bizarre but fitting and flattering.

'No child – of whatever age – could wish for a better mother-father-friend,' Pip proclaimed, missing Django and Derbyshire enormously and deciding right then to visit him that coming weekend.

'Your father?' Ruth asked.

'He died when I was small,' Pip revealed softly.

'Your mum?' June asked quietly.

Pip paused. Sipped her tea. Dabbed a crumb of cake and licked her finger thoughtfully. June and Ruth were lovely. Why shouldn't she tell them? All her friends knew. What was so secret? 'She ran off with a cowboy from Denver when I was even smaller,' Pip shrugged.

Ruth and June gasped. The concept of an almost-orphan was so unbelievable it was almost theatrical. The concept of maternal defection was inconceivable. Actually, it was horrific. Criminal. Instinctively, both mothers looked over to their sons. If the boys had been nearer, they'd have hugged them close. But they were larking about, clambering on the fake rocks that really shouldn't be clambered on. They were happy and safe.

'It's fine,' Pip assured them, 'it's cool. I suppose we've never known any different, you see. I barely remember her. Certainly, I never think about her. Honestly – it's just a concept to us. It seems it's more upsetting for others!' Ruth and June raised their eyebrows, sighed, stared at their laps, lifted their eyes to gaze at Pip benignly.

'Are your sisters married?' June pressed on, having glanced at her watch, dismayed by how much she and Ruth had yet to achieve and by how little time there was to do it in.

'Fen is assessing the credentials of two rather different men – one town, one country; one rich, one poor; one young, one much older.' June and Ruth looked most impressed. 'And Cat has finally fallen in love with the right man, having been disastrously involved with the wrong one.'

June and Ruth nodded and hummed and stirred at the vestiges of froth clinging to the sides of their empty mugs. It's coming, it's coming.

'And you?' Ruth asked casually.

'Me what?' Pip replied ingenuously.

'You married? Divorced? Living in sin? Just plain sinning? Celibate?'

Pip stared at the specks of Earl Grey clinging to the base of her cup like dirt. How should she answer them?

I'm in love with your brother-in-law. Your ex. The father of your child. Of your nephew. I behaved badly and I'm paying the price. I really like you both. But you'll loathe me when you know more.

'Nah,' Pip said, nonchalant and dismissive, 'no one in my life at the mo' – not even on the horizon.'

June and Ruth tipped their heads this way and that. 'By choice?' Ruth pressed. Again Pip glanced away, looked deep into her teacup but way beyond the dregs of tea, finding much interest instead in the speckles of sugar grains left on the table by the previous customer.

'No,' she said, flicking the sugar with her finger, 'not by choice, if I'm honest. By my own –' She stopped.

Stop it, stop it! Stop it now. Shut up. Go home.

'Sorry,' she said breezily, standing up, 'I really have to go home. I completely forgot, I have to –' She arose from the table without finishing her sentence.

You have to what, Pip? Run away? Hide? What?

'Must dash,' she chirped. 'Thanks so much for the tea! Ta-ra! Say "bye" to the boys! Ta-ta!' Merry Martha had suddenly taken the place of Pip, who had performed a disappearing act so fast, so seamless, that the Davids Blaine or Copperfield would pay top dollar for her method.

'Shit!' said Ruth, frowning at Pip's teacup.

June raised her eyebrows in agreement. 'I guess you could say that our sauce has curdled.'

Ruth thought for a moment and then disagreed. 'A little more stirring might just rescue it. You pay and retrieve the boys. I'll meet you at the car.'

Ruth comes across Pip walking through the car park.

'Pip!' she calls, because she refuses to let Merry Martha fool her. 'Hey! Pip?' Can she hear her? Is she feigning deafness? Ruth doesn't care. She walks briskly, jogs a couple of steps, marches up behind her. 'Pip?'

Pip turns. Rivulets of grey course down her white face like rain in a London gutter, like the messy smudge on a school book made by a bad eraser. 'I've had a sneezing fit,' Pip announces defensively. Ruth gives her a tissue and says 'Bless you'. Pip blows her nose so noisily that momentarily, Ruth wonders if it's an occupational hazard – that sound effects for bodily functions become unintentionally exaggerated even when the act is off. And then Ruth wonders if the act is off. If it's all gone off.

The two women stand in the vast parking lot whilst the ubiquitous jeep-style vehicles of the North London mothers slalom around them.

'That's better,' says Pip, dabbing her eyes, then honking her nose again, 'ta. Must be delayed hay fever or something.'

'Of course,' says Ruth.

'Better go,' says Pip and she grins fleetingly before walking off.

'Phone Zac,' Ruth blurts out. Pip is rendered immobile. She can't even turn to regard Ruth with horror and insult. She's too gobsmacked to tell this woman to mind her own bloody business. Though, actually, Pip knows it is partly Ruth's business. Ruth walks up to her and stands at her side, focusing on the same discarded crisp packet as Pip. 'Just give him a call,' Ruth suggests in a voice that is at once wise and caring. There's silence. She wonders why this one manufacturer puts salt-and-vinegar crisps in a green packet, when most use blue. 'Give him a call,' she repeats, 'for me, for June.' She scans Pip's face. 'For Tom.' It's impossible to read her reaction, not just because of the make-up. 'For Zac,' Ruth shrugs. 'Whenever. But do it. I mean, we could do it – June or I – but it wouldn't be the same. He'd rather hear from you. Believe me. Trust us.'

'I really, really have to go,' Pip says firmly and she walks off. Ruth tells herself that it's Pip's cumbersome comedy shoes that make her stomp so.

After supper, June phones Zac to arrange Tom's weekend. Courteously, she asks after Juliana, assuring her sceptical ex that no, she's *not* taking the piss.

'Of course I'm not being facetious,' she remonstrates. 'I'm being nice, you sod! She seems very, um, *alluring*. And she's an absolute stunner, too! You must be the envy of your male friends.'

Zac doesn't know how to respond. Weird that Ruth said pretty much the same earlier. He'd presumed that she and June had disliked Juliana for the very reasons he liked her – her beauty and her aloofness. For Zac, just now, surface details suffice. Burrowing beneath takes too much effort for too little reward. Like *crème brûlée* – crack through the glossy caramelized crown and it can be disappointingly bland underneath.

'We saw your clown today,' June says conversationally, anticipating the ensuing silence. 'Zac?' she chirps. 'You there?'

'What?' Zac pretends he hasn't heard. 'My mobile phone is ringing,' he fibs. Says he must go. Says 'See you on Sunday'. June knows he's been taken off his guard. Why wouldn't she know? She's his ex-partner. She knows what makes him tick. And what doesn't. And if he was over the clown, he'd've just said 'Oh, really?' and if the clown had never meant much anyway, he'd've just said 'Oh, really?' He wouldn't have been struck silent. He wouldn't have lied about his mobile phone. June feels encouraged and of course she phones Ruth directly.

The next morning, Zac wakes to a slumber-hazy image of Pip lying next to him. Pigtails jutting this way and that. A little residue of face paint here and there. A glimpse of rosy nipple. Silken shoulder. The sound of her breathing softly. The sensation of the warmth from her body; the scent of it. He indulges himself and lets the apparition linger awhile. Then Juliana sighs from the other side of his bed and a sharp toenail catches his ankle. He's wide awake now and Pip is banished. Or did she vanish? Hard to tell. But she's certainly gone.

THIRTY-TWO

*D*jango knew it was impor-
tant to feign delighted surprise at Pip's announcement of her
impromptu visit. However, pre-emptive calls from both Cat
and Fen had, of course, furnished him with the bare bones
of his eldest niece's situation almost as soon as they were
known. He was rather stunned to hear that she who had so
famously denounced love, sex and all the incumbent
panoply, was now licking her wounds, racking her conscience and nursing her heart, having apparently fumbled
with a few too many men in too few months. Django was
pleased that Pip wanted to come home and rest up. Though
he was confident that her sisters would offer limitless
emotional comfort, he knew he could provide help of a
practical nature that they could not. Django had always
championed the necessity of distance from London, the
merits of Derbyshire air, the importance of three large home-
cooked meals a day, the refuge in the solid walls of one's
childhood home. Contemplation and game plans might well
be achievable in the wine bars of London surrounded by
one's contemporaries, but true healing and intrinsic belief in
the right way forward, were best done at home. And home,
for the McCabe girls, would only ever be Derbyshire.

Down in London, so he'd heard, most young people

would lunch on the go on prepacked sandwiches and grab a supper from a conveyor belt of uncooked fish and cold rice squashed into strange shapes. The thought made Django shudder. Meals should be three courses long (if the lemon soufflé was ready first, then have it first – the McCabes often did) and be eaten in a leisurely way at the table. Think of the indigestion otherwise! He'd be the first to concede that his recipes were unconventional, but they were undeniably wholesome. Just look at the health and vitality of his nieces; he could count on one hand the number of school days they had missed – the three of them combined – due to illness. And Django credits their closeness as a family in part to his rigorously adhered-to institution of eating together at the table. That's why the girls have such becoming table manners. The McCabe household in Farleymoor, Derbyshire, has never done supper on laps with fork-loads shovelled absent-mindedly into mouths whilst the focus is on watching television. Instead, they've always sat at the kitchen table, chatted and argued, conversed and jested long after the meal is over. Even now, on their visits home, Django will unearth the old *Top of the Form* general knowledge quiz books at the girls' request, grilling them on the capital city of such-and-such a country while they wait for the soup to heat up, or the casserole to cool down, or the ice-cream to melt a little so that it can be spooned out.

Django went to the vast chest freezer in the only outhouse with a weatherproof roof and rummaged around for the racks of lamb that the Merifields had given him. He'd been saving them for a Special Supper, wondering when that would be and now knowing without hesitation that it was tonight. He smacked his lips at the thought of gravy, his secret recipe which called for eye-watering quantities of Tabasco and a good dollop of Bovril. He'd have liked to do his celery and stilton soup for starters. But he'd forgotten the celery. And the stilton. So he was going to experiment with apple and cheddar instead. If ingredients went well together in the raw, he was confident that they'd cook up a treat when together in the pot. And anyway, it wasn't as if a good slosh of Worcestershire Sauce couldn't help where necessary. Maybe a dribble of sherry if he hadn't drunk it all. He couldn't remember. He had a feeling that he'd finished the Scotch but that the sherry was still half full. He could be mistaken, though. If that was the case, he knew there was an unopened bottle of Madeira wine that would do very nicely instead.

Whatever. Pip coming home was a very sensible plan of action. He was touched and encouraged that she obviously knew what was good for her. To catch her breath, catch up on sleep, have a think, eat hearty meals, decide what to do. To have her old bedroom, and her old uncle, all to herself. To be fed and cared for. To choose London over Derbyshire. To have the moors as her thinking space, the solidity of her childhood home to embrace her. To sit in the lap of the old cedar. To sit in the wind-breaks provided by the lichen-licked drystone walls. Solitude and space and comfort and company. She'd feel safe, enveloped by reminders of the enduring stability in her life even if her present was tense. Soon enough, she'd know where she'd been and where she'd be heading next.

Django checked her room. He'd frequently offered to replace her curling posters of Simon Le Bon and Nick Heyward with a framed Kandinsky or a watercolour from the gallery in Bakewell, or just to redecorate it in neutrals, but she'd consistently resisted. His girls never ran from their past. They embraced it. They were proud of it. The posters stayed put, greasy splodges creeping across the surface from each corner due to the ancient blobs of Blu-tack. Django glanced around the room. He'd made the bed instinctively, well over a week ago, just as soon as Fen had called to confide that her sister was having a spot of bother. This morning, he added the patchwork eiderdown. The nights were drawing in. Already, the moors were sending a slight shiver through the house morning and night.

Looking around him, he nodded at the wall Pip had painted orange with navy spots when she was sixteen. Cat had told him how Pip had recently added colour to her living-room and painted her bedroom ceiling hot pink. Django was pleased. Pip might be broken in her heart, but a cerise ceiling signified to him that she was on the mend. All that bland beigeness she espoused he would rate plain boring. From what he'd heard of her flat in the city, it seemed to contradict his eldest niece's personality. Like someone forcing themselves to speak in dulcet tones when it was far more natural for them to sing and chortle at the top of their voice; like someone training themselves to walk demurely in high heels when trainers or pumps better suited the natural spring to their step. Time out in Derbyshire would put the colour back into her cheeks, too, and she'd stride back to London singing once more, of that Django was sure. He set off for Chesterfield to meet her train, leaving a vast vat of stew simmering on the stove for lunch.

The eldest of his nieces looked younger than he remembered, younger somehow than the other two. It was most peculiar. Though all three girls were slight in physique and with barely an inch or a pound's difference between them, Pip's deportment and demeanour had always given the illusion of stature. All that gaiety and bouncing around and daft make-up and larger-than-life liveliness. Just then, Django was quite shocked. Catching sight of Pip lugging her holdall along the platform, he could see that she looked wan and visibly thinner, her litheness and poise compromised. He concentrated on not letting his concern show. What he wanted to do was scoop her up in his arms, envelop her in his sheepskin coat and support her to the car and beyond. But he didn't. He'd feel awkward and she'd worry that he was worried. She'd back off, fix a smile on her face, pretend that everything was just dandy.

They hugged, as always they did. But though he offered to carry her bags, when she said 'No, no, not with your dodgy back, old man', he respected her dignity and allowed her to manage them on her own, though this pained him far more than his rickety sacroiliac joint.

Pip chatted sociably for the first part of the half-hour journey home, but the closer they came to Farleymoor, the quieter she became, interspersing the odd comment or question with lengthy periods gazing out of the car window to the moors and way beyond. Django was aware that she swallowed hard as soon as home came into view, that she cleared her throat when they swung into the driveway, that she made much of blowing her nose and keeping her face in her handkerchief when they came to a standstill.

'Delayed hay fever,' she explained.

'It's a bugger,' Django sympathized. He took her bags from the boot before she could object, asking Pip to open up the house for him.

All Django can smell is the stew. Chilli powder, specifically. He makes a mental note to dampen it down with oregano and plain yoghurt before serving. Pip, however, standing in the hallway, eyes closed, soaks up the scent of her entire home. It is an olfactory phenomenon. She knows well that it will only be detectable for a few minutes on arrival. After that, it will be so subtle as to go unnoticed. And though it is unique, unchanging and beautifully familiar, it is an aroma impossible to conjure up anywhere else. Back in Kentish Town, she will be unable to remember how her childhood home smells. She could close her eyes all she liked, flare her nostrils and concentrate very hard but it would be futile. And today, once she's unpacked and gone downstairs to the kitchen for lunch, the house's inimitable scent will be at once so familiar and usual that she will not think to notice it, nor be able to detect it.

Right now, though, her senses are filled with it. It's so vivid that it's a taste and a sound, too. She can smell stew, but it's so obvious, so short-term, that it's almost vulgar. Far more potent are the top notes and undertones of the aromas of the house itself. Oh, for a perfumer to blend them for her, bottle them for her to keep and call upon. Wood smoke. Old furniture. Coal tar soap. Django's penchant for piquant condiments. The slightly damp downstairs cloakroom. The overflowing fruit trough in the Drawing-room, which, at this time of day, the McCabes call the Library. The stair carpet, threadbare in parts and revealing the warm, worn wooden planks beneath. Coffee that Django grinds fresh each morning. Pipes and cigars. The cat from the cottage over the way. More than all of these, though – the very fabric of the building itself. The blue-grey stone hewn from the local quarry almost three hundred years ago, the rafters still standing the tests of time, the flagstone floors, the earth way beneath, the cast-iron fire-places, the ill-fitting doors, the window glass with the occasional cracked pane allowing the scent of pine and heather to filter in. All is deliciously salty, earthy and warm. Derbyshire and Django. Salt of the earth. Enveloping warmth.

'I'll just unpack,' Pip says. 'I'm absolutely starving. Something smells good.'

The stew for lunch was interesting. A little chewy but full of flavour – though not of the type usually associated with casseroles. Perhaps it was the addition of tuna, maybe the slosh of Madeira. Pip didn't know, nor did she care. She ate all that Django placed in front of her and even requested a small portion of seconds. Django suggested fruit and coffee in the Library and Pip washed up while he prepared a tray.

'The stew will be even better tomorrow,' Pip said.

'True enough,' said Django, 'though I was thinking of freezing it because I wanted to try a tortilla for lunch tomorrow.'

'Either,' Pip said enthusiastically, whisking a warm dry tea towel from the Aga rail.

Not even Django's potent blend of Costa Rica and French Continental, freshly ground and brewed until utterly opaque, could keep Pip awake that afternoon. With a half-eaten apple lolling in her lap, she dozed off. Django drank his coffee down to the dregs and ate four satsumas, throwing the peel into the fireplace. He read the *Racing Post*, the *Daily Telegraph* and a magazine Fen had left on her last visit, *Art Matters*. He scrunched the newspapers up and placed them in the grate, too, in preparation for a fire later. He'd use the cherry logs he'd been given by the Sutcliffes. The fire would smell excellent. He ate another two satsumas and added their peel to the pyre for good measure. Every now and then, he glanced across to his niece, sound asleep. He wondered whether to remove the apple from her lap – it had rolled over and her trousers showed a growing splodge where the juice was blotting. Pip's mouth was relaxed and ajar, a little drool collecting in the corners of her lips. She didn't look so fragile now. There was colour already to her cheeks. She looked very peaceful and it seemed intrusive to gaze at her. So he left her to her nap and prepared the apple and cheddar soup. He resorted to a fair amount of cornflour and two tins of baked beans as well.

THIRTY-THREE

*A*part from two visits to the Rag and Thistle pub – primarily so Django could show her off – and a couple of trips into Bakewell for provisions and newspapers, Pip happily confined herself to her home and was glad not to go above a walking pace for the duration of her stay. And walk she did. Either briskly up hill and down dale. Or just round and round the garden. Or in a leisurely way over to the folly on the other side of the valley. Or striding with purpose so as not to be late for tea and tart with Old Miss Sydnop. There again, she often merely meandered here and there because destination was irrelevant. Three or four times she raised the pace to a veritable jog when taking next door's flat-coat retrievers for a walk. Her tally over the week was pretty impressive – but will pale into insignificance against the immense distance she's got to accomplish on her personal journey.

Even though I've never had a conventional job – in that I've never done the Monday to Friday, 9.00 till 5.00, commute by tube, sit in an office, take coffee breaks, style of work – yet I find there's something rather decadent about it now being Tuesday afternoon and I'm prancing across Farleymoor. It's bizarre, I feel like I'm playing hooky, bunking off, doing a runner, skiving, taking a non-legit sickie!

What are you doing with your privileged time, Pip?

Thinking.

About?

Stuff.

Specifically?

I'm just taking stock.

A stocktake?

Perhaps.

And what do you find?

That there are things missing. And though I can account for them, they're still missing. I miss them.

Can't you retrieve them?

No. I can't. But I suppose I can try to ensure that I'm not so careless with precious things in future. The thing is, I know when and where I lost them. And why. So I guess that's a start to preventing such negligence from occurring again.

Soon enough, it was Thursday and she'd been back home for almost a week. Her sojourn had rested her and revived her, but she was acutely aware that though home was right here, reality resided, for the time being, back down in London. She felt homesick for Derbyshire though she hadn't yet left.

'You're a bit quiet,' Django probed gently, pouring her a little cherry brandy in the Snug (the Drawing-room had metamorphosed out of the Library that afternoon into the Snug that evening by Django lighting the fire) and offering her a jag of peanut brittle that she just about had room for after supper. 'Didn't the curry agree with you?' He paused. 'I admit I may have overdone it adding HP Sauce to the ensemble. Bloody faulty lid, being so loose.'

'It was delicious,' Pip assured him. She smiled over to her uncle. And smiled inwardly, too. What on earth was he wearing, she marvelled. Corduroy trousers the colour of maple syrup with a pleated waist; a shirt that was so Thomas Hardy, with its intricate smocking, that it might as well belong to Bakewell Amateur Dramatics; a neckerchief that he'd proudly tell you he wore as a bandanna when he was at Woodstock; mismatched socks; and, by the side of the sofa, tan leather boots with an alarming Cuban heel. God, she loved the man! How wonderful to be so charmingly eccentric, so steadfastly idiosyncratic, so utterly unself-conscious. Nothing for show, nothing so as to impress, no statement to make, no nasty quirks lurking.

'I reckon my sisters have filled you in?' she suddenly announced. Django just raised an eyebrow sagely. He didn't want to implicate Cat or Fen, he didn't want to change the subject, he certainly didn't want Pip to feel defensive and thus retreat. So it had taken her almost a week to bring to him what she had no doubt shared with the moors and the cedar tree and next door's flat-coat retrievers. So what? He believed it to have been her prerogative. Right now, he knew the most seemly and encouraging response he could give would be through physiognomic distortions. So he twitched his lips, lowered his eyes and raised them again, regarding her levelly. 'I'd do the same,' Pip admitted, 'if they were in a dither. In fact, I often have, haven't I?' She paused. 'That's what families are for, aren't they?'

Django nodded. 'It's not tittle-tattle,' he said quietly, 'when passed amongst us.'

'You're so right,' Pip said gratefully.

'So, Philippa, my dear,' Django said, peering intently at the cherry brandy label – not that he was reading it, but just surreptitiously to shift attention away from Pip and her traumas, so as shrewdly to put her at her ease. 'Can I top up your tipple?' He reached over to her glass with the bottle.

'I've done stupid things,' she admitted with a grimace. 'It's only now that I don't regret the fling with Caleb – he's the—'

'I know,' nodded Django, 'Fen explained.'

'I don't even regret the one-night stand with Alex,' Pip admitted. 'He's the—'

'Yes,' Django interjected, 'Cat explained.' He peered

briefly at Pip, then rose from his chair to fiddle with the fire; as if to say that the one-night stand with Alex really didn't warrant further discussion.

'The only regret I have is over Zac.' She looked at Django. He settled himself back into the tub chair, sipped his brandy slowly and then returned her gaze. His expression was open. 'Did Fen or Cat tell you about him?'

'A little,' Django said, actually knowing an awful lot but also knowing it was wise to encourage Pip to proclaim it all in the open to him.

'He's the one who –' she paused. Django refused to assist her. She'd just have to think and finish her sentence on her own. And out loud. Pip glanced at the fire. Glanced down into her brandy balloon. 'Well, he's actually, simply, The One. Is Zac Holmes, Django. Actually.'

Django raised his glass. 'To Zac,' he toasted, 'actually The One for our Pip.'

Pip shook her head forlornly. 'He's gone,' she whispered, a tear so full, so brackish and heavy, that it splashed fast and noisily straight down into her glass. She took a gulp of liqueur as if to hide the evidence. The brandy tasted no different. 'I'm not to him as he is to me,' Pip said.

'Why do you say that?' Django asked with a tone of incredulity which he hoped would signify optimism. 'If he's the one for you, why on earth wouldn't you be the one for him?' He let the question hover in the room. As if the question itself provided the only answer. 'Of course you are! Just look at you! You're gorgeous! You're a catch! You say you've lost him? Gracious, girl, out you go to find him again.'

Pip shook her head and tried to sip her liqueur. Her throat was so tight with the knot of tears she was holding at bay that she was unable to swallow. She swished the liquid around her mouth until it had anaesthetized her gums and numbed her tongue.

'Communication communication communication,' her uncle emphasized.

'Won't do any good!' Pip remonstrated histrionically. 'I've fucked up and that's all there is to it.'

'Language!' said Django, though the McCabe swear jar was customarily full on account of his own ripe choice of expletives.

'Pardon me,' Pip said.

Django passed her a peeled satsuma. She picked at the pith and noticed how it made her fingertips scaly. She popped two segments in her mouth and bit down. The sour-sweet acidity zipped along her jaw, making her eyes water and yet helping her tears go away.

'You know what,' she said clearly, 'I've made a mistake.' The proclamation was immense for her, her eyes darting over Django's face. 'Me.' She didn't seek Django's understanding of the situation, just approval of her declaration. He glanced at her and then seemed to find greater interest in Fen's copy of *Art Matters*. Pip would have to elaborate. 'I know that I don't *need* a man,' she said, 'however, I now think I'd rather *like* one – but only this *Zac* one – in my life.' Django regarded her intently. As she let her gaze drop, so, too, did the corners of her mouth. 'However, my ridiculous behaviour and daft principles have made this impossible,' she spat at herself. 'I've forfeited Zac, Django. He's not interested. He doesn't want me. And I don't blame him.' Uncle and niece looked at each other. Keeping her focus steady, Pip continued. 'I must move on and carry forward the hindsight of it all.' She cupped her hands around the rest of the satsuma, as if it might emanate warmth. 'It's time for a change,' she began to conclude, 'so, Zac was my first love. And it's my fault that I have to say "was". But *c'est la vie* and all the other clichés out there. Me and my fucking stupid fear of commitment.'

'Language!'

'Pardon me.'

'Not the word "fuck" this time,' Django clarified, 'the word "commitment", Pip. I've never heard anything so flimsy and feeble!'

'I *have* a fear of commitment!' Pip protests in a chant-like way, as if she's learned it off by heart from an article in *Cosmo.* As if it is a fact as indisputable as her blue-green eyes. As if it is something she was born with and will die with, and to argue otherwise is futile and plain daft. 'I have,' she repeats slowly and somewhat patronizingly, 'a fear of commitment.'

'Bollocks!' Django says derisorily, taking yesterday's *Daily Telegraph* and scanning the television listings as if they are far more interesting than Pip. 'Absolute bloody bollocks.'

'Language,' Pip counters, with not much conviction.

'Overruled,' Django declares, scrunching down the newspaper as if he's supremely irritated that her nonsense is preventing him from reading yesterday's television times. 'It's entirely justified in this instance. You're wrong. You're talking codswallop.'

Pip is pissed off. The room is too hot. It's not yet October. There's no need for a fire, however lovely the smell. Django has poked and stoked and fed it too much. Pip smirks out loud at the parallel. She's been given too much rich food. Too much bloody cherry bloody brandy. She's been poked and prodded and probed. She's bloody well going to go home tomorrow. 'I'm tired,' she says. 'I'm going to go to my room. Pack. I'm off *home* tomorrow.' She cringes. She said that on purpose in her petulance and she regrets it instantly. How childish.

'Philippa,' Django says sternly and, though she's halfway to the door, she stops, turns and lets him lecture her. 'I am telling you that you do *not* fear your *own* ability to *commit.*' He lets the statement hang in the air, the italicized emphasis is blatant. 'Just think about your unwavering dedication to your career, your notion of sisterhood and friendship. You are tireless. That is why we all lean on you. Because you are so totally committed to the lot of us.' Pip finds herself sitting down on the arm of the sofa, staring at the faded knees on Django's corduroys. 'You do not have a "fear of commitment", Philippa McCabe,' he all but mocks, 'that's just an easy way out of all of this. What you have, dearest one, is a deep-seated and totally understandable fear of *other* people's commitment to *you*.'

His conclusion is so strong, delivered so brazenly, that she reads it in her mind's eye as a shout line in capital letters, italicized here and there. She blinks, she closes her eyes, she opens them and blinks again, frowning deeply. She shakes her head vehemently. She's desperate to deny it.

Wait! She's never been in love, for Christ's sake! Not until Zac. So Django's theory is flawed. And she tells him so.

'Don't you see,' she concludes triumphantly, 'I've never been committed to a soul! Before Zac, the blokes I've dallied with have been in love with me. I haven't cared for them and therefore haven't cared when they've ended.' She pauses. She's confused. She fears she's contradicted herself but she's not quite sure how. Is a fear of commitment the same as having never committed to a soul? Her mind is fuddled. It's all boiling down to semantics. She's in a knot and she's squirming.

'I totally, wholeheartedly, agree,' says Django, taking her off her guard, 'you're never been in love. Until Zac, you've chosen chaps whom you've simply liked but who have loved you. So when they're over, it hasn't hurt you. Not that you've ever considered *their* grief.'

Pip has no idea what's coming next. All she knows is that hitherto, Django has made sense and now she's powerless to disagree. It's simultaneously unnerving and yet just a little comforting, too.

'Why have you done this, over all these years?' He's asking it as a question but she'd much rather he'd answer it for her. 'I'll tell you why,' Django obliges. 'Because what *you* actually fear is being left by someone *you* love.'

Thank you, Django. Thank you.

*

Pip just stares at him. It makes perfect sense and it appals her.

'That's why you have attempted to destroy what you had started to unravel with Zac.'

Go on, Django, go on!

'Your fear of *commitment* centres solely on another's commitment to *you*.'

More, Django, more!

'And who can blame you, my darlingest duck,' Django says softly, crossing the room to his niece and placing a hand so gently across her shoulders, 'who can blame you, my dear? Your mother left you! She ran off! You were tiny!'

Django tries to still a shudder when experiencing acutely the pain he still feels at his sister-in-law's abhorrent act. Pip holds tightly on to his hand in both of hers. He smiles down at her, benevolently. 'I know we as a family have it down to a banter – "mother ran off with a cowboy from Denver" – but the reality is so hideous that the only way we can deal with it is by making light of it.' Pip regards him, wide-eyed. 'You tell your Zac that your mother ran off with a cowboy from Denver when you were tiny,' Django says, 'and if he's even half the lad I suspect he is, he'll pull you to him and never let you go.' Pip stares at him. What on earth is she meant to say now? 'Go and pack,' Django says, 'have a good night's sleep – tomorrow you'll be back to that peculiar orangey night-time you lot have in the city.'

Falteringly, Pip goes to her room. There's a part of her that feels she's been let off the hook. There's a growing part of her that knows she isn't thankful for this. She looks at her clothes, her holdall. She thinks about baggage. She inhales deeply and gazes at Nick Heyward and Duran Duran.

What'll I do, boys?

You know what to do.

Pip returns to the Snug. Django is still reading yesterday's television listings in the *Daily Telegraph*. 'Django,' she says, with slight trepidation, 'it's just that I told Zac that we're a big happy family.' She stares at the rug. 'Really big.' She feels ashamed. 'I've not quite told him about my mother,' she reveals, glancing up at Django but, unable to translate his expression, she swiftly stares down to the rug again. 'About the cowboy in Denver bit.' She again scans her uncle's face but he's regarding her intently and waiting for her to continue. 'In fact,' she says quietly, 'I've even referred to her as "Mum".'

Django's heart bleeds for her. She can't tell, though. She feels guilty, as if manufacturing her mother and reinventing the woman as someone called Mum, somehow devalues all that Django has given to her and her sisters.

Django's heart, though, aches for Pip. For Fen, for Cat, too. For his late brother. Damn that bloody woman! No child should have to invent a mother. No child should have to accept an eccentric uncle as a mother. Damn that woman! 'Communication communication communication,' Django reiterates a final time in a slightly hoarse voice. 'You confide in Zac. You tell him about your mother and you will see – if he's half the chap I have a feeling he is – you will see how he will understand and embrace the provenance of your fib.'

Pip hadn't once stopped to think of it like that. All that Zac is flashes across her mind. He wouldn't think less of her, if anything he'd think more of her. And when Django meets him, she realizes, he'll think him double the chap he reckons he is now. She looks at Django with a mix of admiration, relief, gratitude and intense love. ''Kay,' she whispers. At the door, she stops, turns to face him again. 'Night,' she says, giving a small wave.

'Night, duck,' he replies.

'We couldn't have wished for a better mum,' Pip tells him, 'in you.'

Django smiles at her, tells her to stop being soppy, to have a bubble bath and bugger off to bed.

'I could have wished for a better mum for you,' he says

quietly as he stokes the fire and settles it for bed later. 'Damn that woman!'

So Pip returned to London by train. The sway of the carriage, the rumble of the tracks, the blur of the landscape rushing past, lulled her into a final, concluding bout of contemplation. It had taken her but a week at home to acknowledge her lifetime of hiding. She knew now that there was more to self-awareness than merely acknowledging one's character traits. I'm a jealous type; I'm a clingy type; I fear commitment; I fear being left – that's a start, but ultimately they are little more than excuses. Declarations alone do not provide solutions. Self-awareness is the realization that one can neither live in the past, nor run from it. The point of self-awareness is not to let history repeat itself in the future.

'It's not about forgetting the past or demeaning it. I have to actively embrace the past,' she said to herself as the train pulled in to Derby. 'I have to stare it in the face,' she declared as the train pulled out and continued south, 'be neither afraid nor embarrassed.' She sighed and drifted off to sleep with the effort of it all.

'It's not about moving on!' she suddenly said rather loudly, waking as the train stood stationary at Luton. A teenage boy who'd just embarked suddenly decided against sitting opposite Pip. 'It's not about moving on,' she laughed, startling an elderly couple recently seated across the aisle, 'it's about me standing my ground, pleading my case, rolling up my sleeves and fighting for what I want and believe in!'

She felt euphoric. She felt light and lifted, and she felt like dashing straight to Zac's, calling her friends and her sisters en route to meet her there, so she could lavish some sort of verbal group hug on the lot of them. Suddenly, it was all gloriously clear to her – where she'd been, where she wanted to go. Simple, really. She could finally define the cause. She certainly understood the effect it had had. Now, at last, she felt she had the means for solution at her disposal. Bloody train, stop dawdling! Godspeed her home so she can make amends.

THIRTY-FOUR

*P*ip McCabe has headed home with a heart full of hope. Her enthusiasm, however, is ever so slightly deluded. She somehow assumes that in her absence, all has been frozen in time, that everyone will be just where she left them, in anticipation of her return, hoping that she's picked up the pieces and is coming back to take up where she abruptly left off. It's as if, in her mind's eye, she has turned the people in her life into a cast of cardboard cut-outs, suspended in the there-and-then. All she needs to do, she feels, is breeze back amongst them, touch them with her magic wand (the non-collapsible one) and restore them to the here-and-now, ready for her revelations and happy to hold hands and stroll forward. That is, after they've given her a round of applause.

As if they'd put their lives on hold!

And anyway, who exactly is waiting for her?

Certainly not Zac Holmes.

Zac is not the type to allow himself to become stuck in a rut. He's too sensible and centred to languish in the past or rue what-ifs. He knows that time waits for no man and the only woman he currently waits for is Juliana who believes it her prerogative to be always fifteen minutes late. He's neither wondered whether Pip has been pacing the moors, soul-searching; nor has he hoped that all her Derbyshire paths have led her to the Road to Damascus. He hasn't had the time or inclination to think about her at all, actually.

Zac's had a hectic week. Work has been crazy. And there's been an inordinate amount of socializing. In his eyes, the latter provides respite from the former while the former provides the funds to facilitate the latter. For Zac, the two are not just complementary – the one is worthless without the other, not that he's one to analyse or complain. He just goes with the flow, accommodating his clients' particulars and peculiarities, welcoming the social opportunities that come his way, grateful for the funds that enable him to pay bills and enjoy himself. And buy that new painting – the huge green one with the orange blob and blue stripe. Once or twice he's been slightly baffled by how proactive his sister-in-law and his ex have suddenly become. But he's told himself not to be so bloody cynical. He should be grateful for their care and consideration. He should be plain pleased that they wish to include Juliana and welcome her into their fold.

And he is.

He is.

But it is a little odd.

He feels something of a passenger when he is accustomed to being in the driving seat.

It's just a little strange, something to get used to, that's all. Allowing himself to be taken for a ride.

* * *

The mantra that June and Ruth had decided upon was 'compliment compliment compliment' and even if they had to exercise it through gritted teeth or with fists clenched out of sight, they were determined to stick with it. On the day last week that Pip headed home to Derbyshire, Ruth had phoned Zac at work first thing.

'About tonight,' Ruth said, 'just thought I'd double-check we're still on.'

'Er, yes,' Zac replied, wondering why his confirmation the night before hadn't sufficed.

'Wonderful,' said Ruth, 'and as I said, I'd really much rather cook than eat out. It would be my pleasure.' She took Zac's pause as a possible falter so she carried on regardless. 'Just something simple,' she breezed. 'See you both around 8.00-ish?' Again Zac paused, again Ruth refused to allow it to be a vacillation. 'Or 8.30,' she offered, because the 'you both' part wasn't open to discussion. 'Wonderful!' she said, as if he had replied 'See you then!'

Juliana would really rather not have gone. A restaurant was one thing, someone's kitchen table quite another; Holloway was something else entirely. But it was too late to cancel. And it wasn't as though there were many viable alternatives that evening for her. There was a works' party somewhere in Fulham but she was starting to tire of her colleagues in the London office. Distant cousins had again extended an invitation for her to spend the night at their place in Hertfordshire. But though their cottage was cute, their three children under five years old weren't, so once again, she made her excuses. Anyway, she hadn't seen Zac for a week or so – not since his kid's party – and she rather fancied a Saturday morning shopping spree in Hampstead. So, though she had hoped that her time in London would preclude ever having to venture to a place called Holloway, if Saturday morning shopping in Hampstead was dependent on dinner at Zac's brother's there the night before, then fine. They needn't stay long. Certainly not if the sister-in-law's cooking was anything like as lousy as Zac's ex's.

Actually, June does finger food very well indeed. And very often. Fortunately, Rob-Dad and Tom feel very lucky. They think her finger food worthy of the maximum number of Michelin stars. They never go hungry. Meals in their house are always so colourful. And transportable, too! 'Delicious *and* nutritious!' Rob-Dad always marvels. 'Fun *and* yum!' Tom always says.

Ruth, however, is a truly accomplished cook. Ruth likes to

cook with cream. And egg yolks. And French unsalted butter. And not so much a drizzle as a gush of cold-pressed olive oil. And she absolutely delights in desserts. The more sugar the better. More egg yolks. Litres of double cream. Kilos of ground almonds. Ingots of fine chocolate. Sloshings of liqueur.

That Friday night, June, Tom and Rob-Dad watched *The Simpsons* whilst picking from plates laden with cheesy potato croquettes, chicken nuggets in a coating of crisps and corn flakes, bite-sized fritters of carrot, pumpkin and courgette and skewers of cherry tomatoes and mini corn-cobs. One hundred and fifty miles north, Pip and Django sat down at the kitchen table to mammoth portions of the rack of lamb from the Merifields, for which Django had devised an interesting gravy enlivened with marmalade, plus a stupendous mash of interesting texture utilizing every vegetable he could find, together with chopped apricots to brighten the colour. In Holloway, Ruth prepared a veritable banquet for Zac and Juliana. Not a single element of the meal was low-fat or calorie-conscious or cholesterol-friendly. Even the side salad was drenched in a delicious, rich, whipped vinaigrette.

Juliana hardly ate a thing. She met every plate-load of food with a polite 'thank you' but a look of utter disdain while she prodded the food with suspicion. Ruth pretended not to notice. She knew that Zac noticed – that was enough for her. In between mouthfuls, she gamely chatted nineteen to the dozen, as was her wont, and Jim asked polite questions about life in South Africa and the vagaries of Juliana's job. They both met Juliana's spartan answers with grace. Although Ruth's motives were ulterior, on the face of it Ruth was just being Ruth – chatty, vivacious, hostess extra-ordinaire. And Jim was just being polite towards his brother's new woman. Ultimately, Juliana was just being Juliana, too. That, thought Ruth, was precisely the point. Without the dimmed lighting of a restaurant, or the unwanted attention of waiters, or the distraction of other diners, one could see much more clearly what one was getting. Ruth thus considered the evening a success.

When Zac went to collect Tom on the Sunday, June asked after Juliana. 'Ruth said it was a fun evening,' she said.

'The food was amazing,' Zac said, privately wondering whether 'fun' best described the evening. Juliana had been stroppy back at his flat when Zac admitted that he was too full to fuck. And she'd cost him a small fortune at Whistles yesterday morning. Still it was nice to have his ex asking after Juliana. And it was touching that his sister-in-law had made such an effort. Wouldn't it be nice, too, if Juliana enquired after June, after Tom? It would have been nice if she had made more of an effort with Ruth and Jim, as well. Ever the diplomat, Zac put it all down to her having a somewhat awkward manner. Or else that she was on a diet. Or that she had a very high sex drive. He liked to think she was probably just shy under that steely exterior. Or something. He reckoned she was simply not used to the overtness of characters like June and Ruth; to rich food; to men with indigestion.

Tom was scurrying around the house, gathering various components of Tracy Island that he simply couldn't leave home without – even though Zac's flat housed a wealth of paraphernalia connected with Thunderbirds.

'What are you boys going to do today?' June asked Zac.

'Oh, you know, a little bit of International Rescue,' Zac replied drily. 'Thunderbirds are go, and all that.'

June laughed. 'Is Juliana around?'

Zac looked fairly startled. He hadn't thought to include her in his time with his son. Certainly, she'd made no suggestion either. In fact, he didn't even know what she was up to that day. Or the next few, for that matter. 'No,' he told June, 'she has plans already.' June nodded as if this was a good enough answer from him and a good enough reason from her. Tom came crashing into the hall, loaded with plastic toys and brimming with excited energy.

'Thunderbirds are GO,' he proclaimed rather seriously, kissing his mother and taking his father's hand.

'I'll do the school run tomorrow morning,' Zac told June, giving her a kiss. 'OK, kiddo,' he said, ruffling Tom's hair, 'let's go To Infinity And Beyond.'

'That's Buzz Lightyear,' Tom corrected, looking nervously about him to check no one had heard his silly old dad's gaff.

For the week that followed, while Pip traipsed the moors with furrowed brow and heavy heart, Zac had barely a moment to himself at work or play. It was a week in which he hoped to consolidate his bonus and was therefore happy after heavy, fraught days for the evening's entertainment to be laid on for him. On one, Juliana treated him to champagne and strawberries at her flat – partly, he realized, so she could show off her new Brazilian bikini wax which left very little to the imagination because it left very little at all. On another, he treated his brother and Rob-Dad to Chelsea v. Spurs and too many pints after a storming victory. Ruth made sure that the intervening three evenings were organized, too. With Juliana's attendance graciously requested, of course.

Ruth had a feeling that Juliana would turn her nose up at any theatre that wasn't West End with name-droppable cast, which was precisely why she chose a new Scottish play at the King's Head in Islington and encouraged the party to knuckle down to a thorough critique and analysis over spicy food afterwards. The next event she pinpointed was a Spanish film, at the Everyman Cinema in Hampstead. To Ruth's horror, she'd overlooked how kinky Almodovar's films could be. She feared her plan had backfired when Zac and Juliana bade a flushed and hasty farewell, disappearing down Hampstead High Street towards Zac's flat at an alarming pace.

Ruth needn't have worried. Indeed, Zac and Juliana did have sex urgently as soon as they were in his flat. But for both of them, it was little more than assisted masturbation.

The film had made them horny individually, but not really for each other. Come quickly. Then go, please. It was like being famished and wolfing down a fast-food-chain burger and fries. You don't really taste it. It repeats on you later, rather unpleasantly. It staves off hunger without one's appetite being truly sated. The resulting feeling is of being unfull and unfulfilled. So Juliana took a taxi home, did a little yoga and had an early night. Zac half-watched *Newsnight* and did some work.

It's Friday night. Pip has been back in Kentish Town for a couple of hours, has flicked a duster over her flat, done her washing, carefully noted down various messages left on the answering machine and been philosophical over the absence of the voice she unrealistically hoped to hear. She's prepared herself a herb omelette, some oven chips, grilled mushrooms and a dollop of ketchup and is perched on a stool in her kitchen, flicking through the mail. Tonight seems the ideal time to catch up on paperwork, pay bills and balance her bank statements with her cheque-book and carefully kept auto-bank slips. Hopefully, she'll soon enough be far too busy for admin and chores.

Which reminds me! The hallway! I bought the paint before I left so I'll set to transforming it from antique white to funky pistachio just as soon as I've washed up.

Down in Soho, Rob and June, Ruth and Jim, Zac and Juliana have formed a cosy little group in a corner of the private members' club that Jim belongs to. June and Ruth have already spoken two or three times during the day to confirm the subtleties of the sign language and code they're to call upon.

'Right, so if either of us sneezes twice, the other has to go to the loo, then the sneezer has to sneeze like mad and excuse herself for the loo, too?'

'Yup. And if I rub Rob's knee, it means Juliana or Zac are getting too physical and one of us should do something.'

'Like what? Spill a drink?'

'Ruth, you are wicked! But I dare you! No, that's cruel. Remember, we mustn't interfere – we can only assist in making the incompatibility as obvious to Zac as it is to us.'

So the six of them are in the bar, sipping drinks and chatting as casually as a stage-managed, ready-scripted June & Ruth Inc. Production allows. Juliana and Zac are sitting opposite one another and there have been no physical displays of affection, or even casual contact. Unluckily for Rob, June has thus had no reason to rub his knee. Both Ruth and June have already had a sneezing fit apiece and have twice convened in the loos to discuss and plot.

'Compliment compliment compliment,' June reminds them both.

'The thing is,' Ruth remarks, 'they seem somewhat disinterested in each other – don't you think?'

'Maybe it's on its way out naturally,' June theorizes. They consider this and see that such a twist would be rather unsatisfactory in the light of their thoughtful machinations.

'But it must be Zac who does the ditching,' Ruth stresses, for the thousandth time. 'He must clear his slate himself.'

Ruth and June's compliments take many different forms, from paroxysms of delight over Juliana's Gina shoes, to an ardent interest in what exactly she does in her consultancy, to downright inquisitiveness about her friends and family Back Home. Juliana's economic answers, polite smiles and compliments graciously but sparingly received, tell Ruth and June little more than they already know. Ruth and June worry that the men are chatting and drinking and not taking a blind bit of notice. Furtive glances over to Zac reveal little. He just nods and smiles and chats and laughs, as ever he does, whomever he's with.

Juliana goes to the toilet. Ruth leans over to June. 'I want to hit your ex!' she hisses. 'I want to say, "Come on, you dick! She may well look the part but she's as dull as dishwater!" In fact, *he* should be telling *us* that she's as dull as dishwater; begging us for advice.'

June nods, tips her head to one side and taps Zac insistently on the knee. 'So how's it going?' she asks him, repeating herself to force him to break off from an intense debate about Budvar versus Budweiser. 'How's it going?' she asks intently. 'With Juliana?'

Zac regards her a little blankly. He glances at Ruth who has her glass midway to her lips. She shrugs. 'Fine,' he says, 'cool, I guess.' Juliana returns before June can probe into long-term potential and Ruth can dish dull water. 'You OK?' Zac asks Juliana with attentiveness typical of him but which June and Ruth feel she doesn't deserve.

'Sure,' she smiles, touching his knee.

Hands off! Ruth shrieks to herself, unable to withhold a nudge to June.

For fuck's sake! June curses to herself, partly because she now has a slosh of Ruth's Cosmopolitan down her right leg.

When Zac goes to the bar to buy the next round, June and Ruth round on Juliana.

'I really like your bag,' Ruth says. 'So how's it going with Zac?'

'Kate Spade,' says Juliana in a doesn't-every-woman-own-one kind of way.

It means nothing to June who's a loyal leather Mulberry girl herself. 'I love your bag, too,' she says anyway, 'and the colour of your nails – so vampy! So, you and Zac – happy?'

'Chanel,' says Juliana. June and Ruth nod effusively while wondering what on earth it will take for a direct answer. 'Zac's great,' Juliana surprises them, but continues in the same tone as if he's her flavour-of-the-month designer nail varnish. Her audience sits agog waiting for more. 'I'd be bored to hell over here without him.'

Because of Juliana's flat tone and level gaze, momentarily Ruth and June both wonder if she means here as in London, England, or here as in right now in the bar in Soho, with them.

'When are you going back to South Africa?' Ruth asks and it sounds more like an instruction than a question.

'Actually,' Juliana says, 'my ticket is booked for next Friday.' The ambient jazz masks Ruth and June's sighs of relief. 'But I may well end up staying until Christmas now,' Juliana reveals. June and Ruth are stunned and horrified and unprepared.

'Work or pleasure?' June asks, as if dreading the answer.

'Are the two mutually exclusive?' Juliana retorts, irritated that there's a chip in her nail varnish. 'I don't think so.'

Ruth and June forget all about their lexicon of sneezes, the symbolism of rubbing Rob's knees, the coded winks and loaded nudges they'd devised for the evening. When Juliana disappears to the street to search for a signal on her mobile phone, they round on Zac.

'I hear Juliana might be staying on,' Ruth exclaims.

'Until Christmas,' June consolidates.

'Yes,' Zac confirms, 'she might.'

'Does that suit you?' Ruth badgers.

'Sure,' Zac shrugs. 'Why wouldn't it?'

THIRTY-FIVE

Zac awoke in Juliana's serviced apartment the next morning. His head ached a little but through general fatigue rather than a hangover.

I'd rather be in my bed, alone, actually.

Why is that?

No reason, really. Haven't had myself to myself for a while. Plus I'd like to doze off for a couple of hours, fart a fair bit, lounge around eating Frosties straight from the packet and see if Cat Deeley or one of her lookylikey chums are on kids' TV.

Can't you do that here?

Juliana doesn't do Frosties. She does wheatgrass and some kind of organic sprouted non-yeast bread. Hers is a fart-free flat. I wouldn't dare. Ogling Ms Deeley and Co. is out.

Why? Wouldn't Juliana be amused?

No. Not her style.

Can't you just doze off anyway?

I'd rather head off home. Have a doze later.

'God, isn't it Sod's Law not to have a party booking on a Sunday,' Pip bemoaned. 'I so need something else to think about, to stop me dwelling on the fact that I simply don't know what to say. What should I *say*?' Pip implored them. 'Think of something. Tell me what to say.'

What on earth did she mean? Her sisters had no idea. It made no sense to them. How could Pip McCabe ever not know what to say? She *always* knew what to say. What on earth were her sisters meant to say to that? She had stolen their whinge. Whenever they'd inflicted it upon her, she'd come out with four or five expertly constructed phrases, of which one or two would be pure lines of comedy to lighten the tone, make them giggle and see their situation as more daft than traumatic. But now it is Pip McCabe herself, their sister and mentor, who doesn't know what to say and she's pleading for their assistance.

'I don't know,' Fen said softly, confused.

'What do you want to say?' Cat asked.

Pip looked crestfallen. 'Dunno,' she mumbled glumly. 'It all seemed crystal clear back home. Now it all feels ominously murky.' Cat poured her another cup of tea from the pot, Fen snapped off a finger of KitKat for her. 'It's not just that I felt brave and optimistic at home,' Pip furthered, 'but I had all these word-perfect soliloquies which I composed and learnt by rote whilst striding about.' She sipped and munched. 'To tell you the truth, down here, they sound not just out of place, but whimsical and deluded.'

The sisters sat at Fen's kitchen table, or what could be seen of it under the scatter of Sunday papers.

'I tried them out in front of the mirror last night,' Pip confided. 'I sounded like a cross between Gwyneth Paltrow at the Oscars and a six-year-old. Ridiculous. And what a sad way to spend Saturday night.' The sisters stared at the same crumb for some time. 'I returned to London with such optimism,' Pip rued, flicking it away dismissively. 'I was bursting with declarations. Most importantly, I had the guts, the incentive, to go for it.'

'So you *do* know what to say?' Fen clarified. Pip nodded.

'But you've lost the inclination to say it?' Cat asked.

Pip shook her head. 'No, not that,' she explained. 'I'd love to. But I've lost the confidence. In fact, perhaps I've never had it.'

'Just phone him,' Fen said, offering Pip her land-line.

Pip started surreptitiously checking her horoscope in the various Sunday supplements, a pastime she had often ridiculed her lovelorn friends for doing.

'Why not just turn up there?' Cat suggested, trying to read her own stars, upside down.

'And say *what*?' Pip sighed wearily, wondering what zodiac sign Zac was.

'Fucking hell, Pip,' said Fen, 'it's not as if you have to get all nuptial! Forget declarations and poetry – just say "hullo" to the guy.'

'If he blanks you, he's a prat,' said Cat, 'and if he says "hullo" back to you, you can follow it with something else. Like "How are you?"'

'Hullo, how are you?' Pip let the words hang. Then she started to laugh. She wasn't quite sure why and nor were her sisters. Soon, though, they were all giggling. 'You're right,' Pip chuckled, 'you're both completely right. I'll do it.' Cat punched the air triumphantly, Fen gave Pip's forearm an encouraging squeeze. 'First, though, I'm going to finish the skirting-boards. I'm turning my hallway into the inside of an ice-cream cabinet,' she enthused. 'Pistachio walls and lemon sorbet skirting.'

'Whatever,' Fen chided lightly. 'Just get in touch with him, all right?'

'And no Gwynnie-style melodramatics,' Cat warned. 'Just say "hullo".'

It's about letting go.

That's what Pip is telling herself as she prises the lid off yet another tin of paint and stirs the lickable colour to loosen it.

It's about letting go.

She remembers the first time she let go on the trapeze – her first flight unchaperoned. She'd hovered and dithered and hyperventilated on the platform and thought 'Fuck this, what and why am I putting myself through this, I'm a perfectly good juggler and clown, I don't need to do trapeze, too.' Second thoughts, she realizes now as she pours a little paint into a tray and strokes the bristle brush over it, second thoughts are normal and understandable.

It's about letting go. It's about not needing to hold on.

And did you let go, on the trapeze?

I did.

And?

I flew.

Any regrets?

I flew! Of course I had no regrets! I flew! It was so nerve-racking it was utterly exhilarating. I couldn't breathe, I couldn't speak, the sensation sapped me of physical strength for hours after. Days, I think.

It was worth it.

Ah. But I had a safety net.

You have a safety net still – one that many would envy, that some don't have and never will. Your beauty, your health, your friends. Your home. Your family.

So how is Pip going to do it? When? And *is* she going to do it? She's stared at the phone a few times. She's even dialled Zac's number, from both her land-line and mobile phones, though she hasn't dared activate the call. She's restricted her number and dialled his land-line and mobile phones, hanging up before connection. Yet she won't sit down for fear of becoming glum and confused, maudlin and useless.

There's only one thing for it.

He can't object.

She's going to play him at his own game.

She's off to Hampstead.

A little friendly stalking.

THIRTY-SIX

*P*ip McCabe has a great big daft grin on her face but not a scrap of slap. Her eyes sparkle naturally, her cheeks are flushed and her nose tip is reddened by the autumn chill that's slithered into town. Her exuberant grin bestows a shine to her features in general. She is practically skipping down Hampstead High Street, having to remember not to giggle out loud or people will stare. All the heartfelt if histrionic speeches she so fastidiously devised and memorized during her stay in Derbyshire, are no longer necessary – though Pip's enduring commitment to their importance is putting the spring into her step. The only cliché she'll allow herself is that which has brought her to Hampstead – that actions can speak louder than words. And she's off to find Zac. That's her gesture and she really needn't say a word – mime will do.

As she bounds towards his road, she feels that a weight has been lifted from her shoulders and the fog which so obscured and distorted her awareness has dispersed. Now that she knows what she wants, what makes her tick, what has made her behave as she has done; so now she sees Zac in his true colours, not the garb she had previously dressed him in. It is as if she has suddenly awoken to the world at large being in full colour, whereas previously, with eyes protectively half-closed, she'd seen only tonal degradations. Behind all this life-altering awareness is an immediate drive to simply embrace. To surprise him. To beam at him, panting no doubt, but just say 'hullo'.

I know Zac! That's the point – now I know him. He treats like with like – which is why he is so affable, so lovely to be around. If I laid some heavy declaration on him right now, he'd bat a load back at me. If I just bounce up to his front door, grin and brandish my best 'Hullo, cupcake!' he'll grin back and say 'Hullo, Clowngirl' or something.

And he would.
    She's right.
    Zac really would.
    She has him to a 't'.
    We know he would, too.
    He'd be startled and delighted and he'd grin as good as he'd get.

Unfortunately, though, it is Juliana and not Zac who answers the door to Pip's rhythmic chiming. Unfortunately for Pip, Zac is right behind Juliana. Unfortunately for everyone, it all happens so fast that Pip booms out her 'Hullo, cupcake!' before realizing the target of her affection is actually behind his sodding gorgeous girlfriend.
    Hullo cupcake hullo cupcake hullo cupcake.
    The three of them are gobsmacked but rooted to the spot.
    'Oh,' Pip says because she can think of little else to say.
    'Pip?' Zac exclaims, bewildered.
    'Cupcake?' Juliana probes. 'Huh?'
    Pip can't very well say 'Sorry, wrong number' or 'Fancy seeing you here' or 'I was just passing'. In fact, all she can say is 'Oh', but it seems that she is only capable of that the once, and now she stands stock-still, mouth agape, staring concertedly if unintentionally at the nape of Juliana's neck where a rather beautiful diamond nestles.

'Won't you come in?' Zac says because he can't think what else to say and they can't stand in the doorway all day.

'Do,' says Juliana terribly graciously, as if it is her flat. As is all that goes with it – Zac included.

'Oh,' Pip says casually, waving her hand around as if there's a fly or a smell to waft away, 'I was just passing, that's all.' Her toes curl at the sound of it. 'I mean, I was just wondering if I could use your loo.' Her toes have practically looped the loop. High declarations of love and intent are one thing, 'Hullo, cupcake' is quite another. 'Can I use your loo?' is something else entirely.

Juliana baulks a little; the girl's quirkiness offends her in much the same way as Zac's ex's lurid finger food. Where are these people's sense of decorum, of refinement? Zac, though, laughs a little. It is both implausible and yet somehow typical that Clowngirl would suddenly front up on his doorstep calling him a cupcake and asking to use his loo.

'Course you can,' Zac says, ignoring Juliana's frown. 'You know where it is,' he continues pointedly, aware that this turns the frown to thunder.

'Thanks,' Pip says meekly and shuffles in. As soon as she has locked herself in Zac's bathroom, she realizes she has all but trapped herself. She slumps down with her back to the basin and wonders what to think. Bizarrely, she suddenly fancies taking a shower. She doesn't need the loo at all. She notes that there is only the one toothbrush and she's pleased. She half-thinks of cleaning her teeth. She runs her fingertips over Zac's luxurious towels. She sniffs his aftershave balm to see if it springs to mind. She doesn't recall it, but it smells nice. She catches sight of herself in the mirror but glances away and dutifully unbuttons her trousers and sits on the toilet. She really does not need the loo. She puts her head in her hands.

I am sitting on Zac's loo. I've sniffed his toiletries, manhandled his towels and resisted the urge to shower or to brush my teeth with his toothbrush. Good God!

You really ought to leave the bathroom. It'll be a little embarrassing soon.

It's mortifying already. I want to stay in here for ever. I want to magically evaporate – like bubble bath around the plug hole.

Pip – you really do need to emerge.

And then what? What on earth am I meant to do? Or say?

As discreetly as she can, she unlocks the door and opens it. She emerges into the hallway and clears her throat, preparing to enter the sitting-room. Only she remembers that she hasn't flushed the toilet, not that there's anything to flush. But she ought to flush it or they'll think she forgot to which won't look good at all. Not that turning up on spec trilling 'Hullo, cupcake' looks particularly good. So she returns to the bathroom, flushes the loo and goes through to the sitting-room making a big deal about wiping her hands on the back of her trousers – though she suddenly wonders if they'll wonder why she didn't use Zac's fine towels for the purpose.

Juliana is reclining languidly in the Eames lounger, her stockinged legs curled sinuously, the *Sunday Times* 'Review' section in her lap. She looks most at home, very at ease with her Sunday at Zac's.

'Thanks,' Pip says to her in a servile way she regrets at once, 'that's better.'

Shut up, Pip!

'You know how it is when you're bursting for a pee!'

Don't say another word, just bugger off out of here!

'I mean, I could have popped in to McDonald's but I thought hey, why not pop in and say "hullo" to Zac!'

For Christ's sake, just leave!

Juliana smiles cursorily and regards Pip with an all-too-fleeting look of distaste that is all the more pointed for its brevity.

'Tea, Pip?' Zac calls through.

'No, no!' Pip calls back over her shoulder.

'I've made a pot – stay,' he suggests, coming into the room with a tray laid for three. Milk in a china jug.

'Really,' Pip says, locking eyes with him, 'I was just passing. I just needed to have a wee. I ought to bugger off. I mean – you know – Sunday afternoons are precious.'

'Well, if you're sure,' Zac says.

Pip wants to gaze at him, try to detect what he's feeling, see if there is a sparkle to his eyes, a spark between them. But she feels suddenly shy and stupid and incapable of maintaining, let alone instigating, eye contact. 'Sure I'm sure,' Pip nods. 'Ta-ra,' she says to Juliana who looks up eventually from some paragraph or other and fixes her with a synthetically sweet swift smile.

'Righty-ho,' says Zac with a shrug.

'New painting,' Pip remarks, nodding at his recent acquisition as she turns to leave.

'Yes,' he says proudly. 'Do you like it?'

'It's very *you*,' Pip confirms warmly. 'You've moved the blue boobs?'

'They're in the bedroom,' Zac laughs, 'and they're *mountains*, I tell you!'

'Yes yes,' Pip jests, 'and lap dancing is a higher form of ballet.'

I really really have to go.

'Well, porn is educational,' says Zac drily with a nonchalant shrug. He walks Pip to his front door, both of them a little confused by how abstract art had led to porn so seamlessly. Both a little amused, too. But soon enough, awkward again. 'Anyway,' says Zac, frowning momentarily at his door lock.

'Yes,' Pip answers him, staring at his letter-box.

'That was a surprise,' Zac says, but too quietly for his tone of voice to suggest whether he means nice or nasty.

'Sorry,' Pip shrugs. 'It was impetuous. I should have called.'

Zac brushes away her apology and opens the door. 'Take care,' he says.

The sound of the door closing denies Pip the 'cupcake' he adds to his sentence. Juliana hears it, though. It pisses her off, yet jealousy doesn't figure. She feels restless and cooped up. She isn't really remotely interested in the *Sunday Times* 'Review' section, let alone lounging about with a whole stack of weekend papers. She isn't really that interested in the clown with the weak bladder. Certainly, she doesn't feel remotely threatened. Why should she? She denounces the clown as physically uncouth and irritatingly quirky in personality. Furthermore, she feels no threat because actually, she harbours no true possessive affection for Zac. Suddenly, she feels bored beyond relief. And irritated. Christ, if she could use the toilet in McDonald's – that's where Zac had taken her and his kid that lunch-time – why couldn't Pip?

'I'm going, hon,' she says to Zac, testing for attention and an objection. Zac, however, doesn't object. 'Maybe we'll do something later in the week.'

'Sure,' he says.

'Maybe we won't,' Julia poses.

Zac shrugs.

'No doubt your sister-in-law will contrive one of her staged evenings,' Juliana says with a cockily raised eyebrow.

Zac regards her squarely. There's no way he's going to dignify that with a worded response. She's pushing it, she's pushing him, he realizes. But he doesn't want to be shoved into a corner like the bad boy. There's nothing to justify, apologize for or clarify. So he just stands his ground, leaning nonchalantly against his wall, looking at his new green painting, quite happy to have his home to himself for the remainder of the afternoon.

'I'll give you a call,' he says. She sees herself out.

Pip says 'shit shit shit' all the way home. She walks as fast as she can, saying 'shit' with every footfall, straight down Hampstead High Street, through Belsize Park, all the way down Haverstock Hill, turning left up Prince of Wales Road.

Pounding the pavement, her heart pounding, chanting 'shit shit shit'. Only when the Kentish Town Baths come into view does she slow her pace slightly and cease her fulminations. She's given herself a blister. And a headache. And of course, as soon as she's home, the answering machine flashes urgently and the phone starts to ring before she's shut the door and switched on the light. She's not scared of answering it any more. She doesn't wonder who it will be. What will be will be, and all.

'Well?' It's Cat.

'I'm on the other end!' It's Fen as well.

'Well,' Pip tells her sisters, while wriggling out of her shoe, peeling down her sock and wincing at her blisters, 'I did it.'

'You didn't!' says Cat, full of awe.

'You didn't!' says Fen with admiration.

'I certainly did,' says Pip. 'I rang his bell and I said "Hullo, cupcake".'

'Hullo, cupcake,' Cat repeats as if it's a line of poetry to commit to memory.

'Awesome!' Fen says excitedly.

'I did it,' Pip repeats, 'I said "Hullo, cupcake". And that's the point.'

'And he said?' Fen asks.

'What did he *say*?' Cat begs to know.

'Nothing,' says Pip, 'initially. Nor did his girlfriend.' Her sisters gasp. 'So I pretended to need the loo.' Her sisters are too shocked to wonder whether this was a cunning plan or not. 'Then what could I do but leave?'

Fen and Cat try to make sense of the facts. Cupcakes and girlfriends and asking for the loo. They wonder what they'd've done. They wonder what Pip should've done.

'I bet he calls,' Fen says decisively, though deep down she thinks it now sounds pretty futile.

'I bet so, too,' Cat says, privately thinking that asking for the loo on top of the cupcake part would not have done her sister any favours.

'Whatever,' says Pip. 'I did it, that's the thing.' She was feeling enormously tired – as if saying 'Hullo, cupcake' was in itself as complete a declaration as any she had composed whilst striding the moors. Somehow, she feels released from obligation. In truth, 'Hullo, cupcake' had utilized an enormous amount of energy. She needs to preserve a little because she wants to paint the door frame into the kitchen a shade of raspberry sorbet before the weekend is over. She switches Radio 2 on and her mind off.

Zac doesn't clear away the tray of teacups until nearly midnight. His cup has drying sediment on it. Juliana's is still half full with a discoloured scummy film now clinging from surface to sides. But it's Pip's cup that catches his attention. It hasn't been used, of course. But he puts it in the dishwasher nevertheless, as if it has been. Before he goes to bed, he surprises himself by holding the towels in his bathroom against his nose. He can't detect Pip. He tells himself he's not trying to, anyway; tells himself he's just checking to see whether he needs to wash the towels, though he knows full well that they've only been out a couple of days because he put them there.

What a peculiar turn of events. The last thing he was expecting that afternoon – or at any time, really – was an impromptu visit from Pip. He really hadn't thought about her much recently at all. Apart from the morning when she intruded on his reverie though it was Juliana in his bed in reality.

She called me 'cupcake'. What a peculiar thing to say. What an odd thing to do – to turn up here, with a manic smile on her face, calling me 'cupcake' and asking for the loo. What the fuck is a cupcake? I suppose I could ask June – it's the sort of thing she makes, no doubt.

Call June! Do. Call June, Zac. Ask her about cupcakes.

Of course he does no such thing.

There again, I always thought Clowngirl was a trifle odd.

He goes to sleep thinking of audits.

'What's a cupcake?'

Ruth looked at Zac and thought it a most peculiar question to be asked in the interval of *A Streetcar Named Desire*. She looked at Juliana and raised an eyebrow in a hopefully conspiratorial kind of way.

'What's a cupcake?' Zac repeated.

'It's a fairy cake,' Ruth replied, wondering if the gin and tonic wasn't quite as watered down as she thought, 'an individual sponge cake baked in one of those crinkly paper cases.'

'Oh,' said Zac, sipping his G & T and thinking it a travesty that theatre bars should be allowed to so obviously water down their liquor.

'Why do you ask?' Ruth probed.

'No reason, really,' Zac shrugged. The second bell sounded.

'A friend of his fronted up on Sunday afternoon,' Juliana informed Ruth, 'out of the blue. Wanting the toilet.'

Ruth nodded, none the wiser. 'And he brought cupcakes?'

'No,' Zac laughed, 'she called me "cupcake".'

'Who did?' Ruth asked. 'Who's she?'

Juliana remained silent, as if she really couldn't remember the visitor's name.

'Clowngirl did,' Zac told Ruth.

Ladies and gentlemen, please take your seats.

Zac headed for the auditorium. 'Then she asked to use my loo,' he told Ruth who stared at him and couldn't deduce what his expression could possibly mean.

Suffice it to say, Ruth could not concentrate on the second act at all, though the tickets were expensive and Glenn Close was magnificent. She was desperate to call June. Immediately. Also to have Zac to herself and grill him intensively. Phoning Clowngirl herself seemed like a good idea, too, just then.

There had to be more. You don't just turn up on someone's doorstep and say 'Hullo, cupcake, can I use your loo?' There had to be more. Zac couldn't have taken it at face value alone, surely. He must have thought there was more to it, too.

Christ! Pip turns up with cupcakes and a full bladder and Juliana is there, too!

Ruth declined Zac's suggestion of a drink after the play. And she was far too distracted to chat to her husband in the car on the way home. It was too late to phone June. But she sent her a text message anyway.

`pip went 2 z's on sun. called him cupcake & asked 4 loo. j there . . .`

Zac declined Juliana's offer of spending the night at her place. He was tired. There were unforeseen hassles at work. He took a cab home alone. He was hungry. He shouldn't have mentioned the sodding cupcakes. Now he quite fancied an individual portion of sponge cake. He asked the driver to stop at a late-night store. The choice was between Bakewell Tarts and Fondant Fancies. He couldn't decide. He bought both.

THIRTY-SEVEN

'Accidentally on purpose.' Zac loved the expression. He also liked 'almost', because it could instantly cast a positive light on a possibly negative situation. With 'almost', you couldn't deny that you hadn't done something you should have, but you could make it appear an innocent timing issue. 'Accidentally on purpose' enabled you to absolve yourself of a certain amount of responsibility in a situation.

And so it was, accidentally on purpose, that on the Tuesday evening, Zac took the High Barnet branch of the Northern Line instead of the Edgware branch. And of course, the first opportunity he had to retrace his steps meant alighting at Kentish Town. However, as if his careless re-routing wasn't enough, while walking to cross platforms he decided that he might just have forgotten to go to the loo before he left work, accidentally on purpose. He didn't actually need the loo – but there again, just say there was a delay for an Edgware-bound train at Camden Town? What would he do then? Well! Doesn't fortune smile on those in need – look where he is! Kentish Town! What a happy coincidence. He knows someone with a loo. Just round the corner. Who owes him a favour. A quick pee and he'll be home in half an hour. Just a minor detour. No big deal.

When Pip's bell rang, she groaned. Most days, at this time, she had been opening the door to some ragamuffin or other trying to flog substandard household goods in aid of some dodgy cause. Consequently, Pip's kitchen drawers were brimming with luminous orange dusters that left more lint than they picked up dust. She had enough pairs of rubber gloves to kit out a family of octopi though the rubber was so thin that even warm water felt scalding hot and hot water caused holes in the fingertips immediately. She'd bought oven cleaner of which one spritz had got her so high she hadn't dared use her oven for days afterwards. She'd bought sponges that disintegrated on contact with water long before they came in sight of a pan; she'd bought plastic bags that didn't open. Tupperware that didn't close, toilet freshener that smelt toxic and bleach that smelt innocuous. So no, this Tuesday, she wasn't going to open the door. Buying the *Big Issue* was one thing, cramming her change into collectors' cans on street corners was another, sending cheques to charities placing tear-jerking appeals in newspapers was another. But giving her hard-earned cash to the slightly threatening urchins who loitered on her doorstep was something else entirely. She didn't want any more tat. She had no need for any cleaning implements. In fact, she had no more room. Anyway, deep down she didn't believe in their so-called charities and she feared her money was more likely to fund daily inhaling of the oven cleaner or some other solvent. So she was going to stay put. Sit stock-still on her sofa, muting the sound on the TV remote control, chanting quietly 'piss off piss off piss off'.

The bell rang again.

Piss bloody off!

And again, this time a barrage of rings and an insistent flapping of her letter-box. The audacity!

Pip sighed and huffed and cursed that enough is enough.

This time, she was going to ask for ID and tell them she'd check it first and would call if she required a subsequent presentation of their wares – subject to twelve-month guarantees. She stomped to the front door. 'I'm coming!' she barked. 'For God's sake.'

It was Zac.

Nothing to buy, nothing to sell. Nothing to do but stand and stare.

'Can I use your loo?' he asked.

Can he use my loo?
   Her static silence caused his features to soften into a swift but imploring shrug of his lips. 'I took the wrong train,' he explained almost apologetically, 'and I'm dying for a pee.'
   Can he use my loo?
   Pip shook her head to shake off the shock. 'Sure,' she said, realizing he didn't deserve the stern expression she'd fixed to her face in anticipation of the scrounging urchins, 'sure. Sorry. Come on in. I thought you were flogging dodgy dusters.'
   Zac laughed and followed her into the flat. 'I come empty-handed but full-bladdered,' he said, standing in her sitting-room, thinking that something was different but unable to define what.
   They stood, side by side, for an awkward moment or two. 'Would you like a drink?' Pip asked, suddenly mortified that she looked a mess in mismatched socks, jeans and hair that needed a wash. She wanted him to say 'yes' partly because she wanted him to stay, partly because she wanted the chance to duck into her bedroom and change her socks if nothing else. She could pinch along her cheek-bones when she was in the kitchen. She'd learned that from Scarlett O'Hara and, though it made the eyes smart, it certainly put a becoming blush to one's face. She'd scoop her hair back into

a pony-tail – she knew there was a hair-slide on top of the fridge next to the spare keys and the torch.

'Sure,' said Zac, 'why not. Cup of tea?'

'OK,' said Pip and went to her kitchen.

She stared at the kettle without filling it or boiling it or seeing it at all, really. Her focus was elsewhere entirely.

My God. For the first time ever, I wish I could phone someone. I want to tell Megan 'He's in my house, I'm making tea!', I want to phone Fen and say 'I look a right state – what should I prioritize, hair or socks?'. I'd love to text Cat: fuck! z here! wot i do??

But you can't because your phone is charging in the sitting-room.

I know he's only just come, but I almost can't wait for him to go so I can start phoning!

Don't worry about your socks. Just make the tea. Add a plate with a couple of KitKats. The hair-slide is indeed on top of the fridge – you can do a little surreptitious hairstyling in the reflection cast by your kitchen window.

When Pip returned with the tea tray, she found Zac looking most at home, relaxed into the sofa, flicking through *Livingetc*. She was struck by the memory of sitting next to him there, a couple of months ago, asking him if he liked her tights, him liking her knees, them kissing. The way he left, that he then returned. And found her topless. And all the fantastic heavy petting before they went to bed. And he stayed the whole night through.

'Tea,' Pip announced, looking concertedly at her newly decorated walls because Zac didn't seem to be.

'Ta,' said Zac.

They sipped politely, darted little smiles to one another, took delicate nibbles along the length of the KitKat fingers and enquired courteously about each other's work.

'St Bea's today?' Zac asked. 'A toughie?'

'Actually,' said Pip, 'it was one of those sessions where it was infinitely rewarding. Sometimes, being a clown doctor is emotionally draining because it's an occupational obligation to keep the smile and the bounce and the laughter when you'd rather sit still and alone and cry. Today, though, I was in the privileged company of such bravery and dignity and beautiful humour that it was truly inspirational. I felt carried along – I felt sustained by them.'

'You're amazing,' Zac marvelled.

'Nonsense,' Pip brushed away and meant it and Zac thought her all the more amazing for it. 'Anyway,' she said, keen to change the subject – she could talk about her work all night, but compliments she found awkward to handle – 'how about you? Lots of sums?'

Zac groaned. 'Actually,' he said, 'it's a fucking nightmare. Recently, we were soaring – as a company, but even more so as a department. Suddenly – for reasons I'm not going to bore you with – the bonuses look like not happening, we seem set to lose a major client and morale amongst my lot is disintegrating before my eyes.'

Pip wasn't sure how to respond. 'Oh dear,' she said, 'I'm sorry to hear that.' She paused and thought how lame and formulaic that sounded. So she then said what really occurred to her. 'It must be tough for you – because I suppose your staff see you swivelling in your chair in your own office and they wonder if you're with them or just after your own gains.'

'God, Pip,' said Zac, 'that's precisely it. I'm under scrutiny by my superiors and my juniors. No one seems to have faith in my conviction. Honestly, the intricacies of the deal just fade into insignificance alongside the team morale which has been undermined. I'd rather have my team back in spirit, than a windfall in my bank account.'

'So you swivel in your chair, racking your brains how to make things work for them, on their behalf, but they see you swivelling and presume you're protected and don't care?'

'Yes,' Zac sighed, 'it's so enervating. There's fuck all I can do. It's out of my hands.'

Pip hummed in what she hoped was a sympathetic manner.

'I'd better go,' Zac said, placing his cup and saucer carefully on the coffee-table. 'I have work to do. Thanks for the tea.'

'Pleasure,' said Pip, clattering her china a little and rising hastily. 'It was nice of you to pop by.'

They were suddenly both acutely aware that Zac hadn't, in fact, gone to the loo. And to do so now would be all the more conspicuous. So they stood and smiled a little uneasily and Zac did a lot of that gathering-stuff-together-to-leave muttering. Actually, all he had to collect was his *Evening Standard* and his jacket. 'Well,' he said, 'keep in touch.'

'You too, Zac,' Pip said, 'you too.' The formality between them was so pronounced she half-wondered if they were about to shake hands. She paused and cast her gaze downwards. Zac's footwear. She wondered if it was incongruous for a man in soft suede boots the colour of caramel to be an accountant. Shouldn't he be in sensible brogues or slimy slip-ons or naff Nature Treks? But she'd always known there was more to Zac Holmes than met the eye – and she knew it was her own fault that it had taken until so recently for her to see it. 'Um,' she faltered. 'Sorry about Sunday,' she mumbled.

'Sorry?' Zac repeated as if he didn't understand.

'Just turning up like that. No warning. You had company.'

'Don't apologize,' Zac said. 'I'm just sorry you didn't stay for tea.'

'You had company,' Pip reiterated.

I'm sorry I had company, Zac remarked to himself, *I wish I hadn't*.

I wish you had said that out loud because your silence has demoralized Pip.

Pip had her hand on the latch when the doorbell chimed. 'Shit,' she said, 'I bet it's the dodgy duster urchins.'

'Here,' said Zac, 'allow me.' He talked amiably to the scruff peddling crap and had soon parted with five pounds, and found himself with a lifetime's supply of counterfeit J-Cloths. Pip wanted him to stay – for supper, for another cup of tea, for another five minutes. But she couldn't find the words to ask. So she said nothing. So Zac made his exit. He climbed the steps up from her basement to the pavement. He looked back down on her, framed in the doorway, the light behind her bestowing an incongruous halo. Her hair was a mess. Her socks were odd. Her jeans weren't that becoming.

'Bye,' he said.

'Bye,' she said. He walked out on to the street and she watched him go.

Just as he was about to pass beyond the boundary of her building, just as she was about to shut her front door, he stopped and leant over the railings.

'Pip,' he called down, 'what's a cupcake?'

'It's a little sponge cake baked in those corrugated paper cases,' she said artlessly, 'like at kids' parties. Like Tom likes. Sometimes, with icing and hundreds and thousands or jelly shapes. Like June made.'

'Oh,' Zac said, 'thought so. Cheerio.'

'Ta-ta,' said Pip.

Perhaps you oughtn't to have asked what but why, Zac.

Perhaps you oughtn't to have been so literal, Pip.

She closed the door and immediately felt desperately lonely. And rather pathetic. Her flat seemed huge to her. She felt diminished. Out of her depth. Surrounded by the strident colours of walls and skirting-boards, it was like being in some Lewis Carroll scene. Nothing was labelled 'Drink Me'. Just two empty teacups.

He didn't notice. He didn't notice the colour.

But he didn't use the loo, either, Pip.

Sometimes, you have to point out the most obvious things to a person. They know something's different, something's changed, but they just can't quite put their finger on what.

*

Juliana phoned Zac just as he was turning into his street.

'Hi,' she said.

'Hi.'

'You OK?'

'Sure, you?'

'Fine.'

There was a pause. Zac sent a vibe down the phone that he hoped would load the silence, which in turn would say more than speech.

'About tomorrow night,' said Juliana, as if she'd been listening intently.

'What about tomorrow?' said Zac.

'I'm going to cancel,' said Juliana.

'That's fine,' said Zac.

'I'm going home in three weeks,' said Juliana.

'Right,' said Zac.

'There's stuff I want to do before then,' said Juliana, 'and other stuff I feel I've done enough of.'

Zac read between the lines, looked up into the indigo sky of the October evening and thanked his lucky stars.

'Zac?' said Juliana.

'I'm here,' said Zac. 'I understand,' said Zac. 'I agree,' said Zac.

'Cool,' said Juliana. 'I may see you, though, before I go. I may organize a goodbye drinks.'

'Sure,' said Zac, knowing he'd be busy.

'Right,' said Juliana, 'good.'

'Good luck,' said Zac. 'Have fun – and take care.'

She was touched. She hadn't actually thought about wishing him well, or having him take care.

'No hard feelings, hey, Zac?'

'None whatsoever, Juliana.'

When Zac entered his flat, he was flooded with a wave of relief. He pressed his back against his front door and slithered down, squatting with his eyes closed and his arms lolling over his knees. He could either fall asleep or he could jump for joy – just then, he couldn't decide which so he continued to sit and appreciate the stillness of his flat and the sense of calm that one phone call had reinstated in his life. Juliana had spared him the task he'd been putting off. Oddly, it made him feel more fondly towards her now than at any other time in their brief history. It also made him realize how he'd never actually been fond of her – just fancied her and took advantage of what she had on offer. Crucially, he understood that the same went for her and he didn't mind in the least. Whatever it was that they'd had, or shared, or taken, it had been equal and balanced on both sides. They'd used but they hadn't abused. Ultimately, they'd simply used it all up.

Thank God, though, that she pipped me to the post. Even though, deep down, I knew she wouldn't have been upset or even particularly have cared if I'd instigated it, I really didn't relish the task of ending things.

Zac rose. He slipped his boots off and stuffed a scrunch of yesterday's newspaper into each, as they were still damp from lunch-time's freak downpour. Today was one of those rare days that Zac actually rather envied the colleagues who wore suits and stiff-collared shirts to work. At least it meant they had something work specific to physically shrug off when they arrived home. Zac, though, could only change from one pair of Gap navy trousers into another, slip out of one casual shirt and pull on a similar one, albeit in a different hue.

I wonder if many blokes actually envy me? I guess most guys my age are either resolutely single or else safely married. I don't really fall into either category, on account of Tom. I suppose I ought to get used to the fact that this is how my life will be – dalliances here, solitude there. The one constant being Tom. And if that's the case then shouldn't it be me who is envied the world over?

The phone rang. Zac wondered if it was Juliana with a change of mind. In which case he'd let it ring. But it was more likely to be work related. He ought to answer it.

It was Ruth. With a selection of things to do and nights to do them on.

'Thursday sounds good,' Zac told her because he really didn't fancy some art opening tomorrow night.

'Great,' said Ruth. 'Shall I book a table for four for dinner afterwards?'

'Juliana won't be coming,' Zac told her, conversationally.

'Oh?' said Ruth, physically pressing the receiver closer to her ear in her curiosity. 'Everything OK?'

'Very,' Zac assured her, 'we're just not a –' he paused. How on earth could he categorize what on earth he and Juliana had been? We're not two people who sleep together any more? We're not having our casual dalliance any longer? We don't really give a flying fuck about seeing each other again? 'Well,' said Zac, 'Juliana won't be accompanying me to things any more. Run its course, you could say.'

Ruth was so stunned and delighted that she shut her mouth for fear of emitting an excitable squeak, being all she was capable of. She felt if she were to do so, Zac might well see it as her taking credit for the state of his affair. And then he might change his mind. And ask Juliana to take him back. No. Ruth had brought him this far, she wasn't going to allow him even a pigeon tiptoe backwards.

'But I'm still on for Thursday,' Zac carried on regardless, 'as long as you didn't have some kind of couples-symmetry dynamic in mind.'

Ruth laughed. 'Not at all,' she said, though she'd much rather say 'Not a moment too soon' and pry. 'It'll be great to see you.' She was desperate for details. 'Are you cool about things?'

'God, yes!' Zac assured her.

'OK,' said Ruth cautiously whilst she thought what else to say, 'OK.' She craved a post-mortem. 'There didn't seem much of a connection,' she defined, sagely and subtly, 'between you and Juliana.'

'You're right,' said Zac, 'that's why it's no big deal at all.'

'How did Juliana take it?' Ruth asked.

'Oh,' said Zac very openly, 'it was Juliana who did the dumping.'

Ruth was so staggered, so supremely disappointed, so taken off her guard, that she had to stop herself from shouting 'No no no! That wasn't the idea! You were to do the chucking! It was all planned to perfection. Damn! What went wrong?'

'Anyway,' Zac continued, 'I'll see you on Thursday?'

'Sure,' Ruth managed eventually. She knew Zac better than to rummage for further information right at that moment. 'Damn!' she murmured, hanging up. 'Bollocks.' Billy glanced up. 'Mummy just said a naughty word,' she told him, thinking to herself that she could say a lot worse, 'naughty Mummy.' She dialled June, continuing to murmur 'naughty, naughty Mummy' absent-mindedly under her breath. Billy, however, whose vocabulary had been honed in Holloway playgrounds, was neither shocked nor impressed. He went to find his father to play PlayStation. The two of them always had a good and justified cuss at the screen.

'Bollocks,' Ruth cursed down the phone to June, her hand cupped over the mouthpiece lest Billy was still in earshot, 'you'll never guess what's bloody happened.'

Zac had no desire to contemplate Juliana – what it had all meant, if it had meant anything at all. After all, if he had time to think about Juliana, he most certainly had time to think about work and that's where his priorities should lie. Thus Zac really didn't have the time or the space to think about Pip either. It was enough that he had indulged himself in the impromptu detour on his journey home. Now, though, he couldn't really figure out why he had turned up. Actually, he couldn't quite believe he'd turned up at her flat at all. It would take him too long to wonder why on earth he'd done it. Currently, he didn't have time to think why. There was work to be done. Out came his laptop and on came his frown.

*

It seemed like only minutes later that the phone rang. However, glancing at the clock revealed that it was actually nearing midnight now. It could well be work calling. He ought to answer it.

'It's a term of affection,' Ruth's voice declared, dispensing with even a 'hi' to announce herself.

'What is?' Zac said, shutting down the laptop and settling back for an indulgent late-night chat with his sister-in-law.

'Cupcake is,' Ruth explained proudly, as if she'd thoroughly researched it on Zac's behalf in her every spare moment since the theatre bar the previous night.

'Oh,' said Zac, suddenly losing the impetus for the chat and instead feeling just enormously fatigued.

THIRTY-EIGHT

*P*ip felt thoroughly confused by it all. Though it had been a wonderful surprise to see Zac — and though she was keen to read excessively into every second of his visit, every gesture, every short sentence — ultimately, she wasn't quite sure why he'd come. Certainly, he hadn't popped by to use her loo. Mind you, nor had she when she turned up at his last Sunday. She wondered how she could wonder what was going on when her overriding instinct was that there wasn't anything going on at all. How could there be? After all this time? After all that had gone before? After all, he'd hardly been alone on Sunday. Perhaps she should be satisfied with a friendship based on cups of tea and the lavatory. She knew for sure that she didn't want to lose Zac Holmes from her life. She thought he was great. More than great. So, even if she couldn't have all of him, should she settle for just a part?

She also felt confused by how unsatisfactory it had been to share the sparse details over the phone with Megan and Fen. They'd listened and cooed but they could read no more meaning into his visit than she could. She didn't want to hear Fen reason 'He was on the wrong tube and needed the loo.' It was far too sensible and prosaic. She wasn't happy with Megan for saying 'See! He obviously thinks of you as his pal, too' when Pip had told her she wanted him as more than a pal. If they weren't going to say what she wanted to hear, what was the point of her confiding? Texting Cat, who was in Paris for the launch conference of the following summer's Tour de France, was equally frustrating. Her sister was obviously so enthralled to be back in the fold of the Lycra-lad fraternity, and back in the arms of her doctor beau, that Pip's long texts were responded to with the scantiest of abbreviated encouragements.

She went to bed feeling glum, goading herself that there was something rather pathetic about still feeling there was something she could do. However, if Zac's persistence early on hadn't worked on her, how could she possibly expect, at this late stage, with all that had gone before, that any persistence on her part could sway him?

I'm not going to phone, I'm not going to phone, I'm not going to phone.

How often had Pip forced her friends and sisters to chant those words? 'Don't you dare phone him!' she would tell them. 'And if you feel you're going to, for Christ's sake, phone me first!' And though they'd trust her reasons and could see sense, they obeyed only during daylight hours or when in her company. The lure was too great. Sure enough, Pip would be contacted at some point and they'd admit ever so meekly that they had, in fact, phoned. And how they wished they hadn't. And help, what could they do?

'It's not about playing-hard-to-get crap,' Pip had tried so hard to impress on them, 'it's not about games at all. It's about you presenting yourself in the best possible light, from all angles. Phoning to say nothing in particular, or something irrelevant, simply won't reflect well on you at this stage. You mustn't give him any reason to be put off before he knows the real you.'

'But I could just phone to say—'

'No!' Pip would declare. 'Don't! You'll gain nothing and you'll jeopardize the lot.'

And yet, here she is, sitting on her hands, glowering at her phone with a mixture of fear and desire. She desperately wants to phone Zac. She's not sure what she'd say – perhaps just 'hullo' without the 'cupcake'? Or ask how work is? Or Tom?

I know! I could ask if I left my gloves when I popped round on Sunday.

You didn't have gloves with you.

He doesn't know that!

Don't phone, Pip. Not right now. Not if you're not sure what to say. Not to ask about non-existent gloves. Not if you're not sure what's been going on in his life. Anyway, you're running late and you've got ward rounds at St Bea's. It's Thursday, after all.

With enormous self-restraint, Pip didn't phone Zac. But I wish she'd phoned someone because leaving St Bea's late tea-time, she suddenly had a brainwave that to anyone else, whether they knew her or not, would seem utter lunacy. Even if she had phoned a sister or friend, she was so convinced that what she was about to do was inspiration of staggering genius, that no threat or plea or scream from anyone else was going to stop her.

It wasn't stalking! Far from it! It was simply a brilliant idea and a prudent gesture. Far better than a phone call. And it wasn't really going to involve Zac at all, yet she was going to do him a huge favour. It was going to work wonders – for him on a personal level and, hopefully, for the possibilities that might still be salvageable between them.

You see, he'll ask himself why and the only conclusion he'll come to is that I did it because I wanted to prove how deeply I feel for him.

Did what? What are you off to do? You're leaving St Bea's and yet you are still dressed as Dr Pippity. And you're not heading for the tube at all. You're stomping through the City, chuckling and winking at passers-by. You don't mind whether they're laughing with you or at you – they have smiles on their faces and you deem that to be the important thing. Last time you strode this route, you were sobbing your eyes out, remember?

I found that bench. Look! That one right there. And suddenly Zac was beside me, comforting me and looking after me.

And he got you drunk.

And that was our first night together.

What are you going to do in the middle of Finsbury Circus? Cartwheel across the bowling green? Perform on the bandstand? Wave? Wait? Change your mind?

Oh, I'm not staying here! I'm off over there.

Where Zac works? Now? At five o'clock? Without warning, let alone an appointment? Dressed like that? Change your mind!

What a day. Zac Holmes glanced at the clock and knew he had at least another five hours in the office. He swivelled in his chair and gazed down from the window to the green grin of Finsbury Circus. Pigeons mainly. A tramp. A couple of high-heeled power dressers marching with conviction to some meeting or back to their office for a last conference call of the day. A few young flash City bucks already drinking at the bar. In the waning daylight, a businessman was sitting on a bench eating a sandwich – wolfing it down. Zac reckoned it was probably a late breakfast rather than a late lunch or tea. He wondered how long that man would work tonight, what time he started this morning.

Zac recalled that he last ate mid-morning. A smoked salmon bagel. A kingsize Twix. Two cans of Red Bull. Nothing since. No time, no appetite. He sighed. What time would he be home tonight? No point even guessing. He didn't have time for so much as a gasp of fresh air, which he suddenly felt he desperately needed. The circus opposite looked strangely uninviting today. The autumn livery of the trees, so stunning last week, now looked a little drab, the branches rather moth-eaten. The tramp and the pigeons, pecking around. The clocks had gone back. It would be dark when Zac looked out of his window again. He wouldn't even know if the tramp was still there.

There was a sharp rap on Zac's door. A rap like that required no permission to enter. His superiors huffed in. Zac caught sight of his team out on the floor, in Pod-land, all eyes on his office. They looked worried for the most part, some untrusting, others downright livid.

'Right,' said Mr Big Cheese in his lousy suit and naff Nature Trek shoes, shutting the door on the apprehensive audience.

'Let's crack on,' said Mr Slightly Smaller Cheese, in a suit that was shiny in patches from wear, and a pair of scuffed sensible brogues.

'Fire away,' said Zac, taking off his fleece and running his hands through his hair.

'You've hit the nail on the head,' laughed Mr Big Cheese. 'You'll need to cull your team. It's the only way. Thirty per cent.'

At first, Zac could say nothing while his brain stormed around for immediate solutions, persuasive objections and convincing obstacles. None sprang to mind. Only panic helped him strike; his loyalty to the company, his pride in his profession, his passion for his team underscoring every word he spoke. He was an accountant shooting from the heart but his long shots ricocheted back from the Cheeses who were retaliating with their heads. Every solution Zac proposed, every objection he put forward, every obstacle he prophesied, was systematically denounced and overruled by the Cheeses.

'If I have to make thirty per cent redundant, I'll be amongst them,' Zac declared without histrionics. It was no threat. It was honour. Morality. Karma.

'Nonsense,' said Nature Trek Cheese, 'and you know it's nonsense.'

'And you know the redundancies make sense,' said Scuffed Brogue Cheese. 'It's business. It's life.'

'If you leave, you leave a sinking ship,' shrugged Big Cheese. 'That's not the behaviour of a captain.'

'You know you'd do better to stay,' said Smaller Cheese. 'Use your head. Work it out.'

Zac wanted to swear at them both and tell them to stuff their jobs. Most of all, he wanted to divine a way that his team could remain complete. Even if it was bad for business.

The Cheeses left and Zac swivelled in his chair. Maybe it *was* time for a change. And yet, wouldn't that be letting his team down more? If he left in protest, would those remaining sink? And wouldn't those leaving be cosseted by princely redundancy packages and glowing references? What could he do? He could do with a drink. Lucozade – the manufacturer used to say it refreshes a person through the ups and downs of the day. All it did for Zac was quench his thirst. He swigged from the bottle. And then he choked.

What the fuck is that?
What the fuck?

There is an almighty rumpus in Pod-land. A dervish is whirling her way amongst Zac's staff; singing and joshing and squawking. She's knocking spectacles off people's noses, tugging their ties back to front, cartwheeling between desks, sipping their vending machine drinks, helping herself to Extra Strong Mints, trying on jackets slung over chair backs.

'What the fuck?'

Zac doesn't know whether to remain in his office, hopefully hidden, or brave the floor and protect his dumb-struck staff.

'What is she *doing*?'

She's ruffling hairdos, hitting herself in the eye with rulers, drawing pictures on notepads, tripping over invisible cables, swirling between the staff, singing atrociously and muttering madly.

'What is she doing *here*?'

She's leaping upon a desk, performing a handstand that looks dreadfully precarious. Now she's upended herself. Curtsying.

'Oh fuck, not *balloons*.'

She reckons, because these are miserable adults, they won't want balloons in the shape of sausage dogs or tortoises. No. Cocks are the order of the day. For the female staff, at least.

'Jesus.'

Zac watches in horror as his gobsmacked female colleagues are handed balloons in the shape of penises. Suddenly, he dreads what on earth his male staff are in line for.

'Enough.'

Zac emerges from his office at the very moment Pip trills to all and sundry, 'Take me to your leader!' whilst standing on one leg and putting the finishing touches to a final balloon penis.

All eyes are on Zac. His staff look utterly bewildered. Holding their inflatable penises. Picking hole-punch scraps out of their hair. Retying their ties. The clown, though, looks flushed and triumphant. She's far too charged with adrenalin and mischief to detect Zac's expression.

'Mr Holmes!' the clown declares with glee, leaping from the desk, cartwheeling towards him and showering him with bits of stuff from her pockets while the plastic gerbera on her lapel squirts him squarely between the eyes with a blast of water.

'For fuck's sake,' he hisses. His words and his tone turn her to stone. The clown is stuck. She gawps. She can't actually move. 'This way, please,' says Zac, taking a tight hold above her elbow and marching her from the floor.

Zac is seething. His grip on Pip's arm is tight and unfriendly. He stomps down two flights of stairs though she stumbles in her daft shoes to keep abreast of him. On a landing far enough from his floor and also from the entrance hall, he stops. He faces her. He drops her arm and puts his hands on his hips. He is frowning and speechless.

'I thought,' Pip says, rubbing her arm, 'I could cheer your staff up.' She shrugs. 'That's all. I mean, it's half five. I thought it would be a wacky end to a wanky day?' She bites her lip, because she's distressed and also because she is desperate to appeal to Zac's soft side.

Zac laughs but with no heart. It's sarcastic and he's angry. 'They're not kids, for fuck's sake,' he spits, 'they're not kids who need cheering up. For fuck's sake. And the day is hardly at an end – we'll be working through the night if you must know. Christ.'

Pip shuffles. 'Sorry,' she says.

'A third of them are about to lose their jobs,' Zac hisses with incredulity. 'Do you really think some stupid kid's clown larking about their desks, manhandling them, soaking them, is going to make them feel better?' Pip wants to remonstrate that clowns aren't just for kids. But Zac gives her no chance. 'Do you honestly think that handing out fucking balloons in the shape of cocks is going to make my staff think "Hey, I haven't got a job, but look! A balloon like a willy!"?'

For Pip to tell him she did it for him, as a gesture, spontaneous and from the heart, seems to be futile. So she just keeps her eyes trained on his lovely shoes and lets him seethe at her in silence.

'For Christ's sake,' he mutters, 'just go, will you.' He doesn't wait for her response. He can't be bothered with lame apologies. Damage and disruption are done. Zac turns and takes the stairs three at a time. He doesn't look back or say another word.

Only when she's quite sure he's gone, does Pip creep down the two flights and out of the building. She keeps her gaze downcast at all times. Like a child who thinks that if they cover their eyes and can't see, then they're surely invisible. She makes it home. Collapses on to her sofa and sobs. She leaves smudges of her slap all over the calico. She doesn't care at all. She seems to have a knack for dripping cosmetics over her soft furnishings. She's had no luck removing the nail varnish.

THIRTY-NINE

Something is irking Zac, unnerving him, catching in his throat when he's eating, waking him at inopportune moments from an otherwise heavy slumber, making him frown mid-smile. It's burrowing into his conscience like a weevil into a rug. Bugging him. It nips him at indiscriminate times – when waiting for the kettle to boil, or the tube to come, or when he should be concentrating on what the Cheeses are moaning about, or last thing at night when he thought his mind was empty. Actually, Zac knows that he probably understands what the problem is, but he also realizes that once he has acknowledged it, he will then be obliged to face it and rectify it at the earliest opportunity. Opportunity for Zac seems to be in short supply at the moment. So, because he honestly doesn't know where he'll find the time, and because he has other worries that are vast by comparison, he tries to justify that this is just a little niggle, after all. And oughtn't he to prioritize? Or, better still, just accidentally on purpose forget it altogether?

He can't. It's impossible. It may not have millions of pounds and employment law stamped all over it, as his other hassles do, but the niggle is insistent and weighty and has value. It is as if his life is currently plagued by bugs – he's constantly swatting, but missing. The hassles at work can be divided into two species – great big bloody hornets and dirty lumbering bluebottles. The former are dive-bombing him, the latter seem always just beyond his swipe. But essentially, he can confine them to the office, where they buzz around and goad him. Ultimately, he can shut his office door on them, escape them entirely when he opens the door to his home. However, that's where the mosquito awaits him. Hidden. He never knows when it is going to pester him next. It's difficult to see. Suddenly it can hound him, lunging at him during the stillness of sleep, or waking him up a good half-hour before he needs to. It's far more stealthy than the hornets or bluebottles; insistent and controlling. It doesn't take long before Zac knows there's nothing for it but to locate it and rid himself of it.

'Daddy!'

Tom wasn't expecting to see Zac on Monday night. After all, he'd had the whole weekend in Hampstead with him and the entire cast of Thunderbirds, so Mum and Rob-Dad could go to some place called Door Zit to do boring grown-up stuff and stay in a hotel with breakable things. However, here was his dad, on his doorstep, on Monday night, and what excellent timing it was, too, because the fish fingers were just about ready and there were plenty of oven chips to share.

'Daddy's going to have supper later,' Tom's mother told him, 'but he's going to sit with you while you have yours so Mummy can luxuriate in a bubble bath.'

'Will it be fish fingers you're having later?' Tom asked thoughtfully, because if it wasn't – if it was, say, chicken nuggets or mini burgers – he might change his mind, have *his* bath now, and eat with Daddy later.

'It's leftovers,' his mother informed him, which clinched the deal. She went off for her bath and Tom and his father went to the kitchen. Tom insisted his father had a few oven chips because leftovers were not enough for a growing boy, let alone a grown-up dad.

Though June was keen to extract all manner of juicy details from Zac concerning Pip turning up last weekend and the demise of Juliana during the week, she took a good sip of wine each time a burning question threatened. It was rare, but not unheard of, for Zac to call her asking if she could spare 'a couple of minutes'. She had learned that it was his code for needing to confide, to workshop an issue troubling him, something that perhaps his male friends were not quite qualified to do. She knew, therefore, that Zac's casually requested couple of minutes would run into an entire evening. She didn't mind; she loved him dearly. Moreover, she was flattered. Fundamentally, she was intrigued.

Rob was happy to make himself scarce because he could indulge in an entire evening watching the European Cup at the pub near work without having to phone regularly, without having to watch his pint intake, without having to justify or apologize for the evidence of too many Marlboro Lights on his clothes, hair and breath. He liked Zac enormously in his capacity as pub-buddy or co-daddy. However, being party to a possibly convoluted confession was slightly outside the parameters of their friendship. Neither he nor Zac minded at all. They were good-time pals, not soul mates. Theirs was a friendship based on shooting the shit or building cardboard garaging for Tom's trucks. Their easy affection for each other showed itself in friendly insults, not in the opening of hearts and the splurging of intimate details.

At first, June was worried and disappointed that perhaps all Zac actually needed to talk through were his concerns at work. For the first time since he left his last job four years ago, her cursory enquiry about work was met with a full half-hour's monologue of the hassles therein and the anxiety he was feeling.

'So,' he said, 'the redundancies will happen early next

week.' He filled up his wineglass. 'There's fuck all I can do about it.'

'Grim,' June agreed. She went to the kitchen to prepare two plates of food. She knew Zac would mind neither the leftovers, nor the partaking of the meal on his knees.

They munched in silence. 'Coffee?' June asked when the plates were bare, because by definition there cannot be seconds of leftovers.

'Please,' said Zac, stroking the arms of the armchair rhythmically and burping as politely as he could.

But he soon followed her into the kitchen.

June had him stacking the dishwasher to stop him fidgeting. She could sense that the crux of his visit was on the tip of his tongue. To ask him outright what was troubling him so would no doubt see him swallow it down and feign nonchalance instead. To carry on as if he'd just popped round for 'a couple of minutes' was a much shrewder tactic. She clattered around noisily, grinding coffee, boiling the kettle, cursing the chipped mugs and asking him if he'd mind soya milk.

'Er, I'll take it black,' Zac said, rummaging under the sink for the dishwasher tablets. 'You're out of Rinse Aid. Oh, it's over with Juliana – not that it was ever on.'

June didn't falter for a moment. 'I'm sure there's a new bottle somewhere – fuck it, one cycle without won't matter. Just shove it on. That's a shame.'

'What is?' Zac asked, just in case she hadn't heard and was referring to dishwashers.

'Juliana,' said June, as lightly as possible.

'Not at all,' Zac assured her, 'not at all. In fact, Ruth seemed more pissed off!'

'Oh?' said June, filling a cafetière. She of course knew, but she couldn't risk Zac realizing.

'Come on!' Zac laughed, nudging her. 'You of all people must have known what she was up to – all that forced socializing. She wanted to point out how mismatched we were.' June felt rumbled, too, but started frantically rummaging around in the tin foil and cling film drawer so that her blush didn't show. 'She even sounded gutted that it wasn't me who did the dumping,' Zac remarked.

'You know what Ruth's like!' June laughed, leaving the ambiguity floating. She plunged the cafetière, splattering coffee grinds over everything in a half-metre radius in the process. Good. Timely diversion. Zac mopped, June apologized. She placed the coffee and mugs on a tray.

'Anyway,' said Zac, 'the way I see it is that it saved me the hassle. You know how I hate stuff like that. I'm crap at it – I'd rather bury my head and keep the peace. I'm eternally grateful to you for burying "us" – I'd never have had the courage. I like you all the more for it! Thanks, babe.'

'Cupcake?' June asked Zac, regarding him squarely but with a brilliantly contrived expression of total innocence that he was momentarily unable to see through.

But June couldn't hold it. It was far too exciting. She bit her lip. And Zac saw. He turned his head sideways, regarding her slyly through slanting eyes. Then he pinched her, quite hard, on the soft part of her tricep.

'Ouch!' she protested. 'Bastard!'

'You,' he accused, 'are wicked.'

'Look, do you want the sodding cupcake or not?' June asked, her eyes simultaneously sparkling with mischief and smarting with the throb from her arm.

'It's a term of affection, you know,' Zac told her with fake naivety whilst admiring the little cakes on offer, each iced individually to perfection.

'I do know,' said June, placing a few in a careful configuration on a plate. 'And how are you going to reciprocate?'

'I thought of *mon petit choux*,' he said, unable to resist taking a little jelly orange slice from the top of one of the cakes.

'Your what?' June asked, slapping his hand.

'It's a term of affection,' Zac shrugged, 'though perhaps it's somewhat obscured in translation. My little cabbage.'

*

So Zac told June about Pip's impromptu visit on Sunday. And his accidentally-on-purpose detour on Tuesday. June knew it was crucial not to comment, certainly not to judge, nor add any opinion of her own; just to listen. All Zac gave her was facts. Pip stayed fifteen minutes. Went to the loo. Had no tea. Called him 'cupcake'. Noticed the new painting. He'd stayed twenty minutes. Forgot to use the loo. Had tea and a KitKat. Talked about work.

Riveting stuff.

But not enough.

So Zac gave June a potted history of meeting Pip. He told her about when he first saw her. How he must have come across as a mad stalker. About how he had subsequently wavered, fearing she was too eccentric herself, though deep down he sensed there was a potential connection. He told June about the preliminary texting and how long it had taken to set a date. He told her about the mad sisters in Soho, about tea at Brown's, everything she needed to know about swans. About Pip's pale blue trainers and that clown make-up is called slap. About her commitment to clowning and her remarkable skill at it. He told June how he found out Pip had a boyfriend and how his degree of disappointment had surprised him. He told her about finding Pip sobbing in Finsbury Circus because she had been two-timed; he told June that he'd taken Pip to the pub to drown her sorrows and eventually, hours later, after much intense evasion, they had slept together.

'The sex was OK,' he told June, 'nothing spectacular. But what was good was the sleeping together.'

He told her how he'd woken to Pip's slap-smudged face and Pippi-Longstocking-style plaits; how she'd seemed shy that morning but that he had blamed her hangover. That she tries to hide *Heat* magazine and HP Sauce. He told June of the marvellous coincidence at the Maida Vale kids' party – that poor Ruth had had a migraine and he'd gone to pick Tom and Billy up. And there was Merry Martha. And she made him a balloon. And she'd accepted a lift to Holloway. And they'd spent ages steaming up the windows of the Audi before spending a great evening wading through his record collection.

'That's when we had sex for the second time,' Zac told June. 'It still wasn't that great but the sleeping together was. The waking and finding her in my bed. I liked that.'

And then he told her about Pip's peculiarly sudden but extreme change of heart, mind, inclination and intent. And his reaction. And that, until Tom's birthday, they hadn't seen or spoken to each other.

'And damn you for making me pay her in cash,' Zac said. 'I felt like Richard sodding Gere in *Pretty Woman*.'

'In your dreams!' June laughed, pretending to be mortified with hindsight that she'd asked Zac to pay Pip. Cash.

'And that brings it full circle,' Zac told her, pausing to drink down his lukewarm coffee, accepting a refill and another cupcake. 'She showed up on Sunday and what should have been odd and delightful was a nightmare on account of Juliana being there.'

'But *you* then turned up on Tuesday,' June pointed out, 'and I promise you, that won't have gone unnoticed. Especially because you *didn't* use the loo.' June grinned. 'Honestly, believe me – I know these things. Pip'll have been reading all sorts of fairy-tale endings between the lines. She'll have analysed your every gesture and everything you said and didn't say. Trust me.'

'I doubt it,' Zac said morosely.

'Yes, she bloody will!' June exclaimed, carrying on regardless of Zac's sudden solemnity and glum expression. 'I bet you she'll have phoned her sisters and her friends saying "He said he wanted the loo, but guess what, he never went" as if it is as much a declaration of your romantic intentions towards her as any turquoise Tiffany box bedecked with white ribbon.'

'No,' said Zac decisively, 'she won't. Not after Thursday.'

'Thursday?' June asked. 'You saw her on Thursday, too?'

'Yes,' said Zac.

'And?'

'Oh,' says June, wishing she hadn't because it sounds too pessimistic. 'Oh,' she says, unable to prevent herself and the drop in octave.

'Exactly,' Zac says despondently, 'and as mad as I was with her at the time, I'm actually far more pissed off with myself now. I realize I humiliated her much more than she embarrassed me. I flew off the handle simply because stress was at boiling point. My anger was disproportionate to her so-called crime. I was in a vile mood and my head was burning. Suddenly, she's there, making balloons in the shape of willies and squirting my staff with water. You know what my staff are like for the most part – they personify every cliché associated with my profession. Willy-shaped balloons are not their kind of thing.'

'She did it because she wanted to help,' June defines, 'and because she wanted to make a gesture to you.'

Zac pauses. 'I know,' he says, 'I know.' He shrugs. He looks desolate. 'It's haunting me, believe me. It won't leave me alone – like a mosquito with a grudge.'

'I don't think all is lost,' June tells him with encouragement and sympathy and conviction.

'You don't?' For the first time, Zac's expression lightens and he looks to June imploringly. This is exactly what he had hoped to hear. And he knows June well enough to know that she wouldn't tell him what she knew he wanted to hear if it wasn't what she actually felt to be plausible.

'I don't,' June reiterates. 'I reckon you're both evens in the apologies-pending stakes.' Zac is eating his way absent-mindedly through a fifth cupcake, hanging on June's every word. 'I mean, I reckon Pip has some commitment issues,' June defines, 'but fucking hell, Zac Holmes – look at you! We parted over six years ago and you've had no desire to commit since!' Zac nods energetically. 'Anyway,' June says, 'for what it's worth, I reckon if you sit down and hammer it out, the weight of your individual apologies should bear each other out – even if the misdemeanours are so different.'

'You really think I should call?' Zac marvels. 'You honestly think she'll answer?'

'I do,' June says, 'and she'll now be way too nervous to call you.'

'Rightly so,' says Zac. He's had enough coffee. He fancies another glass of wine. He goes to the kitchen and fetches a bottle of Rioja. Alone, June wishes she had a Dictaphone so all had been recorded for Ruth. And then she's pleased she hasn't. It's private. It would be an insult to Zac. Ruth could have the bare bones – she'd pick at them gratefully anyway.

'I like Pip,' June tells Zac, accepting the glass of wine and having a lengthy sip. 'As Dr Pippity, as Merry Martha and as herself. You'd be good together.' Zac raises his eyebrows. 'You may well look stunned,' June laughs, 'you know how difficult I am to be won over.' Zac raises his glass. 'Remember that poor girl – what was her name?'

'Amelia,' Zac grimaces.

'And that other one – with the specs.'

'Rosie,' Zac winces.

'And the one with the weird left eye.'

'Tina,' Zac all but howls.

'Well,' June says, 'Pip I like.'

'I like Pip, too,' Zac agrees.

'Tom likes her,' June points out.

'He does,' Zac agrees.

'She seems to like him, too,' June adds.

'Who wouldn't!' Zac says and he and June chink glasses.

They sit and work their way through the bottle of wine. Though June would love to devise a precise soliloquy for Zac, she knows that even if she did, he wouldn't use it. His style is unique. He'll do things his way, in his own time. As he's done thus far. She really hopes that he and Pip can finally synchronize timing. There's no reason why they can't. They have everything going for them. June feels all talked out, she's worked hard this evening for him and she's tired. The wine is finished and there's only one cupcake left, rather uninterestingly iced, too. She's looking forward to seeing Rob. He should be back soon. She's prepared for him to smell of booze and fags and fried food but she doesn't really mind. Time for Zac to make tracks. Time to change the subject and edge him towards the door. Time for bed.

'You haven't noticed!' June pouts with mock outrage.

'Noticed?' Zac frowns. 'What?'

June waves her arm around. 'We redecorated!'

Zac looks about the room. 'Oh, yes,' he says, unconvinced.

'We went from peach to apricot,' June remonstrates, 'in a day!'

'It's lovely,' says Zac, 'very subtle.'

'You mean you can hardly notice it.' She looks around the room. She loves it. Then she looks at Zac. He's staring at a blank part of the wall as if he's reading some Divine scripture there. 'Zac?'

'Oh my God!' he exclaims softly. He looks at June as if a thunderbolt has struck him, granting him some celestial sign.

'What?' June asks, wide-eyed, correctly assuming Zac's revelation is Pip-related.

'I knew something was different,' he declares, 'I just couldn't put my finger on it.'

'On what?' June begs.

'Do you think it's too late to go round now?' Zac asks her.

'Go round?' June exclaims. 'To Pip's?' Zac shrugs. 'Yes,' June declares, 'it is!' Zac looks crestfallen. 'Look,' June tells him sternly, 'you two have done your impromptu thing – now it's time for some courtesy.'

Zac considers this. He nods. 'You're right.'

'Do not go there tonight,' June warns him, 'do not even think of phoning her tonight.'

'Aye aye, cap'n,' he salutes her.

Zac has to exercise enormous restraint to tell the taxi 'Hampstead'. When he's home, he physically unplugs his land-line and does not recharge the dead battery on his mobile, just in case he wakes in the early hours and is tempted.

FORTY

'*T*he thing is,' Pip said over the phone to Django, 'I tried my best and I failed.'

'The thing *is*,' Django reasoned with his niece, which he'd been doing for the past half-hour with permutations of tone and phrase, 'the fact that you can hold your head high and say you failed and yet not feel a failure – *that*'s the thing.'

'Oh, it hasn't put me off men,' Pip told him, 'it hasn't even put me off Zac. But I can see I have to let it lie. God – if ever a week felt like a year.'

'Was it this time last week that you were gallivanting across his desk, then?'

'Almost to the minute, poor bloke,' Pip groaned, yet with grace. 'Oh, well. I am almost at the stage of being able to laugh and cringe at it all. Give me a month and it may well become my dinner party conversation piece.'

'Dear Philippa,' said Django, envisaging Pip so clearly leaping about amidst all those nonplussed accountants, 'I feel you deserve a happy ending – what's the point of all this hard-wrung self-awareness otherwise?'

'Whatever,' said Pip. 'It's just a pity because I know you'd've liked him.'

'I most certainly would!' Django declared. 'I'd've liked him all the more for a family discount – I pay my current accountant a fortune for him to tell me to pay the taxman a fortune. They're in cahoots, I tell you, *cahoots*!'

'Anyway, lots more fish in the sea,' Pip said, 'every pot has its lid.'

'Hey!' Django remonstrated. 'You've gone and pinched all my clichés.'

'I know,' Pip laughed, 'for good reason.'

'Plenty more cupcakes in the tin,' he said, slyly.

'Django!' she declared.

'Come home soon,' Django said, 'before Cat leaves for the States. Now that Fen's made her choice between her two suitors. Let's have a gathering. I'll cook something special.'

'It's a lovely idea,' Pip enthused, 'I'll talk to the girls. You know what – why don't you come down to London? I want to show you my spruce new flat. You'd approve.'

There was silence. Django loathed the city so much that he now found the briefest of visits took until Christmas to recover from. Regardless of when he travelled. He couldn't possibly afford two months' convalescence! But he'd love to see Pip's flat, mainly because she wanted him to. She sounded house-proud and plain proud of herself.

'The thing is,' Pip said, knowing her uncle would never come but knowing that to invite him anyway was the point, 'I like it. The colour. The change. I mean, I haven't gone from one extreme to another – it's not Day-Glo or metallic or anything. It's just a step away from what it was. And Zac, indirectly, was the inspiration for change.'

'The inspiration for change,' Django repeated, thinking his niece had a very becoming turn of phrase at times.

'All sorts of change,' Pip said. 'I must go – my mobile has just beeped. It's probably Cat and I *must* have a hair wash before we meet up – I forgot to brush out Dr Pippity's plaits before I left today.'

'Come home soon,' Django implored.

'My littlest sister! Off to the States for a staff position on some sports mag!'

Pip is muttering to herself in her inimitable way. She's tidying up whilst the bath is running because she prides herself on her ability to multitask.

'Where *is* my mobile?'

It's not in the bedroom. It wouldn't be in the bathroom. It's in the kitchen. She folds and stores the empty supermarket bags before she retrieves her phone from under a net of satsumas.

'What's mon petit choux?'

She scrolls through. It isn't Cat's number. Or Fen's. Or Megan's. She has a name tag for them, anyway. Whose number is it?

'*Mon petit choux*? Damn, why didn't I concentrate on French at school? My little something or other?'

Fen doesn't know what it means, either. Megan can only suggest choux pastry and profiteroles. Pip tries Cat – all that time spent in France must have rubbed off on her. Cat says 'cabbage' – it means, literally, 'my little cabbage'. Cat and Pip are baffled. So is Fen, when Pip phones to tell her that someone has sent a text about a little cabbage. Megan is amused but confused, convinced that profiteroles must surely be a more seemly translation. She says she'll phone the French teacher at school. She phones back half an hour later. Pip is wrapped in a bath towel, combing product through her wet hair.

'It *does* mean "my little cabbage",' Megan says, excitement creeping into her voice, 'but, though the translation sounds bizarre, actually it's a simple term of affection.'

'A term of affection?' Pip asks, the pace of her heart picking up steadily.

'Yes,' says Megan, 'it is. Like – you know – cupcake.'

Pip sits on her bed, rereading the text message. She's long since deleted Zac's numbers from her mobile phone. But she knows she has them written down in her Filofax. She sits still. Does she dare?

Go on!

She puts on knickers and bra and pads through to the sitting-room. Flips around the pages of her Filofax as casually as she can, stopping to read next week's appointments, skimming over what last week held for her. She doesn't want to rush to H, or Z (she'd filed him under both) because she's convinced that restraint and nonchalance will reap rewards.

It is Zac's number.
    It really is.
    She double- and triple-checks it.
    'What on earth is going to happen now? Am I meant to make the next move? Dare I?'

Go on!

Pip and Cat spent the evening devising increasingly convoluted replies to Zac's text message. The fun was in the composing – none would actually do. Pip then spent until one in the morning texting various options to Megan and Fen, which soon devolved into ludicrous suggestions, ultimately veering off at filthy tangents. The fun was in the sharing. She wouldn't, of course, be sending any of the suggestions. She went to sleep feeling snug and, justifiably, a little smug, too.

Zac's phone beeped on Saturday morning, just as he was hovering in June's hallway waiting for Tom to amass the troops and the trucks that he simply couldn't live without for the next twenty-four hours. With Tom's rucksack in one hand and Tracy Island in the other, plus Woody from *Toy Story* slung over his arm, Zac thought the phone could wait until later. And then he thought that perhaps he might just retrieve it now. He dumped Woody and the rucksack and gave June the task of deputizing over Tracy Island. He found his phone. He read the message. He scrolled through though he had no need to. He was an accountant. He liked figures.

He knew certain numbers off by heart. He read the message again. He laughed. The phone gave him the option 'Erase?' Certainly not! He passed it to June to read.

`cabbage & cupcake??? sounds like a mad combo...`

'Reply! Reply!' June urged excitedly.

'Yes, yes,' Zac said with great nonchalance. 'Later.' And he left June all flustered and none the wiser as to his course of action while he led Tom out towards his car. She stood by the front door blowing kisses to Tom and making a telephone gesture with her thumb and little finger to Zac.

Zac appalled himself by texting whilst he drove. He'd never done so before – he'd never even spoken on his mobile in the car unless his hands-free kit was plugged in. Yet here he was, driving one-handed, texting a message, glancing in the rear-view mirror irregularly, watching the road infrequently, trying to keep up a conversation with Tom at the same time.

`acquired taste - suck it and see . . .`

Did he dare send that?

Go on!

`jamie o? gordon r? cordon b? can't find recipe . . .`

Pip had laughed so long and hard that by the time she sent this reply, Zac was safely parked. He set up Tom with the toys and a glass of juice and went to his bedroom window-sill to compose his response.

`come 4 t? 2day? u can use loo . . .`

Pip didn't keep him waiting for long for her answer.

`it's a d8 . . .`

Zac smiled.

'Tom, guess who's coming to see us later?'

'Um, I dunno. Buzz Lightyear? Lady Penelope?'

'Almost,' said Zac. 'Actually, your clown is.'

'Oh. Brill. Can you do that special noise for Thunderbird 1 now, please? But I mustn't see you. Go behind there and do the noise. Put your phone down, Daddy. Let's play.'

*

Pip tried in vain to speak to Fen, Cat, Megan and Django. No one was at home and the girls weren't answering their mobiles. She wanted to tell them the developments, she wanted to work through what she should wear, how she should act, should she bake cupcakes? Take with her a caddy of Earl Grey? Buy a small cabbage en route? How could she face such weighty decisions alone? Ultimately, she decided to read great significance into the fact that she could make contact with none of them. She'd just have to trust her instincts and think for herself. She knew they'd all kick themselves when they realized she'd tried to contact them, she knew they'd be desperate for details and would want to send her their vibes and advice and encouragement. She texted the same message to her sisters and best friend.

t at z's – wish me luck!!!

After three entire costume changes, she settled for a chocolate brown needlecord skirt, black polo neck and tight black boots with a low heel but dainty nonetheless. She buffed her skin the Clarins way, spritzed a little perfume in strategic places, slicked on some lip balm and waved the mascara wand over the tips of her eyelashes. The ensemble was subtle, but she felt properly dressed and attractive.

'Nicely put together,' as Django would say. If he could see me now. If only he was at home for me to describe how I look over the phone.

She left her flat without noticing which lights she'd left on or that she had not turned off the radio in the kitchen.

Damn! Is it rude to turn up without a thing? Would it really have been corny to have brought a small cabbage? Wouldn't such a gesture be the deal-clincher? Shall I turn back and find something to buy?

She had arrived at Zac's empty-handed but with a stomach now so full of butterflies that, as she hovered her finger over the doorbell, she wondered how she'd find room for tea.

I suppose, though, that tea just might be a euphemism.

This both excited and appalled her. Though she suddenly felt undeniably horny, if Zac was intending to seduce her, might he not be put off by unshaven legs?

To say nothing of my knickers being the colour of well-chewed gum?

Put on your most beguiling smile, girl, and ring the sodding doorbell!

If anyone was to ask Zac about that fabled, elusive moment when he knew, he just knew, that Pip was the one for him, he'd declare it was hearing her response to Tom greeting her that Saturday afternoon. It didn't strike him like a bolt from heaven, it didn't really occur to him at all just then. It was only in retrospect that he credited the impact of her reaction to Tom with consolidating how he felt about her.

'Oh hullo, Tom, how are you?'

Pip's tone was steady and casual. She seemed neither surprised, delighted nor disappointed. It was as if she took for granted that ringing Zac's bell might well see his son opening the door, because she was content that his son should be as much a part of the fabric of his life, the furnishing of his flat, as the Eames lounger.

'I'm fine, thanks,' said Tom. 'Shall I call you Pip today?'

'Sure.'

'Brill. Come in and play. My dad's on the loo just now. He's been in there for ages.'

Pip and Tom wrinkled their noses in unison and then giggled conspiratorially.

'Do you know how to play Thunderbirds?'

'Um, I'm not sure, Tom. Maybe the rules I know are different to yours – let's play your way.'

'All right. You have to go somewhere I can't see you – like behind there – and make a noise like *this*.'

'Like *this*?'

'No! That's rubbish. Like *this*.'

'How about *this*?'

'Yes, that's OK. You'll probably get better at it. Now go over there and every time I lift Thunderbird 1, make that noise. OK?'

'Roger.'

'Roger? Who's Roger? There *isn't* a Roger.'

'I mean, righty-ho.'

So Pip was to be heard and not seen when Zac emerged from the bathroom. And her first indication of Zac that afternoon came from Tom.

'Did you have a runny tummy, Daddy?'

'No, just a bit of wind, Tom. I should have had chicken nuggets, not the quarter pounder.'

In retrospect, that was probably the moment Pip truly fell for Zac. He liked her enough and felt comfortable enough with himself to make his flatulence public. No act. No baggage. And anyway, she herself had always veered to a lavatorial sense of humour. Plus, she was aware that whether or not Zac had wind made no difference to how she felt.

Tom positioned his father out of sight on the opposite end of the room to Pip and commanded him to make the sound of Thunderbird 2 at the given sign. Zac growled from his side, Pip perfected a vehicular grumble from hers and that's basically how they conversed for a good ten minutes until Tom remembered something he'd forgotten to tell his father.

'Oh!' he said. 'I forgot! Come and see.'

He led Zac over to where Pip was positioned. They looked down upon her, crouching and preparing to growl. She looked up. She didn't seem in the slightest bit embarrassed but she did look a little cramped.

'Hullo,' said Zac.

'Hullo,' she responded.

'It's Pip,' said Tom, just in case his father had been duped into thinking Thunderbird 1 was really full of fuel and raring to go on an International Rescue.

'Cup of tea?' Zac offered, offering his hand and hauling her up.

'That would be nice,' she accepted, rubbing her back and cricking her knees. 'Thunderbirds is thirsty work.'

It wasn't that time flew because they were all having fun – which they were – but more due to Tom demanding their undivided attention until he decided he was starving hungry and please could he have his supper. After which, the child was so tired and played out that he promised to brush his teeth for twice as long in the morning if he could go straight to sleep right now. His father wouldn't hear of it. And so, for the first time all afternoon, Pip had five minutes in her own company while her host and his son – or was it her host and his father? – busied themselves elsewhere with bedtime routines. She sat herself down on the Eames footstool and had a good look at the new painting. She did like it. It proved to her that there's a place for everything. And in Zac's flat, it had found a sympathetic environment in which to sing. It would dwarf her flat. The colours were too strident – it would be like a blackbird singing before it is light. Lovely in itself, but somehow sadly incongruous and somewhat lost without an audience.

When Zac came through having settled Tom, he found Pip picking at the leftovers on his son's plate.

'I can spare you a whole fish finger,' Zac offered. 'The freezer is full of them.'

'Actually,' Pip replied, 'I like the crunchy end bits with cold baked beans.'

'How about the cold peas?' Zac asked.

Pip wrinkled her nose. 'No,' she said, 'you can have them. I don't like the way they sort of implode. They look like the footballs you see in skips, or people's fingertips after a long bath.'

'So I'm having leftover leftovers,' Zac mused.

'Yes,' said Pip, 'dig in.'

*

They don't really know what to do. They've played Thunderbirds, drunk tea, eaten leftovers, broken the ice. They're housebound on account of Tom and, on account of Tom, playing old records, at the sort of volume old records deserve to be heard at, is out, too. They did their critique of the new painting last weekend. Currently, neither of them needs the loo, or a drink replenishing.

'Would you like to sit down?' Zac asks.

'Thanks very much,' says Pip. He takes her hand and, awkwardly, they attempt to walk as nonchalantly as they can from the kitchen counter at which they've been hovering, through to the sitting-room. Pip's hands feel clammy to her, but there again, Zac's feel clammy to him. He sits down on the sofa and momentarily, Pip wonders quite where she should sit. She's done the Eames – lounger and footstool. How about the banana chair? She'd like to sit right next to Zac but suddenly, she feels she should wait and see.

Zac pats the space next to him and Pip lowers herself down in a most demure way. The two of them then endure an awkward few moments of unnecessary sighs and picking at the labels on the bottled beer and starting sentences simultaneously, then deferring to each other to the extent that nothing is said. Pip contrives a yawn though she's too excited to be tired. It is only eight o'clock.

'Um,' she says.

Zac stretches one leg in front of him, as if suffering from cramp. He fingers the fraying label on his beer. 'Hmm.'

They smile, shyly and fleetingly, at each other. For two people who were perfecting impressions of the Thunderbird craft that very afternoon – albeit crouching at opposite sides of the room – they are now remarkably formal with each other. Pip finds herself wishing Tom was still up to boss them around and tell them what to do, what to say and when.

Without warning, Zac places his hand on Pip's knee and gives a little squeeze.

'I'm sorry about last week,' she announces, surprising

herself at her brevity. It is music to his ears but a tune he wasn't expecting to hear just then.

'I'm sorry, too,' he says.

'I mean, it was stupid of me not to call,' she elaborates. 'I was just trying to – I don't know – make amends by making contact. But now I feel I'm in some crazy downward spiral, having to make amends for making amends that have gone wrong.'

Zac drinks to that. He's not quite sure which event Pip is referring to. After all, she turned up unannounced on both occasions.

'I thought they'd like balloon willies. Stupid it may seem, but I just thought that as a tough day drew to a close, I'd lighten the tone by lowering it. I meant no harm. And I'm mortified.'

Zac considers her apology and regards her pained expression. 'What's odd,' he defines, 'is that you're apologizing for something I don't think needs an apology. I'd much rather say sorry *to you* for humiliating you – marching you out of the office like a loony or a criminal. Stress got the better of me and skewed my vision.'

Pip reflects on this and looks at Zac. His eyes are burrowing into hers, seeking her response.

'OK, shall we call it quits for the Office Atrocity?' she suggests. They chink beer bottles. She takes a contemplative sip. 'I'm sorry, too, about turning up like that last weekend. When you had company.'

Zac swigs and thinks. 'I'm not,' he says, 'I'm just sorry I *had* company. But I'm very pleased you came. It, er, made me see right through the company that I was keeping.' Pip's gaze flicks around his face. He spells it out. 'It was casual, anyway,' he says, 'so it was simply semantics to end something that was never actually on in the first place.'

'You mean,' Pip deduces, 'you chucked her?'

'Actually,' Zac corrects, 'she suggested we call it quits.'

'Oh,' says Pip, trying not to let her inner voice yell 'Baggage! Baggage! Emasculated! Rebound!'

'Saved me the job,' Zac reveals with a very grateful shrug, and Pip's inner voice breathes a shoulder-dropping sigh of relief. 'We just formalized not to bother with each other any more.' Suddenly, they are both aware that Zac still has his hand on Pip's knee. He attempts to take it away, as if he's being presumptuous, but she places hers on top of his and there they stay.

Pip decides to take her boots off. She wants to come very close to Zac, she wants to sit herself entirely next to him. But she oughtn't to have her shoes on the furniture. 'Pull?' she asks, holding out her leg. Zac eases off one boot, then the other. She settles herself facing Zac, her legs tucked underneath her. She touches his cheek. 'Um,' she says, not knowing what to say but knowing that she has two or three great soliloquies to choose from, if only she could locate them. 'It's just.'

Fuck it.

It seems a very good idea to kiss him gently, soon enough deeply, while her brain tries to find where she's stored all those beautifully phrased declarations. After a good long kiss, she still can't remember. So she kisses him again. And after that one, Zac looks so dazed and lust-soaked that she half thinks she could say anything and he wouldn't really hear.

No. This is important. For myself, if not for Zac.

'Zac, what I'm most sorry for is the dithering,' she says, pulling away but keeping her eyes focused on his lips.

'Playing hard to get?' Zac asks lasciviously, making for another kiss.

'No,' Pip says defiantly, placing her fingertip against his lips, 'listen! I wasn't playing hard to get. The point is, back then I really didn't know if I wanted to be *got* in the first place.'

This makes perfect sense to Zac who feels they both deserve to increase the intensity and geography of the fondling and subsequently takes his hand to her breasts. And soon enough he's easing her down, prostrate along the

341

settee, and they're petting and snogging and feeling and grabbing and his feet are on the furniture and his shoes aren't clean and he'd rather buy a new bloody sofa than spoil the moment.

'The point is,' he says, some minutes later and a little breathlessly, 'none of that matters now, does it? Not how you felt or acted then, nor my Juliana interlude, nor clowning at the office. Because the point is – look at us now. Whatever we didn't want then, we want now. We're allowed to change our minds.'

Pip just wants more kissing. To her, just now, physical manifestations of desire, relief, affection, apology are worth more than anything Shakespeare himself could have penned. She pulls Zac down over her again and closes her eyes, letting his lips touch down on hers, letting her mouth open and allowing their tongues to chatter away in a language of their own.

'The point is,' Zac pulls away again, slightly flushed, panting a little, 'we are currently snogging and humping and making out like a couple of hormone-crazed teenagers. It consigns all the other stuff into the past. It's all just a part of our history – because I'd like to think that we have a future. From now on.'

As Zac kisses her, Pip realizes she's just learned a lesson she'll never forget; that apologies can be accepted without risk of payback, that a shaky start can lead to a sublime journey, that one's history is made of everything one does and that unsavoury or difficult elements can rest in the past peaceably alongside the happy or easy elements. Fundamentally, that there need be no repercussions for the future.

'That we can laugh about our rocky start in times to come,' Pip states, no need for a question mark.

*

'Stay,' Zac whispers. 'I'm about to explode.'

'Not tonight,' Pip says. 'I don't want Tom to see me without my make-up in the morning.'

Zac considers this. 'Tom or you?'

'Tom,' Pip says. 'He's only little. I'm Thunderbird 1 to him at the moment. And his daddy shouldn't sleep with his toys without asking.'

'I'll have a chat with him,' Zac informs her, 'and I know he'll be cool about it. After all, it'll solve his perpetual problem of which craft to launch and when.'

Yet Zac remains on top of Pip, brushing strands of hair from her face, from the corner of her mouth. Gazing and grinning and dipping his lips to hers. He sees she's wearing a little mascara, that it's smudged slightly beneath her right eye. She smells very nice. He likes the way her bottom teeth are ever so slightly crooked. He notices a small mole on her jaw for the first time. He sucks an ear lobe. They're pierced but she doesn't wear earrings. He could buy her a pair for Christmas.

God, he'd love to see her breasts bare right now, rather than having to remind himself how they look by feeling them through her clothing. He'd like to get naked with her immediately. Take his time making love to her. It would be new. He now has but a vague memory of sex with Pip not being all that great. But he has a growing feeling – and not just in his trousers – that making love might be a whole class apart.

And Pip takes her lips to his ear. And she's nibbling. And kissing. And she whispers, 'God, I don't half fancy a fuck!'

Zac laughs.

That's my girl.

And he wonders whether with Pip, whom he fancies the pants off but feels all manner of soft fondness for, making love and having a fuck might well be inextricably linked.

Pip is now snuggled in her own bed, too excited to sleep just yet. She's undecided whether to indulge in romantic daydreams of love, laughter and domesticity while she waits for slumber, or whether she should just reach for her vibrator instead.

There's no reason why I can't do both. Blimey. What a novelty!

Well done, Pip.

FORTY-ONE

Megan, Fen and Cat were all apoplectic with anticipation and excitement when they each managed to contact Pip.

'What did you wear? Did you take cabbage?' Fen shrieked. 'Cake?'

'What did you talk about? Did you have a huge heart-to-heart?' Megan demanded. 'And what about the leggy girlfriend?'

'Did you have rampant sex all night long? Who made who holler for mercy?' Cat demanded to know. 'And are you walking like John Wayne today?'

Pip answered her support group so honestly and calmly that, although Fen privately thought her sister should have taken cabbage and cake, and although Megan felt Pip ought to have revealed her one-night stand, for the record, and although Cat was slightly disappointed that no fornicating had taken place, fundamentally they were proud of Pip and happy for her, believing all indeed boded well for her future.

Fen phoned Pip again at lunch-time, suggesting Sunday papers round at hers. Cat was there when Pip arrived, obsessing herself with the sports pages and wondering out loud if she was a lunatic to have accepted a job in the States, at Team Megapac's Colorado headquarters, and a share in her boyfriend's apartment. Her two older sisters told her what she wanted to hear, that it was a great decision professionally, plus that it gave her a chance to cement her relationship with Ben within the crucial, mundane parameters of day-to-day living. Best of all, they decided, it gave Pip and Fen the opportunity for a cheap holiday to the States and Cat simply must go for that reason alone. The sisters refused to acknowledge out loud the potentially epic link of Colorado, Denver, their mother and her cowboy. Another time. Not now.

Intermittently, during the afternoon, Pip went through the various details of the previous day with Zac; initially when asked, soon enough spontaneously, ultimately somewhat repetitively. Both her sisters noted with delight how frequently she glanced surreptitiously at her mobile phone. Who'd have thought, Pip McCabe, bitten by the love bug!

'Why not phone Megan,' Cat proposed, 'and suggest Thai tonight?'

'Brilliant idea,' said Fen.

Pip, though, faltered. 'But say he calls?' she said quietly.

Her younger sisters looked at her in horror. 'Philippa McCabe!' Fen declared, hands on hips, with Cat similarly posed at her side. 'I cannot believe you just said that!'

'The number of times you've shot me down from a similar standpoint!' Cat proclaimed. 'Saying "Catriona, don't fit your life into him" or "Cat McCabe, say he doesn't call – you'll have jeopardized a perfectly nice evening" or "For fuck's sake, do you have to gain his permission for every action you take"!'

Pip looked bashful. 'Listen,' Fen suggested, 'if he does call, you can just arrange to see him later or tomorrow or something. God, I mean, the deal is hardly going to fall through on the question of your availability tonight.'

'It sounds like it's all set in stone anyway,' Cat defined. 'You like. He likes. Happy ever after.'

Pip laughed. 'I'll phone Megan,' she said, hands up in mock surrender. 'I could murder a bowl of prawn crackers.

All I had yesterday was bits of fish finger and cold baked beans.'

'Yes,' said Fen, 'we know.'

'You told us,' said Cat, adding 'about a million times' under her breath when Pip went into the kitchen to phone Megan from Fen's line so she could keep her mobile free.

A part of me is appalled for doubting whether to practise what I have preached for so long. Yet there's another part of me that thinks all these butterflies, the tenterhooks, the adrenalin, are quite good fun, too.

There was no signal for Pip's phone in the restaurant, nor in their loos, so she didn't pick up Zac's text till hours after he'd sent it. It took a little intensive persuading from the girls in her life that no, of course, he wasn't going to change his mind just because her reply wasn't immediate.

'It's not that,' Pip reasoned. 'I just really, truly, don't want him to think that I'm playing games or subscribing to those daft rules or acting according to the tenets of *Sex and the City* or *Cosmo*.'

'He doesn't sound that sort of bloke,' Megan declared astutely.

Pip's sisters and friend allowed her to go home directly instead of going back to Cat's for coffee and none raised eyebrows at Pip's excuse of tiredness. It was nice for them to envisage her scampering home, curling up on her sofa and working through five thousand possible text responses for Zac before sending one and then waiting impatiently for his reply. They'd hear about it tomorrow, no doubt. Maybe even later on tonight.

Actually, when Pip arrived home, she didn't text Zac at all but phoned him direct, and though her heart thudded in her throat while she waited for him to answer, as soon as she heard his voice, she relaxed.

'I was toying with the idea of popping round and using your loo,' Zac revealed, 'but I guess it's a bit late now – it being a school night and all.' He hadn't read a thing into the tardiness of Pip's reply. He'd simply assumed she was busy. Why shouldn't she be? No other reason had crossed his mind. Why should it?

'Can you keep your legs crossed until tomorrow?' Pip asked. 'I stink of garlic, and peanut sauce keeps repeating on me.'

'How are your sisters?' Zac enquired.

'Fine – they're fine. Cat is now happily ensconced with a bicycle doctor and heading for a job in the States; Fen has finally made her choice between two suitors. It's a long story,' Pip remarked. 'Did you have a fun day? How long did Tom stay?'

'We just hung out and played, really,' Zac told her, 'it was great. Though, dare I add, he was most disappointed that Thunderbird 1 had to dock all day. I told him to keep his fingers crossed for next weekend. And do you know what? He did. Physically. Until he had to hold his fork at lunch. Bless him.'

Pip laughed. 'I'd better perfect my engine impression, then.'

'When can I see you?' Zac asked softly.

'Would you like to do something tomorrow night?' Pip suggested.

'Tomorrow is my day in hell – it's when I'm having to make the redundancies,' Zac revealed wearily.

'Oh,' flustered Pip, momentarily feeling like she'd been stood up already, or turned down. 'Right. Well, perhaps later on in the week, then? Some other time. Whenever.'

'Actually,' Zac said, 'on the contrary. It's going to be such a nightmarish day I'd relish the chance to take my mind off it all. So, if you don't mind dealing with a stressed-out accountant in the midst of a morality crisis, he'd love to sulk on your sofa for a bit.'

Pip was stunned and flattered. She also felt lousy that she hadn't thought to offer to share time and space with him in the first place. 'Actually,' she told him, 'I have the perfect cure for you.'

'I'm sure you do,' Zac all but growled, his mind veering incorrigibly to blow-jobs and all manner of indoor sport.

'Down, boy!' Pip laughed, instinctively knowing along what lines he was thinking and not wanting to disappoint him by revealing she had something else entirely in mind.

'I'll call you when I'm en route,' Zac said, 'it may be later rather than earlier.'

'Whenever,' said Pip.

'Night then,' Zac said.

'Night,' Pip said.

She had something to add. She made a humming noise just to hold him there while she decided whether or not she was going to say it out loud. 'I'll be thinking of you tomorrow,' she mumbled.

'Thanks,' said Zac, touched.

Zac phoned at eight. He was at Pip's at nine. Her flat was immaculate and she glowed with the effects of a bath infused with expensive potions and hair treated to all manner of costly and time-consuming lotions. Zac looked ashen, his eyes rimmed red, his hair not so much fashionably tousled as slightly greasy and messed from all that tugging. He looked as though he'd dropped a stone in weight in two days. She welcomed him in with a kiss and a beer, and allowed him to slump into her sofa, rub his brow and stare intently at the wall for a few moments.

'Great colour, Pip,' he said, looking up at her gazing down at him, 'good choice.'

'How are you?' Pip asked, sensing he was far from good and wondering the best way to soothe him.

'I feel like shit,' he laughed sarcastically, 'which is hardly surprising as I am now known as King Shit, too.' He pinched the bridge of his nose and drooped his shoulders. 'It was foul. Vile.' He looked up at her and shrugged. 'Not nice to be loathed. But even worse having to do something that you really don't want to do — but having absolutely no viable alternative.'

Pip looked at him and sucked her bottom lip thoughtfully. She felt as though she was hovering. She was. Because she wasn't quite sure what he'd like, what would help, what she could actually do. She thought he might like some space. Some peace and quiet. But then she thought he'd very probably like her to act on her instincts. So she knelt down on the floor, placed a hand on each of his knees and looked up at him. 'Poor you,' she said quietly, 'I'm sorry. I don't know how I can help.'

He looked at her and shrugged. 'I could honestly sob,' he revealed, his honesty quite startling, his voice hoarse. He shook his head and pinched the bridge of his nose again, so hard that he left a mark. 'I don't even wear a sodding suit,' he declared, 'I can't physically wriggle out of my day. A couple of times today I thought of you, Pip – dispensing your merriment and care to the sick kids. That's one fucking tough job – however rewarding. At the end of each session, the fact that you can wipe your face off, change out of your daft gear – I'm sure that really helps you rebalance?'

'Absolutely,' Pip said, 'and sometimes, I can't wait to put on my slap and change into my motley – even the hospital foyer can be tough enough.'

Zac nodded. He yawned. He stretched. 'What a fucking horrible day,' he said.

'Would you like a baked potato?' Pip offered.

He hadn't thought about food. Actually, he realized he hadn't even considered food since last night. And back then, he was still full from a tea-time finger-food extravaganza when dropping Tom home so he hadn't actually eaten since then. 'That sounds great.'

'I'll put them in the oven now,' Pip said. 'They'll take an hour. Which gives us plenty of time to take your mind off things.'

Zac smiled at her. What a gesture. He raised an eyebrow at the thought of slipping out of the clothes he was in.

'Down, boy,' she whispered, coming close and kissing him, 'you'll have to build up an appetite for *that*. I had something else altogether in mind.'

*

She puts the baked potatoes in, disappears into her bedroom and clatters around in there. She returns with a bag and a towel.

'I like the way you've decorated the room,' Zac says, 'that one wall in terracotta is striking. And the skirting through there looks great.'

'Not too ice-creamy?' Pip asks.

'God, no,' Zac says, 'it sits brilliantly. It's odd – it isn't like you've *added* colour, it's as if all those neutrals simply *hid* the colour before.'

'I think you're right,' Pip says, wondering if Zac has any idea just how incisive his remarks are, 'I think they did.' She tucks the towel around Zac. 'OK, Mr Cruel Bastard Accountant,' she announces, 'let's get down to the serious business of silliness.'

Into Zac's lap she tips the contents of her bag. It's her collection of slap.

'Whoa!' Zac exclaims. 'What are you going to do?'

'We're going to wipe that frown from your brow and give you something to smile about. You're going to see just how therapeutic clowning can be,' Pip tells him, 'by being one yourself. Until the potatoes are ready, of course.'

Zac is puzzled, intrigued and not averse to anything that will take his mind off his day.

'What'll we call you?' Pip asks. 'You have to build your make-up around your persona, not vice versa.'

'Mr Cruel Bastard?' Zac says.

Pip raises her eyebrow archly. 'And what would the children make of that?'

'OK,' Zac concedes, 'how about Zippity Zac?'

'Pity Zac? Still sounds a little maudlin to me,' Pip says.

'Zig Zac?' he suggests.

'Excellent. Now, tell me what sort of clown you'd like to be?'

'A, um, *clown* kind of clown?' Zac tries.

'Auguste or White Face?'

'Who or what?' Zac asks.

351

'Essentially, there are two types of clown – well, three if you count the American Character clown, Mr Chaplin being its definitive. Basically, White Face's lineage harks back to Pierrot and Harlequin. Graceful and shrewd – the French call them *"Clown débonnaire"*. The physical emphasis is on the eyes. In contrast, Auguste clown means "clumsy" and they're characterized by their daft cheerfulness and charm. They're colourful – the crowd's favourite. Physically, the emphasis is on the mouth, the smile.'

'You're essentially a White Face,' Zac says, 'so I think I'll be Auguste. What do you think?'

'I think that's a fine choice,' says Pip. 'We can really play with colour. Also, traditionally, White Face gets to boss Auguste about. So that suits me! They often come as a pair.' She and Zac regard each other and smirk.

And so she began to transform Zac Holmes into Zig Zac and to take his mind well away from the traumas of his day. He sat still, covered in a towel, and was grateful for Pip demanding he close his eyes. Eyes shut, it was actually very soothing having someone smear and rub and paint one's face. Especially when her touch was so light that it doubled as a caress.

Pip made Zac keep his eyes closed longer than was probably necessary because she could indulge in an in-depth gaze at his face; admire his cheek-bones in her own time, run her fingers across his neat eyebrows, marvel at the veritable pitchforks for eyelashes. She analysed his lips; she vaguely remembered an article in some glossy or other which ascribed great significance to the shape and plumpness of a man's lips. Well, Zac's top lip was as full as his bottom lip and Pip decided that this must point to balance. And kissability. And before she smothered him with slap, she indulged herself with holding his face and kissing him.

'How did you get into the whole clowning thing?' he asked her, eyes closed, and mumbling slightly because he presumed he ought to keep his features as still as possible.

'I think I was probably born one,' Pip answered, 'always felt my *métier* was to make others laugh.' Zac nodded. 'Keep *still*,' she said.

'What about my hair?' Zac declared suddenly. 'I can't go into work tomorrow if you've dyed it green.'

'Keep still and hush up about work!' Pip chided, poking him in the ribs. 'Just wait and see!'

'Shall we do something on Friday night,' Zac muffled, 'with my brother and his wife Ruth, whom I think you've met?'

'Cool,' said Pip, 'that'll be fun. Can you open your eyes for me?'

Zac did so and as Pip concentrated on the intricacies of Zig Zac's facial features, Zac Holmes feasted on her face. 'Can I kiss you, please?' he asked.

'No fucking way!' Pip laughed. 'With all that stuff on your face? Absolutely not!'

'Is that *nail* varnish on your sofa – and, God, on your carpet, too?' Zac asked.

'Yes,' said Pip. 'I'm going to wait for the January sales and do something about it then. Now bloody keep still. Actually, I'm just going to see to the spuds – no peeking while I'm out of the room.'

Zac didn't sneak a look. He quite liked the sensation of the make-up on his face. And the smell of baking potatoes drifting in from the kitchen. And the sound of Pip cursing 'Ouch, shit!' as she checked their progress. And in his mouth, the lingering taste of her kiss. His appetite was growing.

'Did you peek?' Pip asked, hands jauntily on her hips.

'No,' Zac said, 'I promise.' Pip had to bite back laughter at the juxtaposition of his earnestness with his new face. 'Close your eyes,' she said though she didn't really need him to. Zig Zac was nearly done. All that was needed was a hat (she used the one Django termed his 'daft Alec hat' which she'd found in the pea-green candlewick bedspread). A little daub of red just there. A light dusting of talc to his forehead. *Voilà*. 'You can look now,' Pip said.

Zac rose from the sofa and went to the mantelpiece.

'Fuck!' He was staggered. 'Oh my God!' he laughed. 'Look at me!' He turned to her.

'No one,' she declared, 'but no one,' she stressed, 'would ever guess that you are a cruel bastard accountant who spent all day firing people!'

'Genius!' laughed Zac. 'If only Tom could see me!'

'We could do it again, sometime,' Pip shrugged, 'we could do Tom, too.'

'And then hit Hampstead High Street,' Zac laughed, 'the three of us.'

'Why not?' said Pip, who was serious.

Zac thought about it. Why not indeed?

'Keep the hat,' Pip said, knowing that Django had a whole collection of panamas, daft Alecs, the odd fez, and berets in every colour available. 'When you feel it's all too much, plonk it on, think like Zig Zac and just take time out for a while.'

'What about the slap?' Zac asked.

'Well, I suppose I could keep spares at yours,' Pip proposed.

Zac couldn't keep himself away from the mirror, or any reflective surface. He didn't think back over his day at all. He felt lively and a daft voice materialized easily. Pip went through to the kitchen and though she told him to sit and relax, he preferred to follow her there and loiter and get in her way and pinch her bottom and tickle her side and cup both her breasts when she reached up in a cupboard for a new bottle of HP Sauce.

'Zac!' she declared with mock outrage.

'Zig!' he corrected.

'Beans, cheese, HP,' she offered, 'or I could do tuna mayonnaise. Or a combination of any?'

'The way to a man's heart is through his stomach?' Zac posed.

'Actually,' said Pip, 'I rather think it's through his trousers.'

*

354

She'd certainly whetted his appetite and he'd tickled her fancy, too. But she insisted he ate up his supper first. He kept his face on during the meal, checking his reflection in the back of a spoon. They cleared away the plates and before she could protest or duck, he'd caught her in his arms and was kissing her passionately. She couldn't do a thing about it. His kiss was so seductive that soon enough she was happy to submit. She'd never kissed a clown before. How good he tasted. Greasepaint and HP and an indefinable taste that was uniquely his. He was smudged and she was covered. They were both breathless and could have stripped off and got down and dirty right there in the kitchen if it wasn't so small and if there had been more than a breakfast bar to lie upon.

'Bed?' Zac murmured, sucking her bottom lip, grazing his teeth against it, slipping his tongue along it and into her mouth.

But Pip insisted that he take off his slap because she'd changed her sheets that morning. She sent him into her bathroom where a jar of cold cream and a bumper pack of cottonwool balls awaited him.

When he emerged, however, free of make-up if a little blotchy here and there, Pip felt suddenly a little shy, somewhat apprehensive. There was no Dr Pippity or Merry Martha or Zig Zac to puppeteer. There was no Tom to be aware of. There was no ambiguity over whether he'd stay or go. They hadn't had more than a bottle of beer each to be falsely bolstered by. There was nothing more to eat, neither wanted another cup of coffee. There was just Pip McCabe and Zac Holmes on the first Monday in November. It was what Zac termed a 'school night' and, past midnight, it really was bedtime.

How to get there?

Do I ask him?

Shall I just ask her?

'Gosh, is that the time?' Pip says and it sounds so contrived that they both laugh.

'Shall we?' Zac suggests. Pip nods, coyly, which isn't contrived, it's simply the way her face falls just then. But Zac doesn't mind at all, he thinks it rather becoming. She locks up, switches lights off, checks the fridge door and takes a couple of deep breaths on the way to her bedroom. Zac is standing in his boxers. His ankles have corrugated marks from his socks. 'I borrowed your toothbrush,' he informs her, 'hope that's OK?' Pip nods. He comes towards her. 'Thanks for having me,' he says, slipping her pullover off.

'I'm rather hoping you'll have me now,' says Pip with a coquettish grin which this time she employs most knowingly.

'Well,' Zac falters theatrically, 'OK then. If you insist.'

'Oh, I do,' Pip says, 'absolutely.'

Pip's bedside light remains on and they marvel and delight at the sight of each other. They thought they were full, but the taste of each other is so good they could gorge all night. The physical excitement is heightened by the anticipation – not just from the evening, but really from the months leading up to this very moment. Penetration, when it comes, is not an anticlimax but a vindication. And yet, the physical sensation of Zac inside Pip doesn't feel remotely familiar to either of them, though it feels incredible. But there again, they've simply had sex twice before. Right now, they are making love for the first time and it's as intense physically as it is soothing emotionally. Previously, having sex has been about taking gratification. Climax has been anticlimax. Tonight, exploring each other's bodies is what is most absorbing. The more pleasure they give, they more they find they receive. The foreplay lasts longer than the copulating but when they come it is within nanoseconds of each other. It's a wavelength thing. It's a release, a culmination, a climax and yet also a beginning, a taste of what's to come. And as they peel away from each other and pant, side by side, they congratulate themselves on their sexual compatibility.

Pip switches the light off.

Zac switches it back on. 'You don't have any coke, do you?' he asks.

'You've brushed your teeth!' Pip laughs. 'Have water.'

'Who can we phone?' Zac wonders. Pip is confused but she's grinning because she knows from his tone and expression that he's larking about.

'I have Pepsi Max,' she offers, 'those small mixer cans?'

'No, no,' says Zac, 'I was talking "caine", not "cola".' Pip looks confused. 'Cocaine,' he says with a dead straight face.

'What?' Pip protests, sitting up and gathering the duvet against herself protectively. 'I don't do drugs,' she doesn't care how prim she sounds, 'well, I have done – but only the soft stuff. And I don't now!'

'I don't either,' Zac confides, 'apart from Nurofen.' He pauses. Pip is looking decidedly uneasy. 'You see,' he says, 'even though I'm shot away with tiredness, I think we should stay awake all night and not sleep at all.'

'What?' Pip is lost. 'Why? Can't we just do that post-coital cuddle and then fall asleep? I'm shagged – literally.'

'Pip McCabe,' he says, regarding her sternly, 'don't you see? When I've slept with you before, you've run away each morning. Something must happen while you sleep, some demon descend and muddle with your mind. If we stay awake, you can't bugger off.'

Pip doesn't know whether to laugh or cry. 'I'm not buggering off,' she assures him quietly, 'I'm really looking forward to waking up tomorrow morning. And having you here. With me.'

It's 5.00 a.m. She shouldn't wake him on account of his nightmare day yesterday and no doubt another hellish day today. But she needs to.

'Zac?' she whispers. 'Zac?' She puts a hand on his

shoulder. His skin is silky but cold, too. She pulls the duvet gently up to his ears. 'Zac,' she says, 'Zac?'

He wakes with a start. 'Fuck, what's the time?'

'Don't ask,' Pip says, 'it's only five.'

'Are you OK?' he asks. 'What's wrong?'

'Nothing's wrong – I wanted you to see that I'm still here.'

Zac absorbs this information and chides himself that, for his sins, he has lumbered himself with the peculiar girl he always suspected Pip was. How reassuring. He'd got her right. 'Good,' he says, turning his head back into the pillow, 'that's good. Be there in a couple of hours, too, and I'll be very, very happy.'

'There's something else,' Pip announces and her whisper hides the fact that she's tearful.

'Yes?' Zac mumbles sleepily, raising his head from the pillow as much as he can muster.

'I lied,' she says.

'Yes?' he says.

'Yes,' she confirms.

'I forgive you,' says Zac. He'd forgive her *anything* for just two more hours' kip.

'But you don't know what about,' Pip implores, spooning herself against his back and touching her lips against his shoulder, 'you don't know what I've done.'

'Whatever it is,' he says, reaching his hand backwards and giving her a rub along her thigh, 'you had a reason. Tell me about it in the morning. Don't worry. Get some sleep, you mad woman.'

Zac wakes just before the alarm clock and finds Pip gazing at him intently. She smiles. He replies. She looks exhausted. 'Hullo,' he says.

'Morning,' she says.

'Are you OK?' he asks.

'I didn't sleep,' she says.

'Shit, was I snoring?' Zac grimaces.

'No,' Pip tells him, 'no, you sleep in a very ladylike way.'

'Oh God,' Zac groans, 'you're not still harbouring doubts about my sexual orientation, are you?'

Pip laughs and shakes her head vehemently. 'I need to talk to you,' she says and looks serious and sad, 'about my lie.'

The alarm bell trills out.

'OK,' says Zac, 'but would you mind if I took confession in the bathroom? The shower curtain will do as a screen.'

Zac brushes his teeth and Pip perches herself on the edge of the bath. She takes a deep breath. Looks at Zac directly. And begins.

'I haven't seen my mother since I was six years old,' she declares. She pauses, trying to assess his reaction to her bombshell. 'I don't remember her at all, really. She ran off with a cowboy from Denver.'

This, Zac was not expecting to hear. He'd thought at the worst there'd be some lurid confession featuring the Dashing Doctor and ambiguity about the overlap with himself; at best something about not letting him keep the clown hat. But it appeared that she was chaste *and* that he had the hat. 'Your mother did *what*?' The information was so bizarre, it was difficult for him to take in.

'She left us – three girls and our dad – for some bloke from Denver. A cowboy. A ranch owner. Very rich. We haven't heard from her since.' Pip speaks flatly, focusing on her hands lying deceptively still in her lap. 'I'm sorry,' she says.

'For what?' Zac exclaims gently, thinking to himself that it's Pip's mother who should be doing the apologizing.

'For *lying*,' Pip admits.

'Django?' Zac asks.

'Oh God, he's real – you could never make up someone like him. He's been our mother and our father, our guardian angel. We never had to want for a thing – warmth, love, sustenance. Django provided for us and he still does.'

Zac sits beside her though the edge of the bath is unremittingly cold against his bare bottom. She glances at him and sees he has a blob of toothpaste dribble on his chin. It can stay there. 'I'm sorry,' she says again.

'It's *awful*,' Zac says, shaking his downcast head, 'terrible.'

'I'm *sorry*,' Pip says, wondering what else she can say or do to prove it. She knows her background must sound unconventional but she's confident that she and her sisters are grounded, good people. And so she also knows she shouldn't have lied. 'I'm sorry. It is awful. You're completely right.'

'Huh? No, I mean for *you*,' Zac says, stroking her leg. 'I can only imagine and actually, I'd rather not. Poor Pip. And your sisters.'

'But I lied,' Pip says, almost urgently, 'to *you*.'

'And I can understand why,' Zac says. 'No wonder you've trodden so carefully. I don't blame you. It must lurk at the back of your mind that people who should stay, go.'

Pip considers this. Then she sobs, her lips aquiver.

'So, to combat that, you tend to pip them to the post.' He raises her chin gently with his hand. Her eyes meet his. He's gazing at her, benevolently.

Then her nose wrinkles and she sucks at her lip. '*Pip them to the post*?' she says, helpless not to snigger.

'I know, I know,' Zac cringes, burying his head in her shoulder, 'you deliver your great confession and that's what I come out with. Jesus!'

Pip's smile is short-lived. She looks concerned again. Zac sidles up close and nudges her. 'I'm *not* afraid of commitment,' she says as if defending herself, as if he'd be justified to think that she was, as if her revelation and the fact that she's lied to him might well make him change his mind.

'Good,' says Zac, 'because neither am I.' They regard each other. 'Think how I am with Tom,' he tells her. 'If you'll have me, I'll stay.' Pip's eyes smart. 'I know you have your sisters. Your friends. Your crackpot uncle who I am dying to meet,' Zac continues, 'but if you'll allow me, I'd really like to take on some of the looking-after, too. If your nearest and dearest will tolerate me.'

Pip looks into Zac's eyes. Django's voice fills her memory

and her heart – he'd told her that if Zac was even half the chap he thought he was, he would understand and embrace the provenance of her fib.

Django's right. And why wouldn't he be. And Zac's right for me. And why wouldn't he be.

Pip thinks of Cat and Fen. Recently, they haven't seemed like her little sisters. It's not that they've suddenly grown up, Pip realizes, but that she herself has let them into her world, though she had to dismantle some of her barriers to do so. And in they bustled, armed with affection, concern and actually pretty mature, sound advice. Pip looks again at Zac. How they'll all love him! They'll be so happy for her. And he'll fit right in. Pip has not needed a man, but at last she is content to *want* this one. She can practically smell, almost taste, the banquet that Django will no doubt prepare in honour of Zac's first visit.

I want to make it soon. I want to bring Zac into my family's fold.

A tear slicks an oily passage out of Pip's eye and takes a faltering path down her nose to her lips. She licks it away. Zac has let her have her thinking time without intrusion but now he senses he can gently nudge her. 'You can never,' he says, soft but firm, '*never* have too many people looking after you. You ask Tom!' Pip wants to nod and laugh and cry but finds she's only capable of a jerk of her head and a strangled gulp. Tenderly, Zac puts his arm around her. 'I'm here,' he whispers, 'because I want to be. Why would I want to leave?' Pip lays her head against his chest and hears his heart as she listens to his words. 'But,' Zac says, 'I'm late for work and I have a sod of a day ahead.'

Pip walks to the bathroom door. 'Zac?' He pokes his head around the shower curtain. 'I'm sorry I lied,' she stresses a final time.

'You'd have to do far worse to put me off,' Zac assures her. She nods. She looks over to him, he's shivering slightly. She ought to let him have his shower and embark on his night-mare day.

'Tell you what,' Zac says, 'I'll forgive you everything for a cup of tea.'

Pip laughs. 'Herbal?' she asks. 'Or normal?'

'Normal!' Zac pleads. 'And a towel,' he calls after her. 'This one is like the Turin bloody shroud – it has half of Zig Zac's face on it.'

ACKNOWLEDGEMENTS

Theodora Children's Trust, which was the inspiration behind my fictitious Renee Foundation, trains and funds talented artists to work with sick children in hospital every week of the year. The Swiss Theodora Foundation was formed in 1993 and has established Theodora clown doctor programmes in nine countries around the world. In the UK, the Trust (set up in 1996) currently supports nine trained Theodora clown doctors. Eight hospitals, one special centre and almost 30,000 children a year benefit from their visits. I am indebted to the Trust and its executive director Joanie Speers for enabling me to study the work of its clown doctors. It was a privilege to watch them at Great Ormond Street and at Guy's hospitals. I would like to thank Dr Mattie (Matthew Faint) and Dr Doalot (Eliza Neam) for allowing me to follow them on their ward rounds. I know that Pip is a better clown doctor for it.

My research for *Pip* was fun and fascinating. I am grateful to Clown Mattie (again) for all his help and enthusiasm, for opening the doors to the Clowns' Gallery to me after hours and for lending me research material. Also, to Clown Fizzie Lizzie (Elizabeth Morgan) whose knowledge on clown history is encyclopaedic. Other people willing to assist me were: Clown Bluey (Blue Brattle), Gino the Clown (Georgina Hargreaves), Emile the Mime Clown (David Girt) and Clowns International photographer Robert Morgan.

Many thanks are due to Alan McGee for kindly letting me set up my laptop in a relatively quiet corner of his office when my son Felix decided my study at home ought to be his bedroom.

I'd like to thank the team at Random House and the

indefatigable Sophie Ransom from Midas PR. As ever, immense gratitude goes to my agent, mentor and friend, Jonathan Lloyd. Finally, special thanks to Mary Chamberlain for her fastidious editing – and patience.

*'Clowns work as well as aspirin,
but twice as fast'*
                    Groucho Marx

AFTERWORD

*T*he number of people who said to me 'you can't have an accountant for a hero' or 'you can't have a heroine who's a clown' . . .! However, before I'd even started to write this, my 6th novel, I knew Pip herself pretty well through writing about her sisters Cat and Fen in my fourth and fifth books. And as for a hero who's an accountant? Well, why not? I've always been keen that my characters should be down-to-earth, normal people – people my readers will recognize themselves in or know others just like them. It's one of the reasons I started writing – I was bored of reading books where the characters were uber-glam and had careers and lifestyles that meant nothing to me.

Whilst researching this novel, I discovered amongst friends and family just how many people don't much like clowns. But also during my research, it became clear how clowning goes way beyond greasepaint. The Clowns Gallery in east London was a fascinating starting point – colourful, yet odd and eerie too. A huge cabinet contained over a hundred years of painstakingly painted eggs – each documenting and also copyrighting the unique masks of individual clowns.

In March 2003, when my daughter Georgia was just 6 weeks old, my son Felix, then twenty three months, broke his leg quite badly. It necessitated a lengthy stay in hospital, in traction, followed by a period of time at home in a 'spica cast' which went from his waist down both legs. He adapted marvellously – but it was traumatic for me. In hospital, despite being flat on his back, he still had fun with the art therapist – but there were no clown doctors there. When, that summer, I started to research *Pip* in earnest, it became fundamental for me to highlight the incredible work these artists do – and thereby give substance to my book as well. Research is a true perk of my career – but for the first time, through *Pip*, I found it incredibly humbling and enriching too. Watching the clown doctors at work and seeing the effects on patients and their families was profoundly moving. They're a gifted and generous bunch. And, after a day's shadowing them, I'd return home to hug my children tight and be so thankful for my blessings.

I have an adored younger brother but I don't have sisters – and those McCabe girls are the closest I've come to having them. I've often felt like their eldest sister – alternately feeling responsible for them and frequently becoming quite fed up with them! My readers pleaded with me to write about the McCabe girls again. I did so in *Home Truths* (2006) – picking up their stories five years on. I thought I'd tied together all the loose ends in a particularly pleasing bow . . . but still my readers want more! Recently, on my Facebook page, there was a vote for the most popular McCabe sister. It was fascinating to find there isn't a firm favourite. Cat, Fen and Pip each have a fan club of their own and pulled in pretty much even scores. However, it seems Django is the character my readers love the most.

Could I write about the McCabes again? A couple of years ago, I thought not. But I miss them too. I miss

Derbyshire and Django's cooking and the sisters' snipping at each other, offset by their genuine closeness – and I miss their blokes. However, I don't think I could take up where *Home Truths* left off – I'd have to face the inevitable with Django and I'm not robust enough to do so. Perhaps a prequel, then – set in the 1970s when Django first comes by those three little girls . . . Watch this space!

Incidentally, there is one sentence that is repeated in *Cat, Fen* and *Pip* – and it remains my favourite across all the novels I've written.

I know your mother ran off with a cowboy from Denver, but . . .

Freya North
Spring 2012

Sally

Freya North

She's a primary school teacher turned sex goddess.
He's a handsome bachelor from Notting Hill...
It's a match made in heaven – surely?

Sally Lomax is 25 and bored of being homely
and predictable, so she's decided to give the boot
to being conventional and reinvent herself as
a femme fatale. This is all well and good,
but she's going to need someone to practise on.

Along comes Richard; suave, single and fiercely
independent. She's determined to be the one
great erotic heroine of his life. He's going to be
her dream affair – no strings, no scone baking,
just sex and sensuality. Until, that is, a New Year
masked ball unmasks more than was intended...

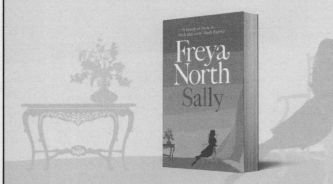

Cat
Freya North

Her career is stuck in a rut.
Her love life has been a tangle.
But fortune favours the brave...

When journalist Cat McCabe lands a job reporting on the Tour de France, she's confident it might give her stuttering career the boost it needs and provide a welcome distraction from a messy break-up. Or so she hopes.

She quickly realises *Le Tour* is not just all about the bikes. Large bulges, huge egos, lashings of Lycra and plenty of sexy shenanigans play their part. And soon enough, her own life starts to mirror the high peaks and perilous lows of the race as she battles for more than just a scoop.

Whatever happens, it's going to be the ride of her life.

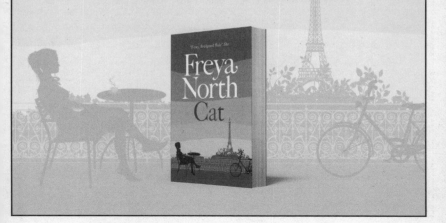

Fen

Freya North

You wait forever for a real man…
Then two turn up at once.

Fen McCabe has only ever been in love once.
So what if he's a long dead nineteenth century artist?
She's an art historian, she calls it job satisfaction,
her friends and family call it insanity.

But then her path crosses not just with handsome
magazine editor Matt Holden, but also with brooding
landscape gardener James Caulfield – twenty years her
senior. Though she fights it, Fen finds herself falling for
both of them in a haze of sex, art and severe indecision…

Does she really have to choose?

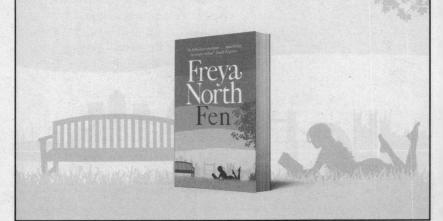

home truths
Freya North

Our mother ran off with a cowboy from Denver when we were small.

Raised by their loving and eccentric uncle Django, the McCabe sisters assume their early thirties will be a time of happiness and stability.

However, Cat, the youngest, is home from abroad to begin a new phase of her life – but it's proving more difficult than she thought. Fen is determined to be a better mother to her baby than her own was to her – though her love life is suffering as a result.

Pip, the eldest, loves looking after her stepson, her husband, her uncle and her sisters – even if her own needs are sidelined.

At Django's 75th birthday party, secrets are revealed that throw the family into chaos. Can heart and home ever be reconciled for the McCabes? After all, what does it mean if suddenly your sisters aren't quite your sisters?

rumours
Freya North

Everybody's talking –
but what's really going on?

Rumour has it that Stella Hutton landed her new job thanks
to family connections. She's guarded about her past
and private about her new life.

Over in Long Dansbury, there's always a rumour circulating
about Xander – but the eligible bachelor shrugs off
village gossip.

Then a rumour starts that Longbridge Hall is up for sale.
Home to the eccentric Fortescues, it has dominated
Long Dansbury lives for centuries.

Stella is summoned to sell the estate. But Xander grew up
there. His secrets and memories are not for sale. He'll do
anything to stand in Stella's way. Anything but fall in love.

Freya North
rumours

Can you believe
everything you hear?

Keep up to date with Freya

Log onto **www.freyanorth.com**

for the latest news, reviews and photographs

You'll also find details on all Freya's books – including sample chapters and what happened next to your favourite characters – plus Freya's journal, an advice page, videos, the chance to win signed copies of her books, and much more.

LM 7/12

Join Freya on Facebook

© Angus Muir

www.facebook.com/freya.north